I0694287

INFINITA BOOK 2
PARALLAX RISING

INFINITA BOOK 2

PARALLAX RISING

CHRISTOPHER HOPPER

HOPPER CREATIVE GROUP

SOMNIUM PUBLISHING

NEW YORK

Parallax Rising
Infinita Book 2

Written by
Christopher Hopper

Copyright © 2022
Hopper Creative Group, LLC
Somnium Publishing

First Edition / Version 1.0

Senior Content Editor: Matthew Titus
Edited by: Jennifer Sell
Proofread by: Christie Strahler, Dan Wong
Cover Art by: Tithi Luadthong
Layout by: G.K. Blackburn

eBook ISBN: 979-8-9850763-4-9
Trade paperback ISBN: 979-8-9850763-5-6
Mass market paperback ISBN: 979-8-9850763-6-3
Hardcover ISBN: 979-8-9850763-7-0

CONTENTS

INFINITA CODEX

For an even deeper experience, keep the Infinita Codex handy while you read. You'll find a vast glossary, organization histories, a character reference guide, timelines, and universe maps all at your fingertips. Proudly powered by World Anvil.

infinita.christopherhopper.com

PROUDLY POWERED BY

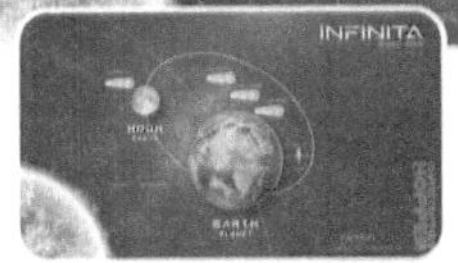

To Netta and Neil

"You could think of this entropy as ignorance of the state of affairs in the black hole interior. The more possibilities there are for what could be going on in the black hole interior, the more ignorant you will be about which configuration the system is in. So this entropy measures ignorance."

— Netta Engelhardt
Massachusetts Institute of Technology
Interview for Quantum Magazine
August 23, 2021

"It may be that intelligence is just the right thing to have to render yourself extinct."

— Neil Degrasse Tyson
92nd Street Y
Manhattan, New York
February 1, 2007

PROLOGUE

Thirty-Five Years Ago
Tuesday, October 8, 2216
Edinburgh, Old Scotland, Norasia

Neon

Maybe it was the mob's anger that drove the men to molest her. Like so much steam built up in a pressure cooker finally blowing the lid. Or maybe it was just that her violators were evil, and she, being fifteen and separated from her father and brothers, was unprotected. Whatever their reasons, Magnolia Birdwhistle knew that she wanted them to stop.

She was afraid—filled with dread so deep it prevented her from speaking. Like being outwardly unconscious but inwardly awake during an operation. Feeling her skin pierced, bones cut, but paralyzed and unable to tell the doctor she could feel every twitch of his tools.

She had to fight back. Had to say something. So despite the crippling fear, Magnolia found her voice and screamed. As loudly as she could. Her cries echoed off the alley walls. Her family would hear. They must. Lewis would come and help. Of all her brothers, he was always looking out for her the most.

Yet how could they hear? The crowd that gathered along Canongate was tens of thousands strong, all chanting to protect Gaia, to rid the Earth of those who only sought to take and never give. She cursed the futility in her belly. If her family believed in virtual cognizance implants, none of this would be happening. But that was the tech of the space farers, not the rock dwellers, and her father would have none of it. So she screamed again.

"Shut up, girl," the smaller man said as he pushed a grease-stained hand over her mouth. It smelled of copper and solder. She saw his Viatoribus tattoo just as his palm cupped her bleeding lips.

"Let her yell," the larger man replied and forced the hand off Magnolia's mouth. His voice sounded smooth and in control. Like this wasn't his first time. "I like it. And no one will hear."

"Right. Right." The little man slid back some. "You want vid?"

"Yeah. For posterity."

Magnolia stared into the sliver of late morning sky between the building tops as the big man's head and shoulders bucked in the foreground. She wanted this to end but felt powerless to stop it. Trapped. Afraid. Wondering what she'd done wrong.

Finally, the big man climbed off her. "Finish her."

"But she's probably got—"

"She's a nobody."

The smaller man stopped recording with his eyes and produced a knife from his trousers pocket. "Whatever you say."

Magnolia's fear went nova. "Please don't," was all she could think to say. "Please don't kill me." But if her pleas hadn't stopped them from raping her, why would her words stay their hand now?

A familiar voice boomed from the alley entrance. "Hey! What's going on back there?" Then boots slapped the wet cobblestones, coming fast. More shouting as the question seemed to answer itself.

The little man turned the knife toward the voices that Magnolia recognized as her father and brothers. The big man was on his feet and securing his trousers when Lewis tackled him to the ground, nearly falling on Magnolia. Jonathan dodged two hasty swings from the little man's knife before throwing a left cross that knocked the assailant off his feet and into a brick wall. Her third brother, Eric, the oldest, pulled the younger brothers away and shouted orders to bind the attackers' hands and feet. But it was her father, Cillian, who hoisted Magnolia off the ground and carried her to a cardboard-covered pallet where he helped put her clothes back on.

"Magnolia, I don't—"

"They…" But that's all she could manage between sobs—the sentence caught in her throat, stuck somewhere between grief and relief. She felt dirty. Exposed.

"It's okay," her father said as he covered her. "I've got you now."

And held her. Tightly. As if the embrace would hide her from the sun and the moon and the face of the Earth. Magnolia never wanted him to let go. But he did eventually when her brothers had finished binding her assailants.

"That's enough," Cillian said to his sons as they continued to kick the big man. "I said, that's enough!"

Eric, Jonathan, and Lewis stood back, panting and wiping sweat from their faces. Knuckles bloodied. Boots glistening.

"Whadda ya want done with 'em, dad?" Eric asked.

"We call the *polis*"—he looked at Magnolia—"and get you to hospital."

Just then, the small man scrambled to his feet. He'd cut himself free somehow. A second knife, perhaps. But Lewis, always the fastest, was on him before the man could get far. They crashed to the stone, and something snapped. It was Lewis who cried out this time, rolling to one side and grabbing his arm. The move gave the adversary just the time he needed to drive his boot knife into Lewis's chest. Once, twice, three times. Eric and Jonathan were on the assailant by the fourth blow and threw him against a curb.

Lewis reached out and said, "Dad... hel-help."

"My God," Cillian sobbed as he rose from the pallet and raced to where his son bled out.

A new sense of helplessness overcame Magnolia as she realized there was nothing her father could do for the son pawing at the wet stones. Seeing her brother race toward death was an agony far worse than she'd just endured. Magnolia clutched her belly, groaning at the bitterness that gouged a hole in her heart. "Lewis! No. *Nooo.*"

"I'm..." Lewis coughed up blood. "I didn't mean—"

"You have nothing to be sorry for, son." Magnolia's father kept one hand on the wound and the other stroking Lewis's damp hair. When the blood pumped less forcefully between Cillian's fingers, he bent down and kissed his son's forehead as if willing the boy back to life with love. But to no avail.

Eyes fluttered.

A deep breath.

"No, no, no," Cillian said.

There came the long sigh, and then Lewis relaxed.

Lewis was sixteen.

Eric was straddling the smaller man and grabbing his throat when Cillian rose from Lewis's corpse and pushed off his oldest son. "He's mine now, Eric."

Magnolia caught something in her father's eyes. Something electric and altogether terrifying. He drove a fist down into the man. A hand calloused, as weathered as the north shore, and hard from years working the land and feeding the herds. Magnolia had never seen him be violent, at least not in the way that some were. His killing was always to feed. To nurture. Or to be merciful in suffering.

But this? This was different.

This would be murder.

Again and again, Cillian Birdwhistle drove his fists into his son's killer's head, cursing and weeping as he did. Each time a hand pulled up, it dripped with a little more crimson; each time one drove forward, it pummeled the target with a little more force. Until Eric and Jonathan seemed compelled to pull their father away. Heartbroken. All of them.

Magnolia hadn't been idle during this time. Her eyes shifted to the big man, and she'd stood, taking everything in, noticing a revolver on the wet stones. It didn't look like any of the weapons her brothers owned, and her father had insisted no weapons be brought to the protest. So it had to be the big man's; perhaps it had fallen from his belt.

Her fingers seemed to wrap around the handle automatically, as if willed by some exterior power. She looked at Lewis and cleared her vision with the back of her forearm. Then she stepped toward the big man, leveling the barrel with his face.

"Magnolia?" someone said. A brother maybe. But she was too focused to know for sure. Too upset.

No, not upset.

Enraged.

These... Viatoribus *spacers* didn't deserve life. They'd raped her, a young woman. They'd killed Lewis, not a year older. And done it all so casually, like it was all just theirs for the taking. So cavalier.

No, there would be no polis involved today. If the government had an important role to play, they would have been here by now. They would have prevented this. And where were they? Not here. Not dead like Lewis. Not wet with men's seed. If there was justice to be dealt, if anyone was going to keep the big man from harming others again, Magnolia would be the one to make it happen. She had the power, and she would not waste it.

Another murder? No...

This was justice.

This was stopping them from ever hurting anyone again.

Someone called for her to put the revolver down. The big man tried shimmying away from her with his arms bound behind his back. But she ignored everyone and listened only to the pain welling up from her heart. Magnolia didn't feel the heat from the flash, didn't hear the crack, didn't notice pigeons rousted from their midday roosts. She only saw the bones shatter in the man's face as she fired point blank again, and again, and again. Hammer striking, drum rotating, barrel bucking in the foreground.

A strong hand grabbed her arm and flung it skyward, but still Magnolia squeezed the trigger. Neon lights exploded overhead, struck by the remaining bullets, until the gun went dry. There, a slow-motion shower of glass and sparks baptized her in the street, washing away the pain and absolving her of guilt. It was, she would later recall, her first true confession, her baptism of fire.

A man pulled her into his chest and pinned her arms to her sides. Her father. Someone else stripped the revolver from her hand. Her brother Eric. No one said a thing. They just stood there. Breathing in the scents of spent gel accelerant, blood, and the residue of the October morning rain.

Magnolia hadn't noticed members of the mob filtering around her father and brothers, what with all her misery and violence temporarily numbing her senses. Neither did she notice people checking the palms of the two aggressors who'd raped her, or her father telling the crowd what he'd seen the dead men do to her. Nor did she see Eric and Jonathan whipping other youth into a frenzy over Lewis's murder. But she did hear the toll of St. Giles's Cathedral. Felt the tremor ripple along Canongate and flow toward Old Parliament.

Magnolia exchanged looks with Eric, with Jonathan who hunkered over Lewis's body, and then with her father, still holding her but less tightly now. Something unspoken passed between them, all while tears streaked down their cheeks and blood dried on their hands. They'd come here to protest peacefully, to try to speak reasonably with the Solum Terram, Preservationist, and Viatoribus leaders gathered for the summit. To make their case that the *Astraea* Station project was a waste of the planet's dwindling resources. But something had snapped in them just as it had in the crowd.

When she'd awakened that morning, Magnolia had known the day would be significant, but she never imagined they'd write songs about it. About her. Then again, few ever do. She only knew that her brother was dead in the street, and that she'd killed a man who deserved to die. She'd crossed a line. They all had. And there was no going back.

"Come on," her father said. "Let's get you out of here."

"No." She raised her chin and then shouted at the mob swelling around them. "We have work to do!" Then, like gathering grapes in a basket to be pressed, Magnolia collected her family and led them forward to Canongate as St. Giles finished tolling twelve.

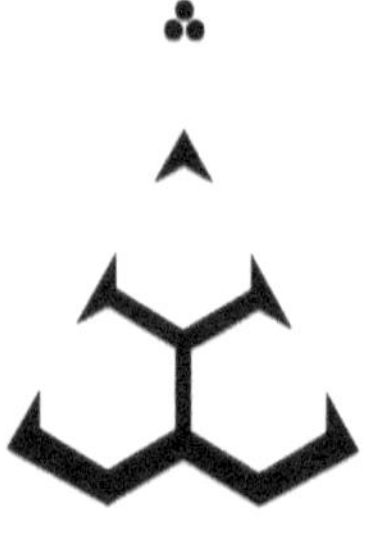

Present Day
Monday, August 18, 2251
Oslo, Old Norway, Norasia

Mary

Preservationist Head Mary Allbrook sat behind her desk and spun a crystal highball glass with her fingers. The grooves scattered prismatic sunlight across the lacquer, tinted amber from the whiskey. She shouldn't be drinking, her doctors said. But as far as Mary was concerned, it was the only thing keeping her alive. Or at least sane. If she won the election, she'd quit then. But until that time, liquor was her friend, not her enemy. She had plenty of those everywhere else.

Votes from the primary election had been cast and tallied the week before, leaving just her and Sir Nigel Sallsworth as contenders for the Secretary General position. Now the Nations of United Earth General Council was just one week away from declaring its new elected leader, and Mary felt assured that the position was hers. Whether or not she wanted it was another matter altogether.

"Since when have you been allowed to want anything anyway?" she asked the mid-fifties woman looking back at her in the old-fashioned glass mirror. Her pear-shaped body, shoulder-length hair, and flat face earned her the nickname Bulldog from her friends and enemies alike—or maybe it was from her tenacity on the council chamber's floor—she couldn't be sure. It didn't matter anyway. She had a job to do, and in the end, life for all leaders came down to duty not personal preference. If it were up to her, she'd be sixty centimeters taller, twenty kilos lighter, and with the cheekbones of a Greek goddess. And she'd have said goodbye to politicking. Of course, aggressive gene editing could have solved all that—the physical, not the political. But she'd been a staunch proponent of letting herself age the way nature intended. Saying goodbye to politicking would also be fine by her.

However, when your family has money, power, and a noble cause, you get raised to extend the money, expand the power, and advance the noble cause. *Damn them for caring*, she thought and then took another sip of whiskey, tasting a smokey note to this bottle that she couldn't quite place.

What else would she have done anyway? Turn a blind eye to wars waged between the spacers and the rock squatters? Acted like the fight over resources and the logic behind space expansion weren't worthy topics of discussion? She could have, she supposed, like so many other elites chose to. Slink off on a fuel-sucking yacht, send very public and very large contributions to one faction or another, and keep aloof from the less fortunate. No. That wasn't her style, even though sometimes she wished it was. But isn't everyone allowed fits of indulgence from time to time?

The truth was, Madame Mary Allbrook was tired of leading the charge for peace and constantly brokering truces. It was like getting parentless children to cooperate but on a global scale. At least with children, they could mature and see reason. But where there was opportunity for profits and bids for more power, clear heads did not prevail. And so it was the endless plight of the Preservationists to be Earth's moral referee.

It wasn't just about fatigue from the constant bickering either, she thought. It was the realization that both sides, in their purest form, had something worth saying. Worth considering. Something true.

Earth was indeed suffering from crippling climate

change, the likes of which had never been seen before —at least for a few million years. She was no historian or climatologist, but she saw merit in the Viatoribus and Sentia Aux arguments for humanity looking for another suitable home. Did that mean that Earth was beyond hope? Surely not.

At the same time, so many of the factors that had accelerated the planet's demise were spearheaded, ironically enough, by the private and public efforts to get humanity "off the rock," as it were. Even brain power— those minds best suited for solving the problems on the planet's surface—had been "stolen by the stars," opponents cried. So she wouldn't and couldn't fault the Solum Terram's populist position to "put Earth first." This was, after all, the only one God had seen fit to grant the species.

Then there was the curious case of the Tantum Terrae. Not that the bastard faction was curious in and of itself. Hardly. She viewed them as ecological terrorists of the worst kind, those who threatened to upset the balance that she and her predecessors had worked so diligently to preserve for generations. No, what made the Tantum Terrae curious now was Sir Nigel Sallsworth's newfound public disdain for them.

Last week's vote on whether or not to go to war against the Tantum—a position Sallsworth had long resisted—had gone unexpectedly in favor of rooting out the illegitimate politicast's leaders and crippling their networks. Sallsworth had suddenly changed his tune, wanting to eliminate the faction and their petulant leader once and for all.

It appeared that the Tantum's connection to *Astraea* Station's catastrophic end had pushed Nigel over the edge. She didn't blame him, of course, but it did seem odd that the legacy hab's demise—a cause he may have championed were it decommissioned and not blown to kingdom come—had inspired him to change his vote. She couldn't put her finger on it, but something was off. Not that Sallsworth shouldn't view orbital sabotage as a war crime; far from! It was simply that he'd turned a blind eye to the Tantum's more illicit operations for so long that this about-face felt... different. There had to be something in it for him, she just couldn't see what.

There was the obvious, of course: that irritating side effect that elevated Sir Nigel Sallsworth in the council's eyes leading up to the election where he stood to unseat her. But at the cost of losing what everyone behind the scenes suspected as the covert arm of the Solum Terram? No, the leverage he gained from black-site deals and secret handshakes was more powerful than anything he'd gain by chairing the council. If for no other reason than none of those activities needed government approval or oversight. To give up the Tantum Terrae now meant he had something bigger in the works. And that worried her. No, it *terrified* her. Because she knew all too well what powerful people were capable of.

Mary rubbed her forehead with tired fingers. She wondered if it was not time to hand the reins to someone else, but certainly not Sallsworth. He'd proclaimed to have grown more centrist, but she sensed the Solum Terram leader would not be as even-keeled as she would want. Mary needed to remain Secretary General for the joint session of politicast heads and world presidents for at least one more term, to continue to carry the Preservationist's mantle of keeping the peace. Especially in light of the provocative new discovery coming out of the Kepler system. While she had her own reservations about what SESI might uncover, she would be remiss if she did not hold true to her politicast's values—Protect. Preserve. Persevere—even when it came to the unnerving prospects of first contact. Not everyone would see it that way. Neutrality often made enemies faster than polarity. And if it came to violence?

"Forgive us," she said into her glass, speaking to future generations. "Forgive us all."

The office door chimed, and a voice came through Mary's V-cog lobby. "Madame Allbrook?"

"Five more minutes, Jeremy. Please."

"But they're waiting for you and—"

"They can wait five minutes more."

Her assistant didn't rebut this, but Mary could practically hear him let out a long sigh directed at her. Such nuances rarely came through V-cog unless the user so desired, and Jeremy knew better.

"May I come in?" he asked at last.

Mary agreed by opening the door but did not turn from the mirror. When he was by her side and the door had closed, she asked, "Tell me. What do you see, Jeremy?"

"Ma'am?"

She nodded at the looking glass.

"Um. A… strong and powerful—"

"Don't bullshit me. What do you see?"

He smiled with the corner of his mouth, having gotten used to her verbal lashes years ago. "I see someone who's been through more than her share of battles, and who, to use your Biblical references, walks with a limp."

"So now I'm a cripple too?"

"That's what you get for wrestling gods."

"Fair enough." She took another sip from the highball and examined the glass. Maybe it was time to stop after all. "Fair enough."

"If I may?"

"Speak," she said with an impatient gesture of her hand.

"I think you come at this wrong sometimes."

"Oh?"

Jeremy busied himself with gathering her suit jacket and briefcase while he talked. "You're thinking about how much work is involved with being Secretary General for another term. Wrestling the presidents, wrangling the politicast leaders—"

"You speak like it's decided."

"Isn't it, though?" His smile faded. "I suppose it will be harder this time around."

"Not exactly the pep talk I was hoping for."

Jeremy let out a small laugh as he took her glass and then helped thread her arms through the jacket. "What I mean is that despite the trials to come, the consequences of you not being here to lead the world are far more grueling."

And there it was: the prospect of the Secretary General's seat falling to any politicast but that of the Preservationists. She and her party had been the even hand on the tiller, the sage in the temple, and the surge wall along the shore for more than eight decades. Without them, she knew, the main politicasts and their factions would descend into endless confrontation. Maybe worse. Maybe war.

"I'm afraid," Mary said after a moment.

"Madame Allbrook, if there's anyone I know who can—"

"I'm afraid if we fail, Jeremy."

And he needed no reassurance of his own point. He merely nodded and handed her the briefcase.

THE CHILLS CAME MORE FREQUENTLY as she read from the prepared speech in her V-cog suite. She mastered simultaneous visual perception in her first year of holding political office; it was an essential skill to anyone in the higher echelons of public life. "Keep one eye on your work and one eye on your enemy" went the adage. Still, her well-practiced skill was waning suddenly, her mind unable to focus like normal.

It bothered Mary that she could not improvise. The council had received and cleared her speech to be recited exactly as prepared. But she was finding it harder to concentrate, and this part was critical.

Come on, Mary. Focus.

"Therefore, the politicast leaders together with the presidents of the Southlands, Norasia, and the American Heights wish to extend an invitation to leaders of the Tantum Terrae to appear before the General Council in the hopes of negotiating terms of peace."

She blinked several times at the cluster of media pixies—Personal Exo-Sensory Environment Experience drones—hovering two meters ahead as their servos and processors chattered in excitement. They represented the eyes and ears of several billion people, and she couldn't afford to let the world down. Still, the pressure was getting to her.

"This action is of particular importance in light of… Excuse me." Mary dabbed at her forehead, took a drink of water, and tried again. "Of particular importance in light of last month's disaster with *Astraea* Station. It's incumbent on world leaders to *respond*, not react, with wisdom and strong leadership. We will even go so far as to say that adding a more tolerant, less reactionary Tantum Terrae to our prestigious body of representatives isn't out of the question, and that we have voted to explore all possibilities that might result in a.... that might result..."

She found herself gripping the lectern white-knuckled. Just then, a medical alert flashed in V-cog, warning her of... an imminent heart attack? Now?

"Madame Allbrook?" Jeremy asked from her right. "Are you alright?"

She waved him off, not wishing to make a scene, but she already sensed the pixies flying closer, like insects looking to feed. "We must react to... *dammit*. We've got to *respond* responsibly in these trying times. And leadership that's..." She licked her lips. "...that's suited for..."

A hand touched the small of her back. "Madame Allbrook?"

She was having trouble seeing. Staying upright. The medical alert began a ten second countdown before it would initiate coordination with an emergency response unit. Was this really the dreaded heart attack her doctors had warned her of? But there was no pain in her chest. No cramp in her left arm. And yet the shortness of breath, the sweating, the dry lips, and panic. She'd also lost her voice.

Five seconds.

The pixies were on top of her now, smothering her —the eyes of the world watching her demise. Jeremy called security, and soon more hands willed her to release the lectern. But she wouldn't. Couldn't. She was the Bulldog of Oslo. She couldn't let the world down now. Not with so much at stake. Not when her death would mean…

Death.

That word grew in her head like the bullseye on a target as the countdown hit zero and alerted the building's emergency response unit housed two floors below. She suddenly realized that, yes, she would die from a heart attack. Eventually. But not today. The symptoms weren't there. At least to her. But to everyone else? The refusal to accept gene editing, the chronic drinking, weight gain, and highly publicized warnings from her doctors had written the narrative on her behalf. All that was needed was…

Was a little push.

Her whiskey glass. She saw it in her hand. Saw the sunlight glinting through the grooves and the prismatic interplay of light against fingerprints and dust. She didn't know how, didn't know when, but with her final moments of life, Madame Mary Allbrook felt sure that this was not a death of natural causes.

It was something far more sinister than fate.

Far more intentional than chance.

So she ventured a guess.

"Nanopoison." Mary clutched her head and fell into Jeremy even as the paramedics burst into the room. Madame Mary Allbrook died never knowing that her last word, one she hoped would activate a legion of investigators, came out as an unintelligible slur.

PART 1

JERICHO

"You excited, Cap? 'Cause I am. It's like meeting a new family or something, ya know?" Kit's bounding down the high-ceilinged corridor like a kangaroo. "And, man oh man, do I love zero g."

"It's not zero g, it's one sixth Earth's. And settle down a little. This is an important meeting we're walking into."

"Don't you mean floating into?"

I take hold of his arm just as he preps for another moon jump down one of Beattie IV's hallways—padded for just such hyperactive guests. "Hold up. Need you to listen."

"Yeah. Sure." He scratches the back of his neck for the tenth time in just as many minutes. "What's up?"

I nod toward the module at the end of the hall, the one marked Executive Offices. We're on the moon base's west end, reserved for NUESSA special projects, which includes the Marquis-Class Initiative that, as of just over a week ago, I'm the new head of. And I'd be lying if I said I wasn't nervous. "This is the big leagues, Kit. Bigger than anything you've done before. Lotta crypto. Lotta resources that the world's invested in this project. Right?"

He nods, his wiry hair threatening to spring-launch his black NUESSA hat into the stratosphere. "Which means you need me cool as a cucumber. Right, Cap?"

"Right."

"Cool, cool, cool. No problemo. Can do, Buckeroo."

"And none of that either."

"None of what?"

I wave a hand at his head.

"You… just gestured to my whole face."

"Yeah. Listen…" I take a second to collect my thoughts. Don't wanna crush his spirit, but I can't afford for Kit to be anything but professional. "I put my neck out for you on this, so I need you carrying your weight."

"And I'm ready."

"For the technical aspects, yeah. But you might not be ready for everything else that comes with it. The pressure, the expectations for results, and—"

"The babes?"

"What? No. Kit…" I let out a long breath. "This is my last shot to get it right."

Kit's face flattens as he seems to pick up my meaning. "Right. The accident."

He can't feel the weight like I do. Then again, he's not supposed to; I'm the new MCI director, not him. But he knows what the last test flight cost me, the mission, and the families of the crew who flew with me. And that's what I need him to keep in mind, because heaven knows that no one here is gonna let me forget anytime soon.

"I asked for you to come along because you're a damn good flight engineer. You have attention to detail, you're a fast learner, and your work ethic is, well… you need less sleep than a wasteland rabbit from Old Cheyenne."

He smiles at the reference to his hometown. "Thanks, Cap."

"But I also need you to keep your head down for a while. Watch what's happening, learn to read the room, right? Don't speak unless I or someone else asks you a question. Because here, decisions are measured in billions of coins, and lives are always, and I mean *always* on the line."

He nods thoughtfully. "So… less bouncing down halls then?"

"For now."

"Aye aye, Cap." He scratches one arm and then the other. "Did you itch this bad with the gene therapy?"

"It was a long time ago."

"Yeah. Ha-ha. Bet you were a kid."

"I was. If it's any consolation, I had so much Polyproxamine on my skin my friends started calling me Whitey."

This makes Kit laugh again. "They call me that without Polyproxamine."

Now it's my turn to chuckle. Poor kid's still one of the pastiest guys I've ever met. I pat his shoulder and point him forward. "We've got someone new to meet, and then we'll get you some more anti-itch cream from medical, roger?"

"Copy that, Cap."

We reach the end of the hall and open the door via the V-cog terminal. The panels separate a second later, and Kit and I find ourselves in a spacious waiting room. The curved walls and ceiling are made of aluminum, while the floor is polished stone. Both materials harken back to the base's origin as the first permanent installation on Earth's moon. The larger dome settlement to the south, Harrison City, is the preferred tourist destination and long-term residence, no small thanks to the state-of-the-art laminar film that houses the 1,000 millibars of atmospheric pressure. Like the legacy habs, the dome settlements are engineering feats worth traveling to see—if a person can afford the fare, that is. Fortunately, this trip has been sanctioned by the Nations of United Earth Space and Science Administration and paid for by our home planet's taxpayers.

There's no laminar film over Beattie IV. Just the hard vacuum of space surrounding the base's collection of metal domes, modular outbuildings, and dust-covered launch pads, all interconnected by corridors and tunnels. It suits the engineers and explorers of the Viatoribus and Sentia Aux; we're not much for creature comforts, just the mission. Find humanity a new home. And fast. While the moon's full-time residents require the open atmosphere that the reinforced nano-lam provides, the wrench monkeys and space jockeys are used to tight spaces.

"Jericho Fox?" asks a dark-haired woman in her early twenties. She's dressed in a black uniform with the orange NUESSA logo down her left sleeve. "My name is Alice Ortega, and I'm your new PA."

We shake hands. "Nice to meet you. This is Leslie Smith, my chief systems engineer."

She extends her hand inked with a VT. "I'm Alice."

"Hi," Kit replies. "I'm Alice."

My new PA narrows her eyes.

"Uh, I mean. Oh sheesh. I'm Kit. But you can just call me Kit." He shakes her hand with two of his and then scratches his neck again. "Or Leslie. Or Christopher, but that's long, so most people just call me Kit, like he said. I guess you could also call me Leslie Christopher if you feel the need to be super formal around here, but that's—"

"I'll call you Kit," she replies.

"Ha ha. Okay. Thanks."

I cast him a wry look as he smooths his shirt. Then he mouths the word "sorry" and takes a step slightly behind me.

"Anyway, welcome back to Beattie IV," Alice says. "Care to see your new office?"

"Lead the way."

She turns and approaches one of several doors along the far wall. An augmented nameplate overlaid in V-cog reads Jericho Fox, Project Director. The tag disappears as the doors part. We step into a circular room with a light machine oil smell, accented by leather from the couch and chair on either side of an aluminum desk. Like most decorative objects on the moon's surface, everything that doesn't need to move is bolted to the stone floor. A single thirty-centimeter quadruple-paned port window adorns the far wall as an ode to pre-V-cog era when glass was needed to see beyond a habitat's walls. If I planned on spending much time in this place, I'd order it replaced. But I don't, so I suppress the anxiety that the weak point gives me.

"Everything to your liking?" Alice asks.

"It's fine, yes." But then I notice a pair of dice on a shelf and walk toward them. Even before I get there, Alice seems to notice.

"I'm so sorry. Those were supposed to—"

I raise a hand. "It's alright. The last project lead?"

She nods but looks hesitant. "Edward Carr. He's…"

"He's been demoted."

She shrugs. "I was going to say that he's a piece of work, but yes, he's been demoted to make room for you. Know him?"

I roll the dice in my palm. "Only by name. But I look forward to meeting him."

"You'd be the first."

"So the stories are true?"

One eyebrow climbs her forehead, and she gives me a look like a schoolteacher peering down at a student who's asked a dumb question.

"That bad?"

"Worse."

She extends her hand to take the dice from me, but I wave her off. "I'll get 'em back to him."

"You sure?"

"Special delivery. And the rest of the team?"

"*Selene* Station, putting on the finishing touches." She raises a finger as if remembering something. "The roster. Here."

I get a ping in V-cog and see Alice step into my public lobby offering me an old school manila folder with the NUESSA logo stenciled across the front. I thank her for the folder and tell Kit to join us. He does, and then all three of us are looking through the printed headshots spread out on the galley table. We're below deck in my 2071 Berret-Racoupeau-inspired Amel 60 sailboat, at least as much of one as I could afford when I first purchased the code. I still have a cold storage coin from Sir Nigel Sallsworth that I haven't brought myself to spend, much less check its balance. Could try to use it to spruce things up around here. But, honestly, ever since *Astraea*'s destruction, I haven't taken much time for myself. It's just been… too painful, I guess.

"This is Nairobi Kinshaw," Alice says as she touches

a photo of a woman in her late thirties with braided hair, wide green eyes, and generous lips. Metadata appears above the printed image, streaming credentials and accolades, along with a full medical rundown and test scores for all the things NUESSA cares to track, which, in my experience, is just about everything. "Graduated top of her class from St. John's Institute of Technology. She was transferred to us after the…" Alice looks up at me as if suddenly finding herself in shark-infested waters.

"After the accident," I say with as conciliatory a tone as I can muster. "We'd better just get used to it, copy?"

She nods. "Nairobi was sent over from *Calypso* Station and made lead propulsion engineer."

"Noted." I tap the next picture. "Mr. Smiley here?"

"That's Adrian Wallace. Code and communications specialist out of Norasia. He's also a respected cryptographer, holds three laser patents, and speaks multiple languages. Knows the *Kogarashi*'s software inside and out. He's a quirky one, but the good ones always are."

I glance at Kit. "I'm gonna want you to shadow him."

"You bet, Cap. Count on me."

Next, I point to the picture of a man built like a tower and has the height to match. "Mr. 2.25 meters here?"

"Torrence Vanderburg, navigation officer. Graduate of Oslo Naval Academy with time on several Navy battleships and one fleet carrier."

"Why'd he leave the Navy?"

"Says he favored the idea of exploration above defense."

"Fair enough. And then there's Mr. Carr," I say, looking at the last file pic for the team's top tier.

"He looks mean," Kit interjects. "And grumpy."

I'm about to scold him when Alice jumps in. "You're not wrong. Wish I could say that behind those hooded eyes and scruffy beard is a heart of gold, but I'd be lying. Instead, you have a no-nonsense senior project engineer who prides himself on results and has the record to prove it."

"He's probably so pissed at you for taking his management spot," Kit adds.

"Not helping."

Alice shrugs. "Word on station is he's gunning for you."

"Well, least I know what I'm walking into."

Alice shakes her head at me until I start mimicking her behavior. Then she changes gears as if the topic became irrelevant. "NUESSA would have fired him years ago were he not so damn good. Anyway, wheels up as soon as you're ready. Commander's shuttle is standing by."

"No time like the present. You good, Kit?"

"Handy and dandy, Cap." He itches his arm again, which reminds me…

"Alice, any chance we can swing by medical before heading out?"

"Polyproxamine lotion?"

"How'd you guess?"

She winks at me and puts a hand on Kit's back. "Come on. Let's get you something for that itch."

"Really?" he replies. "Gee whiz, that would be super swell. Thanks, like, a whole lot."

"My pleasure."

"Careful," I whisper to her. "He might ask you to put it on him."

"Noted."

⁂

"Would you look at that," Kit says as we fly from Beattie IV up to *Selene* Station in a light transfer shuttle. At first, I think he means something in the V-cog game he's been playing here in the passenger compartment since we first took off. But now he's pointing to my fingers, which are tapping on the arm of my chair. "Captain Jericho Fox, nervous. Never thought I'd see the day."

I make a fist. "Happens to the best of us."

"Well, that's reassuring. 'Cause I feel nervous, like, well, pretty much 100 percent of the time. It's when I'm *not* nervous that ya need to be worried, ya know?"

"Noted."

Alice taps my other arm. "We're approaching the station. Port side cameras if you want a first look at the *Kogarashi.*"

I thank her but don't pull up the shuttle's exterior V-cog cams right away. Sure, I followed the ship's closed-doors development for years. Seen thousands of renders that were all part of the X-10 ES *Perseverant*'s development. And ever since Director Johnson reinstated and tasked me with leading the MCI project, I've combed through every schematic layer on file. But suddenly there's this strange battle between reluctance and anticipation… something about getting my first glimpse of the vessel in the real. Or at least via V-cog; real life will come within the hour.

"You're doing it again, Cap."

I pull my fingers in. "Eh, hell with it." I access the shuttle's virtual cognizance passenger menu and bring up the hull cams. Port side. Wide angle. The moment I hit the Initiate button, my head goes full-cortex with a spectacular view of *Selene* Station.

This particular O'Neill-Oberth cylinder, dressed in iridescent white and wrapped with NUESSA's orange insignia, is the newest in Earth's orbital fleet. First came the pioneer of them all *Astraea*, which proved humanity could not only survive in space, but we could also thrive. The forty-year-old ill-fated station also became the strategic stepping-stone for countless other scientific initiatives, including those of building bigger and better legacy habs. *Calypso* came next, followed by *Arete*—the largest ever built. But it was *Selene* that captured the attention of the world as it dared to achieve two unique objectives.

The first was exporting humanity via the hab to orbit an object other than Earth. This meant that *Selene* Station was constructed and took on a full crew in proximity to the space elevator Ascender 1 and its station *Elpis* before being ferried 384,000 kilometers to orbit the Moon. The second was that, like the Greek goddess she was named for who gave birth to fifty daughters, *Selene* carried in her womb the materials to construct Harrison City, humanity's first civilian dome settlement. To everyone's relief, the decade-long venture was deemed an overwhelming success and secured humanity's first great leap in settling our closest orbital neighbor. The breakthrough meant Mars, Ceres, and Ganymede would get dome settlements too, which they did.

Now, at an orbit of 33,000 klicks, just over half the Moon's Hill sphere radius, *Selene* Station is ready to give birth to another venture that will further solidify its place in the pantheon of human ingenuity and expansion: the Marquis-class vessel *Kogarashi*, which means the first winds of winter in Japanese. Far from the stuff of comic books and movies, the Stellar Dynamics-designed vessel resembles a ninety-meter legacy rocket more than it does any of its science fiction counterparts. The ship's compact cylindrical body is devoid of any attachments that cannot endure the high-g acceleration and deceleration burns produced from its Ebrahimi Drive, named after the twenty-first century physicist who first envisioned the plasma thruster. The only protrusions from the cylindrical shape are structurally reinforced modules and armor plating that covers the black and purple hull to minimize the impacts from hypervelocity dust strikes. The skin and all points of entry are constructed with self-sealing nanotech to ensure a seamless shell, while the Viatoribus logo and VT insignia spread across the hull in a silver mini-dot motif.

"You ever see it in the real before?" Kit asks me.

"No. They were finishing construction under wraps when I was assigned to X-10 ES, so our paths never crossed. We knew we'd get moved up after the flight tests but then…"

Then what, Jericho?

My V-cog archive function starts auto-populating memories of McCormick, Kasongo, Yang, Müller, and Khaled. Their smiling faces could fill an entire drive if they wanted to. I stop the feed just before the test-flight that killed them. Damn. I really need to shut off auto-recall for their names.

"Cap? You, uh… spaced out there for a sec."

I rub a hand down my face and refocus on the *Koga*. "I'm good."

"We'll be docking on the transportation hub a few slips away," Alice informs us. "You'll have your choice of getting settled in your crew quarters on *Selene* or—"

"Meet the senior staff," I interject.

"Yes, sir."

The three of us continue to watch *Selene* expand and, by extension, the *Kogarashi* as it rotates with the transportation hub at the hab's end. The docking megastructure is an intricate and complex assembly of trusses, conduits, and personnel passages designed to move people, power, and supplies between ships and the main station. The last time I saw a transpo hub, it was being torn away from *Astraea* leaving a gaping hole in the end.

Kit's knees are bopping.

"Looks like I'm not the only one," I say, gesturing at his legs.

"Oooops, ha ha. Yeah."

"What's your excuse?"

His cheeks fill with air before he lets out a long breath. "*Pffft*, I just... Well, it's... *Astraea*, right, Cap? Like, if they could, ya know, if they could do it once..."

"They can do it again."

"Yeah, ha ha. Exactly. Wait, are you saying that as a turn of phrase or as a statement?"

"Yes."

"Ha, okay. Good. 'Cause for a second there, I thought you... Wait. You saying you think they can do it again? What about the security measures? What about—"

I latch a hand onto his bouncing left knee. "Kit. Security measures help keep us from being the worst versions of ourselves. But someone will always find a loophole if they want it bad enough."

"Is that supposed to comfort me?"

"No. It's supposed to remind you that we need to have faith where we can."

"And where we can't?"

"Stay vigilant."

"Stay vigilant, right, right. Yeah." He winces. "How do we do that exactly?"

The shuttle pilot brings us in nice and easy, matching the hub's inner rotational speed, and gets us docked three minutes ahead of schedule. We unbuckle and push toward the exit, but I notice Kit looking like a wasteland rabbit on high alert. "You coming, pal?"

"Sure, sure." He seems to summon courage from his gut and swallows. Then to himself, he says, "You got this, Kit. You got this. Fierce like a lion. *Grrrrr.*"

Alice gives me a grin as Kit passes between us. "He's an unusual one."

"You have no idea." I gesture for her to go first. "After you."

"Oh, no. I insist."

I push out of the shuttle and fly down the tube to meet Kit. He turns left at the end and leads us to *Selene*'s newest security measure: a corridor-wide clearance ring that emits a blue translucent film. Kit grabs a handhold on the tunnel's side and eyes the two Marines on the other side of the ring.

"They're not gonna bite," I say.

"Unless I'm an incog."

"Are you?"

"No. But if I—"

"Then you have nothing to worry about, do you?"

"Yeah, but…"

I push Kit forward, and he passes through the blue-glowing film. The security ring emits a soft chime, and I notice the green reflection of light in the Marines's blackened visors. "Congratulations, pal. Your genes match your nanos. You're not an incog."

Kit pats himself down like he's just been radiated. "Ha ha, told ya." But he hardly sounds convinced.

Alice and I follow Kit through the checkpoint and then emerge into the transportation hub's sprawling zero-g network of brightly lit plazas, each boasting shops and restaurants trying their best to make good first impressions on *Selene*'s tourists. The savory aromas of fresh pita bread and shaved döner kebabs mix with the sweeter scents of apple pie and candied pecans, all of which tempt me to make a pit stop before we carry on. But I know better. Getting stuck here for a meal is always a mistake; since humans eat first with our eyes, no one wants filet mignon out of a pouch, no matter how nice the printed label looks. Best to wait until full gravity on section one's circumference four klicks out.

But then something stops me: of all things, a Mexican restaurant offering the latest in to-go space burritos. The last time I had one of those—the regular non-space kind—I was with Dr. Evelyn Park. She'd ordered tequila, and I, a beer. We'd celebrated our promotions, hers to lead SESI's research team on the alien transmission, and mine to oversee the *Kogarashi*'s maiden voyage. We toasted many things that night, including how lucky we were to be alive. And the dead. Captain Mombawe, Lieutenant Forsythe, and the Marine EOD unit who stayed aboard trying to defuse Jack Birdwhistle's, aka Inspector Stamos's third and final bomb in the backup power generator.

That night was the last time Evelyn and I talked. Life picked up fast from there, and away we went. As far as I know, she's still in St. John's trying to make sense of the alien data that Parallax intercepted. Better her than me. I'd rather be up here any day. Then again, knowing her, she'd probably like to be on *Selene* too, probing Kepler-1649c for more signs of sentient life. But promotions come with strings attached, and we all have our parts to play.

"This way," Alice says and leads Kit toward an intersection.

"Come on, slow poke," he says to me, apparently having gotten over his fears once he made it through the checkpoint. "We haven't got all day."

"Coming." I avoid a Southland's fish fry employee offering free samples and then continue after Kit and Alice. My new PA steers us away from the commercial hub and down a crew tunnel with restricted access designations in V-cog. Our V-cog privileges grant us automatic clearance, and we pass deeper into corridors reserved for sanctioned NUESSA research and development. The sights and smells of civilian life are replaced by technicians floating about in clean room suits and mechanic's coveralls, each with a place to be, head down, eyes forward.

As we leave zero-g and move toward the transportation hub's outer circumference, I keep expecting someone to notice me, to call me out and label me an impostor. Or worse, a traitor. But between the stories that came out about our "heroic takedown" of the Tantum Terrae terrorist who destroyed *Astraea* and the successful evacuation of the station's crew, public sentiment seems to have swung in my favor. At least for the time being; everyone who's ever been in the verb's spotlight knows how easily public opinion can shift. Of course, the real heroes in that final contest with Jack and the incogs are Master Sergeant Ishaq al Farooq "Rook" and his spec ops unit.

It also helps that Sir Nigel Sallsworth and the Solum Terram released me from the politicast—with a gaudy *meritus distinction* award, I might add. I'm guessing that was just to help cover their tracks with any incog involvement.

What do I think about Sallsworth and the Solum? Not entirely sure. Just that the ST were in bed with the Tantum in ways that got out of Sallworth's control. Do I blame him? Hell, yeah. But do I think he's the Boogie Man? No. He seems to believe his rhetoric and thinks he's doing what's best for humanity. That's worth something, even if I disagree with him.

And then there's the fact that the Sentia Aux has taken me in as one of their own, no questions asked. Sure, it would have been easier to rejoin the Viatoribus. That move would've made the most sense given my appointment to the MCI. But I know too much now, thanks to Dr. Park. We're not alone in the universe. And while I still believe that we need faster ships to explore the nearest star systems, I know humanity's survival isn't just about going farther faster anymore; it's about first contact. And that pursuit belongs to the Sentia Aux. Granted, I'm not as fanatical as Evelyn, but I do have the double concentric rings tattooed on my palm now. Call me a skeptical believer.

Does this mean I no longer believe in the Viatoribus's vision of creating ultrafast ships like the *Koga* that can close the gap to potentially habitable exoplanets? Not at all; I'm leading the most advanced project in the history of human space expansion. The problem, as I see it, is that we're still years away from making such trips feasible for all of humanity—emphasis on *all*.

My goal with the Marquis-Class Initiative right now is to prove that advances in drive core technology can reduce the time needed to get to a star system like Alpha Centauri. Even with the current output of the plasma fusion Ebra-drive that harnesses the power of plasmoids, a technology that blows away our species's conventional chemical engines, a single thirty-two-minute one-g burn reaches a maximum speed of 67,783 kilometers per hour. That's twice as fast as most space stations orbiting Earth, enough to circle the planet's 40,000-kilometer circumference once every thirty-five minutes. And yet, as incredibly fast as this is, it's not nearly quick enough to get us to our next closest celestial neighbor in any reasonable amount of time. Hell, at that speed, it would take us 25,000 years just to get past the Oort Cloud on the outer edge of our solar system.

Which is why the discovery of super plasmoids is so damn important.

Where standard plasmoids travel at 20 kilometers per second, their particle offspring square that speed, reaching an astonishing 400 kilometers per second. This velocity increase starts to open up new possibilities, not because of a higher top speed—in a vacuum, there's nothing to resist constant acceleration—nor because of faster acceleration—the human body can only handle so much before we turn to mush bags—but because of efficiency. That is, specific impulse. In basic terms, a spacecraft with a higher specific impulse means it's more energy efficient, and in an environment where top speed is no issue, and acceleration has hard limits for the occupants, fuel consumption rates and thrust efficiency mean one thing: massive distances become more attainable.

Where before we could only accelerate at one-g-constant for a total of thirty-two-minutes based on current fuel capacity and drive efficiency, hitting a maximum speed of 67,783 kilometers per hour, a super plasmoid drive, or SPD, can maintain that same one-g-constant for *twenty-one* hours, reaching a top speed of 2,668,977 kilometers per hour. This means that our current trip to Mars, what we call a one-g plasmoid run that takes sixty-seven days, will be doable in just twenty hours forty-three minutes—less than a day.

But the potential doesn't stop there, because we still need to get to Alpha Centauri, which is a mind-numbing forty-one trillion kilometers away. Most people have a hard time even rationalizing just how large a *trillion* is, let alone how big space is. If someone wanted to count to one trillion, saying one number per second, it would take a person more than 31,000 years to finish the job. That's a lot of lifetimes. But for a person on a vessel with a standard plasmoid Ebra-drive headed to Alpha Centauri? It's worse. They wouldn't reach it for 69,588 years.

Yeah. Not happening.

Super plasmoids, however, allow us to do the job in a fraction of the time. Again, not because they travel faster per se, but because the reaction they're derivative of is more efficient, allowing us to burn longer. So, instead of reaching Alpha Centauri in some 70,000 years, an Ebra-drive in SPD mode sustaining one-g-constant for twenty-one hours and then coasting, will reach the destination star in 1,767 years. Sure, that's still way too long for a human lifespan, but we're not finished. Because an SPD can burn longer than twenty-one hours, and it can do more than one-g-constant—assuming we can afford the fuel bill.

If let go at eight-g's-constant for eighty-four hours

before coasting at zero g's, an SPD-powered vessel can reach a top speed of 85,407,291 kilometers per hour, passing the Oort Cloud at the edge of our solar system some fifteen trillion kilometers away in twenty years and reaching the exoplanets Proxima b and c in fifty-five years. Yup, that's a long time to go stir-crazy on a spaceship, but it really beats 70,000 years.

With all our drive core advances, however, saving humanity is still a long shot, because even if we succeed with the *Kogarashi*, it's just one ship—one way out for an infinitesimally small fraction of the population. And that's not good enough. Can we build more ships? Certainly, assuming we can finance it all, *and* that human civilization doesn't implode. With the way things seem to be going, the climate could be the least of our problems.

Which is why I've hitched my wagon to the Sentia Aux.

For almost three hundred years, it's been theorized that the universe contains other sentient species— longer if you count some of the early stargazers who were executed for sharing their heretical findings. This postulation alone doesn't mean humanity is off the hook—a favorite accusation of Sentia critics. But it does mean that as our predicative models raised the likelihood of the existence of complex extrasolar life, so too is the probability that at least one alien civilization has progressed beyond our own. And, if they are advanced enough to contact us, they've lived long enough to overcome some of the same obstacles we're facing. Said another way, if we are not alone in the universe, neither are we alone in our misery, and if someone has developed technology to contact us long before we've developed tech to contact them, then it stands to reason they've outlived the odds of their own destruction through something more than chance. It's this "something more" that the Sentia Aux hopes to glean from— hopes to learn about and implement before it's too late for our species.

What's the pot of gold at the end of the rainbow? No one knows for sure. Could be a way to repair our atmosphere, leverage new gene sequencing, or develop faster than light travel—not that my money's on that last one. Physics has limits. Instead, better plans for a bigger starship might be nice. A people mover that we can modify for humans and then make a dent in relocating our species to somewhere better—so long as there *is* somewhere better in all the vastness of the big black. Whatever the gift is, as people have taken to calling the Potential Big Reveal, the minds at St. John's have been working overtime trying to discern Evelyn's discovery of a lifetime—hell, of all our lifetimes. And Lord knows I hope she finds something amazing. The night is always darkest before dawn, right?

This is where the skeptics muscle their way into the conversation. And I can't say I blame them entirely; we have a few centuries of alien invasion tales to populate our imaginations with the gravest of crimes against humanity. Planetary extermination through orbital weapons, shape-shifting sleeper agents who undermine global governments, alien succubus procreation and biological warfare—hell, we have more portal gate enslavement stories than I could read in a lifetime. No wonder the critics think the worst of our alien counterparts: the verb has been peddling those scripts long before any of us were born.

I can't say I blame people for fearing *The Day the Earth Stood Still* as an outcome, but I would hope we're at least as generous to the stranger from the stars as we would want them to be of us if the roles were reversed. Then again, humanity doesn't have the best track record with discovering new worlds populated with those it deemed less civilized. Perhaps our expectations are really just reflections of our own dark preoccupations. But I chose to believe that the survivors are the best of us, those who learn the hardest lessons and are better for them. That if we were the ones tasked with making contact with another species, we would treat them as we would want to be treated. One can hope.

So went the conversations leading up to my pledge of acceptance with the Sentia Aux. Damn, it felt good not to see the Solum Terram mark on my palm after that. Likewise, I smiled when the double concentric rings appeared, thinking of Evelyn and Rook and our shared time on *Astraea* Station. I still keep the challenge coin from Rook in my pocket, ready to gift it to someone else who's looking for a place to belong. Or to get a free beer from a Marine who forgot their challenge coin in their barracks.

As for Kit, he decided to keep his ST ink—with both Sallsworth and Johnson's blessings, assuming the position wouldn't be publicized—since his prospects following this appointment were less assured than mine. Makes sense, even though I'm pretty sure he could stay in space indefinitely so long as he wants to. And that the gene therapy takes. Poor guy. But it was a financial decision too. While I would have liked to see Kit move to the Viatoribus, NUESSA didn't allocate enough funds for his transfer like they did mine. Shelling out 100,000 in crypto isn't anything to scoff at, no matter who you are, and Kit wasn't exactly high up on anyone's hire list like Evelyn and me. As long as Kit keeps his head down and hand closed, he shouldn't get in too much trouble.

"Would ya get a load of this?" he shouts from a wide hangar entrance while taking off his cap and putting a hand on his forehead. "Holy biscuits!"

Like I said, low profile. Easy.

Alice waves me forward to join Kit, and I turn the corner. This is my first in-the-real glimpse of the *Koga*. There, across a hangar bay fifty meters wide, is the starboard side of its hull, sealed off from the big black by a nanofiber membrane around the bay's mouth. Massive docking clamps hold the ship in place while tech crews busy themselves in the main hangar. This is as up close and personal as it gets without doing a spacewalk on the hull.

Alice leads us toward a cluster of large glass panels and holographic displays that form a central work area. In the middle are what looks to be the team leads as pictured in the mission brief Alice provided, only here, they're all in black NUESSA uniforms accented with Sentia and Viatoribus logos. The tallest among them, navigation officer Torrence Vanderburg, is first to spot me and nods to the others. Nairobi and Adrian look up and wave, while the last, senior project manager, Eddie Carr, takes his time turning around.

He locks eyes with me, folds his arms, curls his lip into a scuff-laden sneer, and says in an Old Cockney accent, "Oi. Looks like the wanker finally decided to show up."

Nairobi glares at him and puts a hand on her hip. Lips aren't the only ample parts of her figure. "Cool it, Eddie, would ya?"

"Make me."

"You really wanna do this again?" Then she offers

to shake my hand. "Ignore him, Director Fox. Nairobi Kinshaw, pleased to meet you."

"Nice to meet you. And Jericho is just fine. This is Kit."

My wingman is frozen solid.

Nairobi eventually withdraws her offered hand. "Right. Nice to meet you, Kit."

He gives some sort of jerky nod, but that's all.

"Adrian Wallace," says the next man floating over. "Code and comms."

I shake Adrian's plump hand, as does Kit who's now cupping the side of his eyes to, apparently, keep from seeing Nairobi in his periphery.

"I can also get you just about anything you need, if you know what I mean." This added note from Adrian seems to snap Kit out of his extreme bout of bashfulness.

"What *do* you mean?" Kit asks.

"You know…" Adrian puts his thumb and index finger beside his temple and rotates them like he's turning a dial in his head—universal shorthand for stimming and tweaking.

"All legal, of course," Kit says, suddenly sounding very vigilant.

Adrian smiles. "Oh, sure, sure, yeah. All on the up and up." Then he winks at Kit, to which my buddy pulls back like he's just whiffed something bad.

"Don't mind Wallace," the tall man says. "He won't be here long."

"Oh?" I say, shaking Torrence Vanderburg's hand.

"Eventually someone will kick him out for breaking SOPs."

Adrian scoffs. "Typical. Navy crows are so uptight." He looks at Kit. "You know what I mean, right, Kit?"

"Uh. No, I… I still don't. If you're doing something illegal, sir, you should know that—"

"A pleasure to meet you, Torrence," I say, turning back to our chief navigation officer.

"Call sign, Magellan."

"Because you're good with directions?"

"Not in basic training, I wasn't."

"Noted. Knight," I reply, offering my own handle.

"Roger that."

"Kit, say hello."

This gets my flight engineer back on track, and he introduces himself to the taller man. Then he offers his hand to Eddie Carr. "Leslie Christopher Smith. Pleased to meet you."

"Oi, how daft was yer mum to give you a fucking girl's name when you were born?"

"Jesus, Eddie," Magellan says. "Just shake the kid's hand, would you?"

"You suddenly on Nairobi's side now too, ya twat?"

"No. I'm on the side of common decency. Damn."

Eddie offers a low growl and then shakes Kit's hand. Real nice guy.

Figuring I'll try to help smooth things over, I pull Eddie's dice from my pocket and hold them out. "Found these in my office."

"No. You found them in *my* fucking office, which is where they were meant to fucking stay, Foxy."

This raises more than a few eyebrows, including Alice's. She gives me an "I told you so" look.

Eddie takes three steps toward me and jabs my chest with a finger. "And if you kill any of my people, so help me Jesus, Mary, and fucking Joseph, I'll rip your tits off, stretch them out, and give them as fucking Christmas socks to orphans." Eddie bumps me with his shoulder and exits the work area.

There's an awkward few seconds where no one says anything. Eventually, however, Nairobi claps her hands and takes control. "Right. So, what would you like to see first, Jericho?"

"Well, I'd love a tour of the ship."

"Can do." She steps beside me and looks toward Eddie who's talking with a group of engineers in another work area. "He's a little rough around the edges."

"Hadn't noticed."

She grins. "But he's good at his job. And protective at heart."

"Both good qualities to have when you're in charge of a multi-billion coin project."

"Which is why he doesn't want anyone screwing it up. Including you." She waves to Kit who blushes bright red. "Come on. Let's get you both on the fast track. This way."

As Kit and I follow Nairobi, Adrian, and Torrence "Magellan" Vanderburg toward the *Kogarashi*'s bow entrance, a news alert flashes in V-cog. I swipe it away out of habit, noting just how much I hate active notifications, but the alert comes back.

"Cap, you seeing this?" Kit says, apparently having opened the story.

"No. But it can wait."

"Uh, not really."

I look back at Kit. "What is it?"

"Um." He swallows. "Looks like Madame Allbrook just died."

"She what?"

"Yeah. During a press conference. Saying it was a heart attack. And, and, and… you know what that means?" I do, but Kit is too quick on connecting the dots for me and anyone else listening to be stopped. "Sir Nigel Sallsworth is gonna be—"

"The new Secretary General." Whether or not the rest of my new team has seen the headline, my proclamation gets everyone's attention, including Eddie Carr's. We exchange stern looks—not new for him—and the hangar's activity slows as more crew members read the bulletin. Then we both look at the *Kogarashi.*

If Solum Terram policy becomes the dominant force under Sallsworth's leadership, which it no doubt will despite the General Council's claims that politics isn't a factor in their decision making, the *Kogarashi* has a higher chance of being used as low-income housing than it does reaching Alpha Centauri. Everyone knows it, we just assumed Allbrook would never let that happen, just like the long legacy of Presies had done before her.

"What're we gonna do, Cap?" Kit asks nervously.

I stare at the *Koga* as I'm forced to reconcile my apprehensions with the sudden fear that the mission might get scrapped before we have a chance to maiden the ship. "Fly it," I tell Kit. "Bump up the launch timeline, and fly the hell out of it."

2

EVELYN

"He makes me sick," Natalie Mason blurts out. She's sitting across from me in our breakroom, watching the verb feed on Sallsworth's swearing in taking place in Oslo. "No way he was going to win this election."

"Not without a miracle," I say in agreement.

"And this isn't one of those, I can tell you that. Something stinks."

Natalie, the team's linguist and cryptographer with a minor in astroarchaeology, is as skeptical as she is curious. Add to that tenacious, resilient, and dangerously intelligent, and it's little wonder why she's become one of my favorite assets on the SESI Special Projects Team tasked with parsing the extrasolar sentient transmission.

"I'm telling you right now," Natalie says without turning away from the verb glass on the far wall. "Our funding is going to dry up. You wait and see."

"Have a little faith," says Sebastián Fernández Parra, our most recent addition. "There are plenty of gatekeepers guarding our efforts."

Natalie squints at the dark Spaniard. "More angels and shit?"

"Among other things. Though I trust Hartwell and

Minkosef will rally the full weight of the Viatoribus and Sentia Aux respectively to keep any such things from happening. Our work is far too critical."

Natalie faces him and folds her arms in a playfully defiant posture. "I still can't figure you out, Sebastián."

"Oh?"

"One second you think God will save us, and then next you're lobbying for more crypto for space expansion."

"Even faith needs a little push from time to time."

"So you've said." Her frown deepens. "Tell me again how a former priest turns evolutionary biologist?"

"Anyone who says faith and science are incongruent doesn't fully understand either."

"And you do?"

"I'm just one beggar telling other beggars where I've found food for the day. Nothing more."

Jose Ramirez, who was our chief dynamicist on *Astraea* Station, pipes up. "I think he just wanted to have sex again."

"You would," Natalie scoffs.

"What? People have needs. Sheesh."

I ignore the verbal sparring that ensues and turn back to the verb coverage of Sallsworth's swearing in. Tensions have been high ever since Secretary General Mary Allbrook's heart attack two days ago. Rumors around defunding our division within the Search for Extrasolar Sentient Intelligence had blossomed like some of Sebastián's filamentous fungi in a petri dish. And Natalie isn't wrong to suspect a cut in funding. It has me concerned too. But we're close and getting closer. As soon as the puzzle is solved and we release our findings to the world, no one, not even Sir Nigel Sallsworth, will be able to stop us.

"He's a real twat, that one," Natalie says with her arms folded and glaring at the verb glass.

Ramirez stands and pours himself another cup of coffee. "Well, he's the NUE General Council's head twat now, so better get used to him. And who knows, maybe the new financial pressure will finally get you to crack the algo key."

"Screw you."

"Any time."

"Ugh. Gross."

"Hey," I stand and smooth my SESI uniform. "Anyone seen Sam?"

"Said she had to take care of something," Sebastián offers. "Seemed pretty upset and wanted to be left alone."

Ramirez sips his coffee. "Maybe it's just that time of the—"

"Don't," I say, scolding him with a raised finger. "Unless you want me to shove two ovaries up your rectum and string them together with a garden hose."

Ramirez winces, softens, and then gestures toward the glass. "Maybe she was just having a hard time with the news about Mr. Perfect there."

Mary Allbrook's body wasn't even cold when Sir Nigel Sallsworth was unanimously acclaimed as the General Council's new Secretary General. His acceptance coincided with the promised assault on the Tantum Terrae—a strange about-face for a man who, at certain times, tried to rationalize the group's extremist activities. At the moment, the war was waged with search warrants and crypto sanctions. But everyone knew what was coming; the infamous underground leader, Neon, wouldn't take this lying down.

Not wanting Sam to be alone, I ping her in V-cog. "Hey, Sam?" I step into her public lobby. "You here?"

No reply.

"I'm, uh… just checking in on you. Wanted to make sure you're, ya know, alright, all things considered."

Still nothing.

Maybe she's taking a nap and has notifications off.

I consider using my creds and the building's grid to pinpoint her location. It's not illegal. Stars, locating staff is what it's designed for. But most people don't use the feature because of the voyeuristic connotations and the desire to preserve a sense of trust within the organization. Still, if Sam's hurting, I need to be there for her.

From within my V-cog admin menu, I pull up the name Samantha Collins in my team directory and then navigate to the location submenu. I hesitate just before opening the campus map. I don't want to break her trust. But she's been acting strange ever since *Astraea*'s demise. And she's not alone. Suicide rates have hit all-time highs. Counseling clinics have been flooded. And unemployment has skyrocketed. Despite increased security and the NUE's assurances that no more habs will be falling through the atmosphere, the planet has been in a tumultuous state. Human beings are inherently emotional animals, something I really dislike about us. About myself. If I could switch it all off, I would. But we're stuck with our irrationality, our fears, and our desire to fit in and be accepted by a tribe.

All cytoplasm loves to join. Damn.

I launch the map.

♣

THE MORGUE in NUESSA's headquarters hospital is the last place I would expect to find Sam. I'm racking my brain why she would even be here, but I'm drawing blanks. There is one possibility, of course, but Sam hasn't seemed overly depressed—maybe anxious, is all. However, if she were ever going to… well, end things, it would be just like her to try and make less work for those picking up after her. The morgue would be fitting then. But that doesn't add up for me.

I move down the hall with renewed purpose, growing more convinced that maybe Sam is in some sort of emotional pain beyond the anxiety she's been fighting the last week. As an extra precaution, I double-check her vitals to make sure she… doesn't need emergency help. But everything looks stable. The only things even vaguely notable are an increase in heart rate and raised cortisol levels, both of which could be explained by anything from walking fast to crying. Nothing out of the ordinary. Even so, I pick up the pace.

The white-walled corridor of subfloor two is quiet; apparently the staff are all off watching the inauguration. Which means I'll have fewer people to explain my presence to. That's good, because the only person I want to talk to right now is Sam.

My V-cog clears a security checkpoint and opens the doors leading to the morgue's vestibule. Frosted glass frames a check-in counter occupied with a single secretarial excipion. The android is painted white with red accents and bears the universal medical shield on its shoulder and a white cross on the side of its red-plated head. Round LED eyes glow a soft yellow, and articulated hands and fingers rest flat on the desk.

"Please confirm voice identification with name listed

in virtual cognizance registry," says the bot, its angular jaw moving up and down as it speaks.

"Doctor Evelyn Park."

"Voice print and pheromone signature accepted. Please state your reason for entry."

"Unscheduled meeting with Doctor Samantha Collins."

"Reason noted. Please proceed Dr. Park. Have a nice day."

"You too," I say and then pass through the doors. I could totally take that one in the kickboxing ring. Probably knock its anthropomorphic jaw off its head too, given enough rounds.

The hallway ends at a hub with six doors leading to different rooms, ranging from Pathology and Forensics to Refrigeration and Cremation. Sam's ident places her behind the door marked Arrivals. I push aside any lingering images linked to the room's ominous-sounding title and step through the doors to find Sam standing over a drawer with a corpse in it. "Sam?"

Her head snaps up, eyes squinting at me. "Evelyn? What are you doing here?"

"I came to… check on you. But…" She doesn't *look* depressed. If anything, she looks mad. "Mind if I ask you the same thing?"

Sam's face and shoulders stiffen before she glances at the drawer she's standing over.

Curious, I approach the corpse, but my feet stop as soon as I notice the face, or what's left of it. "Stamos?"

She nods solemnly.

"Sam, what… what's this about? You shouldn't be touching him before the autopsy. The investigation's still—"

"I had to see him," Sam says, suddenly seething

with anger. "I had to look in his face one more time. To try to come to grips with just how many people he's… he's responsible for killing." A tear streaks down her cheek, jawbones pulsing. "I just can't wrap my head around what would possess… how someone can justify all the… the people." She's suddenly overcome with grief and shuts her eyes, weeping at whatever memories she carries from our last hours on *Astraea* Station. I know, because I've done my share of grieving lately. And I can't say I don't blame her either for wanting to see the asshole one more time.

Jack Birdwhistle's naked corpse lies in the drawer half covered by the plastic sheet, his skull splayed open by Rook's weapon as if the shot were fired yesterday.

Sam's next words seem to rise up from somewhere deep inside her. "I hate him, Eves. I hate them with everything I am."

"Them?"

"The… Tantum Terrae."

"Right."

"And yet"—she wipes some of her tears away—"they're us. They're just people too, trying to do what they believe is best, aren't they?"

The sudden shift toward empathy surprises me—proof she's not thinking clearly. "They are people, yes. But what they've done… it's inexcusable. Ends don't justify the means."

"Of course, you're right. I'm just…" She sniffs as if trying hard to compose herself. "I'm sorry you had to find me like this." But then Sam hesitates and cocks her head at me as a thought forms behind her eyes. "How did you know I was here? Did you… did you track my location?"

"Sam, I was only trying to…"

"Spy on me?"

"No. I… was worried about you."

"You could have just asked me."

"I tried pinging you in V-cog, but you didn't an-swer." She looks hurt, so I add, "But I understand why now."

At this, her shoulders relax ever so slightly, and she looks back at Jack. "I'm sorry. I should have told you where I was going. I just—"

"It's alright." My hand goes to her shoulder. "You don't need to explain it to me. And I'm sorry for spying on you."

She cups her hand over mine. "Thanks."

After another few seconds, I say, "You wanna get out of here? End work early and grab some drinks?"

This seems to startle her out of her funk. "That's my line, Miss Workaholic."

"So you do wanna work late then?"

"You're a crafty lady, Eves."

"Back to work it is." Then we both shove the drawer closed and put Jack back where he belongs.

THE LAST THREE days have been a blur for me. None of us have bothered to go home, opting instead to sleep on cots in our respective offices and share meals in the small cafeteria on the fourteenth floor of SESI's Schwarzschild Celestial Research Building on the St. John's campus. That is, when we feel like eating. The excitement mounting around our work is such that most of us need reminding to eat, a task taken up by our ever-watchful biologist, Seb.

"Well at least take some water," he says as he extends a tray while we hunker over a shared workstation. Sam grabs a cup of water for me and a second one for herself.

"Thanks, Seb," Natalie offers as she takes a cup.

Ramirez nods his thanks too.

Then it's all eyes back on the problem at hand.

In the real, the team sits around a nine-meter-square holo table capable of rendering out the cubed space in nanometer pixels. It's state of the art, even for professional physicists. In addition, we occupy a shared workspace in V-cog that takes up a warehouse-sized room filled with white boards, dry-erase glass panes, and countless desks topped with classic notepads, quantum calculators, filing cabinets, and computer monitors. Despite attempts in the last two hundred years to fully convert humanity to imageless existential processing, it turns out we're still tactile learners. Even our most cerebral activities function best when connected to physical objects that can help organize, process, and store our thoughts with spatial benchmarks. Granted, we use virtual spaces to do it in, reducing the amount of natural resources needed to create the physical and sometimes no-longer-made products, but the brain still likes the touchpoints even if they aren't real.

The alpha technosignature that Parallax received from Kepler-1649c and that Lemuel illegally saved on his cold storage device of a Catholic medallion fell within the Hawking-Belmont window—a long-hypothesized range of values believed to be among those most likely used by sentient species—and met the IPCSI standards, that is, the initial proof of communication from sentient intelligence. Our signal, captured on July 30th, was one nanometer in wavelength, three times ten to the sixteenth in frequency, sent in three-second bursts that lasted for 180 seconds, and did not repeat—not naturally occurring and definitely not an accident. Moreover, the power required to be this precise, and over a distance of ninety-two parsecs, means that whoever sent it had the technology to do so three hundred and one years ago, because Kepler-1649c is three hundred and one light-years away. If we can figure out what the signal means and why it was sent in the first place, then hopefully the rest will be answered in time.

At present, we are what feels like one discovery away from cracking the code that will unlock the vault. It's what Ramirez scolded Natalie about when he remarked on the algo key a few days ago. Most complex problems don't require fifty different things to be addressed before the equation is solved. That's because any problem a person faces is relative to their present level of understanding; a human in 1903 was not faced with going to the moon. However, they did need to know how to solve for lift and center-of-gravity in order to fly. Breakthroughs usually come down to one or two elusive discoveries that evade the problem solvers. But if they can find it—that sweet spot, that resonant frequency—then the whole thing starts to sing, and two brothers from Dayton, Ohio can defy gravity.

"We've been at this today for… for…" Sam looks at the wall. "Nine hours without a break?"

"I told you to eat something," Sebastián says.

Ramirez rubs his belly. "I could go for a few burritos. Anybody else?"

"You've eaten plenty of those for all of us, Jose," I reply. But the friendly jab doesn't gain the humor traction it might normally; we're all a bit tense, especially Natalie.

"We're so close though," she says. "I can feel it. It's just… It's right there, ya know?" She thrusts both hands at the centerpiece of our frustrations: a model of the wave transmission, represented in peaks and valleys, accompanied by a veritable mountain of binary code. The sheer amount of ones and zeros that flows from the light transmission is truly mind numbing. Even with my physics background, I can't wrap my head around the number Natalie says the stream contains. But therein lies the problem. The code is so gratuitously random that not even our best quantum computers have been able to parse any patterns, aside from an obvious one that we discovered on day one.

"Alright, let's just step back for a second and review," I say. "Number one, the signal bears all of the significant predicated signs that it was created by a sentient species and directed at us. Number two, the only discernible pattern is the obvious three-second segments that repeat every nine seconds. And number three, we have a treasure trove of binary code that we can't make heads or tails of."

Everyone nods in agreement, as if some mystical form of consensus might reveal a new fact. But it doesn't.

Seb rubs his face with both hands and then looks at Natalie. "You're sure this doesn't resemble one of Sagan's models?"

Natalie shakes her head. "It would make this a whole lot simpler if it did."

By "Sagan's models," Sebastián means an experiment the legendary Cornell University professor conducted on some of his graduate students near the end of the twentieth century. He handed them a printed document of 29,791 zeroes and ones saying it was a transmission from an alien civilization. The students knew nothing of the content beyond the binary code, and envisioned it being anything from music to the script to a film. After several hours of work, however, the sleuths noticed that the sum was thirty-one cubed, whereby thirty-one became the base number for the edges of a cube. Once that was understood, the sequence of ones and zeros fell into place and, to everyone's amazement, formed a three-dimensional orbital representation of a formaldehyde molecule composed of a carbon atom, two hydrogen atoms, and an oxygen atom. The students then deduced that the significance of a formaldehyde molecule was the radio frequency attached to it; in essence, the fictional aliens were instructing observers to recalibrate their telescopes to search within a particular frequency.

The entire premise was as rudimentary as it was sublime, and perhaps a touch romantic too. It made several assumptions, all of which we assume Sagan knew, including that aliens understood binary code, had sensory organs by which to manipulate light, and "saw" atoms in three dimensions—all features we would hold in common. A more distressing reality is that alien life has been attempting to communicate with us for eons, yet we share so little in common ontologically that the transmissions have gone—as it were—right over our heads.

But to Carl Sagan's credit, at least one aspect of his experiment turned out to be true: that whoever sent our message captured now in 2251 understands how to embed data within light as binary code, the simplest of all transmission types. It is either on or off, a one or a zero. But instead of finding a key, like determining the cube of the sum, we have chaos.

"What I don't understand is why it wouldn't be simpler to deduce," Sam says after a moment pacing the lab. "Like, you're making contact for the very first time… don't you want it to be simple? Like, 'Hi. Nice to meet you.'"

"For all we know, this is that simple," Seb replies. "To them, anyway."

"And more complex than our best computers can parse," Natalie adds. "Still, logic says that the sender would know that if we have the technology to detect their signal, we also have capability to discern it." Our resident cryptographer seems like she's going to say something more, but the look on her face falls into more discouragement. Then she pats her cheeks as if trying to stay awake. "The verb is gonna have a field day spinning this one."

"Goodbye funding." Ramirez shrugs his shoulders. "It was inevitable, I guess."

Ramirez isn't wrong, either. Within just three days of Sir Nigel Sallsworth being in power, the Solum Terram has already commenced audits on all SESI projects, ours most notably. I knew it was coming, we all did, just figured we'd have more time.

"We're not giving up," I reply at last in a genuine attempt to rally the room. "We've already made history once, and, stars, we'll do it again. Who's with me?"

Everyone smiles, but I can tell they're tired. Crikey, I'm tired. But we're so close, I can feel it.

"Can we be with you after some chalupas and a nap?" Ramirez asks.

That does sound good right about now. Both chalupas and some sleep.

Just then, something hits me.

"Eves?" Sam asks. "What is it?"

"What?"

"You're tapping your nose. You got something?"

I look at my index finger, pull my hand down, and turn to Natalie. "What you said a moment ago…"

"About?"

"How the verb will spin this."

"And?"

I start typing on my V-cog terminal while I talk. "There's another type of light transmission we haven't considered."

Natalie is quick to wave me off. "Evelyn, we've already gone over the simplest constructs that—"

"Not the simplest for us." I pull up the research file I want and open it for the team. "The simplest for a species who can transmit light ninety-two parsecs and hit a bullseye."

Natalie reads the folder title and her eyes go wide. "Photon OAM?"

"Yup."

She hesitates a moment and then smacks her forehead. "Oh my God. That… that might be it."

"It's a worth a shot if we can—"

"Figure out the right channel demultiplexer. Evelyn, you're…" Natalie's tired eyes have suddenly taken to sparkling. "You're a goddamn genius!"

"Only if this works."

"Hold up," Sebastián says. "Can we go back to Photon OAM please?"

"What he said," adds Ramirez.

"It stands for orbital angular momentum," I explain. "It was a type of light communication pioneered in the early twenty-first century but largely abandoned because it was too cost prohibitive, even though it provided exponentially more permutations for data within a given transmission than conventional methods."

Natalie sees that no one is satisfied with my explanation and decides to elaborate a bit more. "So, in terms of light communication, photons have three basic components that matter: energy, which is determined by wavelength; polarization, which has to do with how the photon spins; and orbital angular momentum, which is a helical pattern that the photon makes around the direction of motion, like a spiral staircase."

"The verb spinning the story," Ramirez says with a wink. "I see the connection."

I smile and gesture for Natalie to keep going, but she doesn't bite. "This is really more your department, Evelyn."

"Okay. Well, the OAM mode order is determined by the number of phase changes in the azimuthal direction, which means beams with different values are orthogonal to each other as a subset of the Laguerre–Gaussian modal basis and—"

Seb cuts me off. "I'm sorry, Evelyn. I'm sure that's all very important, and I won't say I'm not intrigued, but is there a way that you can sum for us so we can test this whole… *whatever it is* hypothesis?"

I push some hair behind my ear and feel myself blush a little. "Sorry. It basically means that, by using a photon's third value, we get a nearly unlimited number of possibilities. Then multiplex three or four beams of light together, and you—"

"Multiplex?" Seb asks.

Sam jumps in this time. "Encoding. It's a way of combining similar types of data, like channels. Makes it easier to send over long distances. If you have the source code on the other end, you can untangle it all."

"Demultiplexing," Seb offers, nodding to Natalie who first used the term.

"Exactly," she replies.

Ramirez looks like he's getting it. "So you think that's what our signal is? That the aliens tweaked the spiral staircases, encoded a few beams together, and shot it our way—assuming we'd be smart enough to decode it?"

I shrug at Natalie and then raise an eyebrow to Ramirez. "That's about the sum of it, yes. But if they're as advanced as we think they are, then it would only make sense they'd use something this…"

"Complicated?" Ramirez suggests.

"No. Elegant." I turn to Natalie. "Which means we have our next goal."

She gives me a fist to bump. "Try to figure what codec they used."

Just then, I catch Sam crossing her arms. For a split second, she looks… concerned, maybe? But it's gone before I can settle it, and Sam flashes me a bright smile. "What are we waiting for?"

3

———

NEON

Mary Allbrook was dead, and Neon had nothing to do with it. That unsettled her.

Neon loathed unanswered questions. What's more, she hated things not going according to plan, especially when it came to wet work. She took assassinations seriously. Contrary to what she supposed people thought of her, none of her executions were flippant acts of violence. Did the murders produce chaos? Certainly. That was the point after all. Without disorder, there would be no call for reform, and without reform, there would be no need for the Tantum Terrae at the table. But the killings themselves were always masterfully constructed moves on the politicast chessboard.

The fact remained, however, that someone had moved out of turn.

Neon's feet were sore. She unzipped her black leather boots and let them tumble off her desk and slap the concrete floor. Then she stretched like a feline readying for a nap and watched her laborers unfurling TT banners from the second level. The factory had produced German automobiles right up until the Hundred Years Migration forced it to close. *What a shame*, she thought. The facility had been a prestigious one, bearing the long-revered AMG logo on the front facade. Now, the Affalterbach plant in the Ludwigsburg district of Baden-Württemberg, Old Germany, was a husk of its former glory. The company lived on, of course, finding new grounds in higher latitudes. But this? This would be her new home. *For now, anyway.*

It had been a week since the traitor Sir Nigel Sallsworth had voted in line with the rest of the council to declare open war against the Tantum Terrae—a move that very much surprised her. It was a good thing she hadn't yet spent valuable resources to assassinate Allbrook. It seemed that Sallsworth had taken care of that too, or so she suspected. It *was* an assassination despite how the verb covered it and what the medical examiner declared as the cause of death: a heart attack. Sallsworth didn't have Gaia's Blood, no one did, so he must have risked the use of more conventional nanopoisons, though one still able to fool investigators.

Clever boy.

Nigel's newfound backbone forced her to evacuate Calvert Isle and give orders to torch the headquarters in Vancouver too. Sallsworth had been to both locales, and she anticipated he would come after her. And Neon was right. Within hours of Sallsworth taking office as the NUE General Council's new Secretary General, now just three days ago, her orbital satellites picked up recon activity on Calvert Isle. His agents would only find the smoldering remains of her enclave obliterated by incendiary devices, but that was beside the point.

Sallsworth had wasted no time in securing NUE resources to do his private bidding. Then again, the council had declared war against her, so using the people's crypto to rout her was perfectly legal. And so who cared if he was overly aggressive in his pursuit of her? Any audit into government action that went beyond the standard rules of engagement could be easily written off as officially sanctioned work against a state enemy. Such was politics. And such was Nigel's cleverness.

Having to destroy her properties was a shame. Neon loved her island estate and vineyards. Likewise, the Vancouver headquarters had been a favorite office space. But she had other safe houses, other islands to cultivate beyond those that the Solum Terram was raiding even now. Her resources were more sizable than Nigel knew. So despite all of Sallsworth's efforts to strangle her, Neon was far from running out of breath.

The game was just getting started.

What possessed Neon now was striking a blow against Sallsworth. She had been so close to the Tantum becoming a recognized politicast. Then, in one fell swoop, it all flipped on her. He would pay for that. She would crush him. Just as she would crush those responsible for slaying her son, Jack.

"Are you here?" Neon said in Olivia Tomlinson's V-cog lobby. She double-checked the quantum lock just to make sure the connection was secure and that no geo-coordinates were being logged. Then she asked again, noting how long it took for the incog known as Dr. Samantha Collins to appear.

The thirty-two-year-old blonde-haired woman stepped into the virtual living room to find Neon already seated on a couch. "Sorry. In a meeting."

"Need me to try again later?" she asked without meaning it. Olivia would know better than to accept the offer.

"Of course not. I said it was my mother calling."

"Quaint. Well, I shan't keep you long, *daughter*. Do you have it?"

"Yes. Just as you asked."

"Where is it?"

"With me. It's… it's safe."

Neon noted the hesitation. "Were you discovered?"

"Almost."

"By?"

"Dr. Park."

"Should I be concerned?"

"No. I played the part. Enraged at the culprit. Needing closure."

Neon cleaned the front of her teeth with her tongue and raised her chin in an effort to steel herself against the answer to the next question. "And how was he?"

"At peace."

"Diplomatic. His body?"

"They hadn't done the autopsy yet, if that's what you're asking."

"Don't avoid the answer, Olivia."

The incog took a deep breath. "His face was mostly gone. The MAW rounds saw to that. He also had—"

"I want to see."

Olivia pursed her lips. For a second, Neon thought the woman might refuse. But then a holo window appeared over the coffee table, and Olivia looked away as her visual memory played out for Neon to see. Interesting that the incog didn't want to view it again… or maybe she was just giving Neon some privacy.

Jack's hand had been severed four centimeters above the wrist and lay beside his naked thigh. Dried blood surrounded several puncture wounds in his torso, while heavy bruising testified of the struggle he'd undergone leading up to his execution. Despite his advanced tweak code, the Marines had overpowered him and eventually shot him in the back of the head with their magnetic acceleration weapons. Her son. Her *baby*.

The cowards.

In the real, Neon dug her nails into the arms of her office chair, but in Sam's lobby, she kept her hands light and delicate on the couch fabric. Eventually, the footage ended, and Sam swiped away the screen.

"I can destroy the ring as soon as I get access to—"

"No. I want it."

The incog furrowed her brow. "But it's too dangerous to—"

"Your place is not to lecture me on danger, Olivia."

"Of course. Forgive me."

"I'll send someone to retrieve it."

"To St. John's?"

Neon tilted her head. "Is that a problem?"

"No. No, of course not. It's just that… security has been ramped up since *Astraea*, and they're matching nanos to genes with bio scanners."

"I'm aware. What about the signal?"

Sam walked to a leather chair and sat on the arm. "It's been slow going."

"But?"

"But we might have a breakthrough."

"*They* might have a breakthrough?"

Sam touched her temple and winced. "Right. Force of habit."

"And you'll ensure the research fails?"

"Of course. I won't have to try very hard anyway."

"Oh?"

"The signal, it's… complicated, as is the tech used to send it, I'm guessing. Not even sure we'll be able to—"

"I need assurances."

Sam straightened. "Their efforts will fail. Whether by me or by their own ineptitude. I'll make sure of it."

"I want a report as soon as it's done."

"Understood."

Neon rose from the couch but stopped short of turning out the door. "I'm counting on you—"

"Thank you for that trust."

"—I'm counting on you to take out Dr. Park and her team if you're unable to keep them from deciphering the transmission. *You* cannot afford to fail me again, Olivia dear."

"Fail you?"

"You need a reminder?"

Olivia's lips parted, then closed.

"I'll take that as a yes. How sad. You failed to keep knowledge of the alien transmission from going public and, worse, you failed to *protect my son*."

"I did the best that I—"

"It was not enough now, was it?"

"No, ma'am."

"Mmmm."

"I won't fail you again."

"I should hope not. For your sake. Whatever Dr. Park's team finds, it must not be allowed to leave their lab. Do you understand?"

Sam stood to meet Neon's eyes. "Of course. I'll take care of it."

"You'd better." Then Neon waved the door open and stepped out of Olivia Tomlinson's V-cog lobby.

⁂

"REALLY, MOTHER?" Gemma asked, striding across the factory floor in bright yellow sneakers and grey orbital fatigues. "So much trouble for his ring?"

"It reminds me of him."

"And so does Klaus, but I don't see you wanting him around."

"He's in prison."

"And breaking him out would still be easier than retrieving a damn ring from SESI headquarters." Gemma wheeled another office chair over, plopped down in it, and kicked her heels onto her mother's desk. "We don't even need it. Gaia's Blood is almost done."

"I need his ring," Neon replied, trying her best not to pull her lips back as she spoke. "It's... well, it's..."

"Because you're sentimental."

"I prefer nostalgic."

"Same thing." Gemma squinted at her mother. "That's why we're here, isn't it."

Neon raised a corrective finger. "You and I both know that Affalterbach is closer to—"

"It's where my stepbrother grew up without you."

"Watch your tongue."

"Am I wrong? And don't give me some bullshit about how it's closer to Helsinki or Oslo."

Neon knew she couldn't outtalk her daughter. If apples didn't fall far from trees, Gemma would be stronger and more powerful than Neon ever hoped to be. That was the plan, anyway. But the sapling had been corrupted along the way, coaxed by foreign winds and nurtured by waters of popularity and fame. Which was why the younglings needed the old trees to stand guard like sentinels until their times came. Deep roots, Neon reminded herself. The aged were not so easily swayed by the winds of change, and Gemma needed correcting as she grew into adulthood.

In a rare show of vulnerability, Neon pulled her feet onto her seat and confessed, "He's dead because of me."

"No, mother. He's dead because he got caught. You had nothing to do with that."

"He was trying to prove himself to me."

"That's what kids do."

Neon looked up. "You didn't."

"Sure, I did. But I was ten when I figured I could kill you in your sleep if I wanted. Jack was twice that when you betrayed Klaus."

Neon massaged her foot absently. "I gave that man what he deserved for stealing my child from me."

"No, you went easy on him because you still had feelings for him. Like I said, sentimental."

"You really think me so inept?"

Gemma took her sneakers off the desk and leaned forward to rest her elbows on her knees. A lock of pink-dyed hair swung over one eye. "I think you like the old ways so much that you forget what needs doing."

"And what would you do? Kill Klaus and everyone else who gets in your way?"

"I'd destroy the system, for one."

"Oh, here we go again. Because that's going to solve everything."

"I never said it would. But we could at least start over and get rid of a back-assward politicast system that—"

"We need it, Gemma. The structure is what enables us to—"

"Trade one oppressive regime for another?"

"The Tantum stands for liberty!"

"Not when it has to play by someone else's rules, it doesn't."

Neon had enough of this. She plucked a boot off the floor with her bare foot and pulled it over her calf with her hands. "Get me Jack's ring."

"I'll do it myself."

"No. Send Jager."

"You don't trust me?"

"I need you for something else."

Gemma sat back, attentive. "Go on."

"I need incogs inside the Solum Terram's headquarters."

Gemma smiled. "We already have plenty who we can—"

"Their new headquarters, within the General Council."

"Sallsworth's office?"

"He had Allbrook killed."

"You have proof?"

Neon pulled her other boot on. "Do I need any?"

"Sallsworth doesn't have the balls. He wouldn't risk getting his hands dirty."

Now it was Neon's turn to smile. For all her daughter's bravado and bullheadedness, Gemma still had much to learn. *"Desperate men in the dark dare desperate deeds in the day."*

"Hippocrates?"

"Matismoto. We need to know who he's working with now that he's decided to part ways."

Gemma sighed. "I'll see what I can do."

"There's more." She didn't wait for her daughter to reply. "I want to rattle his cage."

"How badly?"

"Tuesday Soldiers."

Gemma's body stiffened. "You sure?"

"Yes. It's time. I'll make a schedule and a list of participants."

The first verse of the epic poem played out in Neon's mind as she studied her daughter's face. She tried to imagine herself six years younger than Gemma was now. Tried to imagine such suffering. And the unwanted pregnancy that was to come. Then there was Klaus, so young and fair, finding her outside the ruins of Edinburgh Castle with blood on her hands. They would spill much more together. And raise a son.

> *Tuesday Soldiers of October the Eighth*
> *Stood shoulder to shoulder at the Canongate*
> *When twelve came the toll from Blue Crow's bell*
> *Still shoulder to shoulder, they marched into hell*

Something flickered in Gemma's eyes just then. Neon couldn't be sure, but it looked like reservation. It made her wonder if Gemma was ready for all that was to come. Ready to pull the trigger. Ready to give birth to a revolution.

4

———————

JERICHO

"KIT? YOU BACK THERE?" I ask into one of the *Kogarashi*'s storage holds that looks far from flight ready.

A dull *thud* sounds followed by, "Son of a nut-cracker! Yeah, Cap. We're here."

"We?" I start making my way around open cargo cases and nests of tools and tangled cabling. "And what the hell is this mess?"

"Leftovers. Seems some of the team need to be taught lessons on keeping their workspaces clear. And until I can find out who did this, I'm taking responsibility since it was on my watch."

"You're too good for the world, Kit," I say just as the kid comes into view. He's up to his elbows sorting equipment. Two worker excipions are on either side, apparently attempting to detangle some fiber optic weave but not looking very successful. The blue and grey bots are more slender than their planet-bound counterparts; less mass and size are essential for maneuvering in tight quarters and weightlessness. "Looks like you found some help."

One of the excipion looks up at me and waves. "Salutations."

I ignore it. "Nairobi says she needs you on the bridge."

Kit looks up and blushes. "She does?"

"Says you're not answering V-cog too."

"Oh, um… Yeah, I… I'm just busy."

"Busy?" I look around at the mess again. "You can't ignore your team leader, Kit."

"Who said I was ignoring her?"

I fold my arms.

"Okay, fine. But she's… and I'm like… and then there's this thing that—"

"Kit?"

"What?"

"Focus."

"What do you think I'm doing?"

One of my eyebrows perches a little higher than the other. "I think you're conducting menial tasks better suited for excipions when you should be up front with our lead propulsion engineer. No offense," I say to the bots.

"No offense registered," says the second of the pair.

"But the Ferguses need my help," Kit insists.

"Ferguses?"

"Yeah. Thought I'd, ya know, name them and stuff."

"You named them? Good Lord."

"Good Lord is an improper designation," says the first bot. "Correct name: Fergus One."

I glare at Kit and then the second bot. "Let me guess. Fergus Two?"

The excipion raises a hand in response and waves.

"Oh my God. Kit, you can't go around rewriting their alphanumeric call signs."

"But they like it. And isn't it time we started treating them with more respect anyway?"

"You know who you should be treating with more respect right now? Nairobi Kinshaw, that's who. And if you don't haul your scrawny ass to the bridge ASAP, I'm gonna rewrite your call sign."

"Fergus Three?" suggests the first bot.

I point a finger at the robot's face. "You. Can it. And both of you, get this place cleaned up."

"Acknowledged," they say in unison and then return to their work.

"FOUND HIM," I say to Nairobi as I usher Kit through the door and onto the bridge.

"Where at?" she replies from the captain's chair.

"Helping two excipions prepare for the suffrage movement."

Nairobi gives Kit a pleased look. "Nice. They ready to petition the NUE for voting rights?"

"Ha ha," Kit blurts out and then quickly covers his mouth.

Nairobi winks and then turns back to me. "Speaking of petitions, Eddie's looking for you."

"You don't say." I tap the side of my head. "We have V-cog, last I checked. And unlike some people, I answer my calls."

Kit looks away from my glare. "I was consumed with my work, okay? Sheesh."

Nairobi makes a click in the side of her cheek and then goes back to working through the diagnostic holo screen. "Yeah, well, Eddie doesn't like using the tech when he knows he'll catch up face to face. Says he needs to show you something important before we move up to the launch dock. He's in the command quad."

"Thanks for the heads up."

"Eh, I'm not sure you'll be thanking me, but okay. Kit, a little help here?"

"He he he, she knows my name," he says to me.

I give him another stern look.

"Okay, okay, sheesh. I'm going, I'm going."

"Talk to her, not me. Copy?"

"Of course, yeah. Copy copy."

"We'll be fine," Nairobi says. "Catch you later, Cap."

"Later."

I MAKE my way out of the *Koga*, now just forty-eight hours away from the same test flight that cost people's lives and got me fired as a result, and head across the hangar toward the central square of admin workstations. Eddie is alone, head down, eyes locked on one of four curved holo screens.

There hasn't been much time to get to know my team members yet. We've been too focused on getting the ship operational before any sanctions come down from NUE oversight. Sallsworth hadn't been in office ten minutes before rumors started flying about how he was trimming NUESSA and SESI budgets. I don't doubt the veracity of those rumors either. Where the Tantum Terrae's disdain for space expansion manifests in bombs and bullets, the Solum Terram's emerges in the unseen squeeze of budgets and bureaucrats. Hell, I'm not convinced Sallsworth even won fair and square.

Another reason for my team's aloofness could just

be a defense mechanism… on everyone's part. None of us wanna get attached to people who we might have to say goodbye to prematurely. I encountered that a lot in flight school. But there's another aspect at play, if I'm being honest: this team might have second thoughts about Jericho Fox being in command.

While Nairobi seems the most amiable, Adrian Wallace and Magellan are a little harder to read. Which, I suppose, should make Eddie Carr's opinion of me that much easier to digest because it's at least a known variable. The guy hates me. Better the enemy you see than the one you don't, right?

That said, Eddie is hardly my enemy. I've gone toe to toe with the Solum Terram and the Tantum Terrae. They gunned for my head, literally. All Eddie wants is to keep his crew safe and get his office back. Eh, maybe he wants my head too. Time will tell.

I gain his attention as I step into the command quad. "Nairobi said you were looking for me."

"Oi. Wanted to show you something."

"Alright."

He works the terminal fast and brings up a series of windows. It's all just pages and pages of random data to me until I see a ship schematic.

"What are you doing with that?" I ask, pointing to the window with a rendering of my old ship, the X-10 ES *Perseverant*. The sight of it brings up all kinds of emotions, none of which I need right now.

"Research."

"Listen, Eddie. If there's something you wanna ask me, I already told you—"

"I'm not here to ask you shit, you twat. I'm here to fucking show you something that I need you to make sure you understand."

"Alright. Hold up. I'm all for an education, but you gotta stop being a dick."

"Can't. It's in my nature."

"Then your nature's gonna get you fired."

"Huh. Wouldn't be the first time."

We stare at each other in a stand off until I finally say, "Whadda ya got?"

Eddie circles two different data sets and then sits back, folding his arms. I step in beside him and move the holo screens up to my level. The fields he's identified are from two different sensor systems, one from *Astraea* Station's Special Operations Space Traffic Control Center, the other from the *Perseverant*'s onboard master flight control system. They bear the same category fields, as far as I can tell, presenting identical and painfully long data sets.

"Gonna need you to explain, Eddie."

"Thought you'd never ask. Notice the time stamp?"

"I do." He's called up the *Perseverant*'s telemetry 120 seconds before I ejected. It's not a date or time a test pilot or engineer ever forgets. God knows I wish I could. "If this is your idea of hazing, then you're gonna hate the write up I'll be forced to make."

"No hazing here, Foxy. Just want you to watch." He hits the play button, and the telemetry data starts advancing. Numbers race by to the hundred-thousandth, clocking everything from time and distance to rads and fuel expenditure. It's all there, plotted along the ship's ill-fated trajectory through the big black. And it's numbing, not just because of how I feel watching it, but because there's no way to make any sense of it without AI interpreting the sheer volume of data. It's like asking someone to view raw V-cog code instead of the beautiful panorama rendered in the mind's eye.

Ninety seconds remain until the ship's drive core fails.

"Eddie, this isn't helping your—"

"Watch, you twat."

I pull my lips in and make a fist when a small white error flag appears beside a seemingly innocuous line of telemetry. On its own, the indicator means nothing. A hiccup in the sensors with a thousand benign explanations. But then there's another on the category below it, and another, and another. I glance at the mission clock. Sixty-three seconds remaining.

More white error flags trip, and soon there's a list fifty long, maybe more.

My heart is beating so hard I feel like it might break my ribs. At the same time, I'm having trouble breathing.

"You see it, don't you, you bastard. You fucking see it. Oi?"

"Turn it off."

"No."

"I said, turn it off!" My voice rings in the hangar, but I'm beyond caring. I just want it off. All of it off.

Now.

When Eddie doesn't move, I step in to override his terminal privileges, but he catches my wrist. "Oh no you don't."

I rip my hand away and lunge forward, but Eddie stands and drives his shoulder into my ribcage so hard it knocks the air out of me. Still, I'm straining for the terminal interface. I'm gonna knock this guy out if he doesn't let go. But he's got me locked so I can't stop the data from replaying, and his face is buried in my side so I can't punch it. I can only watch the time count toward the *Perseverant*'s end… toward the Ebra-drive's detonation.

I'm angry.

And afraid.

More error flags run down the Space Traffic Control Center screen while the ship's log shows no deviation. Deviation that the operator on *Astraea* would have seen had he been there. Had *I* been there, instead of on the *Perseverant*.

The weight of the discovery hits me like a hover truck. I'm jarred. My brain is working overtime to explain it. To find a culprit. But all the fingers feel like they're pointed back at me.

Because they are.

"No," I say, biting the inside of my cheeks until I taste blood. "That can't be." My knees give out, and I catch myself on the nearest workstation. A moment later, I'm in a chair looking up at Eddie Carr.

"It was a single sensor anomaly," he says with a cool tone. "Created a time delay that got amplified system-wide. The AI had never seen it before. It didn't know how to flag errors on both systems simultaneously since time-lock had been interrupted. Anyone on the *Perseverant* wouldn't have seen a damn thing. Only the operator at STCC, assuming they could recognize cascading event logs without a traditional warning indicator. A year's worth of coin says you'd have recognized it then because you sure as fucking hell recognize it now. Isn't that right, Captain Foxy?"

I can't respond. It's all too… real. Too simple.

Up until this moment, every person in NUESSA, every lobbyist in the Viatoribus, every NUE investigator had scoured the data and determined that the X-10's drive core had failed without warning. It was an unfortunate catastrophe that no one could have stopped because there were absolutely no indicators that anything had gone wrong.

Until now.

This… this changed everything.

Had I been behind the monitors at *Astraea*'s Space Traffic Control Center instead of aboard the *Perseverant*, I would have seen the warning signs with time to spare. Even though my replacement was overqualified for the position, they wouldn't have seen what Eddie had found, because only the mission designer would have been flipping through every last sensor log… because only the mission designer would be that obsessed with the survival of his crew.

I could have stopped it.

Which means I was to blame.

"Welcome to hell, asshole." And with that, Eddie steps around me and walks out of the workspace.

5

EVELYN

As soon as the idea of using photon orbital angular momentum dawned on us, the atmosphere of our offices in St. John's found a new gear. We'd already been sleeping on cots in our offices—some people even using sleeping bags in the hallways. But now no one is sleeping, and we're all hopped up on legal stimulants, both coded and liquid, racing from meeting room to workstation and giving orders to staffers like starship captains to deckhands.

Upon hearing our idea, Doctor Lemuel Brown, the head of SESI, assigned an additional team to our breakthrough. Cracking the language of how the aliens encoded the light streams was going to take everything we had and then some. Every brain, every quantum processor, and—stars help us—every coffee maker in the building.

To be honest, I've lost track of time. Three, four days we've been at it maybe? Hard to say. All I know is that we're getting closer, and the entire team feels it even if they do look a little worn out from the hours we've been putting in. Right now, thirty of us are packed into one of the labs for a late-night group problem solving session. Pressure from SESI and NUESSA, along with my own relentless desire to get this done, means we need to keep pushing. Plus, we've hit a wall and need to make progress before I send everyone home.

"But that doesn't work with the Fibonacci sequence," Sebastián says in a very exasperated tone accented with very Iberian-style gesticulating.

"It doesn't have to work if they're not using a Fibonacci sequence to multiplex the streams," Natalie replies.

"Yes, but shouldn't we assume that a Fibonacci sequence is—"

"I don't think we can assume anything," I interject, feeling a bit more like a referee than a scientist lately. "Other than that, maybe we need a break. Take five, everyone. We'll meet back here at"—I check the time; it's after 1:00 a.m.—"one thirty."

The room clears, and I massage my temples.

"How ya holding up?" Sam asks.

"How does it look like I'm holding up?"

"Considering the circumstances, not bad." Sam pulls a stool around. "Take a load off?"

"Thanks." I catch her smiling. "What?"

"Oh. It's just… crazy how fast things can change, ya know?"

"How so?"

"A few days ago, I was ready to give up. Then we catch a break. And now we're right back to being stonewalled." She shrugs. "And if we don't solve it soon, the project might get scrapped anyway."

"Doesn't matter."

"What do you mean?"

I cast her a dark look. "Even if the council cuts

funding, I won't give up, Sam. I'm taking this one all the way, even if I have to get private investments."

"You don't think termination would be the kiss of death? 'Hey, look at us, not even our own government would keep funding our idea, but maybe you will.'"

"Someone will. But we still have time before we need to look elsewhere. I'm hopeful."

"Yeah."

I work to catch her downturned eyes. "What is it?"

"Nothing."

"Oh, come on. We survived an exploding legacy hab together. I know when something's bothering you."

Her lips part and close twice before she finds her words. "You're gonna think I'm crazy."

"More than I already do?"

Sam chuckles, but then her expression loses its levity. "What if we're wrong?"

I sit up straight as if doing so will help me zero in on the meaning of her question. "About what?"

She gestures to the holo screens lining the walls, each filled with diagrams and data. "About them. What if they're not... benefactors?"

"Sam, you can't be—"

"I am serious. What if the whole reason we're having trouble deciphering the signal is because it wasn't meant for us. And what if the science fiction writers got it right, and we're hastening humanity's demise?"

I pull away. "Who are you right now? Stars, Sam. You're freaking me out a little."

"You haven't thought it too?"

"I..." My mouth shuts.

"See?"

"Of course I've thought about it. Who hasn't? But—"

"But what?"

"But the probabilities work in our favor."

"Yeah? And it only takes one negative probability to end us."

"Sam."

She gives me one of her trademark smiles that has a way of easing tensions. "Told ya you'd think I'm crazy."

I smile back. "Yeah."

"There's something else, if I'm being totally honest." She brushes some hair behind her ear. "It's about the funding."

"Oh… kay?"

"Is this really the best use of taxpayer money?"

"Are you serious right now? You sound like a Solum spokesperson."

"Just… hear me out, okay? I think that—"

"I think you need a break, Sam."

She waves me off. "Maybe we can still accomplish the same goal of deciphering the signal, but do it with those private funds you were talking about. Off the grid, so we don't raise any suspicions, and then when it's time—"

"Sam, the whole point of this project is to keep it *in* the public consciousness. It concerns all of humanity."

"I know. But the longer we go without having answers, the more conspiracy theories take root. And the last thing we need is mob logic undermining the greatest discovery in history. Don't you agree?"

I narrow my eyes at her. Her arguments bug me. Maybe because there are real elements of truth behind what she's saying, even though I disagree with her. But that's science, isn't it? To assert, to vigorously challenge, and then to bravely conclude. It's just… it feels like she's doubling back on me.

Then again, this hasn't been the easiest of months, and we don't exactly have a lot to show for all the money being dumped into our division. Even I know the amounts are exorbitant. Still, to believe the worst about alien life trying to make first contact? That goes against everything the Sentia Aux was founded upon. Which leaves me with a hard question to pose.

"Sam. I need to ask you something."

"Sure. Anything."

"Do you want to be here?"

She balks. "Excuse me?"

"Do you want to be here? Do you want to be on this team? I understand that things change. We change. And I'll be the last person to keep you from—"

She grabs my hand. "Eves. I want to be here."

"You mean it?"

"Of course."

I take a deep breath. I was hoping she'd say that because, after all we've been through, I can't imagine not having her with me. She's become like… well, like family… part of the blanket that you know you belong under. And after fighting so hard to find people I click with, the thought of losing one now unsettles me.

Sam squeezes my hand tighter and then catches my eye. "You're pretty interesting, Dr. Park. You know that?"

"How so?"

"Because for an atheist and a card-carrying pessimist in humanity, you sure do have a lot of faith in a sentient species you haven't met yet."

"Just as long as I'm not the only one."

"You're not." She looks down. "Sorry for all the doubt. I just… guess I'm tired."

"It's alright. No one ever said we weren't allowed to question what we do. Just makes it easier when we can examine it with people we trust, right?"

"Right." Her eyes suddenly look melancholy. I didn't mean to make her emotional. "Thanks, Eves. For tolerating me."

"Hey, I'm not exactly the easiest person to be friends with either."

"No kidding."

"Hey!" I punch her shoulder playfully. "Watch it, sister."

She looks down at her arm. "No wonder you always lose to the sparring excipions."

Our team starts shuffling in from their break looking only slightly less haggard than they did when I dismissed them. But, to my surprise, my conversation with Sam has actually sparked a new line of thinking. It might not merit anything, but it's more than I had before the break.

Once everyone's in, I call our team meeting back to order and then start pacing across the front of the room. "Okay, so I have another idea. We're all making a lot of assumptions here, right? Guessing at the ways and means of how some sentient civilization is trying to communicate with us. But what if we're not looking at it from the right angle?"

"Can you clarify that?" Seb asks.

I nod and then glance at Sam. "We think they're not hostile, right? Because we choose to believe the best about them. But we still need to be cautious. Still careful not to expose ourselves to *the great alien invasion* scenarios we all grew up with." This gets a smattering of laughter. "Well, what if they're thinking the same thing?"

Sam is first to pick up my train of thought. "You think they've encrypted the signal against hostile reception?"

"How would that even work?" Ramirez asks. "Now we're talking about adding ethics to an already alien signal we can't even decipher? How do we know what they think is and isn't hostile, let alone the type of language they would use to describe it?"

"I don't know," I say. "That's why I'm throwing it out here. I'm merely suggesting because maybe all our conventional puzzle-solving techniques are failing for a reason."

"The obvious ones aren't the right ones," Natalie concludes and then starts scratching her neck. "That's not bad, Evelyn. Might be something there."

Seb echoes her positivity. "It's safe to assume that the ideas of preserving life are universal, especially to a species who has evolved enough to send a signal like this. Some ideas are transcendent, and it's usually the simplest ones."

"There ya go." I look around the room. "Break into groups of three and four and start compiling lists of every possible way you could convey an ethic of peace, harmony, friendship—whatever—but only using binary code. And don't forget: you're aliens trying to keep your signal from falling into the wrong hands."

"Easy peasy," Natalie says sarcastically but then offers me a smile to lessen the tone. "Challenge accepted, boss."

"Good. Let's sprint for fifteen. SESI says you're the best and the brightest. Let's see if that's true." I clap my hands. "Time starts now. Let's go!"

Fifteen minutes later, I ask each group to present their best idea to the room. Most are crap. A few are clever. But only one gets Sebastián to sit up straight.

"So we thought, how can we show the promotion of life in the simplest form possible?" says a post-doc student from the Helsinki Science Institute. Enni Mäkinen, I think her name is. "By binary fission."

"Go on," Seb says. Enni is the first person he hasn't dismissed.

"Well, our team got thinking about the differences between bacteria and viruses. These are some of the most basic organisms we know of, regardless of what kind of gasses or light they do or don't need, right? So, the question is, how do they reproduce? One uses its own material to sacrifice itself, while the other essentially hijacks its host cell's protein synthesis pathways to reproduce. What we're wondering is if, by trying to infer our own methods for deduction on the signal, we're actually acting like a virus."

"Trying to pick it apart to suit our own needs," I say.

"Whereas we should be letting the host material reproduce on its own," Seb says as he stands and runs a hand through his thick black hair. "Ay Dios mío."

"Si," Ramirez replies. "It's the most basic way of saying we not only accept you, but we also see you. And we want more of whatever it is you're trying to say. Instead of trying to interject our own meaning, like a virus."

"We just allow it to divide and reproduce on its own," Seb says. "The ardent promotion of life."

"I think I'm following," Sam offers. "But what does it mean practically?"

"It means," Natalie says, stepping to a workstation and drawing on the room-wide holo screen with a virtual stylus, "that we take the entire signal and duplicate it." She starts gathering the raw signal data and grouping it together.

"But without instructions, doesn't that just create more of the same?" someone asks a few rows back.

"Not if we follow their instructions," Natalie replies. "And we've been staring at them the whole time."

"Where?" Sam asks.

"Binary fission," Seb answers. "We split each repeated phrase in half."

"Exactly." Natalie enters the resulting sequence of numbers as an algorithmic function in the command prompt window. "We see you," she says. "And we want more." She hits the enter key.

All at once, the grouped data set starts dividing and multiplying, a reaction that quickly spirals out in three dimensions as fast the computer can generate the model.

"Ho-ly shit," Natalie says in awe as the formula starts spreading over all the holo screens like ice crystals. "It's a fractal."

"Indeed," Sebastián replies. "And it's glorious."

We watch as the self-replicating fractal, designed and encoded by an advanced alien species, overtakes one holo window and appears in adjacent ones. Sam gives me a side hug, and then I point at Enni Mäkinen and give her two thumbs up. She smiles and gestures to her team. It's an intuitive solution to an elegant puzzle.

"Alright, listen up," I say to the room. "This is just the first step. It's a good one—"

"A great one," Seb interrupts.

"—but one of many, I'm quite sure." I look back to our resident cryptologist for confirmation.

Natalie shrugs. "You're not wrong. I don't even think this is the message proper. It's more like"—she tilts her head at the sprawling fractal that's overtaken the room's screens—"it's just the beginning. If our theory about photon orbital angular momentum is right, it could be the multiplex codec that unlocks everything else."

"Nothing like solving one puzzle to start the next," Sam says.

"Anyone still tired?" I ask the room. They shout me down, so I roll my hand through the air. "Then let's keep it going, people."

The words are barely out of my mouth when the lights go out and the holos go black.

JERICHO

I CAN'T TAKE my eyes off the dice on the table. I gambled. I made wagers that I didn't have the ability to back. The dice scream at me like the families of the dead, demanding that I unroll the throw and give them their loved ones' lives back. But I can't. The die has been cast, and the only winner? The only one to walk away?

Me.

Eddie Carr was right.

And I was wrong.

What's more, the attorneys in the cases against us were wrong too. Sure, they'd accused me of being in the wrong place, but they'd said I should have been in the *pilot's* seat to order mission shutdown; no one said I should have been in the STCC on *Astraea*'s bridge. No one but Eddie Carr.

"Cap? You there?"

It's Kit. Guess it's his turn to come hunting for me.

"No."

He laughs from the other side of my office door. "Ha ha. Good one." There's a pause, and then the inevitable "Mind if I come in?"

"Yes."

"Yes, you mind? Or yes, I can come in? 'Cause you know how sometimes when you answer a question, it's hard to tell which—"

"Kit!"

"Coming in." The doors part to my Beattie IV admin office and in bounds my faithful Labrador retriever. "Oh, geez, Cap. You look terrible. Like, *oooph*. You, uh, need me to get you something? Deodorant or a toothbrush?"

"Just your progress report." I hold out a hand without looking away from the dice.

"I sent it via V-cog like an hour ago, but you… haven't confirmed receipt. That's sorta kinda why I'm here. 'Cause normally, you're like really on top of reviewing everything. Unless you're in the head; then there's like a five-to-ten-minute delay. Or when you're in the shower. That's more like twelve minutes. And then when you…"

I ignore the rest of Kit's memorized timetable of my personal habits and pull up his report in V-cog. Sure enough, he logged it an hour ago. Just sitting there, waiting for me to read and accept. Dammit. This whole thing's really getting to me.

The holo windows spread above my virtual galley table, and I scan them quickly. Engines, fuel, nav, power, comms, life support, nanostructures, hull integrity—it all checks out. Everyone's on schedule.

"Cap?"

"What?"

"You… wanna talk about anything?"

"No."

"'Cause I find that sometimes the best medicine is—"

"I just need to be left alone right now. Copy?"

"Oh. Sure, yeah. Okay." His head droops and he turns toward the doors. But that's all. No bouncy step away, no shuffle. He just stands there. Finally, when I'm about to ask *him* what's wrong, he looks over his shoulder with the biggest dopiest sad face I've ever seen.

"My God, Kit. You're insufferable, you know that?"

"Does that mean I'm too caring for my own good? 'Cause my mom says that sometimes I need to—"

"Shut your mouth?"

He clamps his lips together and nods once.

"Jesus. Take a seat."

He gives me a wide smile and a frantic nod as he glides into the nearest chair. He really does look like a lab sometimes. And now he's just staring at me, like he expects me to throw him a treat or something.

I take a deep breath and sit back in my chair. "I was talking to Carr yesterday—"

"What a fudge nugget, right? Wow. He's so intense."

"—and he was sharing some information with me that—"

"Is crossing into other people's fields, right? Biscuits, that guy is nosey."

I close my eyes and take another breath. "Kit."

"Yeah?"

"Do you want to know what I'm going through or not?"

"Oh. Right. Ha! I'm so sorry. It's like, 'Whoop!' there I go again. I'll just listen though. Go on."

After studying his face for another few seconds, I decide to keep going. "He brought up the X-10 accident. Which I get. People do it a lot, and I don't blame them.

But Eddie found something. Something that... that's important."

I wait for Kit to interject, but he doesn't. He just sits there.

"It was a data discrepancy between the ship and command. The log accurately showed a small malfunction in the Ebra-drive, one that eventually cascaded into... well, into what we all know." I swallow and look back at the dice. "Point is, had the operator at mission control been paying attention, they would have caught in advance of the failure. In time to stop it."

I lift my eyes from the desk. Kit's knees are bopping, and his lips are pressed tightly together.

"Do you... wanna say something?"

He lets out a lungful of air. "Oh mash and gravy, yes! It's not your fault, Cap. I mean, you were on the *Perseverant*. How in the world could you have seen... what those in the traffic control center saw... because... because... Holy biscuits, you were supposed to be in STCC." His face goes pale. "You... you could have caught it."

All I can do is purse my lips and nod, slowly.

Confessing this to Kit hurts like hell. Sucks knowing you're wrong about something. Sucks even more when you have to confess it to someone else, especially when you know they look up to you. But as hard as it is to have this conversation with Kit, I don't even wanna begin to imagine the pain and humiliation of telling this to the victim's families. Not for my sake. For theirs. Because it means the tragedy was preventable. It means their loved ones didn't need to die. All because I wasn't in my seat.

"What's that?" Kit asks.

Must've been mumbling again. "I wasn't where I needed to be."

"Yeah, but you—"

I raise a hand. "You asked to see behind the curtain. That doesn't give you commentary rights."

"Sorry."

I lower my arm and look back at the dice. "Problem is, I always wanna be in the action. I wanna be a part of work that matters. That moves the ball down the field and gets humanity where it needs to go. But this time, that desire did the opposite. It pushed humanity back. Cost more than we can afford. And now I've got a team member I'm not sure I can lead, a mission I'm not sure I can execute, and I'm pretty sure I need to bring this up to Johnson and then tender my resignation."

When the only thing that fills the silence is Kit's shoe heels patting the concrete floor, I say, "Alright. What is it?"

He raises his hand at the same time that he opens his mouth. "Ooo! But Mr. Carr hasn't taken this to Command, right?"

"Meaning?"

"Well, if he really wanted to jeopardize your career and take his place back, he'd have done so, wouldn't he?"

"I guess, but—"

"And chances are that he's been holding on to this information for quite a while; after all, he's *Eddie F'ing Carr, oi?* So if he has something to say, nothing will stop him."

"You're suggesting that the fact that he hasn't made it public is a good thing?"

"Totally."

"Then what's his angle?"

Kit gives me a sheepish smile. "Isn't it obvious? He already said it. When you met. 'If you kill any of my people, so help me Jesus, Mary, and f'ing Joseph, I'll rip your—'"

"Yeah, yeah. Christmas socks to orphans. Got it." I squint at Kit. "You really think a guy like that is only concerned about the well-being of his crew and not leveraging anything he can to get what he wants? Who's to say he's not just waiting for me to end my own career?"

"You really think that's how people work, Cap?"

"Don't you?"

He blushes. "No." Kit rubs the back of his neck and seems to think of something else. "Kinda a rough way to live, if you ask me."

"It's kept me in the game this long."

"Maybe. But it doesn't seem fair."

"I'm only doing to others what they—"

"I meant to you."

This stops me. "What?"

"Eh, my dad once told me that the faults we see in others are normally the same things that bother us about ourselves. If that's true, Cap, then I don't think you're being very fair to yourself. 'Cause you're amazing, and you don't need an angle to justify a mistake or prove that you belong on a great team. We're people. We make mistakes. Sometimes big ones. You just gotta... well, you gotta own your crusty hankies, make amends, and keep going until you get where you need to be to help the most people, right?" He seems to consider something else, then adds, "Sometimes, the only person out to get you, is yourself."

Kits stands, smooths a hand down his uniform, turns for the door, and then stops halfway there. "If you, uh, smell something, I… I passed gas a second ago. I got nervous. Sorry." Kit walks out of my office and leaves me alone with more thoughts and methane than I bargained for.

WHATEVER CONFIDENCE BOOST Kit gave me during his pep talk vanishes the moment Eddie Carr waves me to the side of the hangar bay. We're just t-minus ten hours to the *Kogarashi*'s inaugural test flight, and the last thing I need is more drama.

"Oi. So what's your plan, Foxy?"

"Why don't you be more specific, Carr?"

"I don't need to be more fucking specific. You bloody well know what I mean, you wanker. You re-signing or what?"

So much for Kit's wishful thinking. "Nope. You?"

"Come again?"

"If you're so worried about me making another costly mistake, why don't *you* resign?"

"'Cause I'm not the one in the habit of fucking killing people, is why."

"It's hardly a habit."

"Second time's the charm." He looks me up and down once. "So you didn't tell Command then?"

"I figure you already did that for me."

"Oh, come off it. I expect people to own their own shit. That's on you, mate."

"How magnanimous of you."

"Oi!" He grabs my arm as I turn back to the ship. "I'm not done with you. You'd better tell the crew."

"And you'd better get your hand off me before I fire your ass, Carr."

He complies, but his scowl is no less menacing. "They deserve to know, Fox."

Suddenly, Kit's words come back to me. He's right. I do deserve to be fair with myself. And I don't have anything to prove to Eddie Carr. My quarrel isn't with him anyway, even if he was the bearer of some Earth-shattering news.

"No, Eddie. The people I killed deserve to know. And their families, when the time comes. I will not be suckered into apologizing to people who I haven't wronged. 'Cause if that's the case, then you and I need to make lists a few klicks long and prepare to air all our dirty laundry to everyone on *Selene* together.

"No, I owe apologies to very specific people, and I have you to thank for the intel. Other than that, we have a mission to conduct and a test flight to prepare for. So if we're done here, I need to get back to work. And so do you. Unless *you'd* like to tender your resignation?" I hold out my empty palm and wait for a second. "No? Then here's my gift to you." I grab his hand and drop two dice into it. "Careful who you bet against."

"EVERYTHING OKAY OUT THERE?" Nairobi asks me as I enter the reactor's control room.

"You mean my heart to heart with Eddie?"

She nods.

"We're dandy."

"No one is dandy with Edward Carr."

"Then consider me the exception."

"I'm sure." She looks back at the team doing final checks on the propulsion systems. "Anyway, everything's on schedule here. You taking the helm for the move to Launch Position One?"

"No. We'll let the man of the hour have the controls. I'll be in the STCC."

"Roger. What about for the main test in the morning? You, uh… joining us onboard?"

"Negative. My place is with Command."

"That's understandable." She looks up in embarrassment. "I'm sorry, I… didn't mean to—"

"It's okay. I'm not doing this one out of fear, Dr. Kinshaw. I'm doing it because it's where I need to be, just as your place will be here in propulsion."

"Right." She seems to think something over, then asks, "Did he bring up the *Perseverant*?"

Curious. "Why?"

"Well, Eddie always said that he had questions he wanted to ask you if your paths ever crossed, but…"

"But what?"

"He never gave any more details than that. Said it was between you and him."

"You don't say?"

She shrugs and casts me an aloof look. "He can be funny like that. Playing his cards close to his chest and all. Weird bird. But good at his job."

"That he is," I say, looking out the door as if I might see through the ship's hull and spot Eddie. Despite his lack of bedside manner, I'm beginning to think the man isn't all bad.

"Anyway, we'll be good for the transfer at 2115, right on schedule. Then it's all systems go at 0700. Adrian and Magellan are prepping on the bridge now."

"They're next on my list. In the meantime, I need you to look over a few lines of new code."

"Oh?"

I pop into V-cog and initiate a file transfer to Nairobi.

Her eyelids flutter as she attends to the notification without closing her eyes. "What am I looking at?"

"It's something Kit wrote to fix a bug with a potential sensor anomaly."

I can tell she's reading the code fast. "A delay override to maintain time lock?"

"You know your languages."

"It's my job." She snaps back to the real. "No offense, but this is pretty small."

"Then you won't have any problems implementing it?"

"Not at all." Nairobi holds my eyes for another second as something passes through her mind, and I wonder if she suspects. Wonder if she'll ask. "It's important, isn't it?"

I nod, hoping she doesn't press me. "Very."

"Then consider it done."

"Thank you. I'll see you at the briefing."

"Roger that."

I leave Nairobi in engineering and head down the *Kogarashi*'s spine to the bridge. Adrian Wallace hovers over the comms workstation with two other engineers, while Magellan looks like a bona fide giant seated in the nav chair. A pair of techs greet me as I step onto the bridge, and Adrian is first to look up at the exchange.

"Director Fox, we're just wrapping up here," says the stout man says in surprise.

"Excellent." I turn to Magellan. "Same?"

He nods in the stoic manner of a former Navy man turned African sage. "Standing by, Knight."

"Any issues that I need to know of?"

"Only that Adrian insists Kit is cheating at *Vesper Siege IV*," Magellan says.

"It's not true," Kit blurts out over the senior team's shared V-cog lobby. "I'm just faster with manual aim than most people are with all the assists turned on. Adrian's the one who's cheating because—"

"Because the only advantage I have over someone who plays twenty-four seven is brute-force," the comms officer protests. "I have a life."

"So do I," Kit replies. "And it's not 'twenty-four seven'." He lowers his voice. "It's like twenty-one. And a half."

"So long as we're good to go," I say, hoping to avoid any more gamer talk.

Magellan gives me a thumbs-up and a wide smile. "Ready and awaiting your orders, Knight."

Adrian nods too. "Same here."

"Okay. Briefing in twenty." Back in a private V-cog channel, I add, "Kit? You doing okay?"

"Sure. Fine."

"Uh huh."

Kit throws his hands up in the air. "He's just really chapping my backside, ya know?"

"Wallace?"

"Yeah. I just… Ugh, I hate saying it."

"What?"

"I don't like him. Something slimy about him. If he's willing to cheat like that in video games, then what else is he willing to do, ya know? Wink wink."

"Kit, you don't actually say wink wink. You just… Jesus, never mind."

"He's up to no good, Cap. Like maybe his tenure has given him license to be a freeloader. Just do the minimum amount required to get by, ya know? Maybe we wanna look for a replacement and let Adrian coast on his pension. Gosh, now look at me, talking nasty about people behind their backs. Ma would be so cross."

This makes me laugh. "Listen, why don't you take a pee break or something."

"Already on it."

This makes me pause. "You're… playing and—?"

"Tinkling at the same time? 'Course, Cap. It's way easier than you think. Just gotta make sure you're shaking the right stick when you're wrapping up."

"I'll take your word for it." Back on the general channel, I say, "Twenty minutes, people."

OVER 220 STAFF of NUESSA's Marquis-Class Initiative are gathered in the main hangar, while another hundred or so join the briefing in V-cog. The more notable figures present virtually include NUESSA Director Eric Johnson, Stellar Dynamics CEO Cal McNeely, and Malcolm Hartwell and Abu Minkosef, politicast leaders of the Viatoribus and Sentia Aux respectively. I'd heard rumors that Evelyn might be present too, but apparently her team is in the middle of something important and can't be disturbed. Kudos to her, assuming it's a breakthrough of some kind. Hoping I get one of my own. Before that, however, I'm expected to make some sort of speech.

"Thanks for coming, everyone," I say from the ramp leading up to the *Koga.*

"We had a choice?" someone in the hangar calls out. It gets a few laughs, but eventually peers shush the speaker. "Sorry."

I smile and glance at my prepared remarks in V-cog.

"I think it goes without saying that tomorrow morning is a big day for all of us. Countless work hours from you, the best and brightest in the business, a whole lot of perseverance, and a hell of a lot of coin from our donors has made this possible. You all deserve a round of applause."

The sound of clapping comes swiftly, both virtually and in the real, but then dies out as the audience looks to me to continue.

"This endeavor isn't without its risks. I, for one, know that all too well. And just to address the elephant in the hangar bay, no: I will not be on board the ship for the inaugural run. Apparently, they already have enough egos onboard for that." The self-deprecating jab does its job and makes a few people laugh—some genuinely, some nervously.

"I consider it a rare honor, however, to be invited to witness this historic event not once but twice in my life. We made history already, proving that the Ebra-drive could accelerate us faster than we ever imagined. It cost us a great deal… cost me a great deal. But each of us knows the risks we undertake. Knows what can happen if things go wrong. That's part of being on the leading edge. But we also know what can happen—what will happen—when things go right, when the harnessed power of super plasmoids takes us to the stars."

Now spontaneous clapping bursts out in the room. The unprompted praise helps buoy whatever lingering doubts I have. That is, until I see Eddie with his arms crossed, glaring at me. I stare right back and then chose to ignore him.

"We've learned from the past, now it's time to lean into the future. The hardest work is behind us, built on the genius and the lives of those who have sacrificed so we could be here tonight. Now, let that investment yield what it will: a breakthrough that will open a new door to the cosmos."

This summons another round of applause even though I didn't mean for it to. When the wave dies down, I conclude with, "We've got a big day tomorrow, people. So let's get some sleep. We're engines hot at 0700. Dismissed."

As one final round of applause ripples across the hangar and saturates V-cog audio, I can't help but wonder just how Evelyn's doing with her work on the signal and hope she's okay. It seems like only a matter of time before both our projects come under government pressure that forces humanity to abandon our expansion into the big black.

7

EVELYN

"Everyone stay calm and just sit tight," I yell above the team's growing sounds of uncertainty. Most aren't over-reacting, but a few are beginning to panic. A power outage on an entire floor, which is what this looks to be, isn't a normal occurrence. Combine that with daily security briefings on radical groups ranging from the Tantum Terrae and the Bemba Militia to Radio Ultra and Leonidas X, and you understand why some people in the room are scared. Sir Nigel Sallsworth's sudden rise to Secretary General has pro-Earth rock squatters foaming at the mouth, while anti-politicast factions see it as one more reason why the entire system needs to be brought down.

As for me? It's weird how surviving an orbital legacy habitat catastrophe makes everything else pale by comparison. Even still, I'd be lying if I said the power outage wasn't concerning.

I step into V-cog and pull up a scan of our floor's systems. Strangely, however, I get nothing. Even my nanos are having to move down the network priority list. Eventually they acquire a grid signal on a third-tier system—off campus. That means something has not only knocked out the Schwarzschild Celestial Research Building's V-cog net, but it's also hit the whole mainframe. Not good.

"Lemuel?" I say as soon as I enter the director's oak-finished study in V-cog. "Lemuel, you here?"

No response. Granted, he's probably sleeping at this hour. Still, I need him.

"Come on, Lem. Talk to me."

A hand pulls my arm forward. "We should probably move, Eves." It's Sam.

I step out of Lemuel's lobby. "Not until we know more about what's causing this."

"But it might not be safe up here."

"*Or* this is the safest place to be and trying to leave is dangerous."

Sam doesn't have time to reply before something shakes the floor. I catch the reflection of an orange glow off one of the buildings to the north, followed by thick black smoke rising past our floor's exterior windows. I don't know if it's the night sky making everything brighter than it is, but the fireball seems big.

"We're under attack," someone shouts in the back of the room. A moment later, half the research team is running toward the exit while the others are looking for ways to barricade themselves in their respective offices.

So much for staying calm.

I realize just how much the years spent on the streets of Bukjeong Village in the Seongbuk-gu District of Seoul prepared me for moments like this. Instead of panicking, you start thinking; instead of reacting, you start planning.

The two most imposing people on my immediate team are Seb and Ramirez. I call for their attention. "See if you can keep people from moving toward the exits until we have a better idea of what's going on. And if you can't keep them from leaving, at least try to get them moving up instead of down. If we have terrorists in the building, it sounds like they have the ground floor."

Both men nod and then head out.

"Nat, see if you can raise anyone in headquarters."

"What about me?" Sam asks.

"I want you surveying from the windows. See if you can make sense of what's going on down there."

"Got it. And you?"

"I'm gonna try calling security if they aren't already on their way."

While my staff get to work, I slip back into V-cog, pull up the St. John's emergency index, and ping the first entry.

As soon as my request is taken, I appear before a woman in a blue NUE Emergency Response Unit uniform behind a translucent standing desk. "Emergency Response Dispatch, what is the nature of your emergency?"

"We've got explosions inside our building. Lower floors. Total number unknown," I say.

"I have you at the St. John's SESI campus, Schwarzschild Celestial Research Building, fourteenth floor."

"That's correct."

"Please stand by."

The agent's fingers move overly fast, which, given the lack of realism in this escalated virtual environment, is way faster than anyone could type in the real. Were the circumstances not dire, the rendering would annoy me. But in this instance, I'm grateful for the unrealistic speed.

"Local law enforcement, fire and rescue, and NUE

Marine units are moving on your position now, Ms. Park. Please stay online with me until help arrives."

"Marine units? Can you give me any more information about what's going on below me?"

"We are monitoring the situation as it unfolds and will keep you apprised of—"

"Agent Bossard," I interrupt, using the name on her uniform. "I would appreciate brutal honesty in case I need to make decisions to ensure the survival of my staff."

Bossard seems to take this into consideration. My guess is that people in her position are only allowed to divulge so much information before it becomes a liability issue, or a public safety one. I only hope that between my V-rec credentials and maybe the directness of my tone that she decides to break protocol just this once.

"I can confirm multiple sightings of hostile forces in your vicinity, yes."

"Are any other structures under attack on the campus?"

Bossard hesitates. I can't tell if she's checking or stalling. Then she comes back with, "Yours is the only one."

A hundred coins says this is in fact an attack directed at us, which means the assailants are rock squatters: Tantum Terrae or Bemba Militia. And only one of those groups has enough crypto and balls to attempt a stunt this brazen.

"Estimated force allotment?"

"Uncertain." Bossard narrows her gaze. "Sounds like you've served."

"Negative. Just been around my share of those who have."

"Copy."

"Listen, I know I need to stay on the line and all, but—"

"Ms. Park, you have an incoming call."

I give her a surprised look, but before I can reply, a second figure appears in the ERU's lobby. It's a Marine decked out in space combat armor with his helmet tucked under one arm and a MAW rifle in the other hand.

"Forging paths," he says in his proper British accent.

"Through the darkness. Rook! What are you…? I mean, how are you—?"

"I'm circling overhead and have one squad eight floors below you, taking care of some unwanted guests." His rendering glitches for a split second as the grid buffers the link. "But they might not get all the tangos before the enemy reaches your floor."

"So we're the target?"

"Seems so. I need you and whatever personnel you have to move toward… Stand by." His image freezes for a second. At the same time, I hear a loud exchange of automatic weapons break through glass several levels below. Another explosion sends a shudder through the floor while an aircraft rushes by our windows. As soon as vibrations subside, Rook's rendering reanimates. "I need you to put as much distance as you can between your people and the enemy. Make it to the roof if possible. We'll be waiting."

"Already sending people that direction. I'll get the rest moving now."

"Roger. Dare I ask if you have any weapons for self-defense?"

"Do holo calculators count?"

"Only if the terrorists are CPAs." He winks at me. "We'll see you shortly, Evelyn. Stay alive."

"You too, Rook. Good to see you."

He nods, and then his body blinks out of the lobby.

"Sounds like you need to get moving," Bossard says. "I'll monitor your progress with your permission; let you focus on what you need to do."

"Permission granted. And I welcome any insights you get along the way."

"Certainly."

I step out of V-cog but make sure to leave the stream open for Bossard. "Alright, everyone, we have orders to get to the roof."

"The roof?" someone exclaims. Another voice tells them to calm down and start moving toward the nearest stairwell.

"Yes, the roof. Marines are in the building, but we still need to move up as safely and fast as we can."

"Are we gonna die?" a frantic voice yells behind a desk.

"Someday, sure. But not today. Just… stick together, watch your step, and keep your heads down, okay? We got this."

Stars, do I hope we've got this.

By the time I reach the stairwell, bringing up the rear, social notifications stream down the side of my vision faster than I can read. But I only need to see the first entry in the augmented field of view to know that my name is being published like wildfire in the verb's emerging stories categories. Anyone with a pixie has deployed outside the St. John's campus and is pumping live vid for the whole world. Only the area's secure no-fly grid is keeping them from zipping right up our asses for a close up.

Which gives me an idea for how to satisfy my curiosity about the developing situation below us. I select the first headline in the augmented V-cog list, *Suspected Terrorist Bombing at SESI St. John's*, and expand the developing story, complete with live video coverage. The news company's own footage is supplemented with individually sourced footage from private users who will be compensated according to whatever the day's market price is combined with the number of views it gets—all incentives for eyewitnesses to risk life and limb, or just their pixies, to get the best shots possible. In this case, it's a wide shot of my building's north side, highlighting fire and thick black smoke pouring from the ground floor. Floors two, three, and five have shattered windows and bear the signs of lesser explosions. The conflict is definitely moving up, just as Rook said.

I round the landing between floors sixteen and seventeen when more verb notifications displace the lead story I have opened. I assume they're just competing listings paying for top position when I notice the headlines:

- *Developing Attack on NUESSA Christchurch*
- *Calgary Blast Kills 56*
- *10 Hostages Held at SESI Research Lab Oslo*

"You seeing all this?" Natalie asks me over V-cog.

"Yeah. Just… stay focused."

"It's like it's coordinated or something."

"We'll figure it out later, Nat. Right now, we need to keep everyone safe."

"Passing twenty-first and… I'm at the exit."

Another rumble in the floor gets accented by a delayed flash of light in the verb feeds. Several windows blow out of the building's west side about two thirds of the way up. Oh shit… that's our floor. I think that's our lab!

"SITREP, Evelyn," Rook says over V-cog. *Situation report.* He needs an update.

"We're… almost to the roof."

"Roger. You're going to see several Marine gunships inbound followed by a troop transport. That's for you. Encourage your people to stay calm."

"Okay, will do."

"And whatever you do, don't stop moving up."

"Got it."

A low hum fills the stairwell and grows louder by the second. I check in on the verb stream again and find pixies swiveling to track four incoming aircraft. Three of the drab-colored vessels seem hunched over like raptors ready to drop on their prey. Hawk-like wings spread to the sides, boasting vectored-thrust engines with blue exhaust flame. The Devil Dog outline of the NUE Marine's logo adorns the hull, accented by mounted weapons—the teeth and claws of the military gunship. The fourth vessel is larger than the others and looks more like a flying boxcar with weapons in doorways on the sides. Already, a ramp is opening from the rear, and the aircraft is slowing on approach to our building.

Over our staff V-cog channel, I say, "The Marines have sent a rescue ship for us. Wait for it to land, and then approach slowly. Stay calm, and watch for instructions from the crew." A few people ping me back in acknowledgement, but most are probably too preoccupied with the stress of the situation.

I round the landing headed up to level twenty and catch verb footage of two gunships descending toward the fourteenth floor while the third circles the transport, presumably standing guard. At the same time, I see the first members of my staff emerge from the exit corridor like tiny ants. They cover their heads as the transport's engines send gusts of wind across the rooftop. Fortunately, the building has a dedicated landing pad, which helps everyone know their places; my staff stays clear while the Marine ship touches down in the designated area.

Below, something bright flashes from a blown-out window and sends out a streak of light. Maybe if I was more attuned to military ordnance, I'd be able to name the projectile. Something rocket-propelled, and clearly not a weapon the gunships want to tangle with. A blue shock wave from both vessels pumps the air. The enemy weapon's thrust dies from the electromagnetic pulse countermeasure, but the munition still has enough momentum to carry it toward the left gunship. The round touches the hull on the starboard side, and the building face radiates with reflected light from the resulting explosion. Engines flare, the ship lurches, and a second streak leaves the building. Turrets on the aircrafts spine and belly spit out torrents of automatic fire. The streams converge on the rocket, detonating it in a bright explosion that washes out the camera feed.

At the same time, a series of pulsing lights erupts from the gunship on the right. It's opening fire on the enemy, in a civilian building, spitting red hot bullets like dragons spewing fire. The rounds obliterate the windows and tear through the interior. It goes on for several seconds—carpet, furniture, and bodies being chewed to smithereens. Then, just like that, the weapons stop shooting and the gunships pull back, the left one hemorrhaging smoke but still aloft.

I step into the light and I'm about to follow the remainder of my team across the landing pad and toward the waiting transport when someone on the landing below me yells, "Hands up."

I consider running, but the voice sounds too close, so I raise my arms, bathed in spotlights from the transport and sentry gunship.

"Turn around and come back inside," the enemy says.

I comply with the first part, only because I want to see the asshats responsible for all this. He's dressed in a black jumpsuit with matte black composite body armor and matching open-faced tactical helmet. A hot pink TT logo is stenciled on his chest, and he's got a face mask over his nose and mouth.

"I said, back inside!"

"Not happening, asshole."

"Don't make me shoot you!" It's the last thing he ever says. Three magnetically accelerated weapon rounds thump into the man's chest and neck, spraying the door well with blood. His body shudders, then he collapses.

I could split for the transport, but his automatic weapon is just a meter away. It's a non-biolock conventional gel propellant rifle, one I can use right now. If more enemies come up the stairs, I might need the gun, so I lunge forward, retrieve it, and then backpedal out of the doorway.

Bullets ping against the metal frame. I duck under

the sparks, squat run toward the transport, and catch sight of four, maybe five men rushing from the shadows to take positions on the roof. At least one shoots at me, throwing concrete bits into my legs. Pissed more than scared, I turn around and shoot in the general direction of the incoming fire. I'm not good enough to be precise in these kinds of conditions, but I figure general retaliation might buy me and the last of my staff running toward the ramp an extra few seconds.

More bullets zip by my head. Feeling overwhelmed, I abort my run toward the transport and slide behind a squat metal housing. The panels ping and pop under enemy fire while I cover my head. I'm pinned down.

"Over here, you assholes," a voice shouts a few meters away. It's Sam. She's standing in the open and waving her arms.

"Sam! Get down!" The words are barely out of my mouth when a bullet slashes her arm. "*No!*"

I point my weapon over the housing and spray the enemy. The recoil catches me off guard, but I fight it and continue depressing the trigger. Between shots, I scramble to my feet and run after Sam. She's on the ground holding her arm but looks alive.

I can barely hear the sound of my own voice when I yell, "I've got you! Come on!" I reach a hand under her armpit and shoot back at the enemy with the other.

Then my magazine goes dry.

But my weapon isn't the only one to fire at the terrorists. Marine MAW projectiles peppers the industrial HVAC housings, showering the roof in more sparks. I would join them, but without a fresh mag, my magnetic acceleration weapon is useless, so I drop it and use both hands to help Sam to her feet. The Marines are better shots anyway, dropping one, two, and then three enemies behind us. Their firing positions have also moved from the gunship to the rooftop. Four Marines run past Sam and me to create a wall at our rear while a fifth one comes up beside me.

"This way," says Rook's familiar voice. "Keep moving!" He slips an arm around Sam and points me forward.

I nod and focus on running toward the ramp now fourteen meters away. The guns keep spitting bullets, making my ears ring, and I hear people yelling, but everything's too loud to make any sense of it. Rook's coaxing us forward while checking behind us with his weapon aimed. He doesn't seem nervous, at least as far as I can tell—just another day at the office.

Finally, we reach the ramp. I help Sam run up, all while squinting against the engine wash. The sound is deafening, and it takes me a few seconds to realize that someone is shouting at me at the ramp's top. It's another Marine in combat armor.

"Ma'am, I said I need you to—"

"Is everyone here?"

"Affirmative. You need to get seated and buckle in."

"You're sure? There were thirty of us in total, and I don't want to—"

"Thirty-one counting you." He thrusts a hand at an empty seat. "Please secure yourself."

"Okay, yeah." I look back down the ramp and see Rook. He gives me a nod and then disappears around the transport's side. If he's content to get out of here, then so am I. The rest of his fire team have cleared the stairwell door and look to be jogging back to their gunship. So I sit and try buckling myself as fast as I can. Something's stuck, or my nerves are shot.

"Here, I gotcha," Sam yells beside me. One handed,

she lifts a shoulder strap and then the five-point receiver at my groin. "Down there."

"Got it." I insert the buckles and then tug on the straps to make sure everything's secure.

"You're hit," I say to Sam, stating the obvious.

Her right hand covers her left bicep, which is soaked in blood. "I think I got grazed. But it hurts like hell."

I look the rest of her body over quickly to make sure she isn't bleeding anywhere else. "You know you're bonkers, Sam. Right?"

"Says the woman who grabbed a gun and shot back at the enemy."

I laugh once and then ask for one of the Marines to help Sam.

The rear ramp has been closing behind us, and for the first time since the incident began, I wonder how many more SESI and NUESSA employees are in the building. The thought embarrasses me as it seems like something I should have considered before, but I'm guessing Rook and his Marines were way ahead of me there. Fortunately, it's late. Most everyone went home hours ago. Which means this could have been significantly worse.

Stars, I need a drink.

"You okay?" Sam asks.

I'm holding the shoulder straps tightly. Probably from the butterflies in my gut. Which you'd think I'd be used to from all my space travel. Evolutionary reflexes are hard to beat down. Verb access shut down the moment I entered the transport, but I don't need the pixie footage to know we're flying away from the Schwarzschild Building.

"I'm pissed, is what I am," I say to Sam.

She pulls back and gives me a look like I've gone mad.

"What?" I say. "You aren't?"

Sam seems to think things over for a second as the engines continue to rattle the hull. A medic has removed her sleeve and wraps her arm with gauze. "I'm… I'm afraid, Eves."

"You're gonna be fine. Looks like the bullet just—"

"For our team. You think they were coming for us?"

"Yeah." I remember the other headlines. We weren't the only ones assaulted. Which makes the time of our attack irrelevant since the other events were scattered around the globe. But I suspect our work was a focal point since all the attacks do seem to have at least one thing in common. "They've targeted space settlement devs." But that doesn't seem to settle another lingering question: Why did that enemy operative tell me to raise my hands? Why didn't he just shoot me where I stood?

"Maybe we need to stop this, Eves," Sam says as the medic finishes his work.

"What are you talking about?"

"The research, I mean. Maybe we need to… you know, take a break or something. This is… it's too much."

I stare at her eyes until she looks away. I'm just gonna write that comment off as shock related. Feels pretty premature to make that kind of a judgment call, especially given how close we are to cracking the signal. Stars! We're right there. How can she even consider stopping now?

Then again, she did just get shot for the cause. Maybe I'm the one out of line. How many times has Sam reminded me about my fixations on problems "at the expense of all else"? Okay, so I can be a bit intense. Sue me. But it doesn't mean I'm wrong.

"Just relax, Sam. We're gonna get through this."

"Unless we don't." She looks like a deer in headlights. "If the Marines hadn't shown up, if we hadn't gotten out of there, we could be—"

"They did show up, and we did get out. "

"Yeah but…"

"Plus, I had you to distract the bad guys. Who needs Marines?"

This gets her to smile. "I don't know what came over me."

"Totally mad."

"Yeah." She rubs her bloody hand on her pants. "Still, Eves. I think maybe we need to consider—"

"We don't stop, Sam. We don't ever stop."

She nods, but it looks forced. Stars, the hull isn't the only thing being rattled here. I want to get to the bottom of this with her, but now's clearly not the time. Instead, I opt for placing my hand on her thigh and giving it a firm squeeze. She grabs my hand in return, hard. At the same time, a tear races down her cheek, glinting in the red bay lights.

"It's gonna be okay, Sam. Promise."

Without looking up, she says, "I'm not so sure."

8

NIGEL

"Is that the best you've got, father?" Malcom said to the man he normally shared with the rest of the world. But this particular morning, the nine-year-old boy, a single batsman, had Sir Nigel Sallsworth all to himself, bowling stumps. At least in theory. In actuality, Nigel was dodging verb requests for his thoughts on Allbrook's death and his subsequent landslide acclimation. The reporters even found ways around many of his V-cog filters to the point that the intrusions were downright alarming.

"Father. Come on!"

Nigel sent a note to his wife, Esther, and his personal assistant, Rowan, stating that he was going dark and would only be reachable in person on the back lawn with Malcom for the rest of the hour. If something was "that urgent," they knew where to reach him. He owed his son this much; his daddy-daughter date tonight with six-year-old Fiona would require similar treatment. This was their day, what little of it he could give.

Satisfied that he was alone with his son at last, Nigel bowled a beamer more suited for his uni days than for a child. The ball blew past the batter and knocked down the left wicket and bail.

Malcom, having not even swung, looked up in scorn. "You know I can't hit those."

Nigel blushed, realizing his mistake. He'd taken out his frustration on the ball... and on the boy. "Forgive me." He bent over and fetched another ball off the soft pitch. "Ready?"

"Uh huh." Malcom took up his best form, while Nigel lowered his mental intensity and bowled a predictably bouncing ball toward Malcom's sweet spot. The boy stepped into the swing and struck the ball squarely.

"There it is," Nigel said with a hand over his brow, tracking the ball as it sailed toward the boundary. "Bravo."

"Now you're not trying at all."

"Come again?"

"I'm not a baby, father." Malcom retook his ready stance. "Again."

"Fair enough."

Over the next several bowls, the Secretary General forgot himself, at least as politicast leader, business mogul, and statesman. For just a few minutes, he was a father... and maybe a somewhat decent cricket player if the ribbons in the basement had anything to say about it.

Malcom hit two out of every three bowls, and father and son worked together in resetting the wicket until, at last, the sun had gotten to them, and refreshment was required. Rather than fall prey to the temptation of reactivating V-cog simply to summon one of the family stewards and risk verb inundation, Nigel bade Malcom sit in the shade so he might venture back to the summer kitchen. "Lemonade?"

"Extra sugar."

"Is there any other way?"

Malcom smiled. "Nope."

Nigel was halfway to their estate, just past the giant oak, when someone shouted his name. It was Miriam, head of the house, and it was quite unlike her to raise her voice. She'd only ever done that to the dogs and sometimes the horses. But now she was running around the northwest balcony with her hands motioning for him to come. Or stay. Or… hang it all, he couldn't tell.

"Out with it, Miriam." His first thought was Esther or Fiona. But the housekeeper was running on about things he couldn't distinguish.

When at last she was near enough to stop running—hands on her knees—she said, "Attacks! And she's on… everywhere."

"Attacks on what? Who's everywhere?"

"Neon! The Tantum Terrae are… are claiming attacks on… Oh, just turn V-cog on already!"

Nigel had never seen Miriam like this. He thanked her and reconnected to the grid. The moment his lobby appeared in his mind's eye, it came with a slew of high priority notifications, including summons from the General Council, the Politicast Chamber of Representatives, and the Solum Terram headquarters, among others. Whatever was happening seemed to be worse than what they'd forecasted.

Nigel expected retaliation of some kind. It was inevitable after the declaration of war. But with how quickly the NUE has been cracking down on the Tantum assets and its known low- to mid-level associates, he expected the reaction to resemble a hunted animal in death throes, not whatever was causing this level of anxiety.

"Father?" Malcom's voice said from behind.

"Just a moment, son."

"You promised."

"I know, I… I need to postpone."

"But, father, you said—"

Nigel spun around and knelt. "I'm wrong to break my word to you, and I beg your forgiveness, truly. I hope you'll understand."

Malcom wrung his hands, clearly torn between what had been promised and the hardship that would make his father renege on their date. "People are in trouble?"

"A great deal, yes."

The boy swallowed and lowered his head.

But Nigel caught his chin with a finger. "I would not leave unless it was important."

"I know."

"Do you forgive me?"

"Of course, father. Maybe tomorrow?"

Nigel wanted to say yes, but he knew better. "I need you to go with Miss Miriam."

"Yes, father," Malcom said in a small voice. "Thank you for… what we had."

Those words ripped at Nigel's chest, and he lamented his son's wound. Fiona's hopes would be dashed as well. But it was the price Neon was exacting on the world, and Nigel surmised there might not be any dates with his children for a very long time.

⁂

"Catch me up," Nigel said to Walter Brunell, his chief of staff, over V-cog as he strode into his home office and shut the door.

"Nine different coordinated attacks on pro-space installations across the globe, plus three more in orbit, and two over Mars," Walter replied in his aristocratic tone. "Neon is claiming responsibility."

"When?"

"Still happening. She's on a rant, sir."

Nigel took a seat in his oversize leather chair and dimmed the windows. He would watch this in the real, so he ported the feed—now streaming over every sig path in the verb—to a holo display above his desk. Neon appeared, dressed in black orbital fatigues and a black beret, and wearing her trademark electric pink lipstick. Her jacket's zippered seams only closed halfway up her chest and spread apart, revealing bare skin, a pink strap, and the curves of her breasts. She glared at the camera with a seductive look that somehow communicated both pleasure and violence at the same time. When she spoke, the tone was like the reserved rage of a lioness angered over the safety of her pride.

"...Because the people need protection. And it is amply clear that those in places of power are allergic to wielding their authority in ways that would end the suffering of our planet. Instead, they seek only their own comforts, only their own safety, while casting a blind eye to the inexcusable maladies that plague the world."

"Do we have a location?" Nigel asked Walter. The woman had evaded arrest in the American Heights and could be anywhere given her global connections. But this livestream might be just the slipup NUE authorities needed.

"No, sir. Working on it. The broadcast is decentralized."

Neon continued. "The powerful take what they want, when they want. They prey upon the vulnerable, the unprotected. The innocent. They pin us down, strip our dignity, and use the resources that belong to the many in ways that only serve the few."

"What about the background?" Nigel said.

"Security division is scanning all audio and video signatures for comparative analysis."

"Good."

"And yet"—Neon's eyes sparkled—"by their abdication, they create opportunity. By their bloodlust, they make us martyrs of Gaia. By their deficiencies, they unwittingly summon the weak to become great. To become noble.

"And so we do. We rise to the occasion and call those in power to give an accounting of their misdeeds. Not before tribunals, but before the masses. We plead our cause to the nations and demand that the war against us cease. Therefore, I call upon the General Council of the Nations of United Earth to recognize the Tantum Terrae as a sovereign politicast within the Chamber of Representatives, effective immediately.

"Additionally," Neon went on, her voice finding new confidence—as if that were somehow lacking before, "we demand that the directors at the Search for Extrasolar Sentient Intelligence in St. John's cease all and every attempt to decode the so-called alien transmission allegedly captured from the Kepler system; that the Nations of United Earth Space and Science Administration stop development and testing of the Marquis-Class Initiative ship the *Kogarashi* and all subsequent efforts to expand and settle any space territories; that all currently operational legacy habitats and dome settlements be evacuated and decommissioned; and, lastly, that the traitor Sir Nigel Sallsworth be arrested and tried for treason against humanity and the murder of the late Madame Secretary General Mary Allbrook."

Neon's face vanished. In its place came a wide angle shot of an industrial warehouse. Extravagant furniture filled a central living space, while gaudy drapes flowed from second and third story balconies. It was Neon's hideout in Vancouver. He'd been there on several occasions. And this… this footage was evidence of just such a time.

Only it wasn't right.

"You'll do the job for twenty-five million," the man named Sir Nigel Sallsworth said, standing before the large desk on the lush carpet in the warehouse. His bodyguards faced off with hers… only Neon's men had their hands up, weaponless.

Neon shook her head. "I would never gift wrap an assassination for you. Yet here you stand, expecting me to do your wet work and throw in a big red bow?"

"That's not right," Walter said at the recording. "That's not what you said."

Nigel raised a hand to silence the man. His chief of staff wasn't wrong, having seen Nigel's V-cog recording of the encounter. This wasn't how the conversation went. In a manner of speaking, yes, Nigel has said those words, and Neon hers. But not exactly this way. The presentation was near enough that he could almost replay the words from memory. Even hearing this doctored version corrupted his recall. It was as if someone had poured liquid on a watercolor painting to distort the original art—not so much that the viewer couldn't see the landscape, but too much that they couldn't determine the season or time of day.

The Nigel on video said, "Last chance." His guards raised their weapons. "I always get what I want."

"This is all incorrect," Walter said again, more emphatically this time. Nigel found it curious how the man could be so upset with the unethical nature of Neon's manipulation while completely overlooking the fact that his boss had indeed assassinated a woman. A failure to see in the light was often the plight of those who became too used to working in the dark.

The holo display showed Nigel's head drop a fraction of a centimeter, as if his chin were the pin on the back of a brass shell, igniting the primer and detonating the gel propellant. Instead of Tantum weapons firing from behind the curtains and gunning down his men and women as it had in real life, Solum Terram weapons riddled Neon's unarmed personnel with bullets.

The woman cried out, swinging at Nigel's face, but the action did nothing to stop the TT security forces from falling and drenching the carpet with their blood.

The scene changed from the warehouse to another place Nigel recognized: Calvert Isle, Neon's remote ocean-view enclave northwest of Vancouver. There, she and Nigel had walked, or rather he'd limped, as the terrorist leader explained her obscure worldview of maintaining world order through chaos. Only, in this version, caught on hidden cameras throughout her vineyard, it was not he who suffered the bullet wounds to leg and shoulder, but her. Likewise, Nigel on camera lectured the leader of the Tantum Terrae about chaos, control, violence, and resistance while she pleaded for a respite from his abuse.

"This time tomorrow," he said in the recording, "I'll be on my way home, and my team will be back hastening my election. I will manage distribution for the new epoch, Neon. And you? You will manage the pain."

Neon's face reappeared live in the verb stream. "We, the paladins of Tantum Terrae, are pledged to do what is best for humanity, while the so-called leaders of the nations continue to do what is best for themselves. We will suffer it no longer. If our demands are not met, then what you are seeing now is but the beginning of what we are capable of doing for the sake of humanity. Acknowledge us and our desire to protect the world, and we will be ushered into a peace unseen for over three centuries. Gaia will be renewed. But fail to heed our demands? Then you will reap the consequences of Canongate. There will be no quarter given, no mercy bestowed. Only Earth forever."

The stream reverted to a man and women in broadcast attire who seemed caught off guard by being back online.

"You're live," someone shouted off camera.

The woman straightened her back and tried to wipe the surprise off her face. "Our apologies for what looks to have been a verb-wide stream override. However, everything appears to be back online, and our team here is working—"

"It's not true," Walter said on Nigel's behalf. "None of that is reflective of what truly happened, sir"

"Peace, Walter," Nigel said from his chair in their shared V-cog lobby and then terminated the broadcast.

"But aren't you—?"

"Worried? About what?"

"Sir, she's… Well, she's attacking you."

"The battle is not my concern. Only the war."

Nigel had to hand it to Neon. She'd done to him what he'd done to her: aired footage of culpability. What he'd shown the world was unaltered evidence that connected Neon to *Astraea*'s demise by way of Jack Birdwhistle. Neon, in similar fashion, had just fused Nigel to Mary Allbrook's death. Sure, he hadn't spoken the late Secretary General's name when he'd been in Vancouver: he wasn't so reckless. But the implication was clear, and the damage had been done. There would never be any fair trial now; a planet full of potential jurors had been forever biased. Reprogramming a virgin idea logged in the public psyche was difficult if not impossible. His PR team would need to be cunning. Of course, Nigel's personal V-cog recording would exonerate him. But showing the unaltered footage wouldn't absolve him, only implicate Neon as a collaborator. So he needed something else.

"I want Hannah and Gunter to draft a response condemning this as a deepfake. Mitchell should have plenty of resources to analyze the footage and—"

"But the original version still puts you there."

"I don't intend to show the original, Walter. Mitchell will provide you with ample evidence to raise suspicions about the quantum data lock and GPS log. It will be more than enough to satisfy the authorities initially."

"You mean to dismiss the entire transmission as a… as a fabrication?"

"It will take time. But it's the only way to put distance between us, Neon, and Allbrook. Then, with a little time and ingenuity, I have something more in mind to feed them."

Nigel was indeed guilty. Not just of conspiring with Neon, but of actually killing Mary Allbrook. It turned out he did have the stones after all. Few knew, of course. Only his closest staff. Using the nanopoison allowed Sallsworth to distance himself from the slaying, not just forensically but emotionally. Firing a weapon at someone's head, stabbing them with a knife—those were brutal means. But arranging for an unwitting kitchen steward to lace a whiskey glass? The act felt less like killing and more like an accident… an accident that would rid the world of an inept Preservationist whose policies had run their course. Neutrality, he supposed, killed twice as many people as picking a side.

"What about the ratings, sir?" Walter asked.

"They're of no long-term concern."

"But, sir, they'll—"

"In the end, the public will do what they always do."

"Which is?"

"Forget, Walter. Give them another juicy bone, and the public always forgets."

Two new objects appeared in the home's V-cog security feed: NUE shuttles, heading for the south lawn. They were here to collect Nigel. To question him. Start an investigation. Possibly even to put him under house arrest. Or worse. Cricket play would have to wait, as would Fiona's dinner date. The noose was constricting.

"Take care of my family until I return, Walter. And call Matthews. I need eyes inside that woman's new operation, wherever it is."

9

EVELYN

"You've got an incoming call, Dr. Park," says a Marine in the vehicle's passenger side front seat. Second Lieutenant McGraw, communications officer. I know he's just doing his job, but I really hate all the babysitting and comms blackout. I'm also *hangry* and tired, plus I want the V-cog lock on my team released, and I really want to know where the hell they're taking us.

"You mean, I can answer this one, Dad?"

McGraw smiles at me.

But Sam jabs me with an elbow—the one not in a makeshift sling. "Don't shoot the messenger, Eves."

"He knows I'm kidding." Back to McGraw: "I'm not kidding."

"Smart ass," he replies.

I like this Marine, despite my misgivings about the military industrial complex as a whole. "So, you gonna tell me who it is, Lieutenant? Or we gonna play twenty questions?"

"It's Captain Jericho Fox, ma'am. Currently onboard *Selene* Station."

Sam and I exchange looks. This the first outside call we've had since leaving St. John's, flying who knows where, and now driving across what I assume is a rural military installation in an E-Humvee "I'll take it."

"Stand by." McGraw transfers the call to me, and the next thing I know, a ruggedly handsome pilot in a leather jacket appears in my lobby with a concerned look on his face. My guess is that the avatar isn't reflective of what his new job with NUESSA requires, but such is the benefit of V-cog rendering. Though, I wouldn't mind seeing him in *Selene* Station engineering uniform. Just saying. "Fox. Didn't expect to hear from you."

"Same. You, uh… okay? Heard things got a little rough at the office."

"We're doing fine, all things considered."

"Tried reaching you earlier, but they have you locked down pretty tight."

"You can say that again." I refrain from kicking Mc-Graw's seatback in front of me. Again, not his fault. But all anger needs a target, right? "I'm not even sure what all I'm allowed to say. And… how come you're my first call anyway? No offense."

"Apparently, NUESSA and SESI Command are busy putting out several fires, figuratively and literally."

"We caught wind of more attacks. Not a whole lotta details yet."

"That's why I'm calling. And, anyway, you, uh… put me down as an emergency contact."

"I did?" Damn. Forgot about that. A holdover from the *Astraea* debrief.

Jericho gives me a sheepish shrug. "Surprise." Then he changes his tone. "Lemuel asked that I bring you up to speed."

"You? Isn't your test this morning?"

"So you do have cameras in my bathroom."

"You wish. I just have a good memory."

"Okay, Miss Emergency Contact."

I glare at him but eventually break a smile.

"The launch is in five hours, but interdisciplinary communications during a coordinated terrorist attack on two planets takes precedence. Command thought I was the best to—"

"Did you say two planets? Mars?"

Jericho nods grimly. "They hit manufacturing in Mawrth Vallis, and destroyed two of the landing pads in Columbia Hills."

"Stars."

"We're up to ten total hits on Earth. More likely as incoming reports get processed."

"I saw some headlines about Christchurch, Calgary, and Oslo as we were being evacuated." Out loud, I add, "Until the military blacked out V-cog on us."

Jericho furrows his brow but continues. "Add to that some minor assaults on *Calypso* and *Persephone* too, but nothing as bad as…"

"As *Astraea.*"

He nods. "Tantum has claimed responsibility."

"Yeah, I figured. Caught the pink T's on one of the terrorist's body armor."

"Good for us all that NUE security didn't let them get very far. Heard you decided to shoot back too?"

"Somebody dropped a gun, and I was pissed."

"Say no more. Anyway, you're currently riding across Elmendorf Air Force Base in Anchorage."

"Alaska? But St. John's is—"

"Is no longer an option for you. Not after the attack."

My brain kicks into high gear. "No way. I'm not surrendering this to the military."

"I don't think that's what they—"

"We're not conducting research with them, Jericho."

"Lemuel said—"

"Lemuel would never sanction this."

Jericho raises an eyebrow but doesn't speak.

"Oh, say it ain't so."

"You wanna know why Rook had a squad in your building?" he asks.

I rub my forehead with one hand. "No. But I think you're going to tell me anyway."

"They were en route to escort you to Anchorage. The higher ups already had intel that something was in the works, they just didn't know what or when. And since the TT are now listed as a terrorist organization, thanks to the vote, under the NUE's charter…"

"It means the military is employed for defense."

He nods. "Command made the decision to move you in advance so you could continue your work where you'll be safe. And when reviewing options, SESI and the Security Council saw Rook's performance with you on *Astraea* as noteworthy. Figured it would be easiest on you."

"No, they figured I would be more easily manipulated if I was approached by someone I trusted."

"We just thought that—"

"*We?*" I open my eyes as wide as I can. "Stars. You're doing it too, aren't you!"

"Evelyn, listen, we all just—"

"No! No, no, no. Uh uh. I get a say in these things too, dammit. And everyone can just go to hell if they think—"

"Evelyn, please."

"—if they think I'm gonna sit around and let other people make decisions for me and my team."

"They're trying to keep you alive."

"Well they shouldn't. What they need to be worried about is the research."

"You are the research!"

I open my mouth to say something, but no words come out. Then I glance at Sam in the real. She looks concerned even though she's not privy to my conversation. Jericho basically just said the same thing that Sam did when we were in custody back on *Astraea*.

"Evelyn, listen," he adds in a softer tone.

But before he can elaborate, as I know he will, I say, "I get it."

"You do?"

"Yeah. We each have a part to play, and this one's mine." I take a deep breath. "But I want it known how much I hate being whisked off to some black site inside a military base."

"I'll… be sure to let Lemuel know."

"You can tell all of Helsinki if you want. Call up Sallsworth while you're at too, because that guy is—"

"He's under house arrest at the moment."

"What?"

"Neon addressed the world while you've been off grid. Well, she did more like a system-wide takeover. Claimed responsibility for all the attacks and then showed a shitload of evidence damning Sallsworth for arranging Allbrook's death."

"Actual evidence? And people believe her? If there was one person I would trust less than Nigel Sallsworth, it would be Neon."

"The footage she provided passed as undoctored. Granted, a lot of people don't trust her, and we have yet to hear how Sallsworth's people will try to spin it. But after the videos she showed? Seems pretty legit. Looks like Allbrook was assassinated by poisoning. I'm sure NUE authorities have their work cut out for them."

"Stars, that's… that's next level."

"Sure is."

After a few seconds, I ask, "So, what now?"

"You get comfortable in your new lab and find out what our alien friends are trying to say."

"And you?"

"Going through with the test flight."

"You're not worried?"

"Security's pretty tight up here."

"Tell that to *Calypso* and *Persephone*."

"Still, we've got people counting on us and can't afford delays or else we might not get another chance, same as you." He pauses for a moment and studies my face.

"What is it?"

"You close?"

"Heh. More than you know." I lean in. "I think we figured it out, Jericho."

"Really?"

"Won't know until we run some new tests we are working on… well, *were* working on, up until the attack."

"But you're hopeful."

"Yeah." I can't resist smiling. "We're really close. Feels… well, it feels fucking amazing."

He laughs. "I'm glad. Listen, I gotta go. You keep your head down and watch your back. And stay close to Rook."

"My favorite Marine."

"You like more than one?"

I wink at him. "And you stay close to Kit, okay?"

"I'll keep him safe."

"For *your* safety, dummy."

"Sure." Jericho seems to think of something, then adds, "Forging paths?"

"Through the darkness. Later, Fox."

"Park."

CRAZY TO THINK THAT TODAY, NUE Marines rescued my team, wiped out an entire floor of bad guys, and whisked me off to Alaska, all without blinking an eye. Respect. What's more, the Air Force worked with NUESSA and SESI to set up an entire lab for my research team twenty levels below the surface in a part of the base that doesn't even use augmented reality to name the rooms. Just old school placards with words SUB 20 followed by the room number engraved in plastic.

The hallways and cleanrooms are well-maintained, well-lit, and populated with the latest high-end equipment courtesy of the world's taxpayers—no expense spared. I do my best to suppress the side of my brain that's already calculating waste and doing cost-analysis for each piece of gear according to what we'll actually use against what they assume we'll use. But the other side of my brain reasons that the money is already spent, and we might as well make use of it. Waste not, want not.

Bottom line, these people get things done. And I have my life because they stepped in. For that, and the new opportunity to finish our work in peace, I'm grateful.

I walk into the purposefully dimly lit SUB 20 Lab 1 —no frills in that name—to find my team broken into two groups, one writing across holo glass screens and hovering over workstations projecting the fractal models, while the other is crunching large number streams with three dedicated V-cog quantum computers along the back wall.

I scan for Sam and Natalie as I rub my fingers through my still-wet hair from my shower. I'd needed a few minutes by myself after arriving on post, so I figured a shower in our new barracks would refresh me while everyone else went to set up in the lab.

"Over here," Sam calls. She and Nat are behind a freestanding holographic display of the fractal we'd uncovered just before the terrorists invaded the building.

I join them and inspect the three dimensional, slowly rotating render. "How's the arm?"

"Fine. Doc gave me some good stim code for the pain."

"You gonna share?"

"No way." Sam smiles at me and then nods at the fractal. "Like it?"

"It's prettier than I remember."

"That's because we colored it a bit. To make it easier to see the patterns."

"Well, it's working." Sure enough, the hexagonal shape is composed of multiple sub-shapes, each colored in varying shades of an iridescent rainbow. The texture itself reminds me of a snowflake, only this one is blown up several hundred times. It also has multiple layers that seem to move underneath one another.

"That shifting," I say. "From the signal replication?"

Natalie answers before Sam. "Yes. Consensus is that it has something to do with unlocking the photon orbital angular momentum streams. Team Two is working on that now, but initial applications of the patterns aren't producing anything."

I rub my hair again to speed up the drying and take a step closer to the fractal.

At the same time, Sebastián enters the workstation and folds his arms beside me. "Beautiful, isn't it?"

"That's an understatement." I catch him tilting his head one way and then the other, studying the geometry with particular keenness. "What're you sitting on, Dr. Fernandez Parra?"

"With the cryptography end? Nothing. That's a bit above my pay grade."

"How 'bout the biology end?"

He gives me a grin as his eyes sparkle with the projected image. "They used light to create a fractal."

I think I'm following him, but I say, "And?" just to keep him going.

"And… a fractal is something we see in nature stemming from physical processes. Minerals. Ice. Organic tissue. But they managed to do it with light. Granted, it's data-driven, as far as I can tell, but data is a construct, relative to the sender. The point is, these beings managed to create something organic in nature from light waves. Or… particles. You're the physicist."

"We'll say it's both for now," I say, giving him the standard line that every scientist loves to torment students with. Pesky thing, light. Won't make up its mind. "You think it gives us a glimpse into their nature?"

"I do. What, exactly, I can't say yet. But they are advanced, at least relative to us. As far they're concerned, this could be a finger painting. However…"

"Go on."

"…this creation assumes a few things. The most obvious of which is that they perceive light in ways that are similar to our own."

"So they have eyes."

"In a manner of speaking. Though I would be quick to warn us all against any attempts to anthropomorphize them. We can't help some of it, of course. We can only interpret from where we stand. But the more objective we can be, the better."

"So they have… light sensory organs," I try again.

"For now, yes. Again, we have to prepare ourselves for the fact that these creatures could be entirely ontologically *other* than us. But the fact that we at least share light transmission in common is a very good sign, I wager."

"You're a gambling priest too?" Sam asks.

"*Former* priest. And don't we all? Gamble?"

Sam's eyes grow a little wide, but she quickly goes back to work.

"The other things this tells us are less clear, but they cause me to be optimistic," Seb continues.

"Like?"

"They perceive organic shapes in three dimensions, esteem patterns, order thoughts in layers, and utilize puzzles for communication, just for starters. These are all clues that I… Ha! I think I'll spend the rest of my life trying to deduce!"

"Well, if we're lucky, you can just ask them all your questions yourself."

"I savor the prospect, Dr. Park." He folds his arms a little tighter. "And then there is this grand thing."

I look between him and the display twice, expecting for him to pinpoint something new. "What grand thing?"

"They assume."

I can guess at what he's getting at, but it's best not to leave observations to chance. "How so?"

"They assume that we are of a technological maturity to not only catch but decipher their message. And this, I dare say, is the most robust argument of all for why we cannot fail."

"We sure he's not a philosopher?" Sam mutters to me.

I wave her off behind my back. "Go on, Seb."

In a somewhat awestruck tone, he says, "If there is a signal worth sending then there is a people worth sending it to. They value us even before meeting us. They ascribe worth to the recipient by the endowment of their attempt."

"Meaning?"

"They consider us worthy."

For some strange reason I can't quite place, a shiver runs up my spine and down my arms. Excitement. Wonder. Curiosity. I don't even know if Sebastián is right in his assumptions. But the fact that he believes he's right is what moves me. And I'd hate to disappoint him.

I pat him on the back. "We'd better hurry up and figure this out before they lose faith in us, eh, Dr. Fernandez Parra?"

I leave Team One and inspect Team Two's progress, but I'm not halfway through reviewing their computations when I see the door open and a figure step into our dim lab. If it's who I think it is, he's swapped out orbital combat armor for the Marine woodland working coat and trousers. "Rook?"

The man looks my way. "Evelyn."

He extends his hand, but I sidestep it and give him

an around-the-neck hug. Screw professionalism. "Stars, am I glad to see you."

"Same." He pats me on the back once.

I release his neck. "You and your unit… You okay?"

"Everyone did their jobs. No casualties. Which is a lot more than I can say for the enemy."

"Tantum."

"Roger."

"Yeah, I saw the TT on—"

"On the hostile you grifted a weapon from?"

"Ha. Yeah."

He smiles and shakes his head once, either in appreciation or bewilderment. I can't tell. "Thanks for having my back up there."

"I figure if you had some body armor and more ammo, you would've been just fine."

I avoid the recruitment topic. "Jericho said Neon claimed responsibility."

"You caught up with him?"

"We talked on the way here. It was… good to see a familiar face. Same for yours."

"Well, you're going to be seeing a lot more of it. I was just assigned—"

"To escort me here."

"That, yes. But now I'm your shadow."

"Shadow? You mean like security detail?" So *that's* what Jericho meant by staying close to Rook.

"Yes, ma'am. Twenty-four seven."

I make a quick show of looking around the lab. "No offense, but a top-secret underground lab in a remote military base isn't secure enough?"

"After the fireworks show? Command won't take any unnecessary risks, and that's from the top."

I turn and survey my team again. The thought of

what could have been hits me hard. We were a minute away from being gunned down. From losing everything. Back to Rook, I say, "I'm grateful. Thank you."

"You might change your mind after a few weeks. But I'll do my best to stay out of your hair. Speaking of which, you need a towel or something?"

I spot a few wet strands base jumping off my forehead and push them behind my ear. "Nah. But thanks. I need to get back to work."

"What about Jericho's test flight?"

That catches me off guard. I check the time. "That's now? But the media blackout…"

"Not for one of Sentia Aux's biggest VIPs." Rook sends an invite to my V-cog lobby: Secure viewer permission invitation, *Selene* Station, Space Traffic Control Center. "Membership has its privileges."

"Oh, Rook! You're the best."

"Some have said."

I stretch up and kiss him on the cheek, which seems to do the job of jarring him, just a little. "Thank you."

"You better join. The *Kogarashi* is being ferried into position now."

JERICHO

"Hɪ, Dᴀᴅ."

"Son. Thanks for taking my call."

I've got him on audio only since the majority of my attention is needed elsewhere. "Literally about to launch here."

"Figured. Just… wanted wish you luck."

"You sure you're not secretly hoping we fail?"

"I may not agree with what your politicast is doing—"

"Which is what I'm doing too."

He lets out a sigh. "I don't want anyone to get hurt. Never did. I'm just glad you're not… Eh, I hope it goes well… for your sake."

"Thanks. Listen, Dad, I gotta run."

"I know. Go get 'em, Knight."

I end the call and then open the V-cog channel to all those gathered in mission control and aboard the *Koga.* "Alright, people. We are T-minus three minutes and counting. Coming up on final preflight in two."

Selene Station's bridge, secondary command rooms, and V-cog suites are packed with NUESSA and MCI senior staffers and mission support specialists. Behind us, dozens of investors, politicast reps, military brass, reporters, and special guests fill observation balconies and virtual decks. It's a veritable zoo of the important and the curious. But none of the pixies, the shouts and pings for quotes, or the verb interview requests matter to me right now. I've got a ship to test and a crew to keep safe.

The captain of *Selene* Station stands off my left shoulder with her hands clasped behind her back. The rest of the station's nav and sensors crew are at the ready, but it's my team who has control authority over all systems. *Selene*'s full power is at our disposal, and the eyes of St. John's Spaceflight Tracking and Data Network Stations are on us… on the technological achievement that is humanity's hope for leaving our solar system's heliosphere: the *Kogarashi*.

The ship's black and purple, armor-plated body is parked 300 klicks ahead of *Selene*'s orbital trajectory around the moon. The crew, consisting of Mission Commander and Captain Eddie Carr, Lead Propulsion Engineer Nairobi Kinshaw, the towering Navigation Officer Torrence "Magellan" Vanderburg, and Code, Life Support, and Communications Specialist Adrian Wallace, are all seated in their respective crash couches and awaiting orders. Beside me, Kit, one of his excipion pals, and my PA, Alice Ortega, are busy filtering what I need to know from what I don't and feeding it to an augmented reality heads-up display in my natural sight line.

The presence of Kit's recently modified and overly friendly maintenance bot has gotten him plenty of suspicious looks; advanced AI in anthropomorphic robots was banned long ago. But having one of the Ferguses on the bridge doesn't bother me as much as it might others. I've had lots of time around them in hangar bays. More than that, I know it can come in handy on this test, spotting things that a human might miss.

I pair Alice and Kit's incoming feeds with V-cog windows of onboard camera shots of the *Koga*'s crew, external views of the ship, and all the most essential system sensors—including the data log that evaded me the first time. Sure, there's a qualified specialist watching it, and all the key people have been briefed on what Eddie found. I'm just… added redundancy. Because I can't afford to—

"Jericho?" someone says in my V-cog lobby.

I'm about to send the user to Alice when my brain recognizes the speaker's voice. I switch to my virtual suite. "Evelyn. Everything okay?"

"I just wanted to wish you luck."

I smile. "Thanks."

"We're all rooting you on down here."

"I appreciate that." After a moment of awkward silence, I add, "Listen, I gotta go."

"Right, of course. Just… you got this. It's gonna be different this time."

Way to be subtle, Evelyn.

Everyone's kept their lips sealed about comparing the two test flights. Well, everyone but Eddie. Whether the team's silence has been for decorum or superstition is anyone's guess. Probably some of both. But Dr. Evelyn Park? She just walks headlong into the issue. Apparently she's not done either.

"Oh, and just so you know, no one's dying on this run."

"Jesus, Evelyn. I—"

She raises a hand. "Don't pretend you're not thinking about it. Everyone is. We're all trying to suppress those images. But I just wanted to say that's all bullshit. The comparison, not the tragedy. Pain makes us better people if we let it be a teacher and not a tyrant. And I think you've let it change you for the better. So… yeah. You've got this. That's all I wanted to say." She tucks some loose strands of hair behind her ear and then just stands there, looking at me with those deep dark eyes.

Damn. "Uh, okay."

Another awkward second passes, then she says, "I'll see you later."

I grab her arm just before she leaves. "Evelyn. Thanks. For the…"

"No problem. It's the truth." Then, as abruptly as she entered my lobby, Evelyn blinks out, and my hand falls to my side.

"Everything okay in ye ole cranium there, Cap?" Kit asks.

I step out of my lobby and look over at him. "All good."

"Okay, because we're good for"—he lowers his voice—"you know… pre-flight?" He gives me a thumbs-up to indicate that all systems under his observation are nominal. Alice does the same.

"I, too, have reviewed and verified all preflight protocol procedures," says Kit's excipion and holds up its mechanical thumb.

"Didn't ask you."

The thumb lowers.

Kit pats the bot on the shoulder. "It's okay. He's not mad. It just takes a while to, ya know, learn social cues."

Back to the mission, I assign my voice to all command channels again. "This is Mission Control Director Jericho Fox. We are a go for NUESSA and Stellar Dynamics *Kogarashi* preflight check." I glance at my V-cog prompts for plasma test conductor, launch processing system test conductors, flight coordinator at *Selene* Station Mission Control, and St. John's Spaceflight Tracking and Data Network Stations. "PTC?"

"Go," says the first of all corresponding specialists.

"LPS."

"Go, flight."

"SFC."

"Go."

"STJO."

"Go, flight."

Next comes the support test manager, safety console coordinator, and ship project engineer. "STM?" I call out.

"We're a go, flight."

"Safety Console."

"Go."

"SPE."

"Go, flight."

As I say the last three categories on my list, memories flashback to the *Perseverant*, only I wasn't saying these. I was on board. With the crew. Listening to the answer-call cadence of the mission director with his choir of congregants. Capture and recovery director, superintendent of range operations, and then crew's mission commander.

"CRD," I say.

"Go, flight."

"SRO."

"Go."

"And CDR."

"We're a fucking go, flight," Eddie Carr says over comms. A spate of nervous laughter spreads across the bridge. I'm sure all the parents and teachers with kids watching the verb are loving that one. Good thing there's a seven-second broadcast delay. Lord, help it.

"*Kogarashi*," I reply. "You are good for main drive test alpha, mode one. T-minus thirty seconds."

"Confirming main drive test alpha, mode one," Eddie echoes. He and Magellan are in the captain and first officer seats. They swipe through windows and double check systems as the mission counter ticks past the twenty second mark.

I cast a wayward look at the streaming data log window in my vision's lower right. I should close it out, I know. It's a distraction at this point. But, again, I can't help myself.

"T-minus fifteen seconds," calls the flight coordinator.

"Out and back," I add to the ship's crew. "Nice and easy."

"It's a light jog," Nairobi replies, probably more for my sake than anyone else's. "And she's purring like a kitten."

The flight coordinator calls out, "T-minus five... four... three... two... one..."

The *Koga*'s main drive core fires and produces seven brilliant blue cones of light from the stern. At the same time, every diagnostic monitor in real and virtual command spaces lights up with activity. It's like bringing a hospital patient back from the dead. Specialists start calling out their scheduled interval check-ins, while holo windows cycle through the demands of operators who busily cross reference multiple sensor reports.

The bridge's energy is electric. Half of me enjoys the rush, thrilled at the sight of the Marquis-class exploration starship accelerating for its first nine-minute burn. The other half of me is sweating bullets, because I've seen this before. Lived it. Survived it.

I feature the crew cams in my V-cog, away from the prying eyes of the public. Nairobi, Adrian, Magellan, and Eddie's bodies are pinned in their crash couches. Unlike conventionally powered atmospheric flight, the pure straight line thrust of magnetically contained plasma through hard vacuum exerts little distortion on the crew. No massive shaking or head bobbing. Just skin pressing over bone. Were it not for vitals trending upward, a casual observer might assume we're looking at a bunch of old folks who spent their retirement on fancy space suits and not plastic surgery.

"Time, sixty seconds," the flight coordinator calls out. "Acceleration at 7.55 g's and holding. Range, 133 kilometers. Speed, 4,442 meters per second."

"CDR," I call out to Eddie.

"All systems nominal," he replies in a tight voice.

"Huh," Kit says. "He didn't even swear at—"

"You wanna fucking hold my hand too, Flight?"

I glance back at Kit. "You were saying?"

"Ha ha. Yeah."

"Looking good, people." I walk toward the bridge's main display. Hundreds of drones have been set up along the *Koga*'s flight path to provide constant close-up visuals of the ship as it accelerates. The transitions remind me of watching RDX-60 sport class races on the verb as the ship whizzes by in an ever-quickening progression. Likewise, the drones are logarithmically spaced to account for acceleration.

My eyes continue to flit across all the core command

screens. I keep thinking I'm gonna find something. Spot an anomaly, catch a flag. But I remind myself that the world's very best people are watching for these things even more carefully than I am, especially after the last test flight. Instead, my job now is to let everyone else do their work and be ready to process the big decisions if and when they arise.

I glance at the crew feeds again and bring up medical, checking with the mission doctor in charge at the same time. "Safety Console. Medical. Status?"

"Heart rates and blood pressure are up, but everything is within range," Dr. Friedman says in his old Yiddish New York accent. "Acceleration holding at 7.55 g's, flight."

"Roger." I put my hands behind my back and pace along the main display as the *Kogarashi* rockets forward. In one shot, I catch *Selene* Station disappearing in the background, along with a section of the moon and a crescent Earth. Glimpses of *Calypso* and *Persephone* dot the spacescape, as do the V-cog ident tags hundreds of smaller stations and spacecraft. The scene reminds me of sunbathers gathering on a beach to watch a boat race, each bystander struggling to get the best view over the heads of those in front. The image calls me back to just how important this moment is for humanity. For our future. Because if the *Kogarashi* is a success, there will be hundreds of other super plasmoid-powered vessels in its wake in the decades to come.

The flight coordinator's voice breaks my train of thought. "Max speed of 40,000 meters per second reached. Total distance, 10,798 kilometers. Time to drive core thrust suspension and ship rotation in five... four... three... two... one... Mark."

On screen, the blue cones of light vanish behind the

Kogarashi. A moment later, the vessel's side thrusters kick in and begin spinning the starship 180 degrees. The only things that betray the Marquis-class ship's speed are the telemetry readouts and the continually switching drone shots. Otherwise, the *Koga* might as well be sitting in suspended animation.

The rotation takes less than fifteen seconds to complete. As soon as the maneuver is stabilized, Eddie confirms the order for the slow down. "Main drive burn toward zero velocity in three… two… one…" Blue cones reappear in the drone feeds, but this time with the Earth and moon in the distance. Energy meters spike, and velocity graphs begin their long trend lines down as the starship fights to nullify the speed it acquired just moments before. The entire process appears identical to the one that got it 11,000 klicks away, but instead of burning to accelerate, the *Koga* is burning to slow down. Nine minutes later, the ship and crew are stationary at a total distance of 22,396 kilometers.

"*Kogarashi*, this is Mission Control. Status report," I ask over comms. At this range, there's little more than seven one-hundredths of a second signal delay, so the answer comes back fast.

"Mission Control, this is *Kogarashi*. We read you loud and clear. All systems nominal."

A few high fives and pats on the back spread around the room, but nothing signaling that this was anything more than a routine engine check. For me, however, every klick gained is one closer to the SPD test coming up, so the high fives and back slaps are welcome.

"Copy that, *Kogarashi*." I check the flight itinerary and confirm that the ship is exactly where the computations predicted it would be. "Adjust to bearing 105 mark 012 and prepare for SPD test beta, mode two."

"Bearing 105 mark 012," Eddie replies, and then sets to maneuvering the *Koga* into position.

"How you holding up, Cap?" Kit asks in my ear.

"Jesus, Kit." Somehow he edged closer without me knowing it. "I'm fine."

"'Cause, ya know, this next part is like—"

"I know, pal. Can you just… go back to your station?"

"Sure, sure. Me and Fergus One here just wanted to see if you needed anything."

"How may we assist you?" the excipion asks.

I cast it a rueful look and then turn back to Kit. "You can take your positions and keep your eyes on your work."

"But His Esteemed Magnificence has indicated that you—"

Kit grabs Fergus One by the arm and starts backpedaling. "We got it. Nothing to see here, Cap."

As the odd couple shuffles to their shared workstation, Alice says, "Esteemed Magnificence?"

"He doesn't get out much."

"Hadn't noticed."

I rub the back of my neck. It's sore, and I haven't even had my third cup of coffee yet. "All you people are making me more anxious than the ship is. God." I raise Eddie on comms. "How's propulsion looking?"

"Oi. Ask her yourself."

Nairobi's face appears in engineering. "Everything looks good, flight. Didn't even break a sweat."

"Don't get used to it."

"We won't."

By comparison, the next test we're about to do with the *Kogarashi* is a hundred times more dangerous and more difficult than what my crew did with the

Perseverant. Instead of a five-minute burn of the super plasmoid drive, we'll attempt to push the core for a full ninety minutes at the same 7.55 g's as before, but this time reaching a max speed of 400 *kilometers*—not meters —per second. That's crossing the Old United Kingdom in the time it takes to blink twice. When the *Koga* turns and finally reaches a stop at the end of the ninety-minute deceleration burn, it will be a whopping 2,167,748 kilometers from *Selene* Station—that's more than five and a half trips to the moon, or fifty-four times around the Earth.

This also means that the crew will be pushed to that same 7.55 g's for a total of three hours one way, and another three hours during the return trip—a feat impossible for humans to endure before the advent of gene editing and bionano reinforcement. The stresses on the heart, brain, lungs, and bones alone would be crippling. Granted, space expansion flights, when they come, won't subject their occupants to these rigorous test-flight extremes, not unless there's an emergency. Commercial passengers will benefit from SPD-powered engines, not because the drives can accelerate like a bat out of hell, but because they can sustain one-g-constant much longer than any other power unit ever made. They'll be nice and comfortable reaping the benefits of high specific impulse while our test crews get the stuffing knocked out of them. Take risks today so fewer people die tomorrow—that's what test flights have always been about.

But there's more to it than that for us with the *Kogarashi.*

Part of the accelerated schedule is thanks to major advances that Stellar Dynamics and NUESSA made to the Ebra-drive following the X-10 failure. The two entities claim that the *Kogarashi*'s propulsion system is safer and more efficient than what we had on the *Perseverant*. Based on everything I've seen to date and the preliminary tests we've run, I don't doubt their claims one iota. We wouldn't be pushing things this hard if those findings hadn't met our standards—*my* standards.

The other reason for all the hurry, and specifically behind opting to push the *Koga*'s drive core to two ninety-minute tests out and back, is because of time. If there was cause for concern about a Sallsworth-led NUE General Council before, those sentiments have been exacerbated by the sudden events surrounding his supposed assassination of Mary Allbrook. With an investigation comes a seizure of projects. Not that the NUE has leveled any austerity measures. Not yet, anyway. But we all sense they're on the way. With tensions rising planet-side, it's only a matter of time before government leaders rein in "fringe spending" abroad in order to better focus on global stability at home.

I get the rationale. International unrest summons its own apocalypse—faster than climate change, if I'm being honest. And I'm all for efforts to secure regional stability. But for those who argue that NUESSA is a hoarder of government crypto, I always feel it's important to note that the Space and Science Administration spends two percent of the NUE's budget, while forty percent goes to the military. Forty percent. The rest gets earmarked for special interest groups and politicasts. So, it seems to me that if our leaders really want to put more into stemming the tide of global poverty, disease, and in-fighting, there are much better places to take it from than NUESSA. Because the sooner we can give the planet hope, the better.

Which is why we're here.

Eddie inputs the change in direction and points the *Kogarashi* on its scheduled path parallel to Earth's orbit around the Sun rather than perpendicular. It's a precautionary move that sends the ship on a slightly acute trajectory near enough to Earth's future position to minimize recovery distance should anything go wrong. Once the first accel-decel burn is finished, the *Koga* will head back for *Selene*, giving us a massive amount of usable data.

Knowing that the crew has four back-to-back ninety-minute burns ahead of them, I jettison the uptight professionalism required by NUESSA and switch to a non-public broadcast channel with them. The only other people on this stream are Kit and Alice.

"How's everybody feeling?" I ask.

"I mean, I feel pretty good," Kit replies first. "Kinda got an upset tummy, thinking maybe I shouldn't have gone for the extra breakfast dumpling, but then again it was awfully—"

"Kit. Not you."

"Oh. Right, sorry."

"So far so good over here," Nairobi says.

"Same," Magellan adds.

"Anybody know where I put my gummies?" Adrian asks. "Can't find 'em anywhere."

"Oi. You're probably sitting on 'em, you fat fucking lard bowl."

"Ha! Yup. There they are."

To Eddie, I ask, "You feeling good, commander?"

"What's that supposed to mean? I'm about to hurtle through fucking space faster and farther than any human in history because we're strapped inside a rocket with a specific fucking impulse higher than my grandmum's tolerance for malt liquor. How the fuck do you think I'm feeling, Flight? Oi, and don't fuck this shit up either, 'else I'm gonna be riding your dreams like granny panties on a nun."

"Well there go my plans for the day." This gets a laugh from the rest of the crew. Eddie Carr, however, is still as straight faced as they come.

"Christ, lighten up, Eddie," Magellan says.

Adrian adds, "I have something for that."

"*Kogarashi*, this Mission Control. You are clear for super plasmoid drive test bravo, mode two. T-minus sixty seconds."

"SPD test bravo, mode two confirmed," Eddie replies.

Despite the first phase's success and the resulting banter, the bridges on both *Selene* and the *Kogarashi* as well as all the viewing rooms go quiet. I can't tell if maybe I accidentally hit mute on my virtual peripherals or if everyone's just gotten really still. A quick survey of the space confirms it's the latter. Only the sound of mechanical feet shuffling behind me stands out. It's Fergus One, and he's offering me something.

"For good lucky," he says.

I peer at the cigar in his palm and then look over the robot's shoulder to Kit, who forcefully whispers, "It's not *lucky*. It's just luck."

"For good just luck," Fergus One replies and offers the cigar again.

Not one to turn down some good luck, let alone what looks to be a half decent cigar, even if it is from a tongue-twisted maintenance excipion, I accept the gift, thank the bot, and salute Kit with the rolled tobacco. Don't even wanna know where he got this. Adrian, if I had to guess. I stuff the smoke in my uniform's breast pocket. Which reminds me…

"Hey, Eddie," I say. "Check your chair's right hand pouch."

He fumbles with the Velcro flap, reaches inside, and then holds up a black chess piece. Yup, a knight. "Is this a fucking joke?"

"For good luck," I reply and give him a wink.

"Oi, I got something for you too, Knight."

"Oh yeah?"

"Pretty sure I took two dice and shoved them up your—"

"T-minus five…" the flight coordinator calls out. "Four… three… two… one…"

As before, blue thrust cones burst from the seven engine nozzles. Drone cameras auto-adjust speed and aperture to account for the sudden shift in light balance. A second later, the washed-out shape of the *Koga* comes back into view. Once again, I scan the crew's cams and medical diagnostics along with simultaneous glances at telemetry. Unlike the last burn, however, the energy readings are off the charts.

"My God," Alice says under her breath, but forceful enough for me to hear. "Look at the potential output curve."

"I take it you've never seen an SPD in action?"

"No. Just… simulations. Never in the real, like this. They've got active reducers engaged?"

"It's the only way to run this hot without having the drive core run away on you."

"My God," she says again, but without attempting to conceal her astonishment.

The Ebra-drive's super plasmoid mode is so efficient that it can sustain eight g's of acceleration with the given fuel load for up to eighty-four hours, which means it could expend a lot more energy more quickly and push the crew to fatal acceleration speeds, reaching up to 136 g's. That's pancake-grade, right there. The forces involved are violent, but everything from the containment field to the hull's superstructure have been designed to handle the loads. NUESSA, Stellar Dynamics, and the combined leverage of the Viatoribus and Sentia Aux have engineered a power unit that essentially loads a star in a ship's ass, pulls the trigger, and then sips from the output. It's a dangerous balancing act, but there's no way to get humanity out of the system without it.

"Better to tame the beast than chase the dragon."

"What's that?" Alice asks me.

"It's an expression the designers used when first drafting the first Ebra-drive."

"Sounds fitting."

My eyes are glued to the mission clock. The numbers advance but seem to slow down as the timer nears twenty-four seconds.

That's how much time we had before things started to go wrong.

There's a lump in my throat.

Alice says something, but I hold up a hand.

Twenty-two…

Twenty-three…

Twenty-four…

"Flight Co? Acceleration?" I demand.

"7.55 g's and holding."

"Thrust Containment?"

"Nominal, flight," says the ship project engineer.

At the same, I glance at the random data log window that Eddie unearthed and pinned to the corkboard of my soul. This is it. The exact moment when things went critical. Where the fates of me and my crew changed forever. But right now, everything's…

…it's good.

No anomalies. No systems discrepancies. No error logs.

The *Kogarashi* is behaving exactly like we designed it to.

"Safety Console, how's the crew?" I ask.

"Heart rates and blood pressure looking good, Flight. Acceleration still holding at 7.55 g's."

"Copy that."

The good doctor comes back with, "But your vitals are climbing, Director Fox. I suggest that you—"

"I'm fine, doc. Thank you."

"Sure, but you really should think about—"

"I said, I'm fine."

Dr. Friedman doesn't try again.

"Guess Eddie isn't the only touchy project manager we've had," Alice says for my ears only.

I shrug off her attempt to be funny and flick my attention between diagnostics, camera feeds, and telemetry. It's like I'm… just waiting for something to go wrong.

But not wishing it, right, Jericho?

The voice in my head is my own. And not a weird one, like I'm going insane or something. Just the deep dark part of the subconscious that always seems to have a running commentary about the more negative aspects of life. The voice that needs to be fought off more actively when having a bad day.

The trouble is, I don't like what it's suggesting. There's no way I'd wish harm on my crew. Not in a million years. Everything I've done leading up to this moment has been about preventing that. About preserving their lives and ensuring the mission's goals.

But if something did happen…

And you're not on board but where you're supposed to be, doesn't that prove your innocence, Jericho?

What in the hell is my brain doing right now? God, I'm sweating profusely too.

"Cap?"

"*What?!*" I swing around and nearly strike Kit in the head with my elbow, but Fergus One pulls him a few centimeters back to avoid the accidental collision.

I run a hand over my hair and feel sweat on my forehead. "Sorry."

"I'm okay. But you, uh… Doc Friedman over there says you need to sit down, Cap."

Without invitation, the excipion takes a knee and produces a flat foldout seat from its thigh. "Please, allow me to accommodate you."

"Yeah, I'll pass."

Then I catch sight of Friedman moving toward me like a parent who really wants to scold their kid but doesn't want to do it in public. "Director Fox, your vitals indicate that you are—"

"In perfect health."

"Sure. Right up until you go into"—he hides his lips with a hand—"cardiac arrest from a myocardial infarction." He pulls an aerosyringe from his coat as discreetly as possible. "We need to address this, Director. You're on the line."

"I'm fine."

"Like my *fershnickered bubbeh*, you are." He smiles at those watching around the room while stabbing my forearm from under his coat. "Wow, what a lovely day we are having here."

"That your idea of being inconspicuous?"

"I'm a doctor, not a theater major." He turns back to his audience. "Just loving the weather."

"We done?"

He conceals the spent syringe and steps back. "Yes. But you're going to need a full work up when this is over."

"I'll be sure to drop by."

"And I'll be sure to look annoyed."

I rub the tender spot on my forearm only to find Alice and Kit glaring at me. Even Fergus One seems put off that I didn't take him up on his porta-seat offer. "Back to work, everybody." Likewise, I turn my attention back to the bridge's main holo display and reorder my V-cog augmented reality windows.

The crew is safe, relatively speaking.

The ship is still intact.

And the drive core is humming just like it's supposed to.

No errors. No anomalies. No emergencies. And we're five mikes into the ninety-mike accel burn.

Back on the private channel to the *Koga*, I ask, "Everyone still good?"

"Oi! I'm trying to sleep here."

"Under eight g's? Like hell you are," Nairobi replies. "Shoot."

"Aye, because no one wants to fucking shut up on comms, or else I would be."

"Nah, you wouldn't."

"Would too."

"Would not."

I cut in. "Nice to see everyone's getting along. And that your high-g base editing is worth the price NUESSA paid for it. If you need anything, you know where to reach us. In the meantime, sit back, relax, and enjoy the journey to 400,000 meters per second. You're about to make history. Congratulations to all of you."

"And congratulations to you on not blowing us the shit up, Foxy."

"Eh, it's a long flight still. A lot can happen." I shoot Eddie a dark grin.

For the first time since meeting him, I catch something in his eyes that suggests he might not be a complete asshole. A glint. The hint of humor. That somewhere, behind that foul mouth and bitter soul, there's a heart that just might—

"Fuck you, Knight."

Meh, I take it back. "Right back atcha, champ."

I let the crew return to uninterrupted gravitational suffering and take stock of the mission overview. To the relief of my psyche, everything is still nominal. Everyone's doing their job, and the hardware and software are running flawlessly. Just like it was designed. It feels so good that I don't want to say anything for fear of jinxing our progress. Still, every team needs encouragement, and the crew aboard *Selene* is no exception.

"Everything's looking good, people. Nice work. Let's keep it up." My words seem to break some of the mounting tension in the room. I can't tell if the unease was just from the mission or the incident with me and Doc Friedman. Either way, staffers and spectators alike seem to relax a little now that I've bestowed my blessing on our progress. "Eighty-one minutes to go. Stay focused, and keep your eyes—"

"Captain Jericho Fox?" interrupts a man in my V-cog lobby.

"The hell?"

"My name is Agent Tucker with the NUE Law Enforcement Office, American Heights Division." The LEO flashes me a leather-bound badge and returns it to his jacket pocket just as fast. A quick sig auth crosscheck confirms that Agent Tucker here is the real deal. Whether or not the guy looks this way in the real is almost irrelevant: he's playing the bit of dark outfit, dark hat, and dark sunglasses to a T. Predictable as hell and twice as tacky. I say "almost irrelevant" because if this V-cog render really *is* how Agent Tucker looks in the real? Somebody needs to buy the guy a drink, 'cause damn if he isn't taking his job way too seriously. "Are you or are you not Captain Jericho Fox currently onboard *Selene* Station?"

"I'm kinda in the middle of something, Agent Tucker. And who the hell gave you V-cog override permission? This rec is locked."

"I have orders to arrest one of your crew and remand them into NUE custody."

I glance around the bridge in the real, wondering who he might be here for. "Can this wait a few minutes?"

Agent Tucker dispenses with the physical renders and goes straight to displaying a virtual law enforcement crime record and subsequent judicial warrant for the arrest of one Wallace, Adrian M., residing at— It doesn't matter. What does matter is that everything about this document looks legit, and that it's been signed by none other than the American Heights Deputy Attorney General herself. "Captain Fox, I need to know the exact whereabouts of Adrian Wallace. Do you know where I can find him?"

"Have you checked the verb lately?"

"I don't need the sarcasm, Captain. Just asking for your assistance."

"Oh, it's not sarcasm. I know right where Adrian Wallace is." I pull up two camera feeds and push them to Agent Tucker in V-cog: one of Adrian in his crash couch, jiggling from the high-g burn, and the other of the *Kogarashi* hurtling past the next drone. "He's breaking the human speed record as we speak."

"Well, that's not the only thing he's broken. You need to call him in ASAP."

"I'm afraid that's not possible."

"Captain Fox, need I remind you that failure to comply with NU—"

"I'm not pushing back on you willfully. I'm saying that this test has to run its course or else a lot of very important people are going to be really upset. I'm sure that whatever Adrian has gotten mixed up in can be sorted out when the test—"

"How important are the lives of your crew, Mission Director?" Tucker's change in tone and the use of my more formal title suggests that he means business, even though I'm still having a hard time taking him seriously in his getup.

"Very important, sir."

"Then I suggest you do whatever you can to get that man off that ship before your very important crew is harmed."

"Is this about his stimming? Because I can assure that our chief medical examiner has cleared him for—"

"Captain, this is about Adrian Wallace, aka Thomas Pugh, being identified as a known Tantum Terrae collaborator and member of Radio Ultra. Aside from crypto laundering and the sale of illegal stim code and physio, he's connected with at least three high profile bombings in the last four years, all arranged remotely via Black Grid."

Blood drains from my face as images of *Astraea* hurtling through Earth's atmo flash in my mind. But how? We have safeguards. New policies. New equipment and personnel. In that weird backwoods part of my brain, I hope to high heaven that maybe this is a mix-up. That we're not actually repeating the tragedy that was *Astraea* Station. That we learned our lessons and corrected the problems at the root. But who am I kidding? Policies don't change the hearts of bad people wanting to do bad things. The most they do is put off the inevitable.

"This can't be right," I protest. "There's no way. He's been on this team for—"

"Nine years, six months, three weeks, and two days. His tenure exceeds the maximum record checks."

Son of a bitch. "So he would have skirted the most recent safety scans. Which means…"

"He doesn't even need to be using incog tech to exploit the system."

"He just needs to be… himself. Shit."

Tucker nods in agreement. "With these long-term embeds, agency is saying it's gonna get worse before it gets better. Not until new recommendations can be drafted. Wallace is just an old school spy doing bad things behind the scenes. No nanotech needed."

"You're sure about all this," I state instead of ask.

"I wouldn't be here unless I was 100 percent sure."

I run another hand over my hair and realize I'm doing the same in the real. I feel embarrassed that I was duped. That the whole agency was duped. We all were. Except Kit.

"Everything okay, Cap?" he asks, which is followed not half a second later by Fergus the Annoying as Hell One saying, "I concur, Cappy. Is there something we might rectify promptly?"

I dismiss both of them for the time being and look back at Tucker. "Who else knows?"

"Outside of my office? Only Director Johnson."

"I need to speak with him."

"He's being briefed by my superior as we speak."

"Don't care. Need to speak with him *now*, Tucker."

"Stand by."

11

JERICHO

"Cap? What's going on?" Kit asks from behind me as I close out with Johnson and Agent Tucker. The latter is going to be monitoring from V-cog, while Johnson has more fires to put out, leaving me in charge of stopping a potential terrorist attack on a ship accelerating faster than anything humanity has ever made.

Perfect.

"Cap?" Kit asks again.

"Need to talk to you for a sec."

"Sure." He accepts the invite to my Berret-Racoupeau-inspired Amel 60 galley and takes a seat on the leather couch behind the sailboat's dining room table. "What's up?"

"You're gonna wanna stand."

"Sorry. Okay, what's up?"

"You were right about Wallace."

A moment of surprise followed by anger. "I knew it! I knew he was cheating in *Vesper Siege*!"

"About being shady, Kit. I've got a LEO Agent on V-cog overwatch right now with evidence from the NUE that Wallace is a member of Radio Ultra with strong ties to the TT."

Kit's mouth lolls open wide enough to stick a fist into and then freezes.

"You still there?"

"Yeah," he says, mouth still agape. "I was just… I was right?"

"Yes. Now, listen. It's not clear what Adrian intends to—"

"I was right."

"Yes."

"About Adrian."

"Yes. Kit." I snap my fingers. "Need you to focus."

"Sorry."

"We don't have enough info to know exactly what Adrian intends to do, but the NUE doesn't want to take any chances, and I agree. So they're ordering that we restrict his movement and suspend his V-cog access to the ship."

"But he's in charge of comms."

"Which is why I need you to distract him while I get the rest of the crew onboard with a plan."

"What plan?"

"Haven't gotten that far yet. But the main thing is to keep everything looking normal."

"Cool, cool, cool, cool, cool. But even if we can lock him out, how are they gonna physically restrain him?"

Kit's not wrong. Even with advanced gene editing, no human fights eight g's. "Good news is that if the rest of the crew can't move, then neither can Wallace."

"Unless he's tweaking."

Well shit. Hadn't even thought of that. "Then we need to keep his suspicions low so he doesn't try anything until we cut the engines."

"Okay, okay. I can do that. And, how, exactly?"

"Use your imagination."

"Right. You gonna tell Alice?"

"Yeah. But I wanted you to know first."

"Gee, thanks, Cap. I didn't realize—"

"Get in there, Kit. We've got a ship to save."

AFTER BRIEFING Alice and updating Tucker and Johnson, I check in on Kit before pinging Eddie. To my astonishment, Kit's actually got Adrian playing video games. Only in 2251 can you slay virtual enemies in your cerebral cortex while breaking space speed and distance records with your body. Smart guy. Genius actually, because Kit's hiding his disdain and nervousness in plain sight.

"No, no, no! You jerk face! You shot me in the back of the head."

"What did you expect, Kit?" Adrian replies, just as fired up. "You walked right in front of me."

"Only because you were too indignant to take the shot earlier."

Indignant, Kit? Really? We're gonna need to have a talk about his language. Speaking of language.

"Oi, fuck me, mate. I thought you was gonna leave me alone for a few," Eddie exclaims in our private lobby.

"It's important."

"So is *Claire Wood's Return to Briar Lane Live*, but you don't see me interrupting *your* dailies, do you?"

"Eddie. We've just gotten word that Adrian Wallace isn't who he says he is."

"The hell?"

"He's Radio Ultra, with a history of pulling big jobs for the Tantum Terrae. The High Top Uranium hit in '47, Embraer Aerospace Despedida in '49, and—"

He sits up to full height. "You mean to tell me that I've got a fucking assassin on my ship?"

"That's what the LEO agent in my lobby is saying."

"Always figured him for a manky plonker, but not this."

"No one's sure of his exact intentions yet, but we need to cut him out of V-cog and then get him secured."

"Little hard at eight g's, Foxy."

"I'm working on that."

"Then again, if we're not moving, neither is he."

"Unless he's tweaking."

"Aw, bloody hell."

"We have Kit to thank for that insight."

Eddie scratches the stubble under his chin. "We can cut the engines, but it will take sixty seconds for the re-action to subside. He'll see the order if he's still on V-cog."

"And if we cut him off before that—"

"He'll know something's gone awry."

I nod. "Which means we're looking at a full minute where he could go ballistic. *If* he's tweaking. And if he's prepared some other surprise we're not sure of, then he'll have plenty of time to activate it."

Eddie studies my face for a second, then says, "If they sabotage the *Koga*, they win again. No telling how far back this sends us, mate."

Just when I thought there was no liking this man, he goes and puts NUESSA's larger mission ahead of his own life. "We're gonna figure it out, Eddie."

"We'd better. 'Cause if we don't, I'm fucking tying your naked ass to the front gate of a convent and then honking my horn with headlights on you until the nuns come out."

"What, you just… you write these quips down in a journal or something and save them for later?"

He doesn't answer.

"I'll take that as a strong maybe. Run this by the rest of the crew, quietly. See if anyone has ideas on how to secure him and if they've noticed anything unusual. And then I need you to do your Eddie Carr thing."

"My Eddie Carr thing?"

"Being a total dick at finding anomalies in the ship's system logs."

The corners of his lips curl up. "Oi."

TEN MINUTES LATER, the crew have all been briefed on the situation, and I've given Agent Tucker, Alice, and Kit updates. Still, no one has any ideas on how to subdue Adrian Wallace while not simultaneously tipping him off and starting a potentially bad chain of events.

The truth is, Adrian could just be a "manky plonker," as Eddie put it, which I think is something akin to a worthless idiot. Granted, the master coder is far from being unintelligent. Annoying? Clingy? In need of showering more frequently than he does? Sure. But he's no idiot, even though I understand what Eddie is trying to get at. If anything, Adrian's managed to blend in with the Viatoribus's NUESSA alum for at least a decade, probably more, and no one's been the wiser. Well, save Kit. Takes a nerd to catch a nerd.

Bottom line, we need a solution, and fast.

"Pardon me, but would you care to take a burden

off?" says an excipion's voice behind me. It's Fergus One, apparently free of oversight while Kit's lost in game land.

I turn around to see the bot on bended knee again, offering a place for me to sit on his thigh. "No thanks. And it's 'take a *load* off,' not burden."

"Vernacular phrase updated. Thank you, Supreme Mission Director Fox."

"Supre—? Who told you to call me that?"

"His Esteemed Magnificence, Leslie the Great."

"Well, makes sense."

"You seem dissatisfied. Would you prefer I utilize another title?"

"Just… drop the Supreme. And go back to your station, would you?"

"Affirmative."

I watch Fergus One turn and walk away when something dawns on me. "Kit," I say aloud. He's too far engrossed in whatever game he's playing with Adrian to hear, so I have to walk over to his workstation and gently touch his shoulder. "Hey, Kit?"

"Hold on." His eyelids flutter for a few more seconds and then he looks up. "Sorry. Everyone expects you to just *pause* and shift gears, but it's like live grid play, ya know? Ya can't just *pause*. Your squad's counting on you, and there's a whole—"

"Need you to focus."

"Sure, right. What's up?"

I lower my voice. "Did you leave one of the Ferguses on the *Koga*?"

"Oh, basket of biscuits. Was I not supposed to? I thought the flight manifest said—"

"Kit!"

"I'm so sorry, Cap. Yeah, I did. And it won't happen

again. Promise."

"No, you did good."

"I… I did? I mean, yeah, I totally did." He blinks at me. "How exactly?"

"We can use it to secure Wallace."

Kit's eyes dart around for a moment before he connects the dots. "Of course! It's rated for high-g operation!"

I put a finger to my lips. "Quietly. Need you to establish connection, but not on anything Adrian might be monitoring."

"But he's, like, over everything, especially all grid-to-hardware transmissions via V-cog."

From over my shoulder, Alice says, "What about his video games?"

Her presence surprises me, but I wave her into the conversation. "Go on."

"Well, since maintenance excipions use shipboard protocols redundantly against V-cog failure, couldn't you—"

"Communicate with it from inside the game," Kit exclaims. "Holy biscuits, Alice. You're a genius! I could kiss you right now."

"Um…"

"But I mean… I won't 'cause, whoa, right? Unless… you want me to. But I've never kissed a girl, I mean *woman*. You're a lady. And I'm…"

"Got a job to do, Kit," I say, saving the poor guy any further embarrassment. "See if you can access the Fergus—"

"Fergus Two."

"See if you can access Fergus *Two* from inside *Vesper Weave*—"

"*Vesper* Siege."

"God. Just… see if you can get it up and moving. Then we'll talk strategy in a second. I need to brief the crew and update Tucker."

"Right'o, Cap. You can count on me."

"I can help him if you want," Alice says to me and then glances at Kit. "If you want an extra hand, that is."

"You… you know *Vesper Siege IV*?"

"Level 150, with a KD of 5.2."

"Five point—? Are you kidding me right now?"

"Kit," I say. "Voice down."

"Are you kidding me right now?"

Alice shrugs. "Beattie Station nights can get long and lonely."

Kit lets out a nasally laugh that's somewhere between ecstasy and a gaging spell. "Hnef-ef-ef-ef-ef, yeah."

"You gonna be okay, pal?" I ask.

"Sure. Fine. I'm just… fine."

"Alright. Make it happen, you two. I'll be back in a sec."

"I MAY HAVE FOUND SOMETHING, KNIGHT," Eddie says in my sailboat's galley. "It's small but has major implications."

"Hit me."

Eddie brings up a status window monitoring the ship's super plasmoid drive core. He expands a corner tab and then opens a second window with a related data log plus a real time 3D graph with red, yellow, and blue lines in a constant dance with the drive's main output tangents. Lastly, he taps on a single node on a peak in the graph and opens a third window. In it, a double helix spirals gently, not looking in any way out of the ordinary to me. "Found this in the reaction suppression matrix."

"And it's notable because…?"

"It's too steady."

"But that algorithm maintains thrust consistency. It's supposed to be steady."

"Oi, but not *that* steady."

"Explain."

"You know as well as I do that it's like a shock absorber. And what do all springs do?"

"Absorb aberrations in energy."

"Aye. They modulate." Eddie brings up a V-cog rendering of the *Kogarashi*'s actual helm control. This is highly secure; no one can do this but him, me, and authorized users who we both agree to give control authority to. A shiver goes up my spine thinking about the power under our care.

"I'm just gonna give her a little nudge, eh? One quarter of a percent. No one notices." And by no one, I know he means Adrian. "But watch…" He enters the thrust adjustment, lasting only two seconds, and then returns the ship to normal. At the same time, I glance at the double helix. It should have immediately sped up to act as a dampener. But it didn't.

"No change," I say. "Son of bitch. If he initiates any sort of output increase…"

"It runs away from us. Maximum acceleration, no brakes. He'd send us right into the god damned sun. But we'd be fucking pulp before we ever got there."

"Jesus." I square with Eddie. "You're really a dick with systems analysis, you know that?"

"So I've been told."

"Can you undo it?"

"Only if he's distracted. The twat's got it tethered to his analyzer. The only way to keep him from activating it—"

"Is to isolate him from the system entirely with the V-cog suspension."

"And I can only do that in the window of time that Kit and Alice make for Fergus while playing fucking Ring Around the Rosy with Miss Universe."

"Miss Universe?"

"You'll see."

"Can you do it?"

"And risk losing my dick card if I don't? Fuck yeah."

"So what's the plan?" Tucker asks me in his private lobby.

"We're attempting to gain access to a maintenance excipion in the cargo bay that we can use to restrain Wallace," I reply. "I don't wanna terminate the test flight if we don't have to."

"I understand, Captain Fox, but you might not have any other choice. Even if you can subdue him, there's no telling what he's done to onboard systems."

"Actually, there is. I've got one of the best sleuths on that job right now."

"Oh?"

"Seems Wallace has essentially sabotaged the ship's emergency brake."

"Can you fix it?"

"Me? No. Above my pay grade. But Eddie Carr? He'll get it."

"You're sure?"

"Tucker. You ever have that guy on the force who's a total prick—and I mean the worst of the worst—but for the love of everything, you just can't bring yourself to fire the guy because he's made more arrests than everyone in your precinct combined?"

"I could name one or two."

"Well, that's Eddie Carr for us. So if he can't do it, it can't be done."

THE NEXT FIVE minutes have me pacing the bridge, hands behind my back. With every second the *Kogarashi* accelerates, that means a corresponding second is needed to decelerate should the mission need to be scrubbed. That's assuming we can stop the ship at all. And if we can, because Eddie overrides Wallace's exploit, all the politicast turmoil surrounding Sallsworth and the General Council means it could be months if not years before a new test is possible. That said, I'll do everything I can to avoid losing another crew member.

"We got something, Cap," Kit says from his workstation. His eyes are closed and twitching, signaling that he's hard at work in game land. Alice, too, has taken a seat beside him and seems just as focused. "Probably best if I just show you though."

"Alright. Where do you want me?"

"Sending you observer privileges to my POV… now."

I get a V-cog invitation to monitor a live in-game session for *Vesper Siege IV: Age of Carnage*. Been a while since I did any of this. Kinda miss it too. Life's had enough adventure in the real the last two years or so to leave much time for entertainment beyond catching one of my favorite shows. But I admit to missing the appeal of gaming and the community around it. It's probably why I liked racing so much. Fun, friends, and fast.

I click Accept and instantly enter a lobby hosted inside a medieval castle. Cracked stone floors, red drapes on the walls, and wood crackling in a far fire pit with two axes crossed over the mantle.

"Cap?" says a three-meter tall Viking with arms the size of my torso. He's got tribal tattoos across his biceps, a beard that looks like half a wolf pelt, and breeches made of rawhide. The whole ensemble is finished with an axe strapped to his back and domed helmet with horns atop his head. The only reason I know it's my flight engineer is because of the squeaky voice. Talk about incongruent.

"Kit?"

"Yeah. Follow us."

"Us?" I turn to see an old wizard with a long beard. "Alice?"

"They never suspect the old guy in the corner," she says and gives me a wink—or, *he* gives me a wink. This is why I only did racing sims.

"Come on. This way," Kit adds.

The castle vanishes in a flurry of swirling lights. The motes eventually materialize into a battlefield alight with burning pitch, bodies, and ruins. All manner of fantasy characters are dueling it out with broadswords, bows and arrows, and magic, filling the scene with the sights, sounds, and—as only V-cog can provide—*smells* of a hellish medieval landscape.

"How do you stand this? God, it smells horrible," I say, looking through the Settings menu to reduce my olfactory sensitivity.

"Just makes you fight harder," Kit's Viking says.

Alice's wizard adds, "'Cause you know what awaits if you die."

"Oh… kay. What is it you want me to see?"

"This way." Kit and Alice lead my non-bodily presence around the back of a skirmish line boasting orcs and ogres in a bloody melée. Half hidden in a stand of dead trees, I spot a new warrior, this one looking like the overly muscled form of every Conan the Barbarian actor to play the part for the last three hundred years. "Captain Jericho Fox? Meet Fergus Two."

"I bid thee a greeting, immortal god of the air," Fergus Two says in a grandiose tone.

"Why is it talking like that?" I ask Kit.

"To play the part. He's gotta be able to get close to Adrian in the real and in the game."

"And Shakespeare here won't raise his suspicions?"

Alice lets out a laugh. "Have you looked around?"

"Fair point. But you know giving an excipion a verbal lexicon and voice print—"

"Breaks the robo-anthro laws, I know," Kit says. "But we can just undo it as soon as this is over."

"Why do I feel like I'm going to regret this?"

Kit crosses his heart and holds up three fingers. "Scout's honor."

"Fine. What's the plan?"

Alice pulls Mr. Muscles from the stand of trees. He's got a massive broadsword on his back, oiled biceps, and a six-pack that only exists in the movies. And video games. "We have Fergus Two approach Adrian in the game at the same time that he's approaching him in the real. If Adrian is monitoring any system diagnostics, which he surely is, they'll look so similar he won't notice any differences."

"At least until it's too late," Kit adds. "Then Fergus

Two will bind Adrian's character in the game at the same time that he's securing him in his crash couch on the *Koga*."

"Huh. No flags. That's not bad," I say.

"Thanks," Alice replies and puts a hand on Kit's character. "We came up with it together."

Kit's Viking blushes, which I didn't know was even an emote in this game.

Before he can do another one of his snorty laughs, I say, "How long do you need?"

"Three minutes, maybe?" Kit's Viking rubs his arm like a brainiac behind a mic in a spelling bee. "Kinda all depends on Fergus Two's performance." He pats the brute on his shoulder.

"I am Fergus Two, the Ardent Conqueror of Malquith," the excipion proclaims.

"Yeaaah… might wanna do something about that name, Kit."

"But it fits, Cap."

"I don't mean the last part."

"Oh. Ha ha, right. We'll get him a new first name."

"You hear that, Eddie?" I ask after bringing him in. "Can you undo the exploit in three minutes?"

"It'll be tighter than slipping a seal through a fucking keyhole, but I'll make it work."

Kit widens his eyes and raises his palms in the form of a question. "Who puts seals in key holes?"

"Never mind. Alright everyone, let's take back our ship."

To the rest of the spectators on the observation decks and those watching on the verb, the *Kogarashi* is halfway through its first scheduled 7.55-g accel burn with no earth-shattering news to report. Viewership has dropped significantly as there's not much to see. Part of me wonders if most spectators were waiting for another *Perseverant.* Our fascination with catastrophe is truly odd. But I can't blame them. One reason I love watching hover racing so much is because of the remote possibility that something could go wrong. I suppose it's why gamers love grid combat too: there's entertainment value in death, or at least the prospect of it. I don't believe most people actually want to see anyone die, but the possibility intrigues us. So we wait to see.

Meanwhile, a very select group of people know what's really about to happen on the *Kogarashi*—know death is far more possible than the public realizes. Should anything go wrong, the broadcast feeds will be terminated. In the meantime, looped footage is replacing the live feeds in the crew compartments as well as here on *Selene*'s bridge.

With Tucker on overwatch, now joined by Director Johnson, and Kit and Alice synchronized with the *Kogarashi*'s crew, it's time to make things happen. "Everyone ready?" I ask.

Confirmation icons race down my V-cog chat log.

"Kit? You're up."

"Aye-aye, Cap." His Viking form turns toward the game observation camera. "Or should I say, *Odin eier dere alle!*" A text translation appears in the lower third reading: Odin owns you all!

Kit, Alice, and Fergus Two the Something of Somewhere march toward the battle line where several hundred grid players are engaged in close quarters combat with spears, swords, crossbows, and electrifying displays of exploding light. Gamer tags follow each player like glowing pixies, and spotting Adrian Wallace's isn't too hard, even though it does catch me by surprise:

AdrianaC0D3goddess69

And there, swinging a battle axe into the neck of a fallen cave troll, is a string-bikini-clad warrior with bust and butt measurements perfectly suited to an episode of *Plastic Surgery Gone Horribly Wrong*.

"Told you," Eddie says, clearly referring to his Miss Universe comment earlier.

Nairobi adds, "Everyone stand by."

Kit and Alice approach Adrian's character from behind. At the same time, I spot Fergus Two entering the comms crew compartment in the *Koga* where Adrian is seated in the real. His chair is rotated to lie flat against the deck, facing up toward the bow, and surrounded by curved holo screens, which he's monitoring between spats of living out his fantasy as a supernaturally endowed Spartan heroine. Fergus Two climbs through the floor hatch with the smooth and steady power of servos built to overcome the extreme resistance of high gravity.

"Nice and easy," I say to myself, then consider that the joint motors might give away the bot's presence. "Kit, Alice. Can you distract him with some in-game noise?"

But before either of them respond, I hear music swell over the ship's speakers. It's the latest track from Grum Pocket Downfall, if I'm not mistaken, and has a pretty hot bass line—perfect for covering excipion servo noise.

"How's that, Jericho?" Nairobi asks with a smile. "Read your mind or what?"

"I owe you a beer."

"Gladly."

Fergus Two eases all the way into the compartment and starts to slow-walk toward the belly-up Adrian, still deeply ensconced in his match.

"Eddie?" I ask.

"Need some time."

Fergus Two is closing. But too fast.

"Kit, hold up."

Adrian's head jerks to the side. "Who's this?" he asks Kit and Alice from inside the game.

Before either of them can respond, Fergus Two stops, both in the game and the real, and says, "Behold! I am the Conqueror of Malquith, Borion the Third."

Adrian's war goddess gives him a look up and down, and for a split second, I think he's not buying it. My heart catches in my throat. Dammit. But then Adrian's character says, "Glad to have you on the team, Borion."

"The Third," the excipion adds.

"Right."

"Eddie?" I ask again, my voice tighter than I mean for it to be.

"Almost there…"

"Hurry it up."

I keep thinking that any second, Wallace is gonna open his eyes and see an excipion standing arm's length away. If we're gonna do this, it has to be now.

The war goddess squints at Fergus Two for a moment, but then nods toward an incoming knight on horseback. "Can you handle that?"

"My mother bore me upon the granite of Invandora that I might be endowed with fortune enough for moments of grandeur such as these."

"That's what I like to hear." Adrian's anatomically incorrect and extremely offensive character hoists an axe in the air and yells, "Charge!" while at the same time Fergus Two takes one step too loud.

Adrian's head turns.

"*EDDIE,*" I yell.

"Oi! Got it."

Kit points Borion the Third toward Adrian's avatar and yells, "Now!"

The warrior goddess isn't two steps toward the incoming enemies when the excipion wraps his arms around both of Adrian's forms. In the game, the goddess is pulled off her feet and stripped of her weapons; in the real, Adrian's chair breaks from its base and his body is pushed to the floor.

"The hell?" Adrian hollers as the air leaves his lungs. He exits V-cog and tries to lock eyes on whatever's holding him. Finally, he catches a glimpse of the excipion and starts swearing orders at it to let him go.

"I am afraid I cannot abide by your wishes, Lady *AdrianaC0D3goddess69.* You are suspected of endangering the lives of my citizenry, for which you shall be duly tried if the evidence leaves you found wanting."

"Get off me!" To my surprise, Adrian starts fighting the bot.

The excipion's servos whine above the sound of the music and its metallic limbs chattering as Adrian pushes the machine's arms a centimeter off his chest.

"Holy biscuits! He *is* tweaking," Kit says for all to hear.

Gasps go up around the bridge and echo through the observation decks. Verb viewers still have looped footage, but those with security clearance are getting the real show: Adrian Wallace is fighting an excipion in almost eight g's of accelerated gravity. Had we not sent Fergus Two, I don't even want to think about what could have happened. Then again, it still might, because the bot's arms are moving out.

"I said, get the hell off me, you damn robot," Adrian roars.

"I cannot abide by your wishes," Fergus Two replies and then doubles down on the pressure.

Adrian closes his eyes, looking like he's slipping into V-cog.

To Eddie, I say, "Tell me you've—"

"All locked down, mate."

"You can't do this to me," Adrian roars, pushing back against Fergus Two. But the bot will have none of it and forces Wallace to lose whatever ground he's gained. Finally, the man lets out a breath of defeat, then passes out. And just like that, it's over.

WHEN ADRIAN'S eyes eventually fly open from a not-so-mild shock care of Fergus Two, or should I say Borion the Third, Conqueror of Malquith, he finds himself under the excipion's full weight, still pinned to the deck, and the *Koga* still intact. "What... What's the meaning of this?"

"You just got played, Wallace," I say, appearing as a holo figure in Adrian's crew compartment.

A second later, Agent Paul Tucker joins me. "Adrian Wallace, you are under arrest for the attempted murder of your fellow crew members and tampering with NUE property."

"You can't do this! I'm a member of the Viatoribus!"

"I'm sure they'll have plenty to say about that. Anything you say can and will be used against you in—"

"I want my lawyer! Give me back V-cog! You have no—"

"Hey, Borion the Third?" I ask.

"Yes, Supreme Mission Director Fox?"

"Mind shutting him up?"

"Your royal order is my command." With that, the excipion squeezes Adrian's breath out of his lungs again and then clamps a metallic hand over the man's mouth and chin. All Adrian can do is attempt half-powered cries of muffled protest as the excipion holds him on the floor.

"Wike a 'wittle baby," Kit says with pouty lips and then turns to face Alice. She winces at Kit's unintentional pucker. "Oh, man! I didn't mean that. I'd never intentionally, you know, want to kiss you."

"Why not?"

"What?"

"You're saying I'm not good enough for you now?"

"Uh, no! No, no, no! That's not what I—"

"Uh huh." Alice turns away from him but then winks at me.

Huh. Crafty.

"Nice work, everyone," Director Eric Johnson says from the NUESSA virtual observation deck. "Agent Tucker, the prisoner will be awaiting your security forces when the *Kogarashi* docks with *Selene* Station."

"Much obliged, Director."

"Captain Fox? Why don't we open up the live feeds again and let the verb watch the rest of the show?"

"My pleasure, sir. We'll keep a certain compartment's feed looped, if that's okay with you."

"I doth believe he implies my chamber is to be shunned from the public eye," Fergus Two says.

Johnson's one eyebrow climbs his forehead. "And

would somebody please wipe Shakespeare's quantum matrix before we get written up?"

I look at Kit, who lets out a long sigh. "Fine."

As soon as Johnson and Tucker are away, Eddie says in my private lobby, "Oi, Foxy."

"Go ahead."

"How the fuck did nobody catch the shit that Adrian was up to before now?"

"We should've caught it sooner." I pause for a moment. "No, *I* should've caught it sooner."

"Nah, mate. This one's on all of us. And you didn't even fuck up the situation like you normally do once you found out about him. Not bad, Knight."

Did the *Eddie Carr just pay me a backhanded compli—*?

"Now stop congratulating yourselves like a bunch of five-year-old twats at a coloring contest where everybody gets a bloody ribbon, and let's get back on fucking mission."

I close out the line with Eddie and then turn around to point at Fergus One. "Hey, Fergy."

"Yes, Mission Director?"

"I'll take that seat now, if you don't mind. And a light, if you have one." I hold up the cigar he gave me earlier.

"Your wish is my preeminent endeavor."

As the bot walks forward and takes a knee, I glance at Kit, wondering just how many excipions he installed the verbal lexicon on. "Is there anything I should know about with the rest of the Ferguses?"

"*Pfft.* No way, no how, Cap. Hey, would you look at the time…?"

"Kit?"

"Talk soon, Cap. Gotta hit the head."

"Kit. Come back here! *Kit!*"

12

EVELYN

WITH JERICHO'S successful test flight in the history books, I'm back in SUB 20 Lab 1. I've got a few hours sleep under my belt and a fresh croissant and coffee in my hands. From the little Lemuel was able to tell me, Jericho's team is lucky to be alive. It seems I wasn't completely out of line to be concerned that the TT might attempt something during his test, I just didn't expect it to be—what was it?—a Radio Ultra stim peddler being asked to call in a Tantum Terrae favor? What's more surprising is that the guy, one Adrian Wallace, was willing to go down with the ship. They must've had one hell of a pain point. I'm just glad Jericho's team is safe, and that the *Kogarashi* avoided getting scrubbed. At least now the whole system knows we have the power to reach the stars within a human lifespan. I just hope my team is as successful.

"Did you hear?" Sam says as I take a seat in our work area. The holo desks and light boards are filled with attempts to demultiplex the light streams into something beyond the alien fractal.

"About Jericho? Yeah. Pretty great."

She shakes her head. "Four more attacks in the night. Two on Ceres, two on Ganymede."

"Stars." I set my breakfast down. "Casualties?"

"Ten people in the belt. But over forty dead on the moon, and major equipment setbacks. They're saying it's in response to the NUE raids on a TT facility in St. Petersburg, and for arrests made in Ahuna Mons and Nineveh Sulcus. Mars Nation is already calling in the NUE to increase security, and both the Belt Lands and Moons of Jupiter have filed petitions with the Chamber."

I rub the back of my neck and let out a long breath. "This is insane. They've gotta know they can't outlast the NUE. There are other ways to get your point across besides killing."

"What if you were them?" Sam asks as she rolls her chair over.

"What?"

"*What if you were them?* What if *you* felt like no one was hearing you signal the end of the world, so destroying key installations that also happened to leave people dead in the process was your only hope?"

"You one of them now?" I ask as straight faced as I can, then crack a smile.

"You know me." Sam laughs. "I'm just saying… I think it's unfair to completely write people off until we've walked a kilometer in their shoes. Take us for example."

I look from her to Nat and back. "Oh–kay?"

"People think we're freaks, right?"

"Smart freaks," Natalie says in protest.

Sam accepts this with a bouncy nod and a shrug. "That's fair. But you know what I mean. They don't really understand the value of what we're doing until they hear the arguments of why connecting with an advanced alien civilization might mean for the welfare of our species. They need to sit down with us."

"And you've sat with Tantum?" Natalie asks.

"Heck no, you kidding?"

I eye Sam curiously. "But you'd want to, wouldn't you?"

"Who? Me? No way. You're the curious one, Eves."

"I guess. But the Tantum?" I wave her off. "They're all mad, if you ask me. I can't ever see justifying the loss of human life over my belief in a cause."

Sam narrows her gaze at me, uncomfortably so. "You sure about that?"

For some odd reason, the question penetrates me. I can't tell if it's because Sam is recalling something I'm not, or if she believes I'm not telling the truth.

"Well, I know I could justify it," Natalie interjects. She points her index and middle fingers at an imaginary target across the room, then cocks her thumb. "Someone tries to get between me and our research again? And I do what Evelyn did. Bang!"

The sound startles me, and I flash back to the rooftop. Fortunately, both women laugh and dub me an official badass while sipping from their own beverages.

"Time to get back to business," I say once the tension has eased. "Where we at?"

THE HOURS bleed together as we pass through lunch time and into dinner. The next day comes and goes in much the same way, with all teams checking off scheduled permutation tests using the fractal's geometry as the key against two, three, and four-stream possibilities.

When not working with my staff, I field several interviews with visiting NUE Security Council leaders cleared to check in on our research.

"I'm still unclear on how you're attempting to decipher all this," President Velvet Davis says. She's joined me in V-cog by special request, only instead of using my rather sterile and impersonal lobby, security protocols dictate we meet in her hosted space —an exact representation of the Oval Office located in Calgary. I don't expect the American Heights President, or any other political leader, to understand what we're doing. But I do expect the scientific community to at least try to distill some of the more complex processes of our tradecraft into something others might understand. They don't see me drafting bills for global policies, and for good reason—though, to be fair, I have a few in mind. I'm just not egotistical enough to think they'll settle much.

"Madame President, I understand you're a music fan."

"Please, child. There's music, and there's jazz."

"Fair enough. Favorite artist?"

"Which century?"

"Your pick."

"Donaldson Toussaint L'Ouverture Byrd II."

"Didn't peg you for a trumpet woman."

"Didn't peg you to know your music history."

"Don't you mean jazz history?"

President Davis smiles. "Go on."

"Favorite song?"

"Hard to pick just one, but I'd say, for today, let's go with Lights Out, January 1956."

I take a moment to pull up the song in V-cog, but

the moment I attempt to access the verb, a block notification comes.

"Forgive my Secret Service detail," President Davis says and then waves a hand at one of the three suits around the room. "Things have been a little tense lately, as I'm sure you can imagine."

I share a look with Rook, whose orders include following me into V-cog. "I do."

President Davis gets a thumbs-up from one of her men.

"Try now, Dr. Park."

This time, my search yields the intended result: a file of the specified recording. I port the song through the office's speakers and hit play at a low volume. Instantly, Davis's foot starts to tap to the late-night blues tune that harkens back to New York City in its heyday. I let the song play for a minute as the track swells into hard bop, featuring Byrd's smooth trumpet lines as well as a saxophonist I'm not familiar with. But we'll get to that.

While Davis is enjoying the tune, I make a show of channeling the song into a simple 2D analyzer that displays the data in waveform in the air between us. Over the scatted solos and underlying shuffle beat, I point to the rising and falling peaks. "You know what this?"

"A waveform of the song, I take it."

"It is. It represents the combined sum of all the data you and I are hearing right now."

"Following."

"Now, I know who's on trumpet. But, may I ask, who's on saxophone?"

"Jackie McLean. It's his band."

"Piano?"

"Elmo Hope."

"Bass?"

"Doug Watkins. And Art Taylor on drums, to spare you the question. What's your point?"

"How did you get all that from this?" I point at the 2D wave form.

"I can hear the parts."

"More than that, you know the musicians. And you could probably pick them out individually on other recordings without knowing it was them simply by their signature styles I bet?"

Davis gives me an affirming frown.

I lower the music. "So when individual musicians, whose signatures you know, come together and play as a group, in science terminology, we'd call that multiplexing. And your brain's ability to separate them back into identifiable individuals? That's demultiplexing."

"Which is what you're trying to do to the signal."

"It is, yes."

"But… how do you know how many musicians, how many streams you're dealing with?"

"We don't. At least not yet."

"But you will?"

"We sure hope so."

"How?"

"Well, how do you know how many musicians are playing in this recording?"

"I can hear their parts."

"We're trying to do the same thing. To learn the sound of each instrument. Compare it against other things in the library and teach our ears, so to speak, what to listen for."

President Davis seems to consider all this for a moment and then smiles. "That's a beautiful analogy. Thanks for helping me understand."

"You're welcome. Thank you for reminding me how much I miss this era of jazz."

She raises a hand, palm up, and then motions with her fingers a few times. "Turn it up, Dr. Park. The world needs a little more of this right now."

"IMPROVISATION," I shout to Sam and Natalie.

Nat looks back at me, startled, as soon as I terminate the connection with President Davis. "What are you talking about?"

"In jazz, the musicians improvise."

"And?" Sam asks.

"It's an organic process, just like cellular binary fission, right? We keep assuming this code is going to be some sort of rote static thing. But what if instead of trying to hear the instruments in a band based on the singular type of sound each instrument makes, we're supposed to focus on the parts those instruments are playing. The whole reason we can't perceive the instruments is because—"

"The parts they're playing keep modulating," Natalie finishes and then smacks her palm against her forehead. "My God! That's genius, Evelyn!" Her chair squeaks as she spins around and starts typing, fast.

I wave Seb and Ramirez over, and they join Sam and I as we stand off Nat's shoulders. Rook seems intrigued and leaves his post by the door to join us too.

"What's going on?" Sebastián asks.

"Trying a new idea," I reply. "We've been expecting our demultiplexing to identify stationary streams. In musical terms, you might just say constant drones."

"Like my nephew learning to play the sax with his middle school band?" Ramirez asks. "*Es terrible.*"

"Something like that. Probably pretty annoying but easy to pick out," I add.

He rubs a finger in his ear. "Too easy."

"Only that's not how music is played," Seb adds. "Well, good music anyway. Single performances blend together to create a cohesive composition."

"Right." I point to what Natalie's working on. "But if we tell our system to include, not reject, fluctuating variables, we might actually be able to pick out the streams like a listener picking out performers improvising in a band."

Seb walks to Natalie's chair. "Sounds complicated."

"It is," Nat replies as she continues to type. "Very. But our processors can handle it. Plus, it's not like we're completely in the dark. They've given us the raw components to work with."

"The fractal," Seb says.

"Correct. I'm inputting a range of possible values based on the fractal's movement patterns. Think of it like musical scales. Without that, I suspect it would take a few trillion years to break the code."

This seems to pique Rook's interest. "Did you say *trillion?*" he asks from behind me.

"That I did." Natalie talks and types faster. "Anyway, all we have to do now… is give our system permission to listen for solos based on past performances annnnnnd… done." She hits the Enter key and sits back.

The curved holo display at Natalie's workstation starts streaming code way faster than any human can read.

"What's happening?" Seb asks.

"Computer's crunching new permutations," she replies. "It looks like a mess, I know, but that's what we want."

"I'll take your word for it."

"How long?" Ramirez asks. "Before you think it will give something?"

Natalie folds her arms. "Days, a week. Just depends on how much scatting our cosmic friends have decided to—" The screen stops, and Nat leans forward. "Whoa."

"What's whoa?" I ask.

"We got something."

"Already?"

"A couple somethings, actually. Ho-ly shit." Nat's fingers are flying again, this time copying and pasting long strings of code and three-dimensional shapes into other holo windows like sewing a quilt together, but made of integers and images, not fabric.

"Talk to me, Nat."

"Why don't we let them do the talking." She hits the Enter key again, and our world changes forever.

13

EVELYN

"Wʜᴀᴛ ᴀʀᴇ ᴡᴇ ʟᴏᴏᴋɪɴɢ ᴀᴛ?" Rook asks, his voice tight.

"It's a…" I tilt my head sideways at the new three-dimensional, monochromatic cluster of simple shapes. "Is that an atom?"

Sebastián puts a hand on my shoulder and moves beside me with eyes and mouth wide open. "I… I count six electrons, if so. Two orbitals."

"It's a model of a carbon atom." I point to the dots surrounding what I take to be a nucleus. "You see it?" Heads start nodding. "I think that's the atomic structure of a carbon atom! Stars. Is this real?"

"As real as it gets," Natalie says.

"We… we need the rest of the team over here," I shout. "Everyone!"

Sam reiterates my call, and soon the room is buzzing as some three-dozen people jostle toward our workspace.

I reach for Sebastián, but he's falling into an open chair, trying to steady himself on a desk. "We share atomic understanding," he says, face bewildered. "Dios mío."

"All this from some spheres?" Rook asks amidst the growing murmur in the room. "I'm missing it."

"If they can observe atomic structure like we do, it means we share a basic understanding of the fundamental building blocks of the physical universe," I say, trying my best to contain my mounting excitement.

"There's more," Natalie says and pulls our view a few degrees out of the carbon atom until a cubic lattice appears. "A lot more."

"This's… it's a…" Seb sounds as if he might have a heart attack. "A diamond cubic crystal structure. It's a diamond!"

"And it keeps going," Nat adds, zooming out more. We pass other atomic base layers, including those composed of silicon, titanium, and multiple alloys, as far as I can tell. Then patterns morph into shapes, and shapes into structures.

"Are we looking at a… at some sort of schematic here?" Sam asks, now gripping my arm with both hands and squeezing tight.

"I think so," I reply. "Stars, I think so."

The staff start pointing out details: edges, contours, and then overlapping components of alien design. We're definitely looking at a complex object of some kind. Maybe several. There's no writing, no measurements, no key. Just atoms and molecules building on each other, as if the very laws of nature are measurements enough.

I'm trying to take in what the staff are saying, but everyone's talking so fast I can hardly keep up. Likewise, Natalie is using the virtual mouse to scroll faster and faster as if she's a child on a treasure hunt who's just been told to skip the clues and run to where the pot of gold is.

We pass through monochromatic cross sections of structural bracing lined with what I think are conduits for... well, for something that flows. Hydraulic fluid? Electricity? Stars, who knows! But... it all has shape and purpose and... it's intentional. All of it *designed*. For us to see with our own eyes. All based on atomic structure.

I wipe tears from my cheeks and then sense a communal hush fall over the lab as Natalie's swiping slows to the outermost view of the data set. One complete angular object stands apart from a second of identical form, and then a third. Together, the three components form the distant corners of a triangle—one I can only assume is of immense size. Connecting the three points are shafts... perhaps beams of light? Laser light? Then something like a translucent film spreads from the triangle's corners and fills all the negative space in the middle. Just behind the triangular plane of the interplaying light field is something not displayed. A gap in the data. A hole left out of the render, like a second triangle cut from a curtain with only blackness behind.

"You think it's what?" SESI Director Lemuel Brown asks.

"A gate of some kind," I say, sitting on the edge of a leather chair in his oak-lined study. Normally, I'd be tempted to glance out the windows to the lawn and the meticulously rendered forest beyond, but I'm too wound up. From my V-cog menu, I port what we're calling the A-Level view of the artifact from the lab's mainframe and share it with Lemuel.

His eyes go wide as the triangular object floats in suspended animation over his oak desk. He runs one hand over his mouth, moves the image around with the fingers of the other, and then locks eyes with me. "You got this from the signal?"

"We did." I explain the improvisation idea gleaned from my conversation with President Davis, and then summarize Natalie's code slicing. "It's complete, all the way to an atomic level."

"I… It's…" He intuitively uses his hands to zoom in on one of the corner bases, a component we're already calling an emission node. "This is…"

"Remarkable?"

He laughs. "And then some."

We share the delight of discovery together as he manipulates the object and zooms all the way down to a single atomic layer.

"They haven't even bothered with dimensions or instructions of any kind," I say. "Instead, I think they're relying on the shared language of atomic particles for us to apply our own measurement standards. That will make building it much easier for us."

"Building it?"

"Yes. I've already got the teams converting each atomic layer into 3D modeling so we—"

"Evelyn. We don't even know what it is yet, let alone what it does."

"Which is why we'll use the models to run simulations and then—"

"We can't."

"What do you mean we can't? What else are we supposed to do with it?"

"It's not a lack of desire." Lemuel falls into his office chair and holds his forehead in one hand. "The NUE has ordered a temporary freeze on all non-essential space settlement development."

"No. Uh-uh. No, no, no, Lem. We've just discovered the greatest discovery in the history of humanity, and we're gonna have our funding cut?"

"*Have* had it cut. Effective an hour ago."

"You can't be serious, Lem."

"I am. And I'm sorry."

"Dammit." I look out the windows at the lawn. "Feels like *Astraea* all over again."

"Need I remind you that there's a war on?"

"'Violence is the last refuge of the incompetent.'"

"Asimov," he says.

I nod.

"What were you expecting anyway?"

"Stars, Lem. How about some overwhelming amazement that—oh, I don't know—we just had an alien species *not* made of microbiotic methanogens who only know how to fart send us plans for an Infinita Gate to connect our worlds!"

He raises a black bushy eyebrow at me. "You named it already?"

"Of course!" I remember myself, slide back into the leather chair, and look down. "*Parallax One.*"

"I see." Lemuel touches the model again and turns it about. Something's working behind his eyes. Something defiant. That famous resolve mixed with curiosity that destined him for the role of SESI director. "I suppose the world does need to know."

My heart leaps in my chest, but I keep my mouth shut.

"And we do need to find out what we can about its function in simulations."

There it is. Hope. Even if minimal. While Dr. Lemuel Brown is a scientist, he's also a statesman, making him one of the rare individuals in the upper echelons of the NUE's Space Council who understands both the inner workings of bureaucracy and the extreme value of scientific progress.

Lemuel taps the desktop with a finger. "Perhaps the best way to argue for pursuing this is by securing public support."

"Are you saying you want to build it?"

"I'm not Sentia Aux by accident, Dr. Park." Before I can get a word in edgewise, he adds, "But there are many questions we must answer first, and we have a lot of work to do. *You* have a lot of work to do. We're looking at politicast unrest, international terrorism, resource shortages, austerity spending bills, it's... it's hardly the time to be proposing something of this magnitude."

"Or maybe it's the perfect time."

Lemuel studies my face for a second.

When he doesn't budge, I add, "Come on. You and I both know you have a fat discretionary budget sitting there for rainy days."

A blast of air comes from his nostrils. "How fast do you think you can model it?"

"Triple my department and—"

A raised eyebrow interrupts me.

"Okay *double* my department, and we could have results in a few weeks. Press conference in the first full week of October."

"Figured that out quickly."

"You think I came in here without a plan?"

"Not for a second. But I just cut your staff request."

"Because I knew you would settle at double."

He laughs at me. "You're amazing."

"'Cause I'm such a pain in the ass?"

"Your words, not mine." A few seconds later, he

says, "I'll need to run this through some very private channels. Both the Space and Security Councils are gonna want to know how this works and why. And we'll need to wait until we know as much as we can about it before we go public. The more questions we can answer up front the better."

"Understood."

"With assurances that little green men aren't coming through with blaster guns and light swords to eat our faces off."

"You're… mixing genre metaphors there but—"

"Evelyn."

"I understand."

"And if they ask for more time—"

"Maybe we don't have more time, Lem."

"—if they ask for more time, we'll need to be prepared for that outcome." His face says not to push him.

I got what I need anyway: permission to continue in the midst of interplanetary turmoil. "You'll have daily briefs waiting in V-cog."

"With special development alerts as they come," he adds.

"Of course."

"Good." Then the SESI director gets a twinkle in his eye.

"What?"

"Why is it that every time we negotiate, I think I'm getting what I want but have the distinct impression you got more?"

I stand, offer him a smile, and then turn for the door. "'Cause it's true."

My team of over sixty scientists with top secret security clearance has taken over several more labs on the twentieth subfloor of Elmendorf Air Force Base in Anchorage. We've even moved our barracks down here. I didn't even have to ask the staff; they just did it themselves. Any floor space not used by workstations, extra cable runs, or display hubs is taken up by sleeping bags, toiletry kits, and piles of dirty laundry that will get washed "eventually." Like all noble pursuits of historic importance, creature comforts come last.

"You stink," Sam tells me from her side holo display.

"I'm surprised you can still smell," I reply.

"I can't. That's how I know it's really bad." Then she waves a hand in front of her nose.

"You sure it's not just you?"

"Nuh uh. This has Eau de Evelyn Kick Boxing scent all over it."

"I miss working out," I say as I step back and consider our latest calculations of emission node number two's hydrogen core size. "Think they can send down a sparring excipion?"

"Not until you get your homework done, Miss Park. We can't keep this up forever."

"Yeah. But it is fun, isn't it? Reminds me of grad school."

"Weren't you like sixteen?"

"Like I said, fun years."

"Okay," she says in a dorky tone. "*Brainiac*."

"Whatever, Miss Top of My Class Collins. *Sheesh*." I tap the end of my nose. "Anyway, I don't think we need much longer."

"Oh?"

"Few more days, we can run second phase simulations with all the final specs to appease the higher-ups. Then we'll have enough for the press conference."

"Still seems really fast. Don't you… think we need more time?"

"To tell the world we deciphered the signal? Stars, Sam. Aren't we robbing the public enough by keeping it quiet as long as we have?"

"I dunno. The Manhattan Project was kept secret for something like five years, I think."

"But we're not trying to blow anybody up here."

"Who's blowing people up?" Rook asks a few meters away and then walks into our work area.

I lift my chin toward Sam. "She's just worried about letting the world in on our discovery."

"I'm just saying there's historic precedent for keeping government secrets a secret," Sam says as if the NUE Space Marine will come to her aid.

"She has a point, Evelyn."

"Oh, not you too."

"Thank you," Sam says in victory, then sticks her tongue out at me.

"Real mature."

This gets all three of us laughing.

Feels good. Reminds me that there's more to life than twenty-four seven research. Okay, I admit maybe we need a few breaks more than we've been giving ourselves lately. But then again, I've got this thing in my gut that says we can't stop. There's too much on the line.

"I still don't even understand how it all works, you know," Rook says at last, eyeing the A-Level projection that perpetually fills the main lab's center. "And I've been watching you all nonstop for weeks."

"Well, we don't know either, not exactly," I say in concession. "But we do theoretically."

"At least most of it," Sam says.

"So we do or we don't?" Rooks asks. "You're both confusing me even more."

"It's… complicated." I wheel a chair over for him. "Enter at your own risk, if you dare."

Rook takes the offered seat and cracks his neck like he's getting ready to start boxing. "Alright. Let's go."

"Sir Isaac Newton."

"Ah, bloody hell."

"Stop it!" I punch him in the arm.

"Okay, okay. I'll behave. Sir Newton tells us how apples fall from trees."

"More than that, he creates, like actually invents, an entire language to explain it."

"Calculus."

"Yup. Before that point, the human race knows stuff falls. Sees it. Experiences it. Even harnesses that power to get stuff done. But it's not until Newton that we have a clear understanding of how gravity is acting on the apple.

"Or take Daniel Bernoulli. Up until he publishes *Hydrodynamica* in 1738, we think birds fly because they flap hard enough. But it's Bernoulli's principle that advances our knowledge of fluid dynamics to the place where we understand how a wing generates lift.

"My point is that there's a difference between understanding how natural phenomena work and being able to benefit from them in pursuit of some creative purpose. If we had to wait to walk until we understood the effects of gravity, the human race would have been floating until the seventeenth century AD."

"I'm pretty used to that." He winks at me. "So you're saying we'll benefit from an Infinita Gate even though we don't understand how it works?"

"More or less. Except we do have some theories based on our current understanding of science. We're just acutely aware that our neighbors are far more advanced than we are."

"How do you mean?"

"Well, we already have very old theories about the technology we're encountering in the data, we've just never been able to test them. And those ideas we have tested and proven, we could never execute on the scale we're talking about here."

"Any examples?"

"Sure." I pull up a D-Level cross section of the node we're working on and isolate a spherical cavity on the inside. "So far, we understand that each corner node fires a powerful multi-particle laser into the next node in a clockwise direction."

Rook nods, then folds his arms.

"Alright, so inside those nodes, you have this sphere here. It's the target area for the incoming beam from the previous node. The sphere is essentially the same kind of containment area we have inside our particle accelerators."

"Smashing atoms."

"Exactly. In this case, however, the target area is not only a magnetically shielded hydrogen envelope, but it also contains a silicon lattice, so we have a few different things happening at once."

"There's more?"

I chuckle. "Yeah. Too much?"

"No, just... go slow."

"So, way back in the 1950s in Russia, you have a physicist named Lev Landau who theorizes something called triangle singularity, where two kaons split from an origin particle and change their identities. This is still early quantum physics, right?"

Rook nods but then shakes his head. "Kaons?"

"Oh, it's a… quark-antiquark pair. Uh…" I snap my fingers in the hopes of finding better words, realizing I'm using science speech to explain more science speech.

Ramirez yells from another workstation, "Hydrogen atoms get blown apart, creating new particles that've been hit so hard in the head that they have an identity crisis and exist in two places at once. Boom. First try."

Rook says, "Thanks."

"It's not exactly right," I reply.

"Close enough," Ramirez yells back blindly.

"It works for me." Rooks waves me forward. "Keep going."

"Okay, so, while all this is happening, the lasers are also carrying neutrons and firing them into the silicon lattice I mentioned earlier. Scientists have been experimenting with this kind of semiconductor work for a long time in the hopes of learning more about the fifth dimension."

"As in scifi shit?"

"Well, as in the stuff that some scifi gets all their ideas from. But this is much less interesting. Or, at least it was, up until…" I gesture to the budding model of *Parallax One*.

"So if we've had this for so long, why is any of this a surprise?"

"Aside from it all working together in some life-altering transformational way? Scale."

"How so?"

"Firing neutrons into things is apparently so common even our alien neighbors do it. But on a much,

much, *much* larger scale. Back when the US National Institute of Standards and Technology started experimenting with this, they were able to produce something called Pendellösung oscillations in a scale between 0.02 and 10 nanometers where they could start to see the fifth force at work."

"Alien portals?"

"No. Uh, less sexy, but we're getting there. Think of the fifth force like an explanation that unites our understanding of gravity and electromagnetism."

"Definitely less sexy."

"Okay, but, what our galactic neighbors have produced, we think, is something that utilizes these known phenomena—kaons, triangle singularity, Pendellösung oscillations—to do something else we've theorized about but also can't create."

"Alien portals?" he asks again.

"Einstein-Podolsky-Rosen bridge in a tensor network."

"I have no idea what you—"

"Alien portals," I say reluctantly.

"You see? I knew it."

"Yeah."

Rook claps his hands once and laughs. "Alright, Dr. Park. Give me Einstein's Popular Rosebridge—"

"Einstein-Podolsky-Rosen bridge."

"That."

"It's another theoretical idea—"

"Oh God."

"—an interpretation of quantum theory that suggests the entanglement of spatial coordinates can connect two locations even though they are very far apart."

"In space."

"Anywhere. But, yes, we're talking primarily about space here."

"So, point A, meet point B, get there fast."

"Pretty much. The takeaway from all of this is while we have working theories, even some peer-reviewed and quite historic experiments, we've never put it all together to do what we believe this gate will do."

"And that is?"

I look from him to Sam and back again. "Send us to another part of our universe."

"Alien portals."

"Good grief."

ROOK CALLS FOR A STRETCH BREAK, and I decide to freshen up my apparently stinky self in the ladies' water closet. We've taken over almost all the bathrooms on this and the next two levels, transforming them into something as close to a camping spa as possible. According to Sam, I don't use it enough, but I think she's just irritable at the moment. We all are. Being cooped up down here does need to reach an end. Fortunately, I think it's coming soon.

Sam walks in just as I'm washing my hands.

"Nice tutorial for Rook back there," she says, turning on some hot water. Then she pulls her hair up, removes her shirt, and wets some paper towels to conduct what we've termed a camping bath. She dabs her neck, stomach, bra line, and armpits with the towels and then throws them away.

"Not as easy as the professors make it look. The good ones, anyway."

"You'd fit right in. With the good ones, I mean."

"Thanks."

Sam rubs her face with some water and grabs the soap.

While she works, I say, "Hey, I haven't run this by any of the others yet, but, assuming we get the all clear, I think the earliest we can hold the press conference is the eighth of October."

Sam stops washing her face and looks up.

"What's the matter?"

"Uh… Just, that's kind of a random day, isn't it? Like a Wednesday?"

"Yeah. What's wrong with that?"

She goes back to washing her face. "I dunno. Just thought press conferences were supposed to be held on Mondays or something."

"Does it matter?"

She shuts off the tap, grabs another hand towel, and starts dabbing her face. "No. Just saying. But… don't you think we need more time?"

"Why? We've already submitted the final packets to the Space and Security Council subcommittees as requested. And we have more than enough to move forward with grant proposals if public funding falls short."

The restroom door swings open, and three other women walk past us.

"I'm just thinking we still might want to take it easy," Sam says in a softer voice. "Let things settle in, take our time, see what comes of it."

I squint at her but keep my tone low. "You feeling okay lately?"

"What's that supposed to mean?"

"You just…"

"What?"

I square with her. "You seem reluctant lately. With a lot of this."

Sam holds my gaze for a moment and then looks back into the sink. "Aren't I always the Yin to your Yang, Eves?"

The reference makes me smile. It's true, after all. I am the curious, hyperactive, adventurous one; she's the more reserved, passive, and cautious one. "Yeah. But it's—"

She shuts off the water. At the same time, the three other women laugh at a joke behind us. Sam dabs her face again and then lowers her voice to just above a whisper. "I'm afraid."

"Of what?" I reply in an equal tone.

A long few seconds pass before Sam lets out a sigh. "I'm afraid of you getting hurt."

"Sam, how many times have we been over this?"

"Apparently not enough."

"What's that supposed to mean?"

"That you're not paying attention to just how badly really powerful people don't want this project to go forward. Tantum. Solum Terram. Who knows which other anti-spacer factions? I mean, look at us! We're in the belly of a military base in Alaska, Eves. *Alaska.*"

"We've weathered trouble before."

"This feels different."

"We can handle the Tantum."

She eyes me through the mirror. "Can we?"

"Why? You know something I don't?"

"I just…" Sam gives her reflection a frustrated look. "I don't know."

"Hey. Quit getting hung up inside your own head. What we're doing here is worth the risk." I grab Sam's shirt off the sink and offer it to her. "Ready?"

Sam ignores the shirt and doesn't seem to want to let this go. A tear slides down her face at the same time that the three women behind us laugh again.

"Hey?" I shout over my shoulder. "Could you take that outside, please? We're busy here."

They see Sam crying, apologize, and head for the door.

When the room is quiet again, Sam says, "The Tantum… they seem to be getting more bold. I've lost people."

"As have I."

"Yeah, but… I don't want anyone on our team getting hurt. Or worse."

"And neither do I. But we have to keep going. So I'm not sure what to tell you."

"That you'll be careful." She glares at me through the mirror. "I know there are risks. And I believe in what we're doing now more than before."

"More than before?"

"I don't want something bad to happen to you, Eves. I could never forgive myself."

"Well, I'll try not to disappoint you. But what do you mean more than before?"

Sam spins and looks me in the eyes with tears streaming down her cheeks. "I'm serious, Evelyn. What happened back there at St. John's is only the beginning. They're coming. I can… I can feel it. And if we're not careful, I mean really goddamn careful, then we'll just be more numbers in the body count."

Body count. That jars me. And not for the obvious reasons of the present.

"I know body counts," I say after a moment.

Sam tilts her head, as if in a silent prompt to ask for more.

"Life on the street was hard in Seongbuk-gu District. We'd go days without food sometimes. And there was fighting. Always fighting. Over the stupidest things too. Which led to deaths so meaningless that you... well, you... ran out of ways to explain them. Because you couldn't. There was no point.

"My uncle who got me out of there said I was a survivor. And I guess I was to a certain extent. Keep your head down. Know which streets to stay off of and at what times. Being smart, you know? But *surviving*? That isn't how we thought of it. That makes it sound like you got lucky and knew how to scavenge better than everyone else. Which those things are true; I'm not saying they don't come into play. But I've looked into plenty of dead eyes belonging to people who could scavenge better than me. That's because just getting by, surviving, isn't good enough."

I catch Sam's eye and lean toward her to make my point. "We took it, Sam. Each day, we *stole* life from that city. Made it cough it up, strangled it by the throat if we had to. And that's what we're gonna do here, one day at a time. We snatch life like everything depends on it, watching each other's backs, and sharing what we find. We do that? And we do more than survive. We own it. And we take the world with us." I squeeze her arm. "We'll be careful. And we'll watch out for each other. I have your back?"

She pushes her tongue into the side of her cheek at the same time that her eyes flit about the room as if trying to hold back more tears. Finally, she swallows and takes a deep breath. "And I have yours."

I pull her into an embrace and wait until she returns it. "We got this, Sam."

"I hope you're right."

"Of course I'm right. When have I ever been wrong? Name one time."

This gets a little laugh from her, and I sense her relax.

"And it's gonna be okay." We separate, but I keep my hands on her shoulders. "Focus on the job, let Rook and the others do theirs. Right?"

She smiles and wipes the last of her tears away. "Yeah. Thanks, Eves."

"You know it." I hand over her shirt. "Ready to get back in the ring?"

"Yeah, okay."

14

NEON

"Mother, come. Have a seat," Gemma said to Neon as the Tantum Terrae matriarch entered the lab. "Here."

Neon took the chair and made herself comfortable. A dozen of her biotech engineers had converted one of the old Mercedes AMG automobile design suites into a rather stylish test lab in spite of the facility's disrepair. Most of the valuable components had been scavenged a century before. But some of the original glass walls made for ideal projection canvases, while rows of old school server racks housed new quantum units. Neon was sure Gemma had a hand in dolling up some of the graffiti that adorned the walls too. Newly installed backlights gave a special glow to several images in the background, including old artwork leftover from the company's Formula One era.

"Like it?" her daughter asked, now in pink sneakers —they changed color daily.

"You did well with what you had to work with."

"I thought so too." She activated a battery of holo projectors in the ceiling that cast a 3D Tantum Terrae logo just in front of the main wall. That's when Neon noticed the pig. It wore a collar with a leash tied to a rung in the straw-strewn floor. "Meet Herman."

"Hi, Herman," Neon said to the pig a few meters away. It ignored her, of course, and chose to root around in the straw instead.

In front of the TT logos, Gemma caused several holo windows to appear, each with different diagnostic screens linked to physical points on the pig with projected tethers. The anchor lines moved as the animal did, connecting to windows that displayed synaptic response time, muscle energy dispersion, and several other biomedical measurements. One particular feed showed exactly what Herman saw: a close up of yellowed straw with glimpses of Neon, Gemma, and the other engineers seated in the background.

The most interesting holo screen of all, however, at least to Neon, was the virtual cognizance integration monitor. Herman had V-cog. Probably the only pig in the world with it, Neon guessed. The window displayed multiple features she was used to seeing in her own system diagnostic tools, including grid signal strength, cranial adhesion integrity, and synthetic architecture transference efficiency.

"Has he created a lobby yet?" Neon asked jokingly.

Gemma smirked. "Actually, you'd be surprised."

"No."

"Oh yes." Her daughter called up another display that showcased a small pigpen. "It's almost an exact spatial replica of where we've been keeping him for the last few weeks."

"Smart pig."

Gemma spoke briefly with two of the lead engineers to make sure everything was set. Satisfied, she dimmed the room until only a spotlight shone down on Herman.

A moment later, diagnostic windows appeared around him presenting metrics of his bio functions. Then Neon's daughter presented her mother with an augmented reality tablet that hovered above her lap. The screen bore numerous soft-controls—knobs and sliders—each corresponding to various brain functions. The title *Blood of Gaia 1.0* was listed along the top.

"The extended nervous system override via the frontal lobe and cerebellum is still a long way off," Gemma said. "But the cerebral cortex exploit?"

"It's ready?"

"Why don't you find out for yourself, mother dear."

Neon slid the main "corporal effect" fader to maximum on the virtual controller, then slipped into V-cog, making sure to keep her physical eyes on Herman. She wanted to see how the tech worked in the real, not just the virtual.

"Hello, Herman dear," she said as she knelt in his V-cog lobby and patted his back. The happy pig was busy sniffing for grain hiding in the stray and didn't even bother looking up at her. "Thank you, my love, for giving your life to our cause." Neon stood, withdrew a revolver from her belt, aimed point blank at Herman's head, and squeezed the trigger. Brain matter ejected from the wound, and the pig collapsed with a *wumpf* as the air escaped from its lungs.

In the real, the diagnostics floating above Herman went ballistic. Warnings flashed. The pig's heart rate spiked from a hormone surge of the adrenal glands, and then the animal simply fell over. Pulse flatlined. Brain function null.

Herman was dead.

"Three point six seconds," one of the male engineers called out.

Gemma smiled at him and then at Neon. "That's a new record."

"You've… been decreasing the response time?"

"We think we can break two seconds eventually."

Neon gave her a devilish grin. "Traces?"

"Forensics will list the cause of death as cardiac arrest. For any scientist eager enough, they might find that the brain ceased functioning first, but they'll most likely connect that to the heart malfunction and dismiss the time discrepancy."

Gaia's Blood was just as wicked as Neon hoped it would be. The saying everyone believed as kids was if you died in your dreams, you died in real life. It was a fable, of course. But with this code? Gaia's Blood truly was death through dreaming. All a killer needed to do was be invited into the subject's lobby and overpower them.

"Unlike pigs, we'll actually have to contend with humans," Gemma said after Neon had a moment to collect her thoughts. "But haven't we always?"

"What about insertion time?"

"Right now, we need four and half minutes in the victim's public lobby."

"That's too long."

"We'll trim it down. But the slicing is tedious, and we need experience with victims actually on the grid."

"Have you identified any?"

"Plenty. Just need your approval." Gemma replaced the tablet's control screen with a spreadsheet listing—Neon scrolled to the bottom—178 targets. "They're all Viatoribus members with preexisting conditions, all spread throughout the system and unlinked to each other."

The killings, both those done now in testing and future assassinations, would need to be strategic and 100 percent successful. If word ever got out that such a weapon existed, government computer scientists wouldn't stop until they created counter code. So Neon would need to make sure each target was carefully selected and each death perfectly timed. Her daughter had the right idea, but she was still young. Even with her degrees in advanced bioengineering and virtual cognizance integration, Gemma lacked something that only seemed to come with time. And pain.

"Patience," Neon said to her daughter. "Perfect your tradecraft here. And when—"

"But mother, we need—"

"—and when I give you permission, you may begin real-world trials with my approval."

"But we need human subjects."

"Then take them. But remove them from the grid. No traces."

Gemma seemed reluctant but eventually nodded. "There's a Viatoribus-only bar ninety kilometers north. I know a few patrons who won't be missed."

"Never more than one from the same location. Three day minimums, no patterns. Slurry the bodies."

"Understood."

Neon raised a finger in her face. "And no mistakes."

"Yes, mother. Oh, before I forget..." Gemma passed a verb news notification to Neon in V-cog. "Seems someone isn't keeping you up-to-date as they should."

Neon scanned the headline and clenched her jaw once but said nothing.

"The scheduled date is rather convenient though, don't you think?"

"Perhaps she's doing more than we presume," Neon said.

"Or it's just a coincidence, and she's weak."

"Stick to your work, dear. And leave me to mine."

Gemma shrugged. "Right. Time to butcher a hog."

"Only Earth," Neon replied, staring at Herman's fat corpse.

"Only Earth forever, mother dear."

Sam

"Would you excuse me?" Dr. Samantha Collins said to the small group of scientists and engineers gathered in her shared workstation. "Bathroom break." The team moved aside to let her pass. She thanked them while replying to Neon's incoming V-cog request with a text message of Stand by.

Sam had been testing new code to expedite the repeated tasks of interpolating atomic sizes for three-dimensional printing templates. That, and monitoring the server loads on the simulations Evelyn was pushing hard to complete. She found the whole endeavor of unpacking, analyzing, converting, and preparing to build schematics for *Parallax One* exhilarating. Not only would the final proposal land itself in the scope of a legacy hab, in terms of an engineering feat, but it had the potential to unlock unimaginable potential for the human race. That is, if it were to ever be funded, let alone rendered. For even with all the lab's cutting edge technology and the world's greatest minds, there were still plenty of holes that would need filling… holes that Sam hoped would inevitably stall the entire project and keep it bound to the drawing room floor. At least enough to satisfy Neon. But how did Sam feel about purposely undermining the project? No, that was the wrong question. Sam would never consider such a thing. The real question was how Olivia Tomlinson felt about it?

Instead of turning left into the bathroom, Sam continued down the hall toward a supply closet. Since every square meter of space had been turned into communal living quarters, it was next to impossible to get alone time. Most people used V-cog for that. But there was no getting over the fact that humans needed physical distance from each other, not just cerebral. They also needed privacy, and she'd walked in on more than one couple with their clothes off. So she knocked twice before swiping the utility closet doors apart. And even once they were open, she kept her eyes down and asked, "Anyone here?" before entering.

Satisfied she was alone, Sam locked the closet from the inside—not an unusual thing to do to signify that someone wanted privacy, hello people —and stepped into V-cog. When she finally answered the call, Sam was transferred to one of Neon's suites… one that whisked Sam away to a past she'd tried to forget.

"Hello, Olivia dear."

Sam gave a half-hearted wave while looking around.

"What do you think?" Neon asked, nodding out the window to a breathtaking view of the icy landscape beyond the settlement's iridescent laminar bubble. Etana Dome's hospital faced Ganymede's Grosjean mountain range, which always seemed to glow blue in the twilight hours. The ice sparkled like crystal perpetually cast in the light off Jupiter's imposing southern hemisphere.

"Something the matter, dear?"

"No, I just…"

"Bad memories? Perhaps this was a poor choice."

"It's fine."

"Mmmm." Neon walked toward Sam. None of this was real. Just renders from memories. But Sam's instincts still told her she was dying. Reminded her of a lack of medical care.

"How can I help you?" Sam asked.

Neon ran a finger across the hospital bed's metal railing. "You're not the least bit curious?"

"Should I be?"

"You tell me."

"I don't need a reminder of—"

"Where I saved you?"

Sam felt her heart race in the real but knew better than to let it show in V-cog. "I'm grateful, as ever."

"I'm sure you are." Neon looked at a holo monitor that provided vitals for a patient who wasn't there. Medical lines ran from the wall to the empty bed. "Any update for me? It's been a while."

"Development continues. I've tried to slow them down where possible, but there are so many eyes on the project now, they keep undoing my work."

"Sounds to me like something more extreme is needed."

"I just need more time."

"More time. To decide what, exactly?"

"How to stop the project. I can't just destroy the lab, and the military presence means—"

"You kill her."

The frankness of Neon's words sent a chill up Sam's spine. Assassinating Dr. Evelyn Park was the most direct action, of course. Nothing would derail the project faster than that. But Evelyn was… there were extenuating circumstances. That's what they were, yes. Developing matters that needed a nuanced approach which she alone could—

"Olivia?"

"Kill her, yes. I agree."

"Do you?" Neon studied her face. "What's going on in that beautiful brain of yours?"

Sam walked to the window and studied the ice flats leading to mountains. "If we cut off one head, they'll just grow another."

"Then we make them afraid."

"How?" Sam asked.

"We take her out in public."

"When?"

"The next meaningful opportunity. Can you think of one?"

"Nothing comes to mind. We've been locked twenty stories underground for a month and—"

Neon ripped the medical lines from the wall, and an alarm sounded.

Sam's heart rate spiked again.

"You were going to die up here, Olivia dear."

"I remember."

Neon studied the torn-out ends. "One more casualty of a system that would sacrifice children on the altar of what? Colonization? Expansion?"

"And you rescued me."

"Because you were worth saving. And I knew, when I pulled you from this bed, that we would save so many more together."

"And we have."

"Indeed." Neon silenced the alarm and let the lines drop on the floor. "The question remains, how many more will we save?"

"As many as we can."

"Do you believe that?"

"Of course. Why wouldn't I?"

Neon joined Sam at the window and presented her with a verb headline printed on a piece of paper:

Joint NUESSA, SESI Press Conference to Discuss Kepler Signal Announced for October 8th

Sam's eyes twitched in surprise.

"When were you going to tell me, Olivia dear?"

"Neon, I swear, I—"

"Didn't know?"

"Didn't realize they'd made it official. I'm not privy to those conversations, you know that."

"And that's my fault?"

"No, I… My position doesn't allow me to—"

"Your position was purchased with the lives of a dozen incogs over three years."

"Of course."

"And I should think you would honor all the work done to keep you in place by being a little more forthcoming."

"I have no reason to hide anything from you."

"No?"

Sam squinted at Neon. "You suspect me of something?"

"I suspect that you are growing attached to your work. And fond of this Dr. Park."

"Whatever you see is a ruse. I can assure you."

"Mmmm. I understand that you intervened to save Park's life on the rooftop."

"All part of the act."

"And you were shot."

"Our people should have known better."

"Or you should have stayed out of the way and let them do their jobs."

"I didn't know it was us," Sam lied before she could catch the mistake. Or was it a mistake? Why was she protecting Evelyn anyway?

"Would it have mattered if Park was killed by someone else?"

"No, I… suppose not. I wasn't thinking."

"That much is clear."

"Neon, I—"

"*I* think you need to reassess your priorities, Olivia. First you fail to conceal murders on *Astraea*, then you fail to protect the life of my son."

"I already told you how they—"

"So very many excuses, yes. I recall. Fortunately, *Jack* didn't forget himself amidst the mission's many temptations. And were it not for him, *Astraea* would still be orbiting the Earth instead of rusting below the sea. And yet his killer remains free, and the alien signal seems to promise that even more of Gaia's precious resources will be squandered in pursuit of the frivolous. I'm losing patience with you, Olivia."

Sam turned away from the view and grabbed the hospital bed's railing with both hands. She wanted to leave this place. Abandon this meeting. If she could just lose herself in the transmission work, then she could put off taking the necessary actions a little while longer. But Sam could no more keep the inevitable at bay than she could her body's autoimmune response to the gene therapy on this bed. Neon had intervened then, as a good mother should have, racing Sam to Earth for treatment when her birth parents refused. And if Sam was not strong enough to climb out of her present predicament herself, Neon would intervene yet again. The Witch of Calvert Isle, the Wraith of Ganymede, would execute anyone who dared jeopardize the weak. Whether or not Sam was on board, the guilty would pay. The Tantum always found a way.

"Can I count on you, Olivia?"

Sam caught the woman's brooding eyes in the window's reflection. "Yes. I'll forward my plan soonest."

"And I look forward to reviewing it."

"Feed the rock."

Neon gave a curt nod. "Feed the rock." Then she vanished from the suite but did not close out the render, which left Sam standing in the hospital by herself.

15

EVELYN

"ARE YOU SURE ABOUT THIS?" Rook asks me in the waiting room's silence. The walls are adorned with the flags of the NUE, and the furniture embroidered with the governing body's seal. Outside, beyond the door to the media theatre, I know what kind of clamor awaits me. But here, beside Rook, the quiet holds me in a safe embrace a little longer. And, stars, how I need some peace right now.

I wring my hands once and then put them under my arms. "I'll be fine. Just a little nervous."

"That's not what I meant." Rook, ever alert, stands near the main entry doors and casts a quick glance out the window. He's wearing his planet-side armor, I think he calls it, with multiple weapons on his kit and his helmet tucked under one arm. "Are you certain this whole thing—the gate—is wise?"

"Really? After all you're seen in the last few weeks?"

"I'm not doubting the significance, only the safety."

"I'll be fine." I nod at his armor. "Plus I have Mr. Overboard as my shadow."

"I was talking about the planet's safety, Evelyn."

I tuck a strand of hair behind my ear. "We're back to alien invasion again?"

"Call me a sucker for the classics."

"You're paranoid, that's what you are."

"Keeps people alive in my line of work."

I take a deep breath and reach for a glass of water on the beverage cart. "You know as well as I do that we have to at least try."

"Do we?"

"Rook."

"I'm just saying, you're about to get asked a lot tougher questions from people who like you a lot less than I do."

"And how little do you like me?"

He lets out a chuckle. "Didn't mean it like that. I'm just saying, there're gonna be a lot of very anxious people who are concerned with what happens when and if that gate ever gets opened."

"And you think I'm not one of them?"

"Not really." Rooks rubs his jaw with a hand. "Dr. Evelyn Park is the one who signs up to jump into the ring before the rest of the boxers even have their gloves on."

"Pays to be first."

"Pays to be careful."

I wink at him. Ever the cynical sentinel. "The good news for us is that if we get approval and funding, there'll be a whole lot of highly intelligent people making decisions about operations, contingencies, and first contact. We're just the ones delivering the news."

"And you're okay with that?"

"Why wouldn't I be?"

"Because, let's say unstoppable bloodsucking monsters come out the moment we open it—"

"Rook."

"Can you guarantee it isn't a possibility?"

"Well, no, but the likelihood—"

"Then say unstoppable bloodsucking monsters come out the moment we open it, you have a chance right now to keep that from ever happening."

"The same way I can keep us from ever getting in a grid car again because we might cause a multi-car pileup."

"Except for the likelihood of— Dammit. You and your bloody logic."

That makes me grin. "We can't turn back now, Rook. You know that."

"Do I? Do you?"

"You really want us to keep this from the public? They already know about the signal. And news has already leaked about its complexity."

"It could end right there too. None of us are the wiser, and things keep going the way they have been."

"Someone's bound to leak the real findings."

"Which end up in the verb tabloids, right alongside the mother who birthed a kid with four heads, and the dog who speaks Queen's English."

I point a finger at him. "Hey. I spoke to that dog at length. He's the real deal, let me tell you."

"Christ."

I take a few sips of water, check the time, and then return the glass to the cart. "Aren't you the least bit curious?"

"No."

"Come on."

"Maybe a little. But that shit kills cats."

"Good thing you're not one."

"Cute."

I wipe moisture from the corners of my lips, trying to protect my lipstick. "Wanna know what I really think?"

"I do."

"I think we let our elected officials and politicast leaders make the call."

"And you're just going to abide by that, hands off?"

"No one said I won't fight against what I think is a stupid decision. But I'll do what the law requires. And in the end, if that's what humanity wants, that's what we get."

He folds his arms across his uniformed chest. "Compliance is a side of you we don't often get to see."

"Well... don't get used to it."

"And have your pain-in-the-ass reputation sullied? Wouldn't dream of it." He lets out a sigh, then asserts, "But you think they'll go for it."

I nod. "You know why?"

"Enlighten me."

"Because all our other choices still lead to death."

"But the Marquis-class test—"

"Was a success, I know. But how many people die between now and when there are enough settlement ships to head toward the nearest exoplanet?"

"So die today from an alien invasion, or die tomorrow from solar-system-wide resource failure."

"Which one do you want?"

"None of them. But... yeah, the latter."

"Huh. And here I thought all you Space Marines joined just to fight little green men."

"And women," he adds and then crosses the room toward me. He searches my face like he wants to say something but can't find the words.

After a few seconds of silence, I finally ask, "What?"

"I'm just thinking how much I admire your bravery."

"Come again?"

He nods at the media door behind my back. "Somehow, I feel like aliens will be way easier for you to handle then what waits for you out there."

"That's why I have back up."

"Oh?"

I kiss my fingers and then touch the side of his cheek.

Just then, the doors part, and in walks both NUESSA Director Eric Johnson and SESI Director Lemuel Brown.

"Evelyn," says Lemuel. "Are you ready?"

I turn and smooth my blouse, letting my hands linger on my stomach. "I am. You?"

He shares a laugh with Eric. "I'm not sure any of us are ready for what's coming."

"The good news," Eric adds, "is that we're all in this together. Everything secure on your end, Master Sergeant?"

Rook gives him a thumbs-up. "All sectors secure. All guests check out." But then his eyes shift to me as if he wants to say something else. Or maybe I'm just reading into the look. I can't tell.

Before I have a chance to ask, Eric says, "Thank you, Master Sergeant." Then back to me and Lemuel, he adds, "Let's do this."

THE MEDIA THEATRE in the NUESSA Helsinki headquarters is smaller than it looks on the verb. But it's no less intimidating. Just knowing what kinds of statements have been made in this room by some of the planet's most famous faces makes me weak-kneed—more so because I'm about to be added to the list, if I can keep it together.

The ceiling is a wash of broadcast lighting, and the walls are acoustically treated—no windows in sight. Reporters fill rows of seats on an incline toward a back gallery filled with verb engineers and excipions. No pixies are allowed in here, only conventional servo-driven cameras mounted around the room. There must be two hundred people in the chairs, maybe another hundred in the gallery. And all of them tracking Eric, Lemuel, and me as we take the stage. Rook stands off my right shoulder, and the rest of his unit is stationed throughout the room.

"Good afternoon, everyone. I'm Eric Johnson, Director of NUESSA, and we're pleased to host you here at our Helsinki location given the unfortunate events that transpired at St. John's. It's good to see you all here."

As Eric continues his introduction, I spot familiar faces in the front two rows. There's Natalie Mason, Jose Ramirez, and our favorite priest-turned-evolutionary biologist Sebastián Fernández Parra. There's also Enni Mäkinen and a slew of other team leads responsible for key achievements in the project. I hope to be able to recognize as many of them in my speech as I have time for. They're just as deserving of this moment in the spotlight as I am.

Most surprising of all is the presence of none other than Captain Jericho Fox, fresh off the *Kogarashi*'s successful maiden voyage. I had no idea he was coming down for this. But I'm not complaining. Just seeing him again makes me feel… content. He gives me a quirky smile, and Kit rolls his fingers in a bashful wave. *Playboy*.

Jericho also seems to have a few colleagues seated around him, and I look forward to meeting them after the press conference. But right now, I'm concerned about the one person *not* in their seat. Sam.

I cast Natalie a mildly questioning look, one I hope won't be noticed on camera. Fortunately, Natalie doesn't need any more from me. She mouths back with the word, "Bathroom."

"To speak on that, please welcome SESI Director Lemuel Brown." Eric steps aside to give Lemuel the podium as the sounds of clapping and camera servos fill the room.

"Thank you, Director Johnson. Hello, everyone. Thank you for being here today.

"As you can imagine, it's been a busy number of weeks for all of us at SESI, and we've been looking forward to this momentous day for a while. Even despite the attacks on our facilities, our dedicated and professional staff have labored to achieve what we believe will be looked back upon as the single greatest contribution to human evolution and expansion in history, one we are excited to share with you, distinguished members of the Nations of United Earth and those in the media who are tasked with sharing this discovery to the world, Mars Nation, the Belt Lands, and Jupiter Moons."

I lose track of Lemuel's speech. My eyes are on Sam's empty chair.

Rook, too, is focused on her absence, and he catches me eyeing him. In V-cog audio only, he says, "Did you know she wouldn't be attending the event?"

"She's in the bathroom. Probably just nerves."

"I'll send someone to check."

"I don't think that's necessary."

"Doesn't matter."

I glance over my shoulder again and give him a sideways look, but he ignores me. Back in V-cog, I ping Sam. The soft trill chimes three times before she steps into my lobby. "You okay, Sam?"

"Fine, I'm just… Oh God. I'm… not fine. Not fine! *Ouwalgh.*" Sam doubles over and vomits. Except in V-cog, we don't get any stomach contents or the delightful smells associated with the reflex. After two more dry heaves, she pushes hair behind her ears and wipes her mouth with what I presume is a hand towel. Sam hasn't bothered to turn off virtual mimetic mirroring.

"Nerves?" I ask when she's finally composed herself. She nods.

"Which bathroom?"

"Why?" She grins. "You gonna join me?"

"No. But the Marines might. I'm on stage."

"Oh shit. Evelyn, I'm so sorry. I'll be right there."

Sam blinks out, and I raise Rook again. "She's in the bathroom. Coming back now."

"Roger."

In the real, I spot his shoulders relaxing ever so slightly. Man, and I thought *I* was uptight. But with everything we've been through, I can't say I blame him.

Rook

Master Sergeant Ishaq al Farooq didn't like the fact Dr. Samantha Collins was out of her seat. But he was an equal opportunity skeptic: had anyone else been AWOL, he would have been just as suspicious. Did it bother him that Sam was a part of Evelyn's inner circle? Like hell, it did. That's where saboteurs loved to strike from the most. But he had nothing on the woman to suggest she was anything but loyal to Evelyn, the Sentia Aux cause, and the SESI aim to bridge-build with intelligent sentient species. Nothing, that is, but his gut.

And that rankled every nerve in his Space Marine Corps body.

People loved when their gut corroborated evidence, Rook thought. It made trusting intuition easy. But that was cherry-picking. The real test of a person's sixth sense, the kind that kept a unit alive, that saved Jericho Fox's life when that incog Afumba got a kill order over V-cog, was a willingness to pursue instinct even when there wasn't intel. That no one else but Rook seemed to suspect Sam of... well, *something*, was disconcerting. Acting on it meant he'd risk making enemies with anyone who thought Dr. Collins was innocent. Notably, Evelyn. Park appeared to love Sam like a sister. And why not? They'd worked together for years, discovered the Kepler signal, survived *Astraea*'s demise, and decoded a real honest-to-God alien message.

That was the biggest puzzle of all to Rook. Sam hadn't seemed to do anything that would compromise the mission. Sure, he'd overheard her express apprehension about the physical dangers of continuing the work in the face of Tantum Terrae attacks. But that was a common theme amongst all the scientists and engineers he'd been around. They were academics, not trained trigger pullers. It was normal to be scared. In fact, not being scared would have made her stand out. Instead, she celebrated her team's victories and lamented their impasses. And yet, somehow, that bothered him.

Behind Evelyn's back, he'd tasked his unit with investigating any and every lead that popped up, no matter how small. There was no reason to make Evelyn anxious or to jeopardize the trust they'd built. His were all standard searches and background checks anyway. Still, the constant investigating would make her worried, he knew, but Rook had a job to do: keep Evelyn safe at all costs. He would not fail.

Despite his most faithful efforts, however, there was no progress made in connecting Sam or any other team member to the Tantum Terrae, Leonidas X, or any other terrorist group—not even a competing politicast. They were clean. Which was good, wasn't it? The whole point was to keep everyone safe. Keep her safe. And make sure the project moved forward. Always forward.

As Sam took her seat in the front row again, just in time for Evelyn to be introduced, Rook's V-cog pinged. It was his recently promoted Sergeant and EOD tech for the *Astraea* op, Daniel Geller.

"Go."

"We got a hit on that Canongate keyword you wanted us to run," Geller said. "Looks like it goes all the way back to a protest in 2216."

⁂

Evelyn

"Good afternoon," I say into the mic. Only, it doesn't sound like me at all. So I clear my throat and try again, followed by, "Thank you for being here on what I believe, what we believe, is one of the most significant days in, well, in recorded history."

I keep expecting someone to raise a hand, ask a question, or talk back to me. But nothing comes. Instead, there's just a gaping void that's pulling on me, sucking my words into the verb. I try hard not to think about how many people are watching me right now. *Just focus on the facts, Evelyn.*

"As you all know, *Astraea* Station's celestial exploration laboratory recorded a first-of-its-kind extrasolar transmission from Kepler-1649c, one that Parallax, our advanced quantum network, determined with over ninety-nine percent certainty was sent intentionally from an intelligent species. Today, we can go a step further than Parallax and confirm unequivocally that the Kepler-1649c transmission was indeed sent from an advanced alien intelligence."

The room's emotional baseline rumbles like a seismograph's needle charting a subterranean quake. I see the peaks register in the audience's faces, hear the murmur in verbcasters making involuntary audible commentary over V-cog, and feel the excitement rise in the room.

"Over the course of the past several weeks, NUESSA and SESI, along with support from the Viatoribus and the Sentia Aux, have been hard at work decoding the signal in the hopes of determining its significance and, if we were very lucky, discovering what, if anything, our cosmic neighbors had to say.

"The task itself was indeed… excuse me." I reach for the glass under the lectern, take a sip, and clear my throat. "The task of decoding the signal was arguably the hardest project I've ever been a part of. Doctors Samantha Collins, Jose Ramirez, Natalie Mason, Sebastián Fernández Parra, and postdoctoral xenobiologist Enni Mäkinen, among many other notables on our exceptional team, were instrumental in creating the solutions to a most complex set of problems." I spend precisely sixty seconds of my presentation explaining, or rather dumbing down, the concepts of photon orbital angular momentum and multiplexing independent beams of light. The agency's media coaches explained that anything more would exhaust viewership and that all the peer-reviewed findings would be available in NUESSA's V-cog library.

"Of course, we all had legitimate concerns as to whether or not we would be able to understand anything sent to us. It's hubris and a failure of logic to anthropomorphize our alien neighbors and assume we speak the same language. Even NASA's Voyager message carrying a 1977 phonograph record makes several assumptions that extraterrestrial life-forms would have the mechanical means to spin the disc at sixteen-and-two-thirds revolutions per minute, let alone understand

Sumer Akkadian, Chinese Wu, or a 90-minute selection of music.

"Unlike us, however, our Kepler signal senders decided to use a much more elegant solution to any potential communication barriers by using the language of physics. Or, put more simply, the language of atomic structure. Interestingly, this is not a surprise, as the late great Carl Sagan himself theorized such a possibility during his time at Cornell University in Ithaca, New York. In the end, what we received was akin to a set of plans sliced into easily recognizable atomic layers, much like a 3D printer uses to construct an object, to form a structure we believe will change the course of human history.

"Ladies and gentlemen, today, with the approval of the NUE Space Council, NUESSA and SESI would like to present the fruit of our labor, something we have called *Parallax One*, first of the Infinita Gates from Kepler-1649c."

The theater's lights dim at the same time that a room-wide holo projector casts a three-dimensional model of *Parallax One* above the audience's heads. Familiar to all my team are the three emissions nodes at the triangle's apexes, spanning seven kilometers between points, shown by an accompanying scale. New to the schematic, however, is massive housing, like a stumpy triangular legacy hab extending away from the nodes. Its design is far from complete, but it serves today's purposes.

I join the audience in marveling at the gate. My team looks proud, and Sam seems like she's on the verge of tears. I even catch Jericho in wide-eyed wonder. Kit points to ten things at once, and the rest of Jericho's entourage is almost as enthusiastic—all but one scruffy looking dark-haired dude with his arms crossed.

"What you are seeing here," I say amidst the swooning crowd, "can be broken into two components. The first and most significant is the gate itself, comprised simply of three emissions nodes to form the pre-eminent triangle." The triad lights up and displays identification tags E1, 2, and 3. "The second component is our proposed energy module habitat containing the Wendelstein 7-X fusion reactor necessary to power the emissions nodes." The blunt triangular tube lights up and extends another eight and half kilometers from the nodes.

"This second component is important since the transmission did not include several specifics, most notably how the device is to be powered. But that's understandable since it seems they adhered to the underlying assumption that any recipient civilization with enough advanced technology to receive their signal would also have their own indigenous methods suitable to power it.

"As such, according to the plans transmitted by the alien civilization and what we're able to deduce from the specifications, each node in the gate employs our equivalent of a 20-petawatt extreme light infrastructure laser with a wavelength of 820 nanometers and pulse length of 25 femtoseconds to emit a 100-centimeter diameter beam into the adjacent node in a clockwise progression."

The three points send bright beams of light into one another

"With each laser firing into the next emissions node in a perpetual-style chain reaction, accelerated pions strike hydrogen atoms to produce kaons—yet another kind of quark-antiquark pair—that change their identities in the process to create two new points of a quantum triangle with the original first particle as the base, something we know as a Landau triangle singularity."

Eyes start blinking and heads turn sideways. I'm losing the audience with my science talk, something the coaches warned me about. Even Sam looks like she's squinting in pain. So I advance the visuals. The nodes and laser beams swell with ambient light and produce a phase-shifted membrane in between them, filling in the triangle's center area. The recessed triangular cavity inside the energy module begins to glow too.

"The reaction is contained within each node's internal magnetic field core, forming a massive Pendellösung oscillation window that, in turn, creates an Einstein-Podolsky-Rosen bridge between one location and another in a tensor network. Uh... again, these terms can all be found on the—"

"Where does it lead?" calls someone from the press. I can't see who, but I can tell from the grunts of people around him that this is indeed the question of the hour.

Stars, it's my question too. "In truth, we don't know yet."

"How do we control it?" asks a tall woman, rising to her feet.

"At the moment, the nodes appear to be hard-coded, as if it's fixed to a—"

"Can they turn it on from their end?" someone else asks, fighting over other people trying to ask questions.

"What happens when you go through?"

"And what other specifics didn't the transmission include?"

"Do you think the aliens will send an invasion force?"

This last question opens the floodgates. I pump my hands at the audience. "Whoa, whoa. Please, everyone. *Please.* We'll be happy to take your questions in just a moment." But no one seems to hear me, and the onslaught becomes unmanageable. Lemuel steps in beside me and starts trying to calm the crowd as well. That's when I notice Sam's face go pale, as if she's seen a ghost. Her eyes are focused somewhere in the near distance, like she's cogged out. But then she looks at me and screams my name.

Rook

CANONGATE.

The extremist leader known as Neon had used the word in passing during her verb-wide broadcast weeks ago. Pundits assumed it was either a war metaphor or some play on words about a political scandal and wrote it off. Rook too had forgotten about it. But during a recent re-watch of Neon's ultimatums, he'd noticed a glint in the woman's serene eyes when she'd said the word—a look he'd seen before in dictators and despots who'd, on the surface, appeared to be masters of self-control, but underneath were rage-filled tribalists.

"Then you will reap the consequences of Canongate," Neon had said to the entire watching public. "There will be no quarter given, no mercy bestowed. Only Earth forever."

"What protest?" Rook asked Geller.

"Pretty obscure, held in Edinburgh."

"Old Scotland?"

"Roger. It was an anti-space march that went from Edinburgh Castle down the Royal Mile to the Parliament building. Turned ugly by the end in an old section of town—"

"Called Canongate."

"Bingo. Protesters and security forces were slain."

"I need a better connection than that."

"That's just it. We don't have anything on the people involved, just some old verb posts saying it may have been the unofficial start of the Tantum, but nothing concrete."

"Then what do you have?"

"The date, Master Sergeant. It was Tuesday, October 8th, 2216."

"Son of bitch." Rook looked from Evelyn to the audience, which was now riled up with questions. His eyes searched the crowd like a wolf's hunting prey. "Geller, we're suspending the event. I want the room cleared and Command informed of—" He stopped. The shocked face of one, Samantha Collins, stood out among all others. A split second later, the woman launched out of her seat, charged the stage, and lunged at Evelyn.

Over the team's mil V-cog channel, Rook yelled, "Tango inbound! On me!" and then dove to intercept the assassin.

16

JERICHO

I COULD TELL by the look on her face that she was surprised to see us. Which was kinda the point. Big day for Evelyn—for everyone, damn. And I wanted to be here for her. Kit too. I'm just glad NUESSA and the higher-ups over at Stellar Dynamics saw fit to give me and the crew some leave. We did kinda earn it though. I also thought it was cool that Nairobi and the others were up for making the trip back to Earth. Yup, even Eddie Carr, despite whatever his face tried saying when I presented the opportunity. He's getting easier to read. Well, kinda.

"Wow, Cap. I mean *wow*, am I right?"

"Just keep it level," I whisper to Kit as he points out key features of the Infinita Gate's design overhead. "And pay attention to Evelyn."

"Sure, sure, but… it's an *alien portal*, Cap. And… and have you ever seen a Wendelstein stellarator in person?"

"Yup."

"Of course you have. This changes everything, right?"

"If it works."

"Ha ha, yeah. But it'll work, right?"

"Kit."

"Sorry."

Evelyn's losing me a bit with the laser specs and the atomic physics, but I'm getting the gist of it. The whole thing is mind-blowing, really, and I'm not sure what's more incredible: that an alien civilization has actually sent us blueprints for some sort of portal, or that Evelyn's team has already designed a power unit to support it. My guess, though, is that the energy module habitat we're being shown is just a mock-up. This is primarily a SESI project for the moment, aimed to secure funding and public interest. It's gonna take whole a lot of NUESSA wrench monkeys to design and build out the rest.

"Does he look okay to you?" Kit asks me.

"Who?"

"Rook, on stage. He's making the same face I do when I get a fungal rash down in my—"

"TMI, pal." But Kit does have a point. Rook looks like he has a pole up his ass... more than usual. He's decked out in matte black and grey combat armor, holding his MAW rifle across his chest. Pretty sure it's the Marine standard issue Scorpion SR-90. But I lose focus amid the growing number of questions coming from the press behind me, ranging from the reasonable to the downright paranoid.

"Do you think the aliens will send an invasion force?" someone high-strung verbcaster yells. This sets the rest of the room off, forcing Evelyn to try to regain some sense of control.

"Whoa, whoa. Please, everyone," she says. "*Please.* We'll be happy to answer your questions in just a moment."

But there's no stopping them. Everyone's on their feet, microphones and handheld video cameras extended. The rising level of pandemonium isn't surprising. Finding out we're not alone in the universe is one thing; being told aliens sent us a magic door is another. And the press don't seem to be sharing the feel-good sentiments that Evelyn was probably hoping for.

Just as Director Brown steps in to help settle the room, someone in front of me shouts Evelyn's name. It's Sam. *And she's charging the stage.*

Evelyn's eyes go wide.

Rook steps forward and puts himself between Sam and Evelyn, his weapon rising. Then a sharp noise zips overhead—the sound of a pixie ripping through the air. I catch the blur toward the podium. Sam jumps at Evelyn but collides with Rook just as the drone stabs Sam in the back. She cries out, wrapping her arms around Rook. The Marine looks confused and pushes Evelyn back while the audience reacts to the unsettling sight of a SESI staffer with a drone stuck between her shoulder blades.

I'm on my feet when a second pixie flies toward the stage, this time striking the podium and splintering the wood. A red LED on the back flashes. It's speeding up. And then the drone detonates.

The force knocks me back into my seat. Kit shouts beside me. Others scream. And then the sprinklers kick on, showering us with fire retardant.

I press my eyes hard, trying to will away the blinding light and the sharp smell of gel accelerant. I think something's cut my face. Rook is shouting for Evelyn and the directors to get off the stage while the rest of the Marines call for the attendees to exit the theater. Someone's tugging on my sleeve.

"Time to go!" Eddie nods to the nearest exit.

"I'm staying with her." I point to Evelyn and haul myself out of the chair. "Get everyone else out."

Before he can argue, I bound over the next row, ears ringing, hop onto the platform, and head toward the backstage door. One of Rook's men, Geller, raises his weapon at me. "Fox?"

"I'm staying with Dr. Park," I say, not looking to get shot but unwilling to back down from the point.

Geller nods toward the door and lowers his rifle. "Double-time."

"Me-me too," Kit exclaims, coming from behind.

Geller doesn't look happy but compiles. "Keep your heads down."

Kit ducks, waves his thanks, and follows me out of the theater.

Down the hall, I see Rook, a bleeding Sam being shouldered by the directors, and three more Marines. The drone in Sam's back is on the floor and smashed into pieces. Geller follows Kit and me, and I pick the pace.

"Evelyn!"

She turns around. "Jericho!"

Rook, too, looks surprised. But Geller says, "He insisted." I know he only let us sneak through because we have history together.

"Evac on the roof," Rook says and points to Sam's escorts. "Care to step in?"

I nod and relieve Brown and Johnson, neither of whom seem in good enough physical shape to get Sam up several flights of stairs. "How many floors?"

"Six."

I get Sam's attention as Kit takes up her other arm. Her eyelids are droopy, and she can hardly stand.

…l soaking my sleeve at the
…ured her back. "She needs

…er Marine I recognize,
…ulls two items from a
… He pushes a skin pack
…se of her neck and activates it
…s. Then he presses and aerosyringe
… The injection of nanobots will help alle-
…uin while also keeping the injury from getting any
…vorse.

"Good to move," Grabowski says to Rook.

But Geller waves off the comment. "Anyone else seeing this?"

We follow his attention back down the hallway. Blinking red LEDs hover over the carpet some twenty meters away, looking at us like demon eyes in a dim forest.

Rook demags his sidearm from his hip. It's his Hermann & Gruber HG-11 subcompact pistol.

"Again?" I say.

"Nope." He offers the weapon to Evelyn instead.

She accepts it, pairs the biolock, and then readies the first charge. "Set."

Geller holds his pistol up to me. "I want mine back."

"Roger."

Kit and I follow him, Geller, Evelyn, Brown, and Johnson toward the stairwell door while Grabowski, Rodgers, and Ibrahim raise their rifles toward the pixies on our tail. The moment the drones see us move, they surge forward and let out their telltale whine. But the Space Marines are on it and open fire. Their magnetic acceleration weapons shoot three-round bursts down the hall. The hydraulic sounding *zip-zip-* air, followed by an explosion.

"Scratch one," Grabowski yells as a brigh shadows in the white-painted open stairwell. to the next landing where Rook and Geller are spotting the angles and aiming higher as they move

"Easy does it, Miss Samantha," Kit says, motion to the woman with his free hand. "One step at a time.

"Thanks," she replies, her first word so far.

More automatic MAW fire sounds behind us, followed by three more explosions.

"Clear," someone shouts. A second later, Ibrahim pulls the stairwell doors closed while Grabowski encourages us to pick up the pace since "there could be more."

"Switch to air burst claymore rounds," Rook calls out. His men comply and start swapping out their green color-coded amrods for yellow banded ones. I assume the air burst rounds spread like a shotgun shell.

We arrive on the second landing when something moves below me, coming up through the stairwell's central gap. The red light catches my eyes, and I yell, "Drone!"

Instinctively, I cover Sam and fire off two rounds, but it's not my shots that blow the thing up. It's Evelyn's. The pixie detonates near my feet and blasts my legs with heat. Evelyn's above me with both hands on her pistol and yells, "Keep moving."

Geller opens up on the next wave as more heat and drone fragments pelt us. All the noise makes my ears ring again. What I wouldn't give for Marine combat armor right now.

"Jesus," Grabowski says. "They're fucking everywhere!" As if summoned by his words, the faint whir of more incoming pixies erupts from somewhere below.

"Rodgers and Ibrahim, I want EMPs on our tail," Rook demands.

"At max discharge, these might knock out your V-cog for a sec," Grabowski says to the rest of us. "It's normal and will come back online in a minute."

I thank him for the update and urge Sam to move faster as the sound of the pixies grows louder. But one appears ahead of the others and catches Rodgers by surprise. He sets his lemon-sized dodecahedron EMP grenade on a step just the drone drives a metal spike into his shoulder and then explodes a moment later.

The blast throws me to my knees, as it does to Sam and Kit. Evelyn and the others also hit the deck. Meanwhile, Ibrahim tosses her geodesic sphere on the ground and yells, "Frag out!" A bright blue flash makes my skin tingle, and the persistent V-cog grid strength indicator in my peripheral vision vanishes. The whirring stops. Next thing I know, the sound of hardware clattering off railings echoes up the open shaft.

"You good?" Ibrahim asks Rodgers, whose armor is smoking.

"Christ, yeah." He pushes himself up and examines his shoulder. There's not even a dent. "Little bastard caught me off-balance. I think they're packing shaped charges." Rodgers looks up at me. "You guys okay?"

I glance at Sam. She coughs and nods at the same time. Kit gives me a thumbs-up.

"We're good here," Evelyn adds.

"Let's keep moving," Rook says. "Assume more bogies are inbound."

We start climbing the steps again, and I can't help but wonder what the pixie's payload would've done to Sam if it hadn't been a dud. Hell, I'm surprised she isn't paralyzed. Thing must'a just missed her spine. "You're one lucky lady, you know that?"

"Tell me again when we're out of the woods."

"You got it."

Rook and Geller continue to lead us up the winding stairs while the other Marines peer over the side to watch for more drones.

"Any idea who's sending them?" I ask no one in particular. "The Tantum?"

"That's our current assumption," Rook replies.

Geller adds, "We discovered a connection with today's date to a historical event that may have helped launch the TT movement fifty years ago."

"That would have been nice to know," Evelyn says.

"Yeah, no shit. Sorry." Then Geller looks down at Sam. "Way to save Dr. Park's life, Collins."

More winded, Sam says, "We're all playing our parts."

Rook gives her a resigned look. Almost sad even. Strange. To Evelyn and the two directors, the Master Sergeant adds, "I'm just sorry we didn't make the connection sooner."

"You get us out of here in one piece, and we'll call it even," Brown says.

"Roger that, sir."

The whir sounds return, this time from above and below.

"They're coming from both ends," Grabowski yells.

Evelyn raises her weapon and fires at the first drones that punch out an air vent overhead. The Marines follow suit.

"EMPs ready," Rook yells as the pixies keep pouring out.

Ibrahim and Rogers pull the last devices from their kit and ready the electromagnetic pulse grenades.

"One at a time, devil dogs." Rook steps in front of Evelyn to shield her from the coming ordnance. "First wave is you, Rodgers."

The Lance Corporal nods and then throws his EMP underhanded toward the sixth level. Three pixies zip out of a duct and dash for us, but the grenade is perfectly timed. Rodgers is getting his revenge. The EMP flashes, and again, my hair raises on end. Whatever cool-off time our unshielded V-cog nanos had since the last blast has been restarted, and the grid indicator still reads No Signal. All three drones seize and roll sideways, tumbling away from us.

The next wave rises through the central shaft. Rook orders Ibrahim to toss her grenade.

"Frag out," the Corporal says, releasing the EMP and watching it detonate one second later. The blue flash hits us again, and the drones fall away.

"Do you, ya know, think I'm still gonna be able to have kids after all this?" Kit asks Grabowski who's just beside him.

"Shit, I sure hope not. Keep moving."

"Shut up, Grabowski," Rodgers calls up.

Grabowski gives him the one-fingered salute.

We round the next landing and arrive on the sixth floor. Rook steps past the main level entryway and orders a side door to be muscled open since the EMP disabled the motion sensor. Once the Marines have it open, Rook and Geller check both angles into the next room. It's a utility warehouse with roof access on a platform along the far wall. Massive HVAC units, duct work, and a control station separate us from the exit.

"Stay together. Guns up," Rook orders and then

leads the line down a center aisle bordered by workbenches, sheet metal housings, and conduits. We're not halfway through the room when we hear more drones, this time moving through a one-meter duct along the ceiling. Then, without warning, they burst through the metal and scan the room.

"Guess we know how they get places so fast," Geller shouts. "Open fire!"

The Marines and Evelyn rake the ceiling. The first few drones go down easy, some breaking apart in midair, others detonating. Rook keeps us moving toward the elevated platform and the exit. A new fireteam appears in the door, spots the targets, and joins with our Marines in taking out the hostiles. Whoever's piloting these pixies must sense our escape is imminent because they're sending the units in droves. The pixies are also pushing their way free in new places, catching more than one Marine off guard.

Ibrahim shouts an expletive as a drone dodges her fire. When she finally hits it, the explosion envelopes her head and chest. It's nothing her armor can't handle, apparently, because she steps away unscathed. But I can't imagine what the blast would have done to an unprotected person.

"Don't slow down," Geller admonishes us as Kit and I fall behind with Sam. My back is aching, my thighs are burning, and I'm ready for this to be over. I spot a drone sliding along our left side, so I raise my free arm and squeeze the HG-11's trigger several times. The pistol barely bucks, and the MAW projectiles ping against metalwork in the warehouse. I'm not sure I hit the thing, but it's not tracking us anymore.

I reorient on the platform again. "Just a little bit further," I say for Sam and Kit as much as for myself.

Rook covers Evelyn as she ascends a steel staircase, followed quickly by Brown and Johnson, and then us. We're not halfway up when a lucky pixie weaves between incoming fire streams, shoots through a gap in the railing, and manages to bore into Brown's calf. I'm about to try swatting it away when the device goes nova.

The light blinds me. I'm also free falling. Backward. I reach to grab something but find only air. My ass hits a wall. No, the ground. Air knocked out of me. Head cracked. I gasp, look around. Get only blurry shapes. Focus returns, ears ringing, and my face is hot as hell. I taste blood. Then I shout for Evelyn.

"Jericho," she calls back.

I look up high. She's atop the landing, surrounded by armor. Good. Johnson is on the stairs. And Brown… Brown is missing half his leg. And screaming.

Someone's blocking my view. A Marine. Yelling my name. He grabs my chest and hauls me up.

"I said, can you walk?"

I nod. "Yeah, I… I can walk."

Somehow I'm still holding Rook's HG-11. I look down for Sam. Another Marine is hoisting her over his shoulder. Kit, too, is being helped up by Ibrahim, I think. Hard to… yeah, hard to tell. I'm… damn, I'm covered in blood. But pretty sure it's not mine.

"Move, move, move," someone shouts.

I'm charging up the stairs and see two Marines grab Brown. A thick stream of red trails from his thigh, coating the stairs and dripping between the grates. He's still shouting in agony too. God, help him. MAW fire peppers the warehouse as drones continue to punch their way through air vents, ducts, and access shafts. But more Marines have pushed into the room as well, covering our exit. The moment my eye even catches a blinking red LED, the pixie goes down, either in pieces or in flames.

I clear the top level, get drawn toward an open door, and then find myself in broad daylight, shielding my eyes from the sun. At the same time, my V-cog reboots and connects to the grid. Notifications flood my peripherals. I mute them, choosing instead to focus on Evelyn and Rook who are crossing the rooftop toward a military transport of some kind. The only apparent weak spot in the ship's angular taupe-colored hull is an aft ramp. Marines guard the cargo bay while a turret mounted atop the vehicle sweeps back and forth across the sky. The closer I get, the more I feel the heat pouring off the bird's fusion engines.

I feel like we're in the clear when someone shouts, "Contact," and more weapons start shooting. A quick glance over my shoulder reveals a dense cloud of flying objects that my brain mistakenly designates as a flock of starlings. But birds don't have blinking red LEDs.

Evelyn accepts a new amrod from Rook and swaps it out with her spent mag. "How many of these damn things do they have?"

My thoughts exactly.

Despite the fact that magnetic acceleration weapons don't emit nearly as much sound as conventional guns, put enough of them on a rooftop shooting at explosive drones and you have yourself a veritable New Year's Day celebration. Streams of automatic fire with tracer rounds weave through the air, forcing the pixies to scatter. But seconds later, the drones shoot in from our flanks—all of them dashing for one target.

Evelyn.

I lift my pistol and start shooting into the nearest

swarm, making sure I check the background. Last thing I want to do is hit someone. But I'm doubtful my fire is doing much of anything. That, and my amrod is just about… yup, empty.

Explosions erupt on either side of our line as we race toward the transport, now just twenty meters away. Looks like we're running through a fire tunnel, getting showered with exploding metal parts.

"Thumper going hot," someone calls out from up ahead. Sounds like Rook. I don't know what a thumper is, but I hope it helps.

All at once, a sphere of blue energy pops from the transport, surges through me, and sweeps through the drone clouds. My V-cog goes completely dead, and my nose smells burnt ozone. What little hair I have on the back of my arms is standing straight up. I whirl around and watch the airborne LEDs blink, and all the drones drop like rocks.

"Keep moving," Rooks yells back, waving us forward from the open ramp. "Come on!"

Evelyn makes it up the ramp first, followed by Director Johnson, and then Brown slung over a Marine's shoulder. Sam, likewise, gets carried in, then Kit and I run up, tailed by an ever-constricting semi-circle of Marines, weapons up. The last man gets tapped on the shoulder and turns up the ramp while someone pounds the close button. At the same time, the transport powers up and blows all the drone debris off the roof.

I reach for a strap of webbing to steady myself and then look around for Evelyn. She's being pushed back by medics treating Brown.

"I need to make sure he's gonna be okay," she protests.

"We're taking care of him, ma'am," says a medic. "Please, take your seat."

I move to Evelyn's side and pull her gently toward the bench lining the hull. "Come on."

She blinks at me, face scratched and bleeding from dozens of small cuts, and then lowers herself into an empty seat amidst the Marines. I sit beside her and start helping her buckle in, but she rips a belt out of my hands. "Fuck!" She sits there for a moment, looking across the bay at Brown, and then clicks her buckles together.

Rook walks over and takes a knee. To Evelyn, he asks, "You okay?"

"What do you think?" She hands his pistol back.

"I think you're probably sick of getting airlifted from rooftops. Mind if the medics take a look at you?"

"I can wait for the hospital."

Rook turns to me. "You hit?"

"All good."

"Copy. I'm gonna check in with Command and then the pilots. I'll be back in a moment."

Evelyn and I both nod our thanks, and then she returns to staring at Brown and Sam, both on stretchers.

"She was right," Evelyn says. "Sam. Said somebody was gonna get hurt. Said we should..." She rubs her forehead with hand. "Stars, it... it doesn't matter now anyway. The project—"

"Will move forward," I interject.

"What?"

"You'll see."

"But the Tantum, they... they—"

I take her hand, then relax against the backrest and close my eyes. "Sometimes, when the enemy over-reaches, it's the only push your cause needs."

"But I didn't even make it to the proposal section before they…" She lets out a long sigh. "It all just… feels like a bad dream, ya know?"

"One that you're still kicking ass in. Thanks, for back there. The drone in the stairwell."

She smiles. "You were too slow." But her look fades.

"Hey. We're gonna get through this, Evelyn. One step at a time. And you're getting your Infinita Gate."

"You sound so sure."

"I am."

"How?"

"'Cause I'm gonna build it for you. *We're* going to build for you. You'll see."

Evelyn doesn't answer with words, just squeezes my hand and sits back. Then someone else takes my other hand.

"I love us," Kit says.

I yank my arm back, but Kit tries taking my hand twice more. "Dude. No."

"But I thought we were——"

Evelyn leans across my legs and takes Kit's hand. "I got you."

He gives me a stupid grin. "See?"

PART 2

17

NIGEL

Two Weeks Later
Wednesday, October 22, 2251

Nigel

HE WAS NOT ALLOWED to step outside his home. Not so much as a stroll through the garden or even a sniff of the late autumn air. And yet house arrest had its perks. Nigel never had so much time with his son and daughter before, nor had he seen his wife as often since the NUE mandated he stay put. *Blessings in disguise*, he'd remarked on more than one occasion, particularly after a game night at the dining room table or a family movie. There, in those moments, the suspended Secretary General got a glimpse into the life he could have had were it not for his career with the Solum Terram and the resistance from well-funded and highly motivated spacers. Not to mention the headache that was the Tantum Terrae.

But Sir Nigel Sallsworth was far from inactive in his sequestration. To think otherwise would have been a tremendous underestimation of his resourcefulness.

It had been two weeks since the attacks of Tuesday, October 8th, and already the events had taken on a life of their own. Individually, assaults against private and government entities were certainly newsworthy, to say the least. Thousands had been slain on Earth, the moon, Mars, Ceres, and Ganymede; only the legacy habs and their extreme vigilance following *Astraea* fared slightly better. Collectively, however, the attacks were spoken of under a unified title, one comparable to other significant moments in world history, a point on the human timeline that would be taught to school children for generations to come. Good press or bad, Nigel hated that *October the Eighth* valorized the Tantum Terrae attacks. But he likewise reveled in the opportunities it afforded him. And, if he was wise—truly cunning and ruthless in his dealings—he might just come out on top. The first President of Earth.

"Good morning, Walter," he said behind his oversized desk in V-cog. The room was an exact copy of the home office he sat in now. Oak bookshelves filled with first editions of everything from Emerson, Mac-Donald, and Dostoevsky to Bentley Hart, Holtzneimer, and Matismato. A Persian rug, leather armchairs, and Tiffany lamps that had survived the Great Migration trimmed out the space. "What do you have for me?"

Walter, never to be seen out of his three-piece suit, virtually or in the real, offered Nigel a folio and then took a seat in one of the leather chairs. "Another four percent loss in membership is the biggest public headline."

"Middle class?"

"And lowest. Reasons cited are—"

"A lack of action on our part. I can read it well enough."

"Of course, sir. It's just that with you here, it feels as though the Solum Terram has been…"

"Well? Go on."

"Anemic, might be the best word."

"And the worst?"

"Undone, sir."

"Are they all such bloodthirsty scoundrels?"

"Well, Neon's decisiveness has a certain attraction to it."

Nigel raised an eyebrow at Walter. "You sound intrigued?"

"I'm afraid it's more serious than that."

"Oh?"

"I resigned from the Solum Terram this morning and have purchased a sidearm at the local dispensary."

Nigel tried to keep a straight face. "As well as a tattoo on your ass, I suppose?"

"No. That was already there, sir."

"How avant-garde of you."

"I am quite the rebel, some say."

Nigel browsed the stats on the front page once again. "So they're attracted by action, are they? I wonder how they'll respond to being duped."

"Favorably, one might presume."

"Mmmm. Is the file complete?"

"It is, sir. Ready to air."

"Leak it."

Walter nodded and made a note. There was a

sparkle in his eye, Nigel thought. But it passed. "In your absence, the Space Council has also allocated more funds to—"

"I already know. Let's move on." Nigel flipped to the second page of the brief. It was an update on Tré Matthews's progress. "What's this?"

"Something codenamed *Gaia's Blood*," Walter replied. "He believes it's a new neuronano technology capable of killing from within V-cog."

Nigel looked at his chief of staff as if the man had gone mad. "That was supposed to be impossible."

"So was impersonating multiple people and sending *Astraea* Station to a watery grave off the coast of Old Florida."

"Point taken. But we're talking about something far more advanced than that."

"Indeed we are, sir. But Matthews's intelligence checks out, at least initially. He's risked a great deal to secure it."

"How far along?"

"He believes they've started human trials."

"Christ. I want Lotus on this."

"I'll forward Matthews's intelligence files to them." Walter pauses. "Sir, if I may?"

"Speak."

"Do you think Lotus can crack it?"

Nigel felt his imagination take over. The idea of being able to kill anyone from anywhere through V-cog was... unspeakable. Nay, terrifying. The entire premise of quantum encrypted biological firewalls made physically harming users through the grid impossible. But someone with this kind of power would be...

"Unstoppable."

"Pardon me?"

Nigel snapped out of his daydream. "Yes. Yes, I do. And I want the full writeup as soon as Lotus and Matthews have it. Even if it's just preliminary."

"Of course."

Nigel flipped to page three and scanned the public favorability reports. Despite being under house arrest while the NUE investigation into the veracity of Neon's videos continued, trust in the Secretary General's leadership was growing. "These polls indicate that the caste core already disbelieves the footage Neon aired. They think all this a plot to unseat me."

"Indeed, sir. Progress through reason, not violence, as you've always said."

"If only they knew." Nigel continued to browse the data. "The message is finding a foothold."

"Despite the caste hemorrhaging?"

"I think we've seen the worst. We can increase the re-caste fees as well. But do it slowly. So no one notices."

"Very good."

Nigel stopped at a text block at the bottom from his PR team. It was the summary poll statement, which he read aloud to Walter. "The large majority of Solum Terram politicast constituents believe a leader who champions change within peaceful systems of governance is more desirable than one who seeks political power through fear and violence."

"Just as you said a moment ago."

"Mmm." Nigel took courage in the findings, albeit small. He knew the whims of the mob could change on the wind. *It is a fickle thing, dear Caesar.* But this certainly boded well for him. If only he could address his politicast himself. That might stem the barrage that continued to come from Neon and the Tantum Terrae.

Walter squinted at Nigel and curled one side of his thin lips.

"What are you thinking, old man?"

"The pleasure you'll find on page four, sir."

Nigel flipped to the last page, read the lead line, and looked up Walter in surprise. "Is this legitimate?"

"The Security Council has deemed the evidence against you 'less than credible.' So while you must remain here until it clears the courts, you are at least able to make recommendations to the General Council and—"

"Address the public."

"Indeed, sir," Walter said with a pleased smile. "Indeed."

18

EVELYN

"To us," I proclaim as loudly as my *slightly* inebriated self can muster. I can still read the bathroom placards, and so far the bartender hasn't kicked me out. It's a good night.

"No, no, no," Jericho says, pulling my arm as if to undo my toast. Some tequila spills on my wrist. "To *Parallax One* and the bench jockeys who believe it's a worthwhile cause."

"For now," Eddie Carr says with a pint in his hands. "Until someone here decides to fuck it ten ways to Christmas."

"Oh, shut up, Eddie. What does that even mean, anyway?" Nairobi asks with a hand on her hip.

To Jericho, I mumble, "That one's a real peach."

"You have no idea." He gives a slight raise of his glass to his PA, a woman named Alice Ortega. Must be an inside joke.

Alice smiles back and then addresses the group, "Here's to not screwing the gate ten ways to Christmas!"

This gets echoed by the whole team while our

drinks clink over the round table. Then everyone takes a sip and sits back.

"Hey," Kit says. "*Burp*. It's like Knights of the Round Table, only we're Knight's Knights," he adds, thumbing me. "Get it? *Hu-uh-hu-uh*."

"Would somebody please cut him off?" Jericho asks.

"No way," Sebastián counters with a hand on Kit's shoulder. "I like this guy a bit tipsy."

"I ain't tipsy," Kit says louder than necessary as he stands up and points a finger toward Sebastián. "You're the one who… no, wait. Who said that?" Kit gets a confused look on his face and points his finger from one person to the next, squinting as he goes. When he reaches Alice, he stops and gets a big dumb grin on his face. "Hey, Alice. How *you* doing?"

"Lightweight little fucker," Eddie chimes in.

Kit spins on him. "You're an angry man, Mr. Carr. A big, hairy, stinky angry man. And you could probably use some therapy too. Talking about your mom and how you—"

"Annnd that's about enough of that." Jericho stands and helps Kit sit down.

Meanwhile, everyone seems to be laughing except Eddie. "Wanker," he says and then takes a drink.

"Which reminds me," Kit speaks up again. "What is a wanker anyway?"

This gets a few more laughs, and we all settle back and enjoy each other's company. Which is nice. Because that means we survived. Chalk one more up to beating statistical improbabilities.

Despite the heinous attack on the press conference two weeks ago, as well as terrorist acts against hundreds of other sites across the system, our team has plenty of cause for celebration. I suppose that's what hope is after all: glimpses of opportunity amidst tragedy. The chance to rise above that which seeks to pull you down.

Shit. Maybe I *have* had too much tequila. Freaking poet over here. Eh, don't quit your day job, Evelyn.

First came the news that Lemuel was going to make it. The Marine medics had saved him from bleeding out, which is a miracle—and I don't even believe in those. The way he was losing fluids? No way he was gonna make it. Then again, my PhD isn't in medicine, so what do I know? He's still recovering, and from what I've been told, is a serious candidate for limb regen. That is, if he can endure the downtime needed for the process. He'll hate not going into the office, but that's what V-cog's for.

Our transport flew us to Nor Def, the NUE Military Installation at Espoo, while the rest of my and Jericho's team members were evacuated to Vantaa University Hospital. Fortunately, no one else on our team was seriously injured, nor were any of the press or science community. The assault, it seemed, was meant for me…

Something Sam helped prevent.

Two Weeks Prior

"How did you know?" I ask Sam in the hospital bed beside mine. I'm sitting up, but she's still on her back, fighting the sedatives. When she gives me a puzzled look, I ask more clearly. "How did you know that drone was coming for me?"

"Instinct," she says groggily. Her lips stretch tight,

eyes squeezed shut in pain. Then her face relaxes. "I heard a sound that didn't fit. Like an instrument out of tune in the orchestra. Everyone was yelling their questions at you. But there it was. Weird part is, my brain ignored the discrepancy for a second. Just as fast, another part…" She squints in pain again. "Sorry. I… Another part of me just… couldn't let it go. Then everything clicked. A pixie-free press conference? But I hear a drone? It meant one thing." She rolls her head to look at me. "Someone was gonna take you out."

A pregnant pause spans between us. How am I supposed to respond to someone who saved my life so dramatically? "Thank you" just seems too trite.

"Crazy part is," she continues. "I remember thinking, 'What if I'm wrong?' Here I am, leaping at you during a system-wide press conference. God, can you imagine the field day the verb would have with those headlines?" She tries to hold off a tide of laughter, but the effort sends another wave of pain down her spine. "Anyway, I wish I had been wrong."

"And I'm glad you guessed right." I rise from my bed, cross the gap between us, and take her hand. "Thank you for taking the chance, Sam. Thank you for saving my life."

"Eh, I owed you for Jack."

"Jack?"

"Stamos."

I snap my fingers. "Right. Tried forgetting that bastard had a first name."

"Yeah. So we even?"

"Next one buys tequila."

⁙

The Present

Our main reason for drinking tonight goes beyond the NUE Security Council's recent measures giving the military more broad-reaching power in pursuing the Tatum Terrae. Granted, keeping the faction from committing more *Canongate reprisals*, as they're being called, is certainly something to celebrate. Instead, we're toasting the Space Council's latest special session vote that, truthfully, took me by surprise. *NUESSA Receives Support of* Parallax One *Buildout* read the headline on the verb.

Following our interrupted press conference and the subsequent publication of our summary findings, the vote could have gone either way. And, frankly, I had my doubts. We flew up here to Kyrö Distillery in Isokyrö to put some distance between us and Helsinki just in case we needed to lament the results. But despite Solum Terram opposition, the Sentia Aux and Viatoribus minorities were able to leverage optimism about humanity's "unprecedented opportunity" from my presentation and secure funding.

"I still can't believe it," Sam says, staring into her glass. "Feels like a dream."

"Believe it, sister," Kit says with a hand on her arm.

She gives him a sideways look.

"Sorry."

"While I'm grateful that my flight engineer here thinks so highly of me"—Jericho smiles at Kit, referring back to the *Knight's Knights* comment, I assume—"this whole thing is really Evelyn's show. None of us would be here and now working together were it not for her."

"And my team," I add.

"To Evelyn's Knights," Kit exclaims before Jericho can finish his toast.

He laughs. "To Evelyn's Knights."

We all toast again and drink up, but I pause for a moment to raise my glass in Rook's direction. He's standing by the door, overseeing the Marines assigned to my ongoing military security detail. I'm guessing he'd rather be somewhere in the solar system right now, probably in action against a TT cell, but if so, he hasn't made a peep about it. Instead, he says protecting me is his top priority, and that he's glad he had a say in the matter with his superiors. "You're a humanitarian treasure now," he said to me on the flight up here. "Get used to having bodyguards."

"Baariomistaja?" I call to the barkeeper. "Another round for my friends, please."

The woman behind the counter nods. Meanwhile, I pour a glass of water from the untouched pitcher and walk it over to Rook. "Sorry it's not the good stuff."

"In space, water is always the good stuff." He takes the glass and offers me a smile in return. "Thanks."

"Pleasure."

He and I watch our growing group of mutual coworkers-turning-friends as they get the tall nav officer, Torrence Vanderburg, to read one article or another related to our cause for celebration.

"Are you happy?" Rook asks after a few moments.

"That's a little sentimental for you to ask, isn't it?"

"Legitimate question."

I tap the end of my nose once in serious though somewhat hazy consideration. "Yes. I'm happy. Everyone's worked hard and been through a lot, and here we are, ready for the next chapter. What more could I ask for? Why do you ask?"

He shrugs. "Most of what we see, what Marines see, is the worst of humanity. Tip of the spear stuff. And all this"—he gestures at the frivolity—"isn't exactly part of our normal job description. So it makes you wonder if people down here are ever really benefiting from the calls we have to make out there. And since you're an asset I care about more than most, I thought I'd ask."

"An asset, huh?"

He winces. "Sorry. Job hazard."

"Well, it's better than being a liability." Which reminds me. "Hey, any leads on a possible suspect or launch location for the pixies that hit us? Someone commanding them from a media trailer maybe?"

"Negative," Rook replies. "Nothing conclusive anyway. Footage of the press conference showed no signs of human deployment. Seems all the drones came in via outside air ducts. As for a command site, everything the authorities suspected checked out, so they're guessing a remote site with long range grid connection."

"Understood." I pat his arm once. "Thanks, Rook. For everything."

"Pleasure," he says, echoing my one-word reply from earlier and adding a wink.

I make my way back to our table and hear Jericho ask, "And read that last paragraph again, would ya, Magellan?"

The nav officer stands, raises his pint, and reads from V-cog. "The initial vote, which passed 204 to 171, was ratified late this evening by the Chamber of Presidents, securing the program's first-round funding request and the consolidation of corresponding NUESSA and SESI teams. All of this—"

The table's cheering cuts him off.

Magellan starts again, waving for everyone to calm down. "Several critics of the motion cite the absence of Secretary General Sir Nigel Sallsworth—"

"Boo," several people yell, thumbs pointed down.

"Wanker," Kit shouts, then looks to Eddie. "Did I use it right?"

"Nailed it, mate." He clinks his glass to Kit's.

"—as a leading cause for the vote's pro-space direction. In the meantime, government officials close to the program say plans are already being made to ensure the measures cannot be reversed when the Solum Terram is expected to appeal. The pro-space hopes lie with Preservationist arguments for the recently passed Conversation of Promised Resources bill. Experts expect buildout of the Infinita Gate *Parallax One* to begin in the first quarter of 2252."

"Then somebody better tell those NUESSA engineers to get their asses moving and start designing," Nairobi says. Everyone raises their glasses and downs the rest of whatever they're drinking. A moment later, two servers appear with the new round and start passing glasses around.

On a slightly more serious note, I ask Jericho, "Have you given any thought to where you wanna set up shop, Mr. Project Director?"

"All depends on where the Head of R&D wants to be." He winks at me.

"You two really are *dadorable*," Kit says reaching for his next beverage.

Jericho intercepts the drink. "Nope. Water for him, please?"

The server nods.

"Awwwwwww. Come on, Cap! That was my favorite."

"Water is gonna be your new favorite."

"*Fine.*"

To Jericho's question, I respond, "Seems to me that a lot of what we need is already at Lagrange Point 2. And it's far enough away to keep anxious rock squatters from accusing us of being too close to Earth."

He looks over the rim of his pint at me. "I had the same idea. I even thought we might be able to repurpose *Telemine* Station for the energy module hab."

"They're not even halfway through construction, I thought."

"Exactly."

"Don't you love it when a plan comes together?" Sebastián says.

"You got a name for the aliens yet, Priest?" Magellan asks.

Seb gives the table a wry smile. "I did have an idea or two."

"Well?" Eddie asks. "You just gonna sit there with it?"

"I was thinking the Makriá, at least until they self-disclose. It's the word for far away in Greek."

"I like it," Nairobi says. "To the Makriá."

"Hear hear," everyone else calls, and we drink—one of us, water.

"Cheer up, Kit," I say. "Pretty soon, you might be having a Mai Tai with an alien."

"As long as *Glaricho* over there isn't around to cut me off."

"Because he… glares at you?"

"*Klich.* Nailed it."

"I'll make sure to keep him busy."

"I also knew I liked you best."

"Flattered."

Jericho eyes Kit over his beer. "Traitor."

I'm enjoying the banter and, perhaps, a little too much añejo, when Eddie Carr snaps his fingers and then points to one of the bar's holo displays. The live cricket match is interrupted by a special verbcast. "Oi. Look who it is."

"Sallsworth," Sam says. "I thought he—"

"Shhh," Eddie adds.

"To those of Earth, Mars Nation, the Belt Lands, and Jupiter Moons, greetings from the Sallsworth family home in northern Finland. It's with a heavy heart that I address you tonight, having heard of the NUE's vote to fund *Parallax One* despite the secretary general's profound absence. What's more are the shameful measures taken against me to keep me from speaking to you, my constituency; from participating in this critical vote; and from defending myself against the fantastical accusations devised to undermine my reputation. As ever, I am a man who abides by the rule of law, but I am loathsome of any unjust measure to keep me or any other respected leader from carrying out their duties in service to humanity. As such, I am grateful for this communications stay of my quarantine, and I will endeavor to use it well."

"Why is there a knot in my stomach?" Natalie puts her drink down and casts me a worried look.

Nigel continues. "It should be clear to everyone by now exactly what the Tantum Terrae's intentions are: to commit widespread acts of violence against defenseless targets in an attempt to advance an anti-space agenda. Like you, I am sickened by Magnolia Birdwhistle's deplorable leadership and publicly denounce the Tantum's terrorist activities.

"Conversely, I commend those in the NUE general session who resisted the temptation to pass measures that would further jeopardize the safety of our solar system. The proposed Infinita Gate project not only wastes resources, both human and material, on a frivolous pursuit of—"

"It's not frivolous," Alice interjects, slamming her pint glass down.

"Shhh," Eddie replies.

"—but it also places humanity in the gravest of dangers should the gate become operational. On this point, I agree with the Tantum Terrae. The future of our species is my highest concern. But this is where the Solum Terram distinguishes itself from the treacheries of the Tantum and negligence of the Viatoribus and Sentia Aux. We will use measures of peace to secure our future—the mechanisms of law and order. Not violence. And not melodrama dressed in the attire of scientific discovery. Our success as a species—nay, our survival, lies here and now, on Earth. We win by increasing carbon scrubbing efforts, developing new heat-resistant agriculture, and expanding our sub-surface oceanscapes. We use the resources at our disposal for good, not evil, and to feed temperance, not infatuation. Austerity, if we are to extend ourselves into a bright and lasting future, is what we must embrace, together. As one."

"This is such bullshit." I down my shot. "He's just… so damn slick, it's disgusting." Despite my animosity, however, the verb feed goes on.

"As you and I both know, Ms. Birdwhistle, also known to us all as Neon, brought forth accusations against me, claiming that I was culpable in the death of the late Madame Secretary General Mary Allbrook. She went so far as to fabricate video of me. All lies. All acts by her to attempt to destabilize our system of government.

"I have in my hand two items that I think are of great import for your consideration as the criminal courts prepare to see my case. The first is an authenticated drive from Lotus Labs, LLC provided to me and the NUE Security Council, verifying that the files Neon broadcast to the entire system were in fact complete fabrications. They have no basis in reality whatsoever. I am afraid that we the public have been hoodwinked, once again, by a malevolent, manipulative cultural agent of evil. Neon's desire to create a conspiracy theory around my alleged involvement in an act I would never conceive of, let alone participate in, proves just what lengths she is willing to go to in order that her ultimate agenda of bringing down the government might succeed.

"The good news for us is that we are dealing with a desperate leader hiding behind what will inevitably be a failed attempt at coercion. The second item I hold is more damning than the first: authenticated proof of Tantum Terrae involvement in the slaying of Mary Allbrook. Please note the following footage may be unsettling to many viewers."

"Bloody hell," Eddie says as he stands and folds his arms.

Nigel disappears, replaced by hidden camera footage of Neon dressed as a cook entering a bustling commercial-grade kitchen. Her bright lipstick is unmistakable. But in case anyone was wondering, a superimposed ident window appears, tethered to Neon's head by a streamer, showing her V-rec number and bio credentials. Any suspicion of fabrication, at least as far as the general public is concerned, is not so subtly put to rest by the NUE Department of Virtual Technology Standards quantum seal in the window's lower left corner. If this footage is fake, and I have every reason to believe it is, then I don't even want to know how much coin Sallsworth spent to pay off the DVTS inspectors.

Apparently in the lower kitchen of the NUE's headquarters building in Oslo, thanks to the geo stamp watermarked along the top, Neon pushes a beverage cart to a back-of-house bar stocked with a wide variety of libations. She pulls a whiskey bottle from a shelf, unstops the neck, and pours the amber liquid into a highball glass. Amidst the sounds of constant swearing and clanking dishware normal in any kitchen, a mic picks out the sound of a woman reciting a poem:

"Tuesday soldiers of October the eighth, stood shoulder to shoulder at the Canongate." With the bottle replaced, Neon turns her back to conceal the cart, which is when a new camera angle appears from overhead, one that the conspirator doesn't seem to know about.

"When twelve came the toll from Blue Crow's bell, still shoulder to shoulder, they marched into hell."

Neon withdraws a small cylinder, no more than three centimeters long, from between her breasts. Nigel would add that touch, wouldn't he. The pig. Then she pours the supposed poison—nanotoxin if I had to guess —into the glass.

"Where's the cart for Allbrook?" someone shouts off camera. A new feed shows a middle-aged man in a steward's uniform. "Allbrook? I need the cart for Allbrook!"

"Jesus and the saints! Relax already," Neon replies, sounding like any number of tired, cranky, overworked, and underpaid chefs in the bowels of a government facility. "It's right here. Don't get yourself so worked up, love."

"Who are you?"

"Danny's replacement, brought over from DPES. Why do you care?"

"I don't." The man snatches the cart from her and almost spills the whiskey when Neon catches it.

"Careful, love. Wouldn't want you getting axed over two fingers of whiskey."

"Gimme that!"

The footage segues to a series of hall and elevator shots as the unwitting steward works his way toward what we all know will be Allbrook's Oslo-based office. Finally, when the man arrives at his destination, we see an image of the late Secretary General wave the steward into her office where he moves the glass from the cart to her desk complete with an NUE embossed cocktail napkin. Mary sips the drink and settles back in her chair. But Nigel's face doesn't return.

Instead, a new scene appears, one time stamped nearly thirty minutes later, in which Allbrook is addressing a press conference—a setting the entire system now knows by heart, as well as what comes next. Only this time, we get a second view. Neon is clearly seen in the back of the room. And she's holding a small device in her hands. At first, it looks like a standard verbcaster recording device. But closer inspection, provided by the auto-zoom in the recording, shows the hardware to be some sort of remote. Neon uses the index finger of her other hand to depress a software button on the screen, at which point

Allbrook, seen in a side-by-side window, trembles once.

It looks like a chill.

She steadies herself on the lectern.

And then continues her speech. "Therefore, the politicast leaders together with the presidents of the Southlands, Norasia, and the American Heights wish to extend an invitation to leaders of the Tantum Terrae to appear before the General Council in the hopes of negotiating terms of peace." She pauses, blinking a half dozen times. Something's clearly the matter.

Neon slowly moves her finger up her device's screen as if sliding a fader.

"This action is of particular importance in light of… Excuse me." Mary removes a handkerchief and wipes her forehead, then takes a sip of water. "Of particular importance in light of last month's disaster with *Astraea* Station."

Allbrook continues to speak, and Neon keeps pushing the fader higher. Soon, the secretary general is gripping the lectern with both hands, and a look of panic flashes in her eyes. The world has seen this before. But viewing Neon's equally intense look of satisfaction adds a new level of horror.

"Madame Allbrook?" the woman's PA asks from beside her. "Are you alright?"

She ignores him and then looks back into the cloud of pixies. "We must react to… *dammit*. We've got to *respond* responsibly in these trying times. And leadership that's… that's suited for…"

"Madame Allbrook?" her PA says again.

The woman falters, clutches her chest, and mumbles something unintelligible. Then Mary grabs her head and collapses at the same time that Neon releases the software fader. Paramedics charge into the room, responding to the now well-known V-cog medical alert. But what was not well known was Neon sliding out behind them, covered by the crowd's dismay.

Nigel reappears live. "These are the actual events as they happened. Which means that Neon is no more a champion of Earth-centric policy then she is a law-abiding citizen. She will stop at nothing to secure her endgame, which is not the preservation of the planet's resources or the restoration of our beloved ecosystem, but simply that of power. Power to infiltrate and eventually overthrow the system of governance that has brought stability to humanity in the wake of the Hundred Year Migration.

"Because of her means of violence, I wholeheartedly endorse the NUE's recent decision to increase the use of military force in order to rout out and ultimately end the Tantum Terrae. She will be judged by her own words: There will be no quarter given, no mercy bestowed.

"With the firm expectation that I will soon be exonerated by the high courts, it is my responsibility to set the tone for where we must head as a global and even system-wide civilization, especially in light of the recent vote to move forward with this business of building a gate to allegedly connect us with alien benefactors.

"First, let me be clear that any measures meant to send labor, materials, or finances toward this juvenile project of—"

"Juvenile?" Natalie exclaims. "Why that little—"

"Shut it," Eddie snaps.

"—is a betrayal of human dignity. Not only does the effort undermine the immediate needs of those resources elsewhere, but, should the outlandish proposition ever net true alien contact, it jeopardizes our entire species. Therefore, not only the Solum Terram, but in time, I believe *all* of the Nations of United Earth will work together to stop this misguided and shortsighted endeavor.

"As such, I am drafting calls to sanction all NUESSA and SESI efforts to construct this gate. Likewise, I condemn all presidents who ratified the measures granting said agencies power and means to pursue what can only be described as a treasonous act against the wellbeing of humanity and a threat to system-wide democracy. And while I readily admit the provocative nature of the joint NUESSA/SESI presentation, as well as the seeming legitimacy that the Tantum's violence provides, it saddens me that, in my absence, those pledged to uphold the basic tenets of life and dignity would so easily be swayed by a modern myth. As Saint Paul once wrote to the young Timothy in times past, 'Reject profane and old wives' fables, and exercise yourself toward godliness.' What is this if not a time when a fable has reared its ugly head? And who are we if we do not pledge ourselves to the pursuit of godliness as it pertains to the reasonable preservation of our survival? Thank you."

The surrealness of the moment is punctuated by the sudden return of the cricket match. We all just sit here, unmoving, until Eddie Carr says, "Would someone please tell me what in the flying fuck I just saw?"

19

JERICHO

Four Weeks Later
Friday, November 21, 2251

Jericho

"How we looking, Knight?" Evelyn says to me as she enters our engineering lab on *Telemine* Station for the first time.

"Well look who's shuttle finally decided to show up," I say with a wink.

"We can't all have the fastest ship in the system."

"It's just on loan. How was your tour?"

She rubs her face once. "Remind me to have someone else do all the press conferences next time we make a big alien discovery, would you?"

"Deal."

"Got some good news for me?"

"Funny you should ask."

"You're done?"

"Come see for yourself."

The cargo hold we turned into our workspace is pretty much one of the coolest digs I've ever had. Kit started calling it the Dream Zone, and it stuck. Holo projectors are spread in front of all four walls, sometimes stacked two deep to overlap multilayered schematics. And not just any projectors, but the Samsung UH3D Super Max that shoot all the way to the ceiling, ten meters up, so that at any given time, it looks as though we're actually inside of whatever room on the station we're trying to amend. Since *Telemine* is NUESSA's latest and greatest uncompleted legacy hab, it has all the bells and whistles a technophile could want, including the best in micro quantum computing, seamless V-cog integration, and IDA—intuitive design aid. It means we can work four times as fast and with ten times fewer headaches.

The warehouse also has some fun creature comforts for use when we've spun up the station to 1g, as we have now; that will change as soon as we start the construction phase. In addition to the curved slide that Nairobi added to the second story, Magellan hung bivouacs and hammocks from the arms of the mega-excipions, ones used for hull buildout. Since all scheduled construction on *Telemine* halted when we got the go-ahead to repurpose the station for *Parallax One*, the "Big Fergies," as Kit refers to them, were returned to their berths and put on standby until we gave them new buildout plans. What better way to use a sleeping thirty-tonne, fifty-million-coin construction robot than to string fabric furniture from its outstretched limbs, right? Even though we all have nice crew quarters on station, most of us have taken to burning the midnight oil here in the Dream

Zone, especially as we've gotten closer to completing the plans.

Selling the Space Council on *Telemine* was fairly easy. Despite Sallsworth's calls for sanctions against us, none of them have passed, but we all know it's only a matter of time before they do. Not wanting to wave a red cape in the face of an already pissed off bull, NUESSA made the call to have us repurpose a partially built station at my suggestion. *Telemine* is eight kilometers of superstructure, hull plating, electromagnetic shielding, life support, sickbay, atomic printers, food printers, moisture reclamators, and the all-important fusion reactor—in our case, the latest Wendelstein 7-X with high-efficiency neoclassical transport dampeners. The thing is a work of art.

Since the station's entire central section is open to the deep black from one end, it means we have nothing to deconstruct in order to mount Evelyn's emissions nodes. Meanwhile, section one holds the transportation hub, fusion generator, and all essential systems. All we need to do is design and build out housing for the nodes, along with power runs, emergency systems, and enough structural reinforcement to handle whatever force loads these three devices are gonna dish out. Something tells me it's gonna be a lot. Or maybe that's just my engineer brain talking. Better safe than sorry.

I nod to Kit, who quickly swipes a few windows away in his workstation and then pulls up our main station view and primary cross section. Then he throws them to our main display stretching across the widest wall that's bordered by two Big Fergies. Their hulkish black and yellow bodies look sick on either side of the display.

"You're having fun, aren't you," she says.

"What gave you that impression?" I cast her a mischievous grin and then point to the view of the outer hull. My hands, mapped by the projection system's spatial sensors, rotate the stubby half-built cylinder in the display until the open end is facing us. Then I grab emissions node E1 and expand it.

"After thoroughly examining what we're calling the base plate, we've pretty much deduced that the Makriá designated this as the preferred attachment area for our indigenous support structure. Not only has their design exceeded all of our stress tests, but it seems to have clear conduit channels for power and sensor equipment. We're taking notes too; the atomic structure of this plate is probably the strongest molecular bonding we've ever seen. We're learning a lot."

"Sounds like our department," she says and then points to a new spine that runs the length of the station from E1 to the endcap at section one. "What's this?"

"Each node gets a support spine that runs the length of the station. Likewise, we'll repurpose some of the trussing to create connectors between the spines laterally across the station."

"So, you're building a tubular triangle around *Telemine*'s existing cylinder to account for whatever forces it might generate?"

"Exactly. In design, the only thing better than a circle or a triangle—"

"Is a circle inside a triangle," she completes.

"You sure you're not an engineer?"

"I'm sure." She pushes some loose strands of hair behind her ear. "Then we're powering it with the 7-X?"

"Yup. Similar to the unknown force variables, none of us know exactly how much each node will draw, right? So not only do we need to take into account any unexpected energy consumption, but also things like variable oscillation, node favoritism, and feedback loops. It'll require extra power conditioners from Earth and a hell of a lotta new code, but nothing we can't handle."

"Sounds complicated."

"Just a lot of math and making sure we have the load distribution matrix right. Again, trying to be ready for anything."

"As long as you're happy."

I turn around and yell to the team spread throughout the bay, "Whadda we think, gang? We happy?"

All thirty-eight engineers on my team cheer back at me, some giving whistles, others content to clap their hands a few times before returning to their work. Nairobi, Eddie, Magellan, and Kit have joined me and Evelyn in front of the main display, along with three new faces from Evelyn's SESI division. I introduce myself to Cheng Liu, a digital and electrical engineer, and Igor Kalashnik, an astrobiologist and their resident medical doctor. The last person I recognize but can't quite place. "Jericho Fox," I say again.

"Bhavna Mishra, communications," she replies in her faint Indian accent.

I squint at the woman, feeling a sudden wave of apprehension. Damn. "*The* Dr. Mishra? Suspected of concealing and aiding Tantum activities on *Astraea*?"

"That's me." She's smiling, which is a good sign, if not a bit unnerving.

Evelyn intervenes. "After Bhavna was acquitted of all charges, I decided to fill a gap in our roster left by Adrian Wallace."

I look from Evelyn to Mishra. "Tell me, Dr. Mishra. Do you like *Vesper Siege IV*?"

"I confess I'm at a loss." She looks at Evelyn. "Should I know what that is?"

"Nope," I reply first. "Glad to have you on board."

"I feel like doing real happy dance to be here," Dr. Kalashnik says. "Is most excitings."

"And you?" I ask Cheng. "Happy dance too?"

"I don't think anyone wants to see me dance. I'm just here to lend a hand wherever you find yourself short."

"Fair enough."

Back to me, Evelyn asks, "So how long do you need to build everything?"

"Six months," Nairobi says with her arms crossed and her head cocked sideways.

"Oi," Eddie says. "Five if we don't get held up by bureaucrats waving their cocks around for funsies in Oslo."

"Really?" Nairobi asks him.

"What?"

Evelyn interrupts them. "So this six months—"

"Five," Eddie corrects.

"Does *five* months include construction of the nodes?"

"Assuming you haven't made any changes to the Makriá's designs," I say.

"Nope. All our time has been spent running simulations on them."

"Results?"

She shrugs. "I mean, everything looks good."

"You don't sound sure."

"Well, it's just that... We don't have any precedent for this, ya know? We have predictions. Models. The math works. But since we've never actually created an Einstein-Podolsky-Rosen bridge before—we've never created a Pendellösung oscillation window this big before—we don't actually know what's going to happen. So this big open space you have here in the middle of *Telemine*?" She points at the station-wide hole between her nodes. "We're gonna wanna keep that clear in case the first thing we send in passes straight through."

"Less work for us," Nairobi says.

"And regarding your power question," Evelyn continues. "We've discovered something in the node design."

"What?" I ask.

"They seem to have built in some sort of automatic shutoff."

"Like a timer?"

"Possibly. Or it could just be a fail-safe if it doesn't find a connection on the other side."

"Like a verb call in V-cog," Kit offers. "Makes sense."

"Oi. You saying somebody has to be there to answer on the other side?" Eddie asks.

"I'm not saying much of anything right now," Evelyn replies. "All we know is that there's a descending power curve in the simulations we're running, and we can't get rid of it. At first I thought it was something we did wrong, but now we're fairly certain it's a design element built into the system itself."

"What changed your mind?" I ask.

"No matter how many times we run the simulations, we always get the exact same time."

"Of?"

"Fifteen point one three nine four minutes and change."

"Seems random."

Kit scrunches up his face. "Is that significant?"

"Not the randomness, but the precision," she replies. "My guess is that to them, this time is a round number. But to us, it's obscure. That's because where we determine a second by optical measurement of how many times a strontium atom cycles hyperfine transition, they might use a different atom, or the same and just count the cycles differently. Who knows. Either way, it's extremely precise, and therefore must be intentional."

"Fair enough," I reply.

Magellan strokes his chin and looks at Evelyn. "You still haven't found a way to direct it, have you? And no real idea where it's sending us?"

Evelyn shakes her head. "Afraid not."

"So we just… turn it on and trust the Makriá?"

She nods once at Magellan.

God, I admire her faith in these aliens. But I also get why we have to do this even if there are a lot of unanswered questions. If we don't activate the gate, it just sits there. Forever. We never find out anything beyond what we know now. And that's fine. We keep attempting to save humanity as before. Act like we never intercepted a signal. Life goes on. Until it doesn't, and our species goes extinct. Orrr… we risk activating it and find out what lies behind door number two. In my mind, we're damned if we do, damned if we don't. But I'd be lying if I said I wasn't interested in at least knowing what lies at the end of this rainbow. Faith in the Makriá? Maybe. Some. But faith in Dr. Evelyn Park? Yeah. Lots.

"Hopefully we'll get good data from our probes," she says. "And if all goes well…"

"We send in the Ferguses," Kit says in awe.

"Sure." Evelyn turns to me. "Construction then?"

"Just need to package these latest changes up, get

final approvals from NUESSA, and then we're good to go. Guessing we'll start in the next couple of days unless they flag anything."

"Or Captain Tighty Whities orders the Marines to shut us down," Eddie replies.

Evelyn looks amused. "Captain Tighty Whities?"

"One of his less offensive pet names for Sallsworth," Kit replies.

"It ain't a pet name," says Eddie. "It's what his bloomin' mum put on his birth certificate after she pulled the pole from his tiny baby ass."

Kit tilts his head. "How did it get up there while he was still in the womb?"

"Don't try to figure it out, pal," I say. "Evelyn. You up for lunch?"

"Sure. You cooking?"

I laugh. "Right this way."

⁘

Evelyn

It's good seeing Jericho again. In the real, I mean. We had a few V-cog meetings over the last month, but those were team discussions, and brief ones at that. Granted, every time our paths have crossed physically, something seemed to go boom. Not sure that's a good sign. But, like with Sam, if I were in a life or death situation, which I seem to be finding myself in more of lately, I know who I want with me.

"Swanky place," I say. "You come here often?"

He gives me a sideways glance and pushes his tray along the rails. The cafeteria is just one of hundreds in *Telemine*'s plans, but the only operational one for the time being. Another will probably open up when more engineers arrive.

Jericho opens a clear door on a cubby with a steaming container of something labeled Roast Beef Sandwich, Swiss. That's as much detail as the printer was willing to give. Mine isn't much better. Sushi, Rare. Not even salmon, tuna, or mackerel.

"It's a bit like gambling," Jericho says. "But it's all safe."

"Screw safe. I wanna know if it tastes good."

"That's why we have Beatrice." He nods to a drink station at the end of the line whose spigots have been replaced with homemade looking beer taps.

"You... got alcohol on station?"

"Eddie and Kit reprogrammed the modifier."

"Stars, kiss them."

"You're telling me."

We collect a few more side items of food and then fill up bottles of beer at Beatrice. Satisfied with our fare, we head to the seating area and find a spot away from the rest of the workers.

"So, any real news from planetside *not* on the verb?" he asks.

I open my sushi box to find a California roll, two pieces of salmon, and a pile of pickled ginger. The other boxes contain edamame, a dollop of fried rice, and a salad with ginger dressing. "The presidents are losing traction to Sallsworth."

Jericho stops just before biting into his sandwich. "That bad?"

"It's a perfect storm in his favor." I squeeze a few beans out of their salted shells and pop them in my mouth. "He's going hard after the Tantum. Has the entire military off-leash. And we all know what war does for the economy."

"And his ratings."

"Right." I eat a few more of the edamame beans and then try one of the rolls. Mouth slightly full, I add, "He's still trying hard to shut this down, but the conflict with the TT is actually helping us."

"Imagine that. Hard to fight two fronts at the same time." He takes a bite, waits until he's swallowed, and then swigs his beer. "So you're not worried about a possible shut down?"

"It could happen. Don't get me wrong. I'm more worried about supply chain issues."

"Hopefully that won't be a problem. As someone said a few weeks ago, L2 has most of what we need. It was a good idea."

"I'm not the one who thought of repurposing *Telemine* Station as the gate's foundation."

"Okay." He smiles. "So that was mine. But you brought up Lagrange Point 2, which is what got me thinking. Teamwork. Couldn't do this without you."

"Mind telling that to all my verbcaster critics?"

"Point me to 'em."

"You're sweet."

He looks down at his beer, then asks, "What about Rook?"

"What about Rook?" I parrot, failing to see where he's going with this.

"They could have stationed him on *Telemine* if they wanted."

"You're skeptical of the frigate?"

"Aren't you?"

"As long as Rook's here, it's just another ship in our orbit."

"A ship with magnetic rail cannons, point defense guns, and guided torpedoes."

"You don't actually think they'd fire on us?"

He sets his beer down. "Right now, I think anything's possible. Sure, we're officially a scientific experimental outpost. But if Sallsworth and the Solum Terram have it in their minds that *Parallax One* continues to pose some sort of danger—one we haven't ruled out, by the way—then I don't think they'd hesitate to shoot down anything they believe is part of a system-wide security threat. Do you?"

I look down at my sushi. "I just hate thinking that our own military might intervene."

"Same. Let me handle the politics."

"I can deal with the politics just fine."

"I'm sure you could. Problem is, no one else can do the *Parallax* side."

"Jericho—"

"I'm not trying to mansplain this either."

"Kinda sounds like you are."

"I'm saying this because, once again, I think you're underestimating your value." He pokes his sandwich with a finger. "At the end of the day, I build stuff, Evelyn. I build it, fly it, crash it, and repair it. That's it. That's my gig. But you? Damn. This station? This whole Infinita Gate? Shouldn't be called *Parallax One*; it should be called the *Evelyn Park*. I'm just along for the ride and happen to have the best seat in the house." He stares at me longer than feels comfortable.

"You done?"

Jericho takes another bite of his sandwich. "Yeah."

"Finally. 'Cause that was awful."

He flips me the bird and takes another sip of beer. "So what happens after fifteen minutes?"

"What?"

"You said the gate shuts down after 15.1 something something minutes. You think it reboots?"

"Your guess is as good as mine. Why?"

"Just trying to think strategically. If that's our window, and we don't know how long it takes to reopen, then a quarter hour isn't much time to work with."

"No, it's not." I find myself tapping the end of my nose. "So we'd better get our shit together."

"Now you're talking." He raises his beer and we toast.

20

NIGEL

"WILL you be home for dinner tonight? The kids are asking," Esther said.

"I need to work late," Nigel replied. "The joint session is convening early tomorrow morning, and I still have to prepare for the motion to file an injunction against NUESSA."

"I thought that you were finished on that?"

"Something came up."

"I'll have Miriam make you a plate. It'll be in the fridge."

"Love you."

"Love you too."

Nigel hated lying to his wife. He hated killing people too. But it was the cost of doing business. No one loved everything about their line of work. Hopefully, if all went well after tomorrow, Nigel wouldn't need to do any more of the parts he despised.

All things considered, he was happy to be back in his office again. The high courts had ruled in his favor, something he had pulled a lot of strings to ensure, but he had both the political and monetary capital to spend, so it was well worth the price tag. Plus, the media and the public were loving his new "come out of the corner swinging" posture toward the Tantum Terrae, the Infinita Gate program, and the Chamber of Presidents. Now, he just needed to consolidate his power and keep the pressure on. Easier said than done. "But if ruling an empire was easy, everyone would be doing it," he said to himself and sipped his single malt.

Nigel had turned the lights down in his office and checked the time. The caller was late. He was about to ping Walter when someone stepped into one of his private V-cog lobbies—an art deco styled luxury apartment in twentieth-century Midtown Manhattan.

"Tré. How nice to see you."

"And you." A silver briefcase hung from Tré Matthews's overlapping black-gloved hands. He wore a black leather jacket with yellow stripes on the shoulders and a pair of designer jeans. When he spoke, it was with a suave Janusian air that played well with his young fit body and oiled hair. "I come bearing gifts."

"Please." Nigel motioned to the gold-trimmed dining room table.

Matthews set the briefcase on it, popped the latches, and then turned the case to face Nigel.

"Is this it?"

Matthews nodded. "The vial contains the code for the cerebral cortex exploit."

Nigel reached in and removed the glass tube, then held it up to the light. He knew this was merely a V-cog render of the data, but it felt good to hold something physical in his virtual hands. "So it can be done."

"Your experts should have no trouble reproducing it in time."

"And you've seen it firsthand? In action?"

Matthews nodded once.

"And?"

"It's effective."

Nigel admired the vial again. "Tell me about it."

Matthews slowly rubbed his gloved hands together as if savoring the invitation to expound on death. "Say you're in V-cog with another person and you produce a pistol. You point at their head, squeeze the trigger, and what happens?"

Nigel felt his pulse quicken as he played Matthews's game, suspecting he knew what was coming. "The bullet passes through the target and may or may not interact with whatever's behind, depending on the host's rendering budget."

"But not with this." Matthews pointed to the vial. "With Gaia's Blood, when you strangle the neck, inject the poison, or fire the weapon, the person suffers the same ill effects in their corporal body."

"It can't be."

"It is, sir."

Nigel now held the vial as if the lightning bolts of Zeus had been handed to him in a test tube. "So much power." His eyes snapped up. "Do they suspect your theft?"

"No."

"Good. Very good. What about progress on the body manipulation aspects? This *puppetry* element?"

"They're still working on the nervous system override."

"How soon?"

"Hard to say. Half a year? It depends on how many subjects they're able to experiment on."

"We can take over the research."

Matthews didn't move.

"What is it?"

"I'm afraid the lead designer is quite talented, sir."

"I'm sure. But we have our own in-house talent." When Matthews didn't reply, Nigel asked, "Who is he?"

"*She*, sir. Gemma Birdwhistle."

Nigel took a step forward. He'd only met Gemma once when she was very young. Different father than Klaus—Jack's dad—but same fire in her eyes as Neon. "Interesting. And she's lead on the project? I imagined she was still just a child."

"Time moves on."

"Indeed. Tell me about what qualifies her."

"She holds degrees in advanced bioengineering and virtual cognizance integration. Currently an incog within the Viatoribus even though she's spent most of her time with her mother since the war began."

"She's in Baden-Württemberg then?"

Matthews nodded again.

Few knew about the Tantum Terrae's new head-quarters, and Nigel would keep it that way as long as he could. Despite his ultimate desire to kill the terrorist leader and wipe her radical movement from the face of the planet, keeping Neon alive had its advantages. At least for a time. Matthews, for example, gave Nigel intelligence that the brute strength of the military would never tease out. Sure, they could level Baden-Württemberg with orbital bombardment. But then the Solum Terram might never find out just how deep their infiltration of the politicast went. Likewise, Nigel recognized that having Neon's daughter continue her work in secret would prove far more efficient than abducting her and forcing her to work in confinement. Why end a good thing prematurely? The steady stream of intelligence was too lucrative to cut off now. He would keep the Navy's dogs at heel a little longer.

"Leave her be," Nigel said at last. "For now. But the time may come that I need you to bring her here."

"Understood." Matthews looked down and to the left. A curious behavior.

"You have more."

"There is a catch, sir."

"To what?"

"The exploit needs an activation key."

"This?" Nigel raised the vial, feeling disappointment turn to anger in a flash. "This is useless then? And you waited to tell me until now?"

"Your engineers can still reproduce the—"

"Enough." Nigel's hand squeezed the glass tube as if to break it. "I don't need a lecture on preemptive strategy."

"Of course."

"Where is this activation key?"

"The same place that Neon keeps her master list."

Nigel paused, and his anger subsided. "Her master list."

"Yes, sir. Every incog in the Tantum Terrae's network."

A shiver went up Nigel's spine. He understood now why Matthews saved the bad news about the activation key for last; tying it to something tantalizing was a smart move.

While the public war raged against weekly TT cell discoveries and the arrest or killing of operatives in the middle of terrorist acts, such an incog blacklist would raise Nigel's power to an unprecedented level. Gaia's Blood afforded him an unrivaled assassination tool, yes, but it had to remain a secret. The incog blacklist, however, could serve up a perpetual menu of public enemies, ones that conventional military action would never root out. His image as a savior and public defender would only soar with each and every unveiling. With Gaia's Blood in one hand and the incog list in the other, Sir Nigel Sallsworth would be, he thought, unstoppable.

"I need time," Matthews said when Nigel didn't move.

"How much?"

"Unknown."

"Not good enough."

The spy worked his jaw. "Four months, perhaps. Neither the list nor the activation key are easily obtained."

"You stole code for the greatest weapon known to humanity in weeks but need more time to secure a list of names and a quantum key?"

"She keeps it on her person," Matthews replied curtly. "A micro drive. Rumored to be in a rather… private place."

"The ultimate firewall."

"One might say."

Matthews's reticence became clear, and Nigel eventually nodded in understanding. Regardless of whatever device the data was stored on, Matthews would have to kill, incapacitate, or seduce Neon—none of which would be easy, and all were deadly. If Nigel wanted the list, he knew he was most likely condemning his employee to death. So he would need to incentivize the job.

"Fifteen million," Nigel said at last.

"Done or dead trying."

"Preferably not the latter."

Matthews nodded once and then vanished from the apartment.

Holding the vial up to the chandelier light once more, Nigel marveled at the cloud of swirling nanobots between his fingers. "What beautiful things we will do together," he whispered even as the sound of his words scared the dying part of his moral soul into hiding.

21

EVELYN

Three Months Later
Tuesday, February 17, 2252

Evelyn

"Is this really necessary?" I ask anyone on the verbcast crew who's willing to call off the makeup artist wreaking havoc on my face. "How does making me look like a—? *Ouch*! Dude! Watch it."

"Please hold still," the guy with the airbrush says.

"Dr. Park," says the big shot in an antique director's chair across from me. She's called Willow Shade. The woman, not the chair. Yeah. Actual name, or so I'm told. She's also having a treatment done by a makeup artist. Though I hardly think she needs any more paint on her face. The woman looks like she's had enough gene editing done to turn a finger painting into Sandro Botticelli's *Birth of Venus*. "Just relax. Max is almost done. Our pixie camera and lighting fleet works best with the contours of the human face slightly more defined than you're clearly used to. I assure you, it's completely normal."

Max backs away just long enough to raise an "I told you so" eyebrow before putting on the final touches. When at last he spins me around to face the curved holo mirror, I look like… well… okay, so maybe not that bad.

"What do you think?" Willow asks.

"It's not how I look in real life."

Max puts a hand on his hip. "Exactly. Off you go."

Willow motions for me to follow her toward a floor-to-ceiling observation window. We're on the top floor of our admin building looking north along eight sections, one kilometer each, toward the seven-kilometer-wide opening on the cylinder's far end. It's where Willow Shade and her number one rated show VerbNow wanted to start the interview.

You'll be great, Lemuel said to me. *Nothing to be afraid of. Plus, the whole system wants to hear from you, and it's important we update the world on our progress.*

Just perfect, Lem. Thanks for saying yes on my behalf. Never mind the fact that Jericho has way more experience with the press and does much better on camera than I do.

"Just be yourself," Willow says as we turn our backs to the glass and the lights come on. Her crew and drones gather closer like birds waiting for us to throw seed.

"Your name's not really *Willow Shade*, is it? I mean, come on…"

The woman glares at me and then runs her hands down her hips to smooth any wrinkles in her skin-tight, hot pink, NUESSA/SESI-embossed space suit. For the record? Neither agency would ever produce something so obnoxious.

I can't believe I agreed to this. I cast Rook, who's standing to my left in the shadows, a "please rescue me" puppy face.

"Only if bullets start flying," he says over V-cog audio.

The lights swell brighter, and I hear theme music from somewhere in the background.

"In five… four…" The producer, whose face I can't see anymore because of the blinding lights, throws the last three numbers with his fingers instead of calling them out. Small red lights on the drones turn on at the number one. For the briefest moment, I want to run. To shove Willow aside and dive for cover. To tell everyone to get down, envisioning the whole room detonating.

"Hey, Shaders! It's your girl, Willow, and you're watching the number one latest and greatest episode in the galaxy, *VerbNow*! Zoom zoom! *Bizzzzzow*!"

I hate everything about her.

"Right now, I'm skipping in one g onboard the hottest station in the system. That's right, you know it as *Telemine*, the repurposed legacy hab serving the powerhouse convertor for—"

"Energy module habitat," I correct her.

"—for the brand new Infinita Gate known as *Parallax One*, baby."

"It's called the energy module habitat," I repeat.

"Woah, look at this! *Zoom zoom, bizzzow*. It's none other than SESI's very own Dr. Evelyn Park, head of research and development, here to give us the very first and super-zoomy exclusive tour of the station. And already we're getting taken to school by her! Ouch. Doc

Evy, it's totally fruff-fruff to meet you and be here on this historic station."

The pixies pivot to me. "Uh, hi. Yeah. Nice… having you and all your shade people."

"Shaders. But we ain't haters! Heeeey."

"Oh… kay."

"Check it. I'm told that *Parallax One* is now in its ninth week of construction and past the halfway point. Tell us what we're looking at here, Doc Evy."

"It's Dr. Park. And we're at section one facing north. Behind us is the interior of the station's main cylinder. But unlike other legacy habs you've seen, the inside has been gutted."

"Kinda like how I made Jamie Mann feel when I left him on stage at HydraFest all alone?" Willow makes a pouty face at the cameras.

"No idea. Anyway, we've been able to repurpose the deck plating as exterior shielding along with trussing to support the emissions nodes and their spines."

"Sounds kinky. Tell me, Doc Evy—"

"Park."

"—how have you managed to make so so so much progress in such little time?"

"Several reasons, the first being our incredible interdisciplinary team of scientists and engineers from—"

"And we'll meet them, I know, but what are those?" She points to one of the mega excipions currently straddling some trussing on the ground floor and laser-cutting a deck plate. The human-shaped bot stands eleven meters tall and four wide.

"That's what we call a Big Fergy—"

"Oooo! *Zoom zoom.*"

"—and it's one of forty industrial construction excipions on station."

"I wouldn't mind those hands working me over, am I right, Shaders?"

"It would pulverize you."

"*Bizzzowwww!*"

"No, I mean, it would actually kill you, Willow."

"And who doesn't need a little of that once in a while, am I right? Let's head down to engineering, everybody. And I'm gonna list off just some of the milestones this star-studded team has hit in record time as we go…"

Someone pings me in V-cog. "Evelyn?"

"Lemuel."

"You're doing great. Just try to… you know, relax a little."

"I am relaxed."

"Then inform your face."

I exhale. "I want to kill her, Lem. Couldn't you have sent up Bill Conrad? Or Sylvia Towers?"

"We need her viewership, Evelyn. This is all about capturing the imaginations of the next generation."

"If this is what the next generation is watching, we're screwed."

He lets out a sigh. "Just at least try to sell this a little more. For me? It'll be over before you know it."

"Famous last words." I lead Willow and her crew into one of the freight elevators and punch the button for the hangar bay. Miss Makeup is rattling off items on the talking points list we provided and making up her own responses as she goes. I don't even understand her version of English anymore. Stars, I want this to end. "Hey, Lem?"

"Yeah?"

"How's the leg?"

"Uh, the prosthesis is almost done integrating. Doctors say—"

"Not that one. The other one. Because the next time I see you, I might shoot it to match."

He gives me the classic "disapproving but knows he can't correct me" dad look. "Remember to inform your face. We need this."

"Fine."

Lem blinks out of my lobby just as the elevator doors part on the Dream Zone. Jericho and Kit made sure to activate all the holo screens and even added accent lights to backlight the parked excipions. Some of the crew have apparently decided to lounge in the suspended furniture, a few elevated to ten meters. Looks like a frat party, not a science expedition.

"*Doc Evy-Par-Par,*" Willow exclaims. "You've been holding out on us! Somebody certainly knows how to get her *fooshie* on. This is how we science, Shaders!"

Without warning, the lights start blinking and a loud rhythm track fills the warehouse with thumping dance music. Willow surges into the space with her entourage in tow. She spreads her arms and starts turning to the music while the pixies circle her. I'm sure that if we hadn't spun the station up for her, she'd be floating back and forth, gyrating to the beat in zero-g. Stars, help us all.

"Hey," Jericho shouts from beside me.

I almost punch him in the face. "You startled me!"

"Sorry. Like it?"

"Don't you think this is—?"

"Over the top? One hundred percent annoying as hell."

"But...?"

"The directors said we needed to appeal to the next

generation. Sometimes you gotta do things for the cause."

"You're enjoying this, aren't you."

"A little." He tips his chin toward the center of the room. "But not nearly as much as what's about to happen."

I spot Kit climbing down a Big Fergy's leg ladder and then approaching Willow from behind. I have some sort of strange protective instinct kick in, like I want to dive in front of Kit to save him from an out of control grid car.

Jericho's hand grabs my arm. "Watch."

Kit brings down the volume on a handheld remote and then just stands there with his mouth wide open.

"Bizow, who do we have here?" Willow asks, looking Kit up and down.

He doesn't respond. Doesn't even blink.

"Might we have a starstruck Shader perhaps?" She waves a hand in front of his face. "Ground control to Major Tom?"

This snaps Kit out of his daze. "Ho-ly *biscuits*! Is it… it's really you? Like, *actually* you?"

"In the real," Willow says, smiling at the drones.

"Moses and marmalade, I can't believe it!"

"Shaders, I want you to meet the one and only Leslie Christopher Smith, assistant project engineer here on—"

"You know my name?"

"Yes. —here on *Telemine* Station who's responsible for—"

"Holy biscuits! Willow Shade knows my name. *My* name."

"Uh, of course. And now the entire galaxy does. Say hi, Leslie."

"Actually, it's physically impossible for the *whole* galaxy to know my name. Even with light speed communications, it would take 50,000 years for your transmission to—"

"Oh, you're a cute one, alright." She touches the end of his nose.

"Uhhhhhhhhh—call me Kit?"

"Is... that a question?"

"Uh, no. I mean, you can call me whatever you want, but most people say me Kit."

"*Say me Kit?*"

"Yup." He swings his arms back and forth while rocking on his heels. Then to the nearest pixie, he adds, "Hey, Shaders! Fooshie Crib for life!" and throws some sort of two-handed gang sign, I think.

Jericho nudges me with an elbow and then passes me a verb window through V-cog handoff. "Check it out." A social data map lists what's trending at this exact moment on the verb, and it's updating faster than I can read it. The phrase "say me Kit" is skyrocketing on the keyword graph, while verified celebrities with the most liked updates are contending for top spots. The highest three entries read:

QueenKittyKat: OMG hes 2 adrbs #saymekit

Danko2222: bras got nerd game. we all be jelly

SophiaFlowerLove: no fair! i claim him first #holybiscuits

"Un-fricking-believable," I whisper to Jericho.

"Looks like we have ourselves a bona fide superstar now."

"Universe, help us all."

The upside to Kit's newfound celebrity is that he occupies Willow's attention for the next twenty minutes, which is 1,200 seconds that I don't have to. Not even *the* Jericho Fox has been brought out for interviewing yet. Either Willow genuinely likes Kit or she's getting real time feedback from her producers about how he's trending. We all know which it is. And it's her loss too, because Kit is a billion times better than all the *Shade Blossoms,* or whatever, I'm sure she hangs with.

Willow and Kit, followed by me, Jericho, Rook, and the flock of producers, exit the lateral lift that's arrived at the station's north end and walk toward the observation room that looks out at E3. The wraparound glass not only provides spectators a great view of the emissions node and its construction but also a breathtaking panorama of the starscape that extends to infinity.

"Honestly, Willow, I think you need to talk to Dr. Park again for this part," Kit says.

"But I'm sure you know the answers too, Kitticus."

He chortles. "I mean, thanks, but… she's the expert. Really." Kit starts waving me over, and I watch Willow's shoulders sag.

"Duty calls," Jericho says softly.

"When's your turn?"

"Kit covered all my talking points."

"You're dead to me."

"Have fun."

I trade places with Kit in front of the wraparound window. He gives me a high five as he passes, and I whisper to Willow, "Don't look so disappointed. Your ratings might slip."

Without skipping a beat, she looks at the pixies and says, "Doc Evy, this part looks super salacious. Zazzy! Can you describe what's happening here?"

"Salacious? Really?"

"All those creepy crawlies probing and zapping the emissions hump? It's got fooshie written all over it."

"Okay, first of all, there's nothing sexual happening here. Secondly, it's an *emissions node*, which houses the high output lasers responsible for generating the Einstein-Podolsky-Rosen bridge—"

"Sounds yummy."

"I swear to Sagan, if you—"

"What she means to say," Jericho exclaims from the side and walks into frame. "Is that the big humps will help create the portal that connects our world to the Makriá's."

"Satellites and Shaders! It's the one and only Jericho Fox!"

The producers start clapping, encouraging me to do the same. I want to crawl in a hole and die. But I give Jericho a few golf claps anyway.

"Tell us more, please?"

"Sure, the robots there—"

"The creepy crawlies."

"Yeah. They're actually state of the art atomic printers that move back and forth across the surface, creating Dr. Park's emissions nodes one layer at a time."

She puts a hand on his arm and squeezes. "It seems like a very time consuming and drawn out process."

"It is, even more so than what we're doing to

Telemine. The team responsible for processing the Makriá's transmission into data that our printers can use has spent tens of thousands of work hours ensuring that every single layer is built to the exact specifications that the plans call for."

"I think there are three big questions on everyone's minds right now. First, how much more time before we get to meet aliens?"

"Well, we're not sure who or what we're going to meet yet, but we're currently on track to activate and send probes through the gate in another eight weeks."

"*Fooshie.* Secondly, will the aliens be green?"

I'm gonna throat punch her. "You'll have to ask our resident evolutionary biologist, Dr. Sebastián Fernández Parra, that one, I'm afraid."

"Lastly, are you available for dinner in zero g tonight?" She bites her lower lip, turns, and starts twerking against a stunned Jericho. "Me likey. Zoom, zoom, *bizzow-ow-ow!*"

Just then, a bright blue flash fills the observation hall and sends a shock down my arms and legs. All lights, cameras, and drones go dead—the latter clattering to the floor.

"What the fuck just happened?" she shouts to her crew.

"We're off-line," her producer replies.

Willow whirls on me and shoves a finger in my face. "You did this, didn't you, you little bitch."

I flex my fingers and then make fists. "You wanna try that again?"

"And you…" She scowls at Kit, then Jericho. "You're all just… just… *Argggggh!* I can't stand you people. We're leaving."

"'Bout damn time," Jericho says.

As Willow's team scrambles to pack their equipment, I look from Kit to Jericho. "You cut the power?"

"Nope."

Kit shakes his head too.

Then all three of us turn to Rook. The Space Marine shrugs, holds up a single dodecahedron EMP in his palm, and says, "Sorry. Thumb slipped."

22

JERICHO

Two Months Later
April, 2252

Jericho

"Anybody up for champagne?" Kit asks from the drinks table in *Telemine* Station's observation deck. The room is filled with banquet table and decorated with handmade signs, taped-up streamers, and colorful tooling. And why not? It's celebration day. The marriage of *Telemine* Station Legacy Habitat with the Makriá's three emissions nodes to form what we now call *Parallax One* is complete at last.

The entire team of scientists and engineers is gathered just below level one's command bridge looking north through the room's panoramic window. We all get an unobstructed view up *Telemine* Station's cylindrical interior to the legacy hab's open end eight kilometers away. Normally, another twenty levels would be added to *Telemine*, followed by an endcap to close off the interior and fill it with atmo. But the unfinished end served our proposes perfectly. Barely visible at this distance are the three emissions nodes perched on the rim's circumference, facing away from us. It's there, in the empty space between those three points, that the portal should appear, at least in theory.

As soon as Kit is done helping the wait staff distribute the champagne glasses, I tap the side of mine with a spoon. "If I could have everyone's attention please?" Talk across the observation deck falls away, and all heads turn to me. "Thank you for being here… not that you really had a choice." This gets a small amount of laughter. "We've all worked hard for this day. Long days and nights, overcoming production and material delays, family needs at home, and certainly pressure from those who didn't want to see *Parallax One* built at all—"

"The wankers," Eddie shouts. This gets more laughs than my quip.

"Now now. We each have our opinions." I motion for everyone to relax. "But what can't be argued is that we've accomplished something incredible together, a feat that I believe people will talk about for generations to come. Speaking of talking, you'd better be ready to chat with *the* Mr. Bill Conrad when he shows up here in a few days for the pre-activation verbcast." This gets some celebratory *woots* and catcalls. Having one of the world's more revered verbcasters on-station is a big deal for the project. "And when he comes, I'm sure he'll discover the same thing I have: that you're one of the finest crews that I… Well, that you're… all amazing, and the way that you've pulled together is… What I mean to say is that I'm proud of you. But, uh… since I'm not much for speech giving—"

"You're doing great," Nairobi calls out.

"We love you too, Cap," adds Kit.

"—I'm gonna defer to Dr. Evelyn Park in the hopes that she can rescue me."

Evelyn steps forward. "Captain Jericho Fox, everybody!"

People pound on the tables or clap one-handed against their forearms.

"Like Jericho said, I wish to congratulate you all on the amazing completion of humanity's first but not last Infinita Gate," Evelyn says. "It's a remarkable thing when people of different disciplines, different though certainly similar politicasts, come together to work on something significant. How much more when the subject of their collaborative efforts poses to benefit and alter the course of human history like nothing before."

Evelyn takes a moment to survey the room. "I want you to look around for a second. Look at the person on your right and left. These faces, these people, are world changers. You, me, us—together, we are responsible for building a bridge to another world. Another species. And we believe it will usher in new ways of thinking, of being, and serve as a catalyst to inspire solutions that could save our species from the coming extinction. So, I know it sounds melodramatic… but I don't care. You, friends and colleagues, *you* have changed the course of history with your sacrifice. So please lift your glasses with me… A toast! To the scientists and engineers of Infinita Gate *Parallax One*."

"Hear hear," the room responds and then starts clinking glasses.

Evelyn and I toast, drink, and then stare at each

other for a second. When the look starts to feel awkward, I say, "Nice speech."

"Better than yours?"

"I mean, I wouldn't go that far." Something catches my eye. "Hey, check it out."

Evelyn turns and looks to where I'm pointing. Fergus One is holding a champagne glass in his robotic hand and toasting Kit.

"They make a cute couple," Evelyn says.

"Takes one to know one," I reply. "I mean… That's not what I meant to say."

She raises an eyebrow at me. "What did you mean then?"

"That they're… Well, that you were… Christ." I put the glass to my lips and down the rest of my champagne.

"Looks like you're all out, Mr. Fox. Let me get you some more." She takes my glass and walks away before I can attempt to explain my way out of the awkward comment again. Classy. Me? Not so much.

Fifteen minutes later, dinner is served, but I excuse myself from beside Evelyn when three successive pings come in from my father over V-cog.

"Everything, okay?" Evelyn asks at my sudden standing.

"Yeah, I just… it's my dad."

"Probably calling to congratulate you."

I squint at her. "Or not."

"PLEASE DON'T DO THIS," Dad asks from beside me. We're on my balcony overlooking the Mediterranean Sea. Fishing boats bob in the blue waters along the

Amalfi Coast while the cliff surges up behind my back toward a cloudless sky. Dad's got a beer in one hand, as do I, and I sense he's looking right at me, but I keep my eyes on the horizon.

"You know what I'm gonna say."

"Do I?"

"Not only is this my job—"

"Which you can walk away from at any time."

"—it's what I *want* to do."

He lowers his head and then runs a hand over his deep black scalp. I used to want to shave my head to be like him. Times change. After a few seconds, he looks up. "Aren't you worried about what might happen?"

"Care to be any more specific?"

"Pandora's Box, son."

I take a pull on my beer. "Not sure if you've noticed, but we already opened one a long time ago."

"And we're suffering the consequences, yes. But in time, we'll find—"

"Solutions? Answers to three-hundred-year-old problems that are only getting worse?"

"We're making progress."

"Too little too late. You and I both know it."

He coughs a few times. "Excuse me." Wipes his mouth with the back of his hand.

"You okay?"

"Heartburn."

I squint. It's unlike him to keep virtual mimetic mirroring on. "Anyway. We've been over this ad nauseam. What else do you wanna talk about?"

"What if they come through with an attack force?"

"Jesus, Dad."

"What? People are asking those kinds of questions."

"And we've done a hundred interviews stating that that's statistically and logically highly improbable."

"But what if they harvest our natural resources?"

"Jesus. Then we die." I set my beer on the railing. "What do you expect?"

"Then how can you be for this?"

"*Because we don't know how much time we have before everyone on Earth dies.* And just because you won't be around for it doesn't mean we shouldn't be preparing something for the next generation to escape it."

"That's low."

"But that's how it looks."

"You sound like your mother, ever the fatalist."

"I'm not being fatalistic. Just being real. And she would understand that."

He sips his beer and seems to let the point go.

"All I'm saying is that, for me, the potential pros far outweigh the cons. If you're right, we die either way. But if Evelyn is right, then we might make discoveries that shift our chances of survival for the better."

He doesn't push back on this. Just takes a sip of his beer and then… Coughs it up.

"What's going on with you?" I pat his back out of instinct even though I know it does nothing in the real.

"Thanks. Sorry."

"No need to apologize."

"I called for two reasons."

"In addition to asking me to call off the activation?"

"Well, that's half of the first. Sallsworth's sending the Navy to L2."

"That's just rumors. There hasn't been anything—"

"On the verb yet? That's because it's not public."

"Then it's hearsay."

He leans his forearms on the railing and studies the horizon.

"You know something."

Dad looks sideways at me with a subtle grin. "Nigel selected me to be on his space management committee."

"What?"

"Said that my expertise from all my years with the Viatoribus would—"

"He's using you to get to me, Dad!"

"I beg your pardon."

"Don't you see? You're not…" *Ah shit.*

"Not what, Jericho? Not good enough? Not legitimate enough to be on an NUE committee?"

"That's not what I said."

"You didn't have to." He works his jaw against my implied insult. "Listen, I'm just trying to do you a favor, is all, so that when they arrive, you can help your team to stay calm."

"They already have a frigate up here."

"The *Bellerophon*? That's just Evelyn's and now your security detail. They've called a fleet carrier, three battleships, and five heavy cruisers. More are on the way."

"Jesus. What are they planning to do? Start another war? They've already got one."

Dad jerks his head to the side.

"The war's over?"

"The last of the TT's locations are all on Earth, which frees up the Space Navy. Should be wrapped up by the end of the month."

My bottle misses my mouth. This is news to me. The verb has the Tantum Terrae going toe-to-toe with NUE forces at the top of every hourly broadcast it seems, and there's been no indication that the government is anywhere close to ending the conflict. Then again, that would be just like Sir Nigel Sallsworth to grandstand the whole thing by swooping in with a sudden victory.

"What are the ships tasked with?" I ask after a few moments of silence. "They can't stop the activation. That's been ratified."

"I'm just saying be careful. Nigel knows he hasn't been able to slow your team down through political channels, no small thanks to the off worlders."

"They're members of the NUE too."

"Shouldn't be."

"What's your second reason for being here?"

He straightens to full height, drinks the last of his beer, and looks up at the gulls circling overhead. "You built this with your first paychecks, didn't you."

"Yeah. Why?"

"I thought it was a waste of coin."

"I remember. Made that loud and clear. And *no*, I haven't spent Sallsworth's cold storage coin yet; it's my fallback if my job goes belly up again. Thanks for checking. Anything else you want to critique?"

He squints and then looks away. "I was wrong about this being a waste. It's really beautiful."

"Okay. Who are you and what have you done with my father?"

He doesn't answer.

"Hey. You okay?"

"No. I'm dying, son."

Mouth suddenly goes dry. I wanna say something, but words elude me. So I swallow what little saliva I have and finally get out, "How long?"

"Two, maybe three weeks."

"Jesus. What is it?"

"Pancreatic cancer, stage four. Highly aggressive."

"I can pay for gene editing, dad. Just go see——"

"They've tried, son. My body's attacking the script faster than they can inject it." The skin on his knuckles turns white as he squeezes the railing. "It's moved into my lungs. I know you have your activation in a week, but I need…"

"What? Name it."

"I need you to come home."

"WHAT DO you mean you're leaving to go see your dad?" Evelyn asks me in the terminal outside the *Kogarashi*'s entry corridor. She steadies herself in zero-g by holding a handrail. "We're eight days away from——"

"He's dying, Evelyn."

Her face goes flat. "Stars. I didn't… I'm sorry."

"It's okay."

"Cancer?"

"Inoperable. Probably from all his time in space and hauling uranium."

"Old gene tech couldn't keep up."

"Yeah."

She rubs the back of her neck. "How long do they think he has?"

"Well, let's just say I wouldn't be leaving you if they thought he had a lot."

"You need me to talk to Johnson?"

"Already cleared. Didn't think twice about it. Even said Kit and I could take the *Koga*. Fastest ship in the world means the fastest return once he… once I… I mean——"

She takes my wrist and pulls me into a zero-g hug.

Only I'm not sure what to do with my arms. But the warmth of her body, the nearness of it, gives a measure of comfort that I... well, I haven't felt in a long time. So I hug her back.

I let go after a moment. Not because I want to, but because I need to. "Gotta get going. Kit's already on board."

"Right. Of course. But... trip duration?"

Someone seems like she's stalling. "Five hours back to LEO. Sixteen and a half to the surface on Ascender 1, and then a six-hour flight to Helsikni. I'll call you when I arrive."

She nods, thinking about something.

"What is it?"

"We can postpone the activation. We'll just need to—"

"No. No way. It goes forward no matter what."

"Jericho. I'm not doing this without you."

"Hell yes you are." There's enough defiance in her eyes that I know she's not going to accept this without a fight. "Listen, stuff comes up. We're human. But history isn't going to wait for me or even you. This is happening. And if someone needs to be remembered for it, if anyone needs to see this with their own eyes, it's you."

"I appreciate that. Really, I do. But there's no reason that we can't delay the—"

"The Navy is on the way."

She blinks at me. "What?"

"A fleet carrier, battleships... they're coming."

"*To do what?*"

"I don't know. It's one of the reasons my father reached out to me... along with the cancer update. I think Sallsworth's getting antsy, and since he can't stop us with sanctions..."

"He's going to try to stop us with force."

"Yup."

"Shit." Something new registers in her eyes. "And you're just gonna leave me with all this?"

"You scared of a little conflict, Dr. Park?"

"I'll give you some conflict," she says, holding a fist up.

"There it is. Just give 'em that, okay? I'll be back to help… soon."

"Hey, Jericho? Be careful. The system's a crazy place right now."

I nod once and then do something I didn't plan on: lean in and kiss her on the cheek. Just… came over me. "Thanks. You take care of yourself."

SEEING dad in a hospital bed was a shock. That was three days ago. But now watching him lose consciousness is excruciating.

"I'm going to ping you in V-cog, okay? Dad?"

His eyes are cloudy. Unfocused.

"Dad? Accept the request, okay?"

Eyelids close. No response.

I tried setting this up earlier, but his neurologist wouldn't allow it due to the strain it put on his brain and weakened body. But as the end was becoming more inevitable, some of the medical safeguards were getting lifted.

Come on, answer, Dad.

I realize that we haven't seen each other in person for almost two years. All our exchanges have been in V-cog. But as I squeeze his hand, willing him to answer my call, I regret not having physical contact with him sooner. All arguments get fuzzy. Who's right. Who's wrong. And who the hell started it anyway? Those all fall by the wayside.

"Dad?" I say out loud. He can't host a virtual lobby, so I am. All he needs to do is accept. "Dad, if you can hear me, I'm waiting. I'm here on the balcony. The Med looks beautiful. And I got a beer for you."

In V-cog, I'm holding the beer out for him. Cap popped and all. It's evening, and the lights are just starting to turn on along the water. I'm about to step out of the render when my father appears.

"Dad!"

"Hi, son. That for me?"

I offer him the bottle. "Sure is. You, uh… had me worried there for a second."

He accepts the beer and just stares at it for a moment. "Felt like I was walking through a dark room to get here. Bumping into furniture, stubbing my toes. Almost… lost my way, ya know?"

That image sends a chill up my spine. Is he really this close to death? I mean, his vitals aren't great, but… But who really knows how the human spirit works anyway, right?

"Well, I'm glad you made it. Have a seat."

"Thanks." We toast with the bottles and sit on my cheap lawn furniture. The air is warm, and an oceanic freighter crawls along the horizon on its way to a port in Cyprus, if memory serves.

"What are they saying now? I can't seem to… remember anything. And don't sugarcoat for me. I wanna know the truth."

I let out a long sigh. "Your body's shutting down, they say. Could be a few days. But…"

"But more like a few hours?"

I nod. Can't bring myself to say it. "I wasn't sure you'd even have virtual awareness left."

"Well, beer tastes good. So that's something, right?"

"Yeah. Sure is."

We sit watching the sky grow darker. Stars will come out any second now.

"Thanks for coming to see me, son. I, uh… wasn't sure if you would."

"Jesus, of course I would. You know… over these last few years we…"

"Don't. It's okay. I know."

"No, I wanna say something. Please."

"Alright."

"I know that we haven't been on great terms. You have your thoughts on the politics and the economy, and I have mine. And saying we should both just give those up isn't fair. It would mean the issues aren't legitimate, and it would discredit our own senses of logic. So I'm not going there. I think you're a stubborn son of a bitch, and so am I."

"Hear hear," he says and offers up his bottle to clink.

"But even with all of our differences, old and new, you're still my father. A man whose whole life I respect, and for my whole life I've wanted to be like. So, here's to you, Dad."

He lays a hand on his chest, and I spot something sparkle in his eye. "Thank you. That means more than you know. My turn?"

"Sure."

"I, uh… I want you to know how proud I am of you."

"You tell me all the time."

"Yeah, but… this time… it's different. You've got balls, kid."

I laugh. "How's that?"

"Sometimes, when I see you on the verb, when they're doing one of those stories about your progress up there? Or even back when you maidened the *Perseverant* and the *Kogarashi*? I think to myself, 'Damn. That man has taken on the whole solar system. And you know what? He's winning. And he's my son. No planet bigger, no star brighter than he is.'"

I look down at my beer. 'Cause if I don't, I might lose it right now.

"I appreciate what you've said about not wanting to mix our views into all this. Maybe we shouldn't. But at the risk of sounding like a dying man who's reneging his beliefs on his death bed, I want you to know something."

I feel his hand in the real squeeze mine.

"What's that, Dad?"

"You're doing good, son."

"Thanks. What do you mean?"

"Your work. Your passion. It's… well… it's good. Listen, I'm a stubborn old son of a bitch who gets stuck in my ways. But you? Well, you've got different ideas, new ideas, and..... they're good, son. I'm sorry that I stood in your way."

"Dad, you—"

"*You* chase this one, Jericho. As far and fast as you can go. You know"—his face tightens in pain for a second—"I realized something after watching you bounce back from the *Perseverant* disaster. You have what it takes. If anyone can find a way to rescue humanity… you will. You'll find it."

I swallow the lump in my throat and wipe a tear aside. "I love you, Dad."

"I haven't heard that one in a long time."

"Yeah. Sorry about that."

"It's okay." He sets his beer down. "Now, if you wouldn't mind, I'm feeling pretty tired. Just need to… take a nap for a little bit. Then then we can resume this, okay? Another beer?"

"Yeah. I'd like that." I wipe another tear away. "Oh, and if you need anything, I'll tell the nurses they can take care of you here in V-cog. Just let them know if you're in pain."

"They've already been taking good care of me in here."

"Alright."

He squeezes my hand one more time in the real and now on the balcony. "I loved you the day I met you as much as the day I need to leave you."

"Same. Get some rest."

"Will do."

With that, my father blinks out of my suite. And, somehow, I think he just blinked out of my life.

"Mr. Fox?" a voice says in the doorway.

I leave V-cog and blink twice at the imposing male figure. He's dressed in a dark business suit that looks like the seams are gonna give out from the muscles beneath. I know this man. Bald head, dark complexion, the look of a killer. He saved my life once, and then, when he was given revised orders to take it, Rook let the man jump off the lift in *Astraea*.

"Afumba," I say, body tensing with the words. The

windows are shatter-resistant, and there's no way I can overpower him. Ten to one he shoots me before I have the chance to call for help. The most I can do is send out a distress call over V-cog if he hasn't jammed my link. "Here to finish the job?"

"No, Mr. Fox." He enters and closes the door behind him. In his deep, Old African accent, he adds, "On the contrary, I am here to get you out alive."

"Alive?" I glance at the door. "My life's in danger?"

"Indeed."

"From?"

"Me."

"I… don't understand. You just said—"

"That I am not following orders."

"Seems to be a recurring theme with you."

He nods once. "I am grateful that Master Sergeant Farooq spared my life. His instincts were correct: I had no intention of harming you once I received the kill order."

"But you still went back to your employer."

"For reasons I have no time to elaborate on now, yes. Suffice to say, it seems that we are, once again, revisiting the same situation as before. Only this time I do not need a Space Marine to dissuade me."

"So you did kinda wanna kill me."

"Mr. Fox, please. We have very little time." He peers through the glass pane into the hall and looks both ways.

"I thought you said *you* were the assassin."

"Only the first of many."

"I can't leave my father."

"He is already gone, Mr. Fox. I am sorry."

"But it's—"

"Only a matter of time now. What is done is done.

Let the dead bury the dead, as they say. Come, this way."

I give my dad one more look, kiss the top of his head, and say, "Love you. Bye, dad."

THE CORRIDOR LOOKS NORMAL; nurses, a few doctors, and some visiting family members walking the halls. But then again, I'm not seeing this through the eyes of a professional killer. Afumba, on the other hand, shields me with his body and then turns me right.

"Utility closet. Inside."

The doors slide apart, and I step between rows of metal shelving filled with medical supplies.

Afumba waits outside and calls, "Medical gown. Put one on."

"Stuff isn't exactly in alphabetical order in here, Fumby."

He laughs once. "Use your eyes, Mr. Fox."

"*Use my eyes! That's* what I was missing." Sarcasm aside, I spot a plastic tote labeled Gowns. I also grab a cap, face mask, and a pair of those little booties to complete the ensemble.

"Hurry, Mr. Fox."

"You can't rush beauty. Almost done." I finally get myself put together and then step back into the hall. Afumba's body seems coiled like a python ready to strike. "If you don't relax, my disguise is worthless, ya know."

He gives me a nod, then points toward a stairwell. "This way. Do not make any calls in V-cog. It will give away your location. And from this point forward, do not answer any calls from people who you do not recognize.

This includes speaking to strangers who appear in your public lobby."

"There something I should know about here? New hack?"

"Of the worst kind, Mr. Fox. Please. Focus."

We walk as briskly as we can without raising too much suspicion. Eh, who am I kidding. My gown isn't able to fully cover my leather flight jacket and jeans, while Afumba here sticks out like a wolf in a chicken coup.

We only make it halfway to the stairwell when the first gel-propellent gunshot rings out. Debris from the wall showers the left side of my head, and I duck below a nurse's station counter. Afumba pulls a MAW pistol from his jacket and returns fire. "Get to the stairs!"

I keep crouched and move as fast as I can as more bullets pepper the walls above me. Afumba covers my exit, running backward while draining his amrod on the enemy. When I finally make it to the stairwell doors, I look to see who's shooting: a woman dressed as a grandmother who's way too limber to be above sixty, and a doctor in a white medical coat.

Afumba hits the woman square in the chest. Her feet come up, and her back slams against the floor. The doctor has taken cover inside a patient's room, but the next time he steps out to shoot, Afumba clips his shoulder. The assassin spins, which gives my bodyguard all the target he needs to end the man's life.

"Down," Afumba yells and charges the door.

I take the steps three at a time, speeding around each landing, and then descending the next set of stairs with a bound. New bullets ping off the railings, throwing out sparks and making my ears ring.

"Don't stop," Afumba says. "Basement."

"Got it."

A new sound, that of an alarm klaxon, adds to the auditory mess. More footfalls echo overhead, and even more rounds glance off the open stairwell's surfaces. The good news is that no one is coming from below. I'm no military expert or professional security operative, but I consider the enemy's absence a good sign. The force sent to take me out is small. Plus, I have to assume that Afumba knows his people's strategy and is countering it, therefore this way is the best way.

As we pass successive floors, I keep expecting someone with a gun to pop out of each new door. So far, the only person who does is a nurse on the third level. But he takes one look at Afumba and backs away.

"Service door," my bodyguard yells once we reach the lowest level. A placard on one of three options marks the appropriate door to our left. The panels separate as I approach, and a long corridor extends to a T some twenty meters away. Cardboard boxes, trash bins, a utility cart, and several broken pieces of hardware line the walls and create a wandering footpath.

Afumba orders the doors closed behind him and then enters a code on the adjacent control panel. An LED ring around the surface shifts from green to red. "That won't hold them for long."

"You're an expert on hospital basement security too?" I ask as we start running for the junction.

"Standard Smith and Proctor security lock. I reprogrammed it before coming to get you."

"Somebody thought ahead."

"Keep moving. Right at the intersection."

"Got it."

I slow and take a precautionary peek around the next corner. No movement. There's no klaxon down here, but strobing red lights do make it a little disorienting to walk. Design oversight. At least they're all streaming in line toward the exit.

After another twenty seconds of weaving through the hospital's morgue of lost and found artifacts, we emerge into a parking garage, but one meant for maintenance employees. Several grid vans, two large service trucks, and some ambulances that look like they've seen better days take up most of the available parking spots.

"That one there." Afumba points his weapon toward a grid van with the words Mobile Medical Supplies on the side. "Get in."

I run down the passenger side and open the front door.

"No," Afumba yells. "In the back. They're looking for two people."

"Right." I press the release for the gull wing. The panel registers the input with a chime, and the door opens vertically. I press the close button before my butt's even landed on the back bench and then reach for a seat belt, but none is in sight. This is a supply wagon, not a human transport, and the bench I'm sitting on is a storage locker.

"Hold on," Afumba says and depresses the accelerator.

The electric grid van peels out of its parking spot, and I'm thrown to the right as the Afumba whips us in the direction of the closest exit sign. We round a sharp turn, barely avoiding a passing vehicle, and then accelerate up a ramp toward daylight. For a second, I imagine us launching out of the garage like a scene in an action movie. Instead, Afumba slams on the brakes. We emerge from the facility like any other vehicle driven by an unenthusiastic day laborer tasked with a job that could be done by a service excipion, except that all of the available bots were busy with more important tasks and couldn't be bothered. My driver even adopts a disinterested slouch to sell the part.

We pass right in front of the hospital as emergency vehicles skid to a stop behind us. We're in the clear. That is until a nondescript man on the sidewalk makes eye contact with Afumba.

"*Zoyipa.*"

"Friend of yours?"

Afumba answers by stomping the accelerator to the floor while trying to type on the vehicle's central holo screen. But he can't do both. I also feel the van top out at 100 kph, so I scramble forward to help.

"Let me." At the same time that I start hacking the onboard driving limiters, the rear glass window explodes. A bullet clips Afumba in the ear and cracks the front windshield. Blood spurts onto my arm.

"More speed," he yells.

"Working on it."

Another fusillade of bullets peppers our getaway vehicle as Afumba banks hard, moving out of the enemy's sight lines, at least for the time being. But I have to imagine that the gunfire has drawn the authorities' attention, and we'll have law enforcement on our tail any second. Which, at first blush, doesn't seem that bad. I'm not guilty of anything but trying to stay alive. And where Afumba might be a little more suspicious, I imagine he can claim protection from the highest echelons of the Solum Terram…

Right up until Guy on the Sidewalk back there rats him out. Which he's probably already done.

"We need to ditch the van," I say.

"No. It is our fastest—"

"Where we headed, Fumby?"

"Safe house outside the city."

"We'll never make it. Trust me on this one. Ditch the van and we'll go on foot, but we need to do it now before they have a chance to mobilize."

Afumba works his jaw once, still keeping pressure on his ear, then pulls over and opens his door.

I bring up the autopilot menu. "Which way is your safe house? West?"

"Yes."

I try to select a destination in that direction on the nav computer, but it's being slow.

"Where would you like to eat?" the van's automated voice asks me.

"I need a map of the West End," I say impatiently.

"I can recommend several restaurants on the—"

"End task."

A descending three-bell chime sounds, and I have manual control again. Finally, I'm able to click on a random address, hit enter, and then climb out before the door closes on me. The grid van crawls away from us and reenters traffic.

"I believe that was a mistake," Afumba says.

"Declining its food recommendation? You're probably right."

"Losing the van."

"You're not the only one who knows how to stay alive, pal. Come on."

"But why didn't you at least send it east?"

"Because we want them going toward your safe house. Pick up the pace, big man."

I lead Afumba through the first storefront I see: a café that, according to their signage, has the best chocolate croissants in Helsinki. Noted. Fortunately, the employees are so busy helping customers, no one notices us heading for the back of the store, or the handful of napkins Afumba grabs for his bleeding ear. We file past the restrooms, manager's office, and basement stairwell, and push out the back door into an alley. Police and fire sirens wail in the distance; I even pick out a hover jet inbound—McRand 907-B if I'm not mistaken. Running a little lean on one of the thrusters too. They should get that looked at.

"They won't be fooled by that van forever," Afumba says as I walk toward a dumpster and chuck my hospital attire inside.

"I know."

"But then they will retrace their steps and consolidate their search."

"Yup."

He studies my face for a moment. "And you're not concerned?"

"Nope." I don't mean to torture the guy. Okay, maybe I do little. It's just that… how often do you get to outthink a secret double agent assassin, ya know? "I need you to burn your safe house."

"Pardon me?"

"Give it up," I clarify, realizing that he may indeed have the ability to set it on fire remotely.

"I fail to see how this is relevant or wise."

"Your safe house isn't totally *safe*, at least not forever, right? Sallsworth will figure it out eventually, I'm guessing. And he has enough influence with local law enforcement to direct them there. So if a suspicious location pops up on their radar, one that can be verified against a list in Sallsworth's possession, it should preoccupy the authorities for quite a while, as well as your peers. Plus, you said it's outside the city?"

"Yes."

"Even better. Can you ping it without giving away your V-cog location here? And put it on a delay to account for the time it would take us to get there?"

Afumba pulls a small tablet from his chest pocket and, just before hitting a software button on the face that says Alarm, he squints at me. "You would make a very good agent."

"I'll keep it on my list of fallbacks."

He hits the button, cracks the remote in two, and then throws it in the dumpster. "What is the next part of your improvised plan, Mr. Fox?"

"I have a NUESSA chauffeur on call. Just need to find someone's V-cog we can use."

"Am I allowed to employ force?"

"As long as it's not permanent, be my guest."

He cracks his knuckles and then heads back into the café. Looks like I'm gonna get to try one of those chocolate croissants after all.

23

THE BILL CONRAD INTERVIEWS

"Joining us live is Mr. Edward Carr, NUESSA Senior Project Engi—"

"Oi. It's just [*beep*]ing Eddie."

Conrad raises an eyebrow. "Mr. Carr, our… producers will be bleeping out your expletives."

"Good for them."

"We also have children watching."

"Oi. You must be proud of them little [*beep*]ers."

Acclaimed and award-winning verbcaster Bill Conrad shifts in his chair and then looks back at the camera. "Joining us live is… *Eddie*, NUESSA Senior Project Engineer on *Parallax One*. Nice to have you with us."

Eddie looks off camera. "[*Beep*] me. How long did you say this was gonna take again?"

"Kit, we understand that you're joining us live from V-cog beside Captain Jericho Fox en route from Earth back to *Telemine* Station. If you could, why don't you tell the viewers a little about your job."

"Sure, sure. No problem, Mr. Conrad. But, uh… first off, I just wanted to say hi to my mom back in the American Heights. Hi mom! Also, to all my fellow Shaders out there: Say me Kit! *Zoom-zoom*." He pulls the sides of his leather jacket apart on loan from Jericho to reveal a green graphic tee shirt with a stylized drawing of his face on it and #saymekit across the bottom.

"DR. FERNÁNDEZ PARRA, many in our viewing audience are curious to know what these Makriá will look like."

"They're not the only ones, Bill," Sebastián replies. "And I'd like to point out that Makriá is simply our temporary name for them until we learn how they refer to themselves. In any event, the entire human scientific community wants to know the same thing as your audience. Of course, we have plenty to speculate about."

"Like… whether or not they'll be a carbon-based life-form as opposed to a silicon-based one?"

"Well, not exactly. Molecules of the carbon-nitrogen-oxygen sort are abundant and really good at not only building complex structures but self-reassembly."

"So *not* silicon-based then?"

"I mean, that's a bit of a misnomer. You don't look at a house with a concrete foundation, wooden trussing, glass windows, and fiber optic cable and call it a 'concrete, wood, glass, fiber house,' you just call it a house as long as it fulfills the requirements of housing people. Likewise the, uh, biochemistry of a silicon-based organism is extremely theoretical, and in the off chance that one exists, it's not a being we could ever encounter."

"And why's that?"

"Uh"—Seb looks around at all the cameras—"do you want nerd-speak here?"

"As best you can break it down for us."

"Well, at room temp, silicon is inert. So in order for it to ever possess metabolic functionality, it would need to be at very high temperatures, ones not suitable for humans. And if the *lavolobes* and *magmobes*, as we call them, ever came into contact with oxygen, they'd be, well, essentially be exhaling sand."

"I see. So it's safe to assume then that the Makriá are more like us?"

"That's a relative term, Bill, but I think it's safe to speculate that they are enough like us that the plans for their Infinita Gate—our name for it, right?—makes as much sense to them as it does to us."

♣

"But there are still things about it that we don't understand. Isn't that right, Dr. Park?"

"There's plenty, yes," Evelyn says.

"And that doesn't scare you?"

"No."

"Why?"

"Well, I understand that we all find comfort in things we can be certain about. For instance, I felt confident that when I sat down on this chair for this interview that it would hold my weight."

"You had faith in it."

"More like a basic understanding of elementary engineering and the evidence of quality craftsmanship compared against accumulated personal experience."

"In English?"

"I saw some of my other colleagues sit on it before I did, and many of them weigh more than I do. Therefore, it was reasonable for me to anticipate my own forthcoming experience."

"And yet we don't have any experience with opening *Parallax One*."

"No. But we do have six months of experience with the transmission, and we can say with confidence that the Makriá are a highly intelligent, very advanced species who, based on the thoroughness, intentionality, and integrity of their creation have in mind amiable purposes of at least the same caliber or higher."

"And yet the potential for harm remains."

"Of course. What worthy enterprise lacks it?"

"But you still have faith."

"Scientists don't get paid to have faith, Bill. We get paid to make informed decisions about the realities of the physical universe. And right now, the potential gains of this historic moment far outweigh the cons from a mathematical perspective. If you want philosophy or religion, you'd better bring Dr. Fernández Parra back out here. I believe this moment is a cause for great hope."

"Mr. Vanderburg, you're an expert on celestial navigation."

"I have a small background in it, yes."

"And, by the way, my daughter loves your call sign, Magellan."

"Thank you."

"Does it concern you, and please correct me if I'm wrong, that nowhere on the device are we able to determine where it might take us were we to pass through it? Nor where extrasolar beings might arrive from if they come to us?"

"It doesn't concern me, no. Again, as others have said before, *Parallax One* is a technological wonder beyond anything we could have invented on our own. The fact that another species is even willing to entrust it to us means there's a significant investment on their part. Just because we don't know how it all works doesn't preclude us from using it or concluding that there isn't more control to be had when we receive more information in the future. It would be a little like giving a grid car to a person a thousand years ago and expecting them to drive it. They could climb in and appreciate the novelty of it, but the only way they're going to move from point A to point B is if we activate the car's autodrive function or control it virtually from afar."

"MR. FOX, our condolences to you over the breaking news of your father's death."

"Thank you, Bill."

"Likewise, we understand you escaped an attack that took place at his hospital. Are we to conclude that it was a Tantum sanctioned strike?"

"Uh, the investigation is still ongoing, Bill. I… really can't say more."

"Many in our viewing audience are curious how the conflict with the Tantum Terrae, as well as a recent spike in piracy, have affected the station's build out. Can you at least shed some light on that?"

"Sure. There have been some delays, yes. But thanks to the amazing efforts of the Viatoribus and the

Sentia Aux, any shortfalls due to the conflicts you mentioned have been rectified by sourcing parts and materials locally."

"Can you give us an example?"

Jericho thinks for a second, then says, "Sure. Take power conditioners. They help regulate the flow of energy from the 7-X drive to the emissions nodes."

"An important component."

"Yeah. And we needed a lot of them. But our main provider on Earth was hit."

"The Protavis Industries attack in Hamburg last month."

"Correct. Where that disruption would have set us back several months, if not years, the Viatoribus, in particular, kept us on schedule."

"By?"

"Well, they were able to source conditioners from several legacy habs and dome settlements that either had reserves or, in a few cases, didn't need the ones they were already running. Trimming the fat, you might say."

"Fat you could use."

"Yup."

"And how does that feel for you, Mr. Fox, having your old politicast support you like this?"

Jericho looks from Conrad to the camera and back again. "Feels like the world believes in what we're doing. Like they want to meet this new species as much as we do."

"AND YOU'RE NOT WORRIED about going through?"

"Who, me?" Kit asks. "No, I won't go through. No

way. We'll send drones, right? And then some of the Ferguses."

"Ferguses?"

"Ha ha. Gosh, so sorry. Um, excipion scouts. That's a… force of habit, right there. Ya know?"

"And then we'll examine the data they bring back."

"Yuppo, Billy Bob." He snaps multiple fingers on both hands and then slaps his palm against the open end of one fist. "Nailed it. First try."

"And then you'll be on that first expedition through?"

Kit's confidence vanishes, and he looks blindly into the nearest camera. "I… uh… never…" He looks to the side. "I'm not actually going through, am I?"

"DR. MASON, as the team's chief linguist and resident cryptographer, have you discovered any clues about the Makriá's language?"

"Well, language is a fairly obtuse term—no offense, Bill."

"None taken."

"For instance, we recognize many languages beyond the speaking sort, even in our day-to-day speech. Take, for instance, the language of music, or the observable language of nature."

"The language of love?"

"Certainly. These all contain lexicons that transcend mere words. They require emotions and perspectives based on shared experiences. That's why subgroups throughout the animal kingdom develop ways of communicating that are indigenous and unique to them, requiring deep contextual understanding. Suffice to say that in terms of words as you and I know them, no; the Makriá have given us no dictionary. No verbal cues. Even if they had, how would we have any way to connect them to our world? The nuances alone might be… well, infinite."

"Nuances?"

"Sure, uh…. take for example, I say, 'Bill, I was flying to get here today.' That means what to you?"

"That you were in a hurry?"

"Absolutely. What else?"

"That you… took a flight to get here. I see."

Natalie nods. "How about that I was actually floating down a corridor to reach this room in zero-g? But because I always dreamed of flying like Superwoman as a kid growing up, I prefer the word flying to floating."

"It's complex."

"Quite. Ask anyone who's learned a second language as an adult."

"So no language, no lexicon."

"I didn't say that. Just that our ideas of language are broad. The Makriá *have* spoken to us, but using the language of science. Of atomic structure. In spite of all the things that might differentiate us, we have a common language of how we understand the physical universe, at least in part."

"Which is how you were able to decode and then build what we have today."

"Precisely."

⁂

"DR. COLLINS, you've helped shoulder a considerable portion of the code cracking that went on in the early stages of the translation."

"I wouldn't say considerable. Just one person in a room with lots of other much smarter people than me."

"I think you're being modest." Bill Conrad holds up a tablet. "Dr. Park is quoted as saying that your contributions are among 'the most significant of any team member in the program.' That's high praise."

"Exaggerated, I think."

"Which is understandable, considering the fact that you saved her life. Who can forget this?" The verbcast feed jumps to a replay of the initial drone attack during the October 8th press conference. Sam is seen leaping from her chair and throwing herself between Evelyn and an incoming pixie that skewers her in the top of the back. "Ouch! The public started calling you a hero after that incident."

Sam's face flushes, and she's looking bashful under Conrad's proclamations. "Just… doing my job."

"DR. PARK, turning to a bit of a serious issue here. Several NUE Space Navy vessels have recently arrived and taken up strategic positions around *Parallax One*. As I'm sure you know, rumors have spread across the verb about the reasons for this move. Does Secretary General Sallsworth's request for a military presence here at L2 signal a cause for concern with your or your team?"

"Alright, let me just say that the progress made on *Parallax One* has been extraordinary, thanks to the tireless collaborative efforts of our joint team of engineers and scientists. That's nothing to say of the Viatoribus and Sentia Aux's uncanny power to keep proposed economic reforms at bay either. Moreover, the fact that both private enterprises *and* the citizens of the moon, Mars Nation, the Belt Lands, and the Jupiter Moons have unanimously endorsed our project speaks volumes about what we're doing here and our efforts to learn from and join forces with an advanced sentient intelligent species. Had the Secretary General passed his earlier measures, we wouldn't be sitting here on *Telemine* Station's bridge looking at live drone feeds of the completed Infinita Gate, now would we?

"Does the military presence concern me? Of course it does, Bill. Just as it should every free-thinking human being in our system. Ask yourself, if we sent plans for a gate to another species with peaceful intentions and then showed up only to find weapons pointed at our faces, is that the same kind of reception we wish to give the Makriá? And as for these outlandish claims that they're coming to enslave us and wipe out our planet, how dare we project our own base proclivities upon them? Have we not endeavored to rid ourselves of such colonistic urges? Have we not grown as a species, evolving to more productive and mutually beneficial behaviors as individuals and world communities? The fact that Sallsworth would think so little of our benefactors shows just how evolved he really is."

That last line was a low blow, she knew. But he had it coming. Likewise, this next moment was what she'd been waiting for. Evelyn turns from Conrad and addresses the camera. "If Secretary General Sallsworth has any intention of using the NUE Space Navy assets currently parked around *Telemine* Station for anything other than sentry duty in the extreme and highly improbable case that military action is needed as a last resort, then every spacer, scientist, CEO, and politicast party member will hold him accountable for actions that endanger the well-being of the entire human race. Stand down, Sallsworth. This isn't your show."

"ANY LAST REMARKS, MR. CARR?"

"Oi. You're a [*beep*]ing twat for wearing so much makeup on camera. That bloke back there was double dipping in all the [*beep*]ing catering, and I'm pretty sure he's got a [*beep*]ing head cold. And your producer AJ right there just said during the break that he wanted to [*beep*]ing [*beep*] Dr. Park in the [*beep*], which, in my book, is permission for me to take my [*beep*]ing hand and shove it so far up his [*beep*] that I can make him talk like a bloody puppet on [*beep*]ing Saturday morning kids show. Did I miss anything?"

"Uh, no, Mr. Carr."

"Great. Then what are we doing sitting around here with our [*beep*]s in our hands? Let's get ready to open a [*beep*]ing gate!"

24

JERICHO

Activation Day
Saturday, April 25, 2252

Jericho

AFUMBA HAS BEEN NAPPING for the last hour of our flight. He needs to wake up since we're nearing our destination. I clear my throat and then ask from my captain's chair on the *Kogarashi*'s bridge, "When was the last time you were in space?" Afumba blinks awake. But no sooner is the question out of my mouth than I consider the very real possibility I know the awkward answer. Afumba's long stare confirms my suspicions.

"Mr. Afumba," Kit says. "Cap just asked you when was the last time you… uh… Oh, wow. I guess it was… was probably when you—"

"We got it, Kit."

"Sorry, Cap. You asked the thing, and then he gave you that look, and then I was like maybe he didn't—"

"Kit."

"Shutting up, Cap."

"Thanks." Back to Afumba, I ask, "So you haven't seen it completed, I take it?"

"The gate stuck to the end of *Telemine* Station? No. Only the short clips we get on the verb." For security's sake, NUESSA and SESI placed media restrictions on showing all of *Parallax One* until activation day.

"Well, you're in for a treat, my friend. Take a look."

I fill the curved command wall with a single holo projection of the *Kogarashi*'s stern camera. Blue lens flares caused by the ship's decel thrust obscure part of the image… but not without adding a certain mystique to the spectacular view of *Telemine*'s white-hulled mega-structure. I'm no poet, but the sight is quite lovely. At least if you're an engineer.

"It is bigger than I imagined," Afumba says, sitting forward in his seat.

"Eight kilometers long and seven across," Kit replies. "Ain't she a beaut? The open end on top there is where the alien emissions nodes are, while the capped end at the bottom is where we've been headquartered on level one."

"But the legacy hab is no longer cylindrical."

"It is on the inside. The triangular sides on the outside are for added structural support and shielding."

"I do not follow."

"Well, Cap here figured out that the emissions nodes on the end—when active, right?—might put more strain on the station's superstructure than the original design is rated for. Maybe collapse the opening, or push it apart… we're not totally sure what to expect yet. Another reason we'll need to clear off when we activate it. Anyway, so Cap builds this triangular sleeve around the cylinder to act as additional support and serve all the added power supply needs. It's pure genius."

"I had a lot of input from a very gifted team," I interject, and then look at Kit.

Afumba asks, "So the open end, that's where the portal window is supposed to appear?"

"Bingo! Right between the triangle created by the emissions nodes," Kit replies. "That's where all the magic is gonna happen."

"And you're planning on going through?"

"Negative," I'm quick to reply so I get ahead of Kit. "Not until we've sent probes and gotten plenty of data."

"Assuming they come back," Afumba says.

"Right. No guarantees. You ready to get a closer look?"

Afumba sits back and squeezes his armrests with his large hands. "Do I really have a choice?"

"You did at one point," Kit says. "But Cap kinda saved your life, and then you saved his, and then he saved yours again so… You're pretty much stuck with us, I think."

"Perfect."

"Hey, yeah! I think so too."

I lean toward Kit. "Think he was being sarcastic."

"Oh. Right. Sure sure."

⚛

Evelyn

"CUTTING IT A LITTLE CLOSE, aren't you?" I ask Jericho as he floats through the airlock from the *Kogarashi* to *Telemine*. The words are hardly out of my mouth when I think twice about my opening statement. "I'm so sorry about your father."

"Me too. Just glad I got to say goodbye."

"Hi, Miss Evelyn," Kit says from behind Jericho's shoulder.

"Hey, Kit. You okay?"

"Pssssh. Me? I'm always okay. Mr. Fine and Dandy, right here. Coooool as a cucumber under pressure."

I'm about to ask Jericho about the attack on the hospital when I spot a third figure coming up behind Kit. Guy's massive. "Who's this?" I ask Jericho without taking my eyes off the newcomer dressed in a black NUESSA space suit with yellow trim, signifying him as a registered guest.

"Evelyn, meet Afumba," he says as Kit floats out of the way.

I cast Afumba a skeptical look. I feel like I've seen him before. We shake hands. "You got a last name?"

"No," he says in the rounded accent of those from

southern Africa. His giant hand covers mine past the wrist. Okay.

To Jericho I ask, "There a story here?"

"Small one."

"Has to do with the hospital?"

"Yup."

"Explain later?"

"You know it. Can we get something to eat?"

"I'll tell the cafeteria we're coming."

Jericho shakes his head. "Given today's schedule, let's just have it delivered to the bridge."

Kit says, "Don't worry about a thing, you guys. Leave it to me. You wanna come help, Afumba?"

"I stay with Captain Fox."

"Oh… sure. Yeah, okay. No problemo. I'll just, ya know, do it all myself then."

"I'm sure food services can give you a hand, Kit," Jericho replies.

A new voice speaks up from behind me. "Hark! His Esteemed Magnificence, Leslie the Great! I will aid you in your quest to bring nourishment to your kinsfolk."

"Kiiiiiit?" Jericho says. "I thought I told you to re-format the Ferguses."

"You did. And I did."

"This doesn't sound reformatted."

"I may have kinda, ya know, missed one?"

"Kit."

"There was the planning, and then the building, and then, oh man, your dad. Gol-ly. And now today's activation? I'm like, *woosh!*, and it's just, *phew!*, a lot, ya know right? Listen. You guys get settled in; Fergy and I will be right up with some refreshments. Talk soon, okay? Bye!" Kit pushes off with Fergus—One, I'm pretty sure—and disappears around a bend toward the main receiving hall.

"He talks too much," Afumba says.

"Who?" Jericho asks. "The kid or the excipion?"

"Yes."

That makes me laugh. "I like him already," I say to Jericho. "Come on. We gotta get ready."

"Afumba believes my father was poisoned," Jericho says as we ride the elevator down to the bridge building on the perimeter of section one.

I look from Jericho to Afumba and back to Jericho. "You're being serious."

Afumba gives a solemn nod, but Jericho keeps sharing the story. "Apparently, Sallsworth has come into the possession of some sort of V-cog weapon."

"What's that supposed to mean?" I ask.

"We are not sure yet, Dr. Park." He seems to think twice about his choice of words. "*They* are not sure yet."

"Your former boss."

"Yes."

I turn back to Jericho. "You sure you trust this guy?"

"He saved my life."

"No. Captain Fox saved my life. Twice. Which is why I am here."

"The lat lift on *Astraea*," I say, finally remembering his face from the debrief footage and Jericho's account.

He nods once.

"How do you know this is what killed your dad?" I ask Jericho.

"I realized there was something odd going on when

I asked to set up a V-cog channel for when dad went unconscious. The head neurologist said that it would cause too much additional strain on his brain and body. But as his condition worsened anyway, I was finally permitted to ping him and we shared his final moments together."

"Doesn't sound unusual to me," I reply.

"Just before I left him, I told him to alert the nurses via V-cog if he needed anything. Standard operating procedures, right? Except—and it didn't hit me until much later—my dad said the nurses had already been taking good care of him."

"He could've meant in the hospital."

Jericho shakes his head. "He specifically said 'in here.' As in V-cog. Someone posing as medical staff had already been in there with him."

"You're suggesting foul play? But didn't the medical reports show that it was cancer?"

"Such things can be doctored," Afumba replies.

"It wasn't you, was it?"

"No. I was sent as clean up. The operation was a ploy meant to draw Captain Fox away from *Parallax One* and assassinate him."

Bile rises in my throat. "If this is true…"

"It all adds up," Jericho says.

"He's a…"

"Murderer."

"I was gonna say a fucking asshole who deserves to be publicly executed."

Jericho turns to a surprised looking Afumba. "Told ya she means business."

I lock eyes with Afumba. "And you had nothing to do with poisoning Dad Fox through V-cog?"

"No."

"And you had decided beforehand that you were going to help Jericho get out alive?"

"Yes."

I hold his gaze for another few seconds, but he never looks away. "Alright. But do anything suspicious, and I will personally see you out the closest airlock. You got it?"

"I would expect nothing less, Dr. Park."

"Good." To both of them, I ask, "If he can do this—poison your dad through V-cog—we have to assume he can do this to others, right? Is that how he killed Allbrook?"

Jericho interjects, "Assuming the footage he broadcast was really just a cover for how he, not Neon, took the late secretary general out."

"No," Afumba replies. "That was through traditional nanoposion delivered in person."

"And you know that because…?"

"Because I know. In any event, this technology is only a recent acquisition. Though, I must say, Sallsworth is playing the information very close to his chest. But I have every reason to believe that if he has access to someone's V-cog, he can execute the exploit."

"Stars. It must have cost him a fortune to develop and keep inspectors paid off," I ask.

"Rumor is that he stole it."

"From who?" But even before the question has left my lips, I know the answer. "*Neon.*"

Afumba nods. "I cannot be certain, of course, but that is the likely conclusion."

"And you know nothing more?" I ask him.

"I do not."

"Mmmm." I eye Afumba up and down once as

gravity builds over our descent. I decide to change gears. "What's in this for you, big guy?"

"I do not understand."

"Why turn on your people? On your whole politicast? How do we know you're not on a long play to undermine the activation and kill us? Seems pretty convenient: the timing of it all, doesn't it?"

"I confess the timing is unusual, but not by design. If I wanted you dead, that deed would be done already."

"Cocky. But keep going."

"I lost my partner to Sallsworth's politicking."

"Jones," Jericho says, obviously familiar with the person.

A memory of more *Astraea* footage comes to mind. "After Stamos took me hostage. The gun fight in the hangar bay."

Afumba nods. "While those were Tantum incogs, they might as well have been Solum, because Sallsworth would order me to kill the very asset she'd given her life to protect minutes before." He gets the thousand-meter stare I've seen plenty of times before. "I make no claims of moral high ground about all I have done. But we—"

"Contract killers," I say, just to be clear, and maybe be a little snarky.

"No. We were bodyguards. And we have standards. But that breach was a step too far. I knew that if I carried out the order to kill Jericho when I was with him and the Marines riding up to section thirty, my partner would die all over again, only this time the blood would be on my hands. As soon as the Master Sergeant let me go, I knew then that I would find a way to not only repay you"—he looks at Jericho—"but work to undermine and eventually kill the man who betrayed me."

I stare at Afumba for the better part of five seconds before saying, "You're really intense, you know that?"

"Mmm."

I pat his massive bicep. "Just glad you're on our side now."

By the time we reach the bridge, I've sent a very condensed note about Sallsworth's V-cog poison to Lemuel and included a brief writeup about Afumba so he's not in the dark about the new bodyguard following us around. I expect Jericho's already done the same to Director Johnson, but redundancy about this is good thing. Plus, if Johnson is slow in passing the information on because of his current responsibilities, I know Lem will be right there to make sure it gets to the proper channels. It's too important to fumble.

"Look who's back," I say as Jericho, Afumba, and I walk onto the bridge. "And meet his…"

"Security detail," Jericho says.

"…Afumba. He helped ensure the Director's safe return to us."

Everybody starts clapping for them and their stunning escape from the terrorist attack on the hospital. The media had reported it as another desperate Tantum Terrae strike, even though I knew better now. They would too, in time.

"Thank you, everyone," Jericho says to the command crew. "It's good to be back, and I appreciate the encouragement. But now we've got a job to do."

"Right," I add and check the time. "T-minus four hours and counting. I want everyone out and transferring to the *Sagan Explorer* in sixty minutes. If you are able to move sooner, that's fine. Ferries are waiting at docking bay one bravo sixteen. One hour, people. Let's do this."

"Last ones out?" the shuttle pilot says to me and Rook as we get seated.

"Copy that," I reply. "Inform Helsinki that the station is clear."

"Roger. Confirming with Spaceflight Tracking and Data Network Stations to NUESSA Command at Helsinki that *Telemine* Station is clear."

The shuttle's main door seals, and I secure my harness. Then I offer Rook a fist bump.

"Didn't think I'd miss this," he says after bumping my knuckles. His helmet's combat visor is set to clear, probably so I can see his face.

"I'm not. *Telemine*'s accommodations suck."

"I meant being assigned to you."

It takes me a second to read between the lines. "Wait. Have you…? Did you get new orders?"

He nods.

We both sit there for a moment while the shuttle pilot eases us out of the bay and away from *Telemine*.

"I have to report back to the *Bellerophon* as soon as you're secure on the *Sagan Explorer*."

"Why?"

"Above my pay grade."

"But… isn't my life still in danger?"

He shoots me a sideways look as if to say, "What do you think?" but holds short of actually speaking it.

"They're ramping up, aren't they."

"That's what it looks like."

I turn my head as far as my helmet will allow. "Think they'll try to stop us?"

"The Space Navy follows NUE orders, Evelyn. And so far, I haven't heard anything that would cause me to suspect we'll be ordered to stop you."

"But you also weren't given a reason for why you're being reassigned."

He pulls his lips back and sucks the saliva off his teeth. "Fair point."

"I don't like this, Rook. I don't trust them."

"I don't blame you. But I also understand their cause for concern."

"Not this again."

"Evelyn, listen. If something does come out that gate that means to do us harm—"

"Which is not gonna happen."

"—but if it did, you'll want us here."

"We're agreeing to disagree there."

"That's fine. But I can promise this…"

"Oh, stars."

"I'm committed to protecting you, Evelyn Park, whether here or there."

I study his face again. This seems out of line for a Marine… but what do I know? "But you just said you had orders to follow."

"And I do. And I'll follow them. But to a point."

"You're allowed to do that?"

"Hell, no. But being with you these last few months has made me realize that you're spearheading something that's above all our pay grades. This is historic level shit, Evelyn, the kind they'll write about for generations to come… assuming they survive." He takes a breath and leans back as the shuttle powers toward the *Sagan*. "My job is not to protect the Corps. It's to protect people. So if our government chooses to hang you out to dry? Then they've crossed a line, one I can't abide."

I may not know much about the whole military code of honor thing, but I'm pretty sure Rook is risking quite a bit with what he's saying. A court martial. His career. Who knows what else. But I'm grateful. Stars, am I grateful.

"What's that?" he asks.

I'm talking out loud again. "I was just thinking how grateful I am to have a friend like you."

He smiles. "Same."

The holo screen in the front of the cabin shows the *Sagan Explorer* coming into view. Its long central hull is divided into numerous labs, all of which are surrounded by box trussing that keeps the ship together like an exoskeleton. Support arms radiate from the main body in the aft, extending out to the hab ring that rotates in a constant half-g spin. It houses most of the crew compartments and gravity-dependent experiments. The entire vessel is powered by an early direct fusion plasma drive and painted in the white and red filigree of SESI with plenty of NUESSA logos along the hull in orange.

Long before I was stationed on *Astraea*, the *Sagan* was home, so heading back on board now stirs up good memories and more than a little nostalgia. But I'm sure that will all go away the first time I have to use the water closet. Kinda like how camping is fun up until you dig a hole with a stick and have to use leaves.

"Hey, before I go, I need to say something," Rook says.

"Oh no, you don't. We just got as mushy as I wanna get, thank you very much."

"It's about Sam."

I meet his eyes, trying to discern where this might be going. "What about her?"

"To be honest, I've been really suspicious of her for a while now."

"What? Why?"

He shrugs but seems undeterred. Good feelings, gone. "A lot of her behavior seemed suspicious to me. Like she wasn't always telling you the whole truth about things."

"She saved my life, Rook. More than once."

"I know, I know. And that's the crazy part. I feel like that was legitimately her. But there have been other times where I'm not sold that she was being forthcoming with you."

"Like what? Rook, this is all very—"

"I'd follow her when she said she was going to the bathroom sometimes, back in Alaska."

"Stars! You followed her?"

"And sometimes she didn't go. Sometimes she'd lock herself in a closet and stay there for half an hour."

"Because she probably needed to get some space. From you."

"There were other times that I saw her working on stuff that didn't look like her normal screens."

"Because you're an expert in demultiplexing photon orbital angular momentum algorithms?"

He looks down.

"I'm sorry. That was too far."

"Have you asked yourself why the drone that hit her in the back didn't detonate?"

"Because it was a dud."

"You sure about that?"

"Of course. What else would it be?"

"Someone not wanting to kill their operative."

"Who's suddenly decided to foil her own assassination attempt?"

"Who's having a crisis of conscience," he corrects.

"You're being paranoid, Rook. And you're scaring me. I just… I don't see how you're drawing any verifiable conclusions from all this *speculating*. And I don't mean to question your judgement here—"

"So don't."

I open my mouth to say something but can't find the words.

"All I'm saying is, be careful, Evelyn. If I'm wrong, then I can live with that. I've made plenty of calls downrange that weren't the right ones. But they were always in service of keeping my unit alive. Always better be safe than sorry, because you've got one shot at staying alive when real rounds are flying. So I'd rather be wrong and alive than right and dead."

After another few seconds, I say, "Well, I can tell you that you're wrong."

"And I don't think you're seeing this one straight. But it's not my job to change your mind, just to warn you. Be careful, okay?"

"Of course. I'm always careful."

"Bullshit."

At least we share a little laugh as the shuttle slows and eventually docks on the *Sagan*. I get up while he stays seated. "See you soon?"

He shakes my hand. "Not if I see you first. Take care of yourself, Evelyn. And thanks… for teaching me a few things along the way."

"Same. I'd be dead without you. Forging paths?"

"Into the darkness. Always."

⣀

I'M NOT ten seconds inside the *Sagan*'s midship hangar bay when I spot Jericho and his team floating with their duffle bags. The group of over thirty engineers is gathered on the far side like they're waiting for a grid bus to show up and drive them out of town. They look a bit forlorn too—Kit being the worst. He's floating beside Fergus One with his chin in his hands.

When I get near enough, Kit sounds as if someone's funeral just wrapped up. "Hi, Dr. Park."

"What's the matter?" I say to him and then look over at Jericho. "Nobody let you guys in the amusement park?"

"Just got word from Johnson that he wants us back on board the support ships," Jericho says. "Most are headed to the *Champion Six*. I'll take my core team to the *Kogarashi*."

"That's cute."

Jericho doesn't flinch.

"Hold up. You're for real?"

He nods. "Apparently there's serious concern about firewalling the team in the event of a major disaster. If one of us dies, the others at least—"

"I understand firewalls, Jericho. Why wasn't I notified of this?"

"You were. Apparently you missed the communique. Came in during your ride over just now."

I shake my head. "I was... preoccupied. But why would they do this now? We're three hours away! I'm calling Lemuel."

"It *is* Lemuel. And Eric. And the Space *and* Security Councils. You can check for yourself."

My hands ball into fists as I confirm the memo in my V-cog inbox and see by the title alone that he's right.

"Can't say that I disagree with the orders," Jericho adds. "Makes sense."

"I still think it would be better if we all stayed together."

He seems to agree but doesn't say anything else.

More to myself than him, I add, "Two goodbyes in ten minutes. How do you like that?"

"Who? Rook?"

"Yup."

"Huh. Looks like they're splitting us all up."

"Yeah. But as soon as we finish this first fifteen-minute cycle, I'm filing an official complaint and getting the band back together."

"I wouldn't expect anything less." He offers me his hand as their transport arrives. "See you in V-cog?"

"You better look good."

"Try my best."

Sam

SEEING Evelyn float onto the *Sagan*'s bridge made Sam's heart skip a beat. After all they'd been through together, it bothered Sam that Evelyn didn't know the truth.

About her. About where she was really born, who her real family was, and how Neon had saved her life. Any stories Sam had shared about her past were filled with half-truths—just so much to make them feel authentic *enough*, but never enough to compromise her cover.

And if Evelyn was going to know the truth, then Sam also wanted to tell Evelyn how she'd become skeptical of the Tantum's agenda. That she hated the way the organization justified taking "guilty" lives in the name of protecting the "innocent" so recklessly. The Robin Hood lines had gotten blurry. The lengths Neon was willing to go to exceeded what was necessary.

And if she was going to share all of that, then Sam had to tell how Evelyn had changed her mind about seeking answers among the stars... answers that might bring about the very solutions the Tantum Terrae seemed to want, at least they had at one point in time. Answers that could save humanity.

Now that they were about to activate the gate, why shouldn't Evelyn know? Sam had intentionally stopped communicating with Neon months ago. Part of her had been too scared to face the woman she considered her adoptive mother, even over V-cog. But another part knew nothing productive would come from the encounter... knew that Neon would only try to manipulate her into submission, and that perhaps she hadn't acted as motherly as Sam gave her credit for. The choice to put distance between them was also strategic. The more time and space that separated her from Neon and the Tantum, the more likely it was that Evelyn would see Sam's allegiance as some old and forgivable part of her past.

Right?

Oh, who the hell was she kidding? Evelyn would

never forgive her. Never understand. And Sam didn't blame her. The things she'd done on *Astraea* Station? Acts to subvert the authorities, turn off cameras, and erase data? She'd disposed of Second Engineer Marcus Del Toro's body, heaved Senior Engineer Morgan Hodges from the power level, and framed Bhavna Mishra for as much as she could. She even covered the bombs that eventually brought the legacy hab crashing to the Earth. There was no hell deep enough, hot enough, or eternal enough to burn such guilt from Sam's mind.

And then add to that all the things she'd done to undermine the signal decoding project. Changing logs, misapplying formulas on purpose, even erasing people's data when they were getting too close. But she couldn't keep up with so many staff on the project. And, if she was being honest, she didn't want to. She wanted to see for herself what the Makriá had to say, if anything. Because, somewhere in her eight-year-old self, she knew her parents—her real parents that brought her into the world on Ganymede—would want to know. Because they had been scientists too. Spacers committed to settling more of the frontier.

Sam could never prove it, of course, could never know for sure what her parents intended to do about her failing health. But she was in so much pain, and resources seemed so limited, that nothing made sense in that hospital bed after a while. She felt like thin paper scribbled on by a dry pen. But Neon had changed all that. And in Sam's eight-year-old mind, being pulled from Etana Dome's hospital and promised healing on Earth felt like the greatest love in the world. And when Neon's shuttle whisked her away, seeing the settlement's laminar film rupture meant Sam would never have to suffer on Ganymede again.

"I'll be your mother now," Neon whispered in her ear. "And no spacer will ever cause you harm again."

The conundrum for Sam now was knowing that she couldn't go back to Neon, and that she dared not go forward to Evelyn. For just as execution awaited her with one, the agony of betraying a true friend awaited her with the other. It was the horrible pit in the stomach. That place of feeling stuck. Of knowing there was no way out of the hole.

Save one.

All she needed to do was open the airlock.

But as Evelyn waved at her from across the bridge, Sam felt something in her soul break. Not the will that might cause her to take her own life. And not the will that would keep her from crawling back to Neon. No, the thing that broke in her was the muzzle she'd placed on her true self, that terrible restraint that had kept her from ever opening up to Evelyn.

She wanted to be free.

She wanted to be known.

And she had to speak the truth.

"Anyone else seeing this crow flap his lips on the verb right now?" Jose Ramirez said.

Sam blinked clear of her daze and pushed toward Ramirez's workstation. "Sallsworth?"

"Yeah. Says he got something big. That's what she said, am I right?"

"Turn it off," Evelyn replied. "All hands, we've got a ring to activate and a new species to meet. T-minus five minutes and counting."

If Sam was going to say something, it needed to be now.

25

NEON

SHE LIKED JONAH. Clearly. He was one of the few young men she called upon who could match her stamina. But he was more than a plaything to her. More than a conquest that affirmed her power. Her control. Jonah had potential to be molded into a brilliant leader, one she could build on.

She ordered him to leave while she cleaned herself up in the bathroom. A minute later, the door slid open, revealing an annoyed looking Gemma.

"You're getting sloppy, mother."

"My body, my choices."

"That's not what I mean."

Neon pulled her pants up and slid the suspenders over her white cutoff t-shirt. "Speak plainly. I have no time for riddles, especially from you."

"He's only been with us six months."

"And many even shorter."

"But you… throw yourself at him without knowing anything about him."

"And you don't do the same, daughter of mine? What with your late-night carousing and stim-powered escapades?"

"All my targets are chosen beforehand. And none of them are brought here. There's a difference. You've grown careless."

"Because I have the power to balance it. And I don't need a lecture from you, love. Jonah's more than proven himself. And he saved my life, if you'll recall."

"You won't let us forget."

"And why should I? I'd have been shot in the back without him."

"I still don't trust him."

"You don't trust anyone, love."

"And who taught me that, hmmm?"

"Then you find me evidence of his guilt, and I'll let you have the privilege of dispatching him."

"I can kill him anytime I want. What I need is for *my mother* to fucking wake up and be a more careful leader."

"A more careful leader?" Neon, now fully dressed, crossed the bathroom to within arm's reach and slapped her daughter across the face. "Watch your tongue, love. It may get you into more trouble than you can manage one day."

"And your obsession with men half your age will get you killed."

"Perhaps. But I'll have fun before the climax stops my heart, dear."

"You're unbelievable."

Neon brushed past her and stood in front of a floor to ceiling mirror, fixing her tousled hair. She changed the subject. "Where is he?"

"In his office, monitoring the countdown with his staff."

"Media?"

"A dozen reporters, all ST loyalists."

"Of course they are." Neon picked up a lipstick from her desk, twisted up the hot pink stem, and then painted her lips. "*Pop*. It's time to pay him a visit."

"We'll be monitoring." Gemma walked to her mother's desk, swiveled the chair around, and waited for Neon to sit.

"Good. Maybe you can learn a thing or two. Because when I'm done with Nigel, I'm going after the Master Sergeant and then Olivia."

Gemma's lips curled into a half smile, but the effort was aborted.

"What is it, love?"

"Nothing. I just… I have something else I need to look into. Research, that's all. Happy hunting, mother. Always Earth."

"Always Earth forever."

LIKE EVERYTHING NEON DID, targeting Sir Nigel Sallsworth on this particular day was intentional—the climax of an entire campaign meant to draw him into her web. Even betraying the locations of certain TT strongholds to the NUE military were feints meant to build a false sense of security in the enemy's ego. After all, what good chess player didn't know when to surrender a queen in order to advance a pawn?

Was she worried about losing operatives? Hardly. Their sacrifice was needed and would never be forgotten. Once the system saw the power that she could wield—that she could take out whoever she wanted, whenever she desired—the masses would come. The government would no longer be able to resist her, finally submitting to the protests her family started those many years ago. And with the inevitable recognition would come a new era of NUE leadership under Tantum control, one that put the spacers in their place and revived Gaia's spirit, bringing restoration to creation.

Nigel, she knew, was a kind of first fruits offering—the initial sacrifice on Gaia's altar. His blood would mix with thousands more to follow, but he, Secretary General of an NUE that had pushed her aside, ignored her, and *taken* so much from her, would always be the virgin offering slain before the great goddess.

Likewise, Master Sergeant Farooq had killed her son—her darling, beautiful boy. She lamented how many years they'd lived apart, separated by Klaus's insistence that Neon was mad. A lunatic. But she'd corrected that and reclaimed her son. All he ever wanted to do was please her. "I live to make you proud, Mother," he'd often said. Unable to show favoritism, she required that he make good on his word and proposed the plan to bring down *Astraea* Station. Jack had been only too willing to accept the task. And he would have succeeded too, were it not for those fools. She would visit Evelyn Park and Jericho Fox before the week was through too.

And then there was Olivia. Sweet, dear, but ultimately weak Olivia. Neon had rescued her from a family bent on space settlement at the risk of their own daughter's life. They knew her body could not endure life on Ganymede. Knew that she needed treatment back on Earth. And yet they chose to stay, all in the name of pushing the outer reaches for the betterment of humanity. Ha! And they called Neon a terrorist. Olivia's parents were no better than cult missionaries who'd rather reach those in darkness than attend to their own flesh and blood in the light. No matter. Neon rectified that and became the child's mother in just thirty minutes.

But after all these years, how did Olivia repay her? How did she reflect on the mercy bestowed? The second chance at life? By letting her brother die, by failing to exact punishment, and then... worst of all... by saving the life of the very woman she was sworn to undermine. Oh, the punishment Olivia had coming would not be swift. Neon already had in mind precisely how long she would make the woman suffer: one day for every year that Olivia had been afforded Tantum protection. Twenty-four in all.

Nigel.

Rook.

Then Olivia.

It was time.

Gaia would not be refused her atoning sacrifices any longer.

Nigel

The Secretary General sat on a couch with his wife, Esther, to one side and his children, Malcom and Fiona, on the other. The Joint Chiefs exchanged small talk around the hors d'oeuvres table while numerous reporters waited just outside his office for their turn to ask Nigel questions. And all across the room, holo projectors displayed live images of the Navy ships stationed at *Parallax One*, waiting like attack dogs to receive their orders spoken in a secret tongue.

Nigel resigned himself to the fact that he had to let NUESSA and SESI open the gate. Despite his best efforts to thwart them, his carefully constructed speeches and bills were unable to gain majority approval. Between Tantum defectors decreasing the Solum's power base and the unexpected rallying of the orbital nations, Nigel found his hands tied by the very system he'd publicly pledged himself to. Which was one more reason the whole thing needed consolidating, he thought. The only resort he had left was calling for emergency military intervention should the opening of the Infinita Gate present a clear and present danger, one he was prepared to argue for the moment the project came online.

Sallsworth's V-cog pinged as his family and staff watched the system-wide verbcast of the countdown. Security protocol demanded that every incoming call be routed through his team first. But this request bypassed them. He saw why. "Neon."

"Hello, Nigel, dear." She stepped around the dining room table in his Manhattan apartment. "Miss me?"

Back in the real, Nigel checked the time and then looked at his wife. "I need to take this." His head of security saw him stand and made to intervene, but Nigel stopped the man with a raised hand. "It's okay, Victor. I just need a moment." Nigel walked toward his office window and peered down into the lamp-lit garden. "What an unexpected surprise. Time to surrender?"

"To me? Yes, I accept."

A sharp chuckle came from his gut like a disgusted reflex. "Huh. Ever the arrogant bitch."

"Come come, Nigel, dear. Name calling is beneath our station. Can't we just be civil?"

"Why start now?"

She walked out of the dining room and into his study where a tall glass case held several antique swords. Neon studied them as she talked. "We are like fencers, you and me. Ever thrusting, parrying, and feinting. Moving back and forth along the field in a violent dance."

"I'd love to keep chatting, but I have a thing."

"Quite so. Word is that you're biding your time."

"That all depends on how things play out."

"I'm sure."

"Care to watch?"

"No." Neon pulled open the case's glass door, took the handle of a rapier, and removed it. She examined the blade thoughtfully—even ran her finger down metal until Nigel noticed a red bead of blood appear when she tested the tip. Then Neon sucked at her finger and smiled, holding it between her teeth. "Care to duel?"

"Maybe another time."

She ignored the comment and tossed him the sword while retrieving a second one for herself. "Come, Nigel, dear. Fifteen minutes remain. That's plenty of time for a bit of fun, don't you think?"

He set the rapier on the dining room table. "Good night, Neon."

Neon

SHE COULDN'T HELP but smile at the surprised look on his face when he wasn't able to step out of V-cog. Even if he called for help in the real, eyes open, hands pleading with his security to "Just do something!" they wouldn't have the means. Because what happened in V-cog had more than virtual consequences.

How delectable. How *utterly terribly monstrously* delectable, she thought.

"En garde," she said, raising her sword and pointing her front foot toward her opponent.

"Why can't I leave V-cog? What have you done?"

"I want to play, Nigel, dear. Please don't disappoint me."

"Let me out." He backed away from her advance.

"Pick up the sword, Nigel. Or I'm afraid this will be a very short-lived game." She could tell he was trying to shut down his system. His movements around the high-backed chairs came in fits and starts. "It's no use. You're a prisoner of your mind now. Here"—she slid the weapon across the table, smashing the stemware and knocking over a candelabra—"take your sword and play."

Still, he refused.

"Deus! Aren't you an obstinate man?" She lowered her weapon, marched around the chairs to meet him, and when she was close enough, whipped the tip of her sword across his wrist.

"Son of a…" He looked up in sudden recognition.

There it was.

"That's right," she said in confirmation of his new-found pain—pain more than a virtual placeholder. It went deep, as if the injury had happened on his physical wrist. There would be no blood, but the nerves didn't know the difference. And so neither did the brain. A jolt of adrenaline had no doubt squeezed from his glands. And now he was awake. "Your sword, Nigel."

"What do you mean to do here?" he asked.

"Why, kill you, of course. You think I would go to such lengths merely to make you suffer?"

"But that's impossible."

She took another step toward him, at last provoking him to pick up the rapier. "Really, Nigel. Of all people, you should know better than to put limitations on what you and I are capable of."

"This will… really kill me?" The suppressed terror in his voice invigorated her.

"We'll see, now, won't we. And don't bother trying to leave. I've locked us in." As if to accentuate her point, Gemma pinged her in V-cog. However, the call was auto-muted. It even felt like Gemma tried shaking Neon's arm—the action felt far away—but there was no use now. Whatever her daughter needed would have to wait. The only way out of here was when the host died.

"You're mad, Neon!"

"As is the world." She thrust at his chest.

Parried.

She lunged at his right shoulder.

Slashed away.

Neon then swung at his head—a dramatic, useless, and unsportsmanlike action meant to throw him off guard.

He leaned away, cursed, and pulled one of his expensive chairs over to keep some distance between them.

The game was on.

26

NEON

NEON STEPPED over the downed chair and threw off her military jacket. She could move better in her sports bra. Plus she knew her physique would distract Nigel. It had before. As soon as she was close enough, she slashed at his side. He blocked the sweep and finally—*finally*—manned up and hit back. A weak thrust at her abdomen.

"Come come, love. That's no way to treat a woman." She countered with a jab at his head.

Nigel parried and stumbled backward into the kitchen. His back struck the island, and then he peeled away toward the farm-style hand sink. When he reached it, Nigel grabbed a pan off the overhead rack to his right and flung it at her. Neon sidestepped the ill-aimed shot, closing fast. A beat later, she went for his groin, left shoulder, and center-chest. All parried in quick succession.

"Now we're getting there," she said. "But I still want more."

Nigel continued backing away, this time rounding a corner into the billiard room off the kitchen. He grabbed one of the balls and threw it. His aim was good, but the shot was easily dodged.

"And at last, your cricket days come in handy," Neon said.

"Stop following me."

"I can't do that, dear."

"I'll have you arrested!" He threw another ball from the table's far side.

Neon caught this one. "No, you won't." She threw the ball back and rushed him at the same time. Three quick strides later, she was at his side, aiming for his ribs and leg.

Nigel parried the successive attacks, fell into a book-case, and yelled when she finally stuck him in his thigh. "You're insane!"

"Oh, please. We've already gone over this time and time again. Have you no other insults to use?"

Nigel checked the blood on his palm as if to make sure it was real. *As real as it gets*, she thought. At least in V-cog, though the body would still behave as if the wound was real—sending white blood cells, boosting adrenaline, elevating the heart rate, and shooting pain signals to the brain with each step. Nigel pulled a book off the shelf, flung it at her, and then stumbled into the next room.

Neon followed Nigel into a generous living room with facing couches, a fireplace, and a wall's worth of windows on the opposite side. The man reached for an iron fire poker under the mantel. The combination of the spear point and curved hook made for a nice thrust-and-tear tool; she knew from experience. But Nigel lacked the discipline needed to employ two weapons si-multaneously, at least for very long. It required more mental stamina than physical and years of training. *Overreaching yet again*, she thought.

Nigel parried and slashed Neon's next attacks, defending with one weapon and swinging wildly with the other. The sound of metal on metal broke the living room's serene silence as the pair of contenders danced among the furniture. The poker gouged the coffee table while Neon's sword drew stuffing from an armchair. An antique globe of Mars crashed to the floor, broke from its mount, and rolled across the hardwood.

Yes, Nigel had two dueling weapons, but Neon was the faster swordsman. And she'd been toying with him. Could she suffer the suspense much longer? All night, if she wanted. Patience truly was a virtue, one that paid off in everything from freelance to foreplay. But she had more sacrifices to offer Gaia. Unfortunately, this needed to come to an end prematurely. So she stabbed his bicep, stomach, and forearm in quick succession, the last causing him to drop his sword.

"Did you know, I once imagined we'd be lovers?" she said, tracking his blood along the floor and kicking his blade aside.

Nigel bumped his way out the living room and into the next room. One hand clutched his stomach, the other his fireplace poker.

"We were quite good at making love," she continued, following him into a smoking room that boasted gold-trimmed French doors with a grand view of the city. "And at traveling. We saw everything together."

"*Stay back from me.*" He held up the poker with desperation that made it quiver. But his body was growing weak. "I'm *warning* you. *Stay back.*"

"I also imagined all the things we'd accomplish together. All the laws we'd change, the policies we'd create. A new world. A better one. And rid ourselves of the spacers once and for all. We could, you know." She circled to the other side and then back, pressing him toward the balcony doors, constricting around him like a boa.

"*Leave*, Neon. *Now.*"

"But I realized, in my fantasies, it could never last." She raised her sword at him and started walking forward. He batted away with his prod, but she brought it back up just as fast. Again, he swiped, and she reset, forcing Nigel to backpedal into the doors. He worked the lever with a bloody hand and then stumbled backward onto the balcony until his back hit the railing.

It was a warm summer night, and Neon marveled at the level of detail the billionaire had rendered into this suite. The sounds of traffic echoing from below. The faint odor of cigarette smoke. The underlying sense of grime that lurked beneath the surface of every brick, every square meter of concrete. People talking. A siren wailing. Even the faint rustle of leaves on the treetop just below the balcony. He had spared no expense for this lobby.

But it was more than that.

Neon knew that if she were to wander the streets, the render wouldn't end. Because with his billions came excess. Nigel didn't just have this apartment rendered: he had all of Old Manhattan.

"And do you know why it wouldn't last?" she said, sword aimed at his eye. "Because you're a fraud."

She thrust, and the rapier's point popped his left eye like a cherry. Fluid ran down his cheek. But she wouldn't let him double over, wouldn't let him even raise a hand. Her sword was at the other eye.

Nigel roared in pain, then clenched his jaw in seething rage. "*I am going to kill you.*"

She ignored him. "You say you want change, but you hoard your money. You proclaim that you want a better future, but you spend it on"—she waved a hand about the air—"a better suite. When billions of people cry out for your help, you withdraw into a cave of comfort. No, Nigel, dear. We could never work. Because we are altogether different creatures. Fortunately, history will forget you. But it will never forget me." She thrust at the other eye…

But the action was cut short by the sound of a gunshot.

Nigel

NIGEL WATCHED the smoke curl in front of Neon's face like a candle wick being snuffed out. She looked down at her belly, at his Glock 43, and then back up at him. Her face, white as a bleached sheet.

The Witch of Calvert Isle blinked in dismay, looking left and then right. Suddenly, her wits came back and she thrust her sword at him. But he parried with his prod, and parried twice more.

With a hand to her stomach, she said, "It's not possible. You… You—"

"Have the same power to kill in V-cog? Why, yes. As a matter of fact, I do." He raised the pistol to her face and ordered her to drop her sword, which she did. "And I wonder where I got it from…"

She coughed, then stepped toward the door and caught herself on the handle. "You were developing an exploit too?"

"Oh, no. I wouldn't waste my money on that. Not when someone else was already doing the hard work."

"You… stole from me?"

"*Stole* is such a harsh word. More like I copied your test answers. Looked over your shoulder as it were."

Neon checked her gut then returned pressure. "But you… You would have needed my—"

"Key? Yes, and wasn't that fun for him to retrieve just now."

"For him to—?"

Nigel relished the revelation that seized her face. He also couldn't help but notice how she touched herself, realizing that the micro drive was missing. "*Jonah.*"

"Among his other aliases, yes."

She coughed again. It wouldn't be long now before her brain believed what her imagination was telling it. "You *bastard.*"

That's when Neon raised a revolver at him.

Nigel hardly had time to consider where she'd gotten it before she pulled the trigger. The hammer rocked back and then snapped forward in slow motion. Fire spouted from the barrel. The bullet spiraled toward him. And he knew his death was imminent. But he leaned aside, dodging the round. This was his lobby, after all— his world—and he would not be overcome.

Nigel emptied half his magazine, most of it done blindly. Neon ducked inside the den and retreated through the doorway. Now it was his turn to track her blood across the floor. And it gave him a moment to consider her gun's presence, as there were only two viable options.

A person in V-cog was limited to importing only what they could first appear with in someone else's lobby. It was usually clothes and an item or two. After that, they could only interact with whatever their host had built into the suite. Therefore, Neon could have discovered a pistol while dueling through his apartment. Nigel had, after all, paid a small fortune for architects to build the home out and stock it following a long list of preferences, ones that included hidden weapons. But he had taken precautions for this duel and removed all firearms but his own. Moreover, Neon's 1960 Colt Detective .38 Special wasn't one he would have stocked. Which left only one plausible answer…

She'd hidden the gun on her person when she entered his suite.

Nigel had, of course, predicted she might arrive with a weapon, but something obvious and much larger. Instead, she'd decided to toy with him, even taking him by surprise. At least for a second. Her luck would run out soon as her Colt's cylinder gave up its sixth shot.

Neon leaned out and fired twice down the hallway. The bullets broke a mirror on the back wall, and shards of silvered glass cascaded across the floor. The rounds barely missed Nigel as he stepped into a den. It presented a second entrance to the same bathroom that she'd just entered. He tossed a book into the hallway to draw her attention and then swept into the bathroom, pistol raised.

He saw the edge of her back and shot twice.

Neon screamed, spun like a tigress, and returned fire. Two bullets shredded the door trim. But when Nigel looked again, Neon had fled. He pushed through the white-tiled bathroom and checked both sides of the exit.

"One round left, Neon. Use it wisely." Then he spotted the blood trail leading up the circular staircase.

Nigel took the stairs one at a time, eyes up, weapon up, just as he'd been trained by his security heads over the years. He'd also practiced counting his shots. There were three rounds left in his 9mm magazine. Higher capacity ones waited in his gun safe, but he wanted to end this before they were needed. The world outside was waiting for him, and he had a portal to shut down. Plus, he knew she was mortally wounded and stuck inside his construct, trapped like one of her mice in that infernal twentieth-century lab experiment she so admired.

At the top of the white marble staircase, the blood trail ran to the end of the hall and into the main bedroom, door cracked open. He moved halfway down the corridor but then ducked inside a walk-in linen closet with a back entrance to the bathroom. He slipped off his shoes, moved silently across the polished granite floor, and then peered into the bedroom. There she was, bracing herself against a wall and half hidden by a balcony curtain... facing the wrong direction.

It was too easy.

But so was manipulating the world.

He aimed and fired.

♣

Neon

NEON FELL into the curtains but refused to go down, her fingernails tearing furrows through the fabric. She tried reaching out to her daughter, who was surely looking on, but the lock-in prevented any return communication. The pain of the gunshots wasn't nearly as bad as the pain of being disconnected from Gemma. Of knowing she was probably trying to warn her of Nigel's treachery. Neon only had herself to blame.

But none of that mattered now. Only surviving did. She'd gotten a look at his Glock 43, a preferred sub-compact for concealed carry. If it held the standard ten rounds, then he had two left. And her Colt .38 Special? One shot left. The gun was a perfect replica of the antique she'd used to kill the big man who'd raped her as a child. She'd survived then, just as she would survive now.

With a whip of the curtain, Neon twirled away from the wall and spotted her target. He stood in the doorway, gun elevated. She pointed, squeezed, and felt the gun buck as her final round sped on its way.

The bullet hit him, she thought. But couldn't be sure. Because his pistol fired too. The round punched her like a hover truck to the chest. The force sent her backward through the balcony doors but failed to send over the railing. Neon would stay on her feet. She would meet death head-on.

As Nigel walked out onto the landing, Neon considered her options. She could rush him but knew the distance was too far. She could try reaching for one of the chairs and use it as a club but knew she lacked the strength. She could leap over the side and take her chances with the sidewalk, but she had too much pride for that. Or she could talk him within arm's reach and bat the weapon aside. Just before she addressed him, Neon thought she heard the sound of her daughter's voice somewhere in her subconscious, willing her to beat Nigel. To kill him.

"One round left, Nigel, dear," she said. "Use it wise—"

Nigel

"Everything okay?" Esther asked back in the real.

Nigel steadied himself on the drink table with one hand and touched his eye with the other. "Yes, I'm… It was someone from another department with a question."

"You sure you're feeling okay? You don't look yourself."

"Just nerves is all."

Esther chuckled. "You and the whole solar system. Come on. The kids want you, before you have to be whisked away to make a speech or something."

"Of course." He poured himself a finger of whiskey, shot it back, and wiped his lips with a cocktail napkin. Then Esther took him by the hand and led him away from the memory of a female corpse on the street with a hole in her head.

27

EVELYN

"Eves?" Sam asks from behind my captain's chair on the *Sagan Explorer*. She should be buckled in, helmet on, ready to go. "Can I speak to you for a moment?"

Before I can answer, Bhavna states over the general channel, "T-minus three minutes to activation."

"Go, Sam."

"It's, uh… important."

"Listening. You need to get secured too."

"I know, I just…"

"This guy is freaking unbelievable," Ramirez says, clearly still watching the Secretary General's press conference. "Sallsworth's trying to upstage us!"

"I told you to shut that off," I reply. "Stars, people! Let's focus here." Back to Sam, I say, "Go ahead."

"You know what? It can wait."

"You sure?"

"Yeah. Just a… personal thing."

"Hey." I snatch her hand out of zero g, sensing I know what this is about. "We're not survivors. We make our own destiny by taking it. Plus, if the Tantum try anything stupid, Rook's got our back. No worries, okay?"

"Sure. Yeah, thanks."

"Put on your helmet and get secure."

Sam pushes off and floats back to her seat at her sensor monitor station. I don't blame her for being uptight. We all are. This is the moment we've been waiting for, and yet again, humanity's eyes are upon us. No pressure.

Deep breaths, Evelyn, I remind myself as the crews of both the *Sagan* and the *Kogarashi* start going through pre-activation checklists. I already know everything looks good, but standard operating procedures exist for a reason—to catch outliers. They also help center people, providing a sense of comfort that comes from practice, which is critical when venturing into new territory. And I'd say this operation qualifies as that. Just a little.

The *Sagan Explorer*'s bridge isn't fancy. Why would it be? It's a thirty-year-old Horizon-class science exploration vessel. But it's home. Served my residency here a decade ago; never imagined I'd be in command. For the moment, I'm a captain, which just sounds odd. I don't wear it as well as Jericho does. But the ship doesn't care. The circular deck has me seated in the middle facing a curved wall of command displays—both holo and hardware. Nav is to my left, crewed by Ramirez. Bhavna is on comms to my right. Sensors, life-support, and diagnostics are behind me, tasked to Sam, Seb, and Natalie respectively. Igor and Cheng are strapped in observation crew couches.

Whatever it lacks in luxury and spaciousness, the *Sagan* more than makes up for in utility and precision. NUESSA and SESI have made sure to keep the sensor arrays updated and the drive core well maintained. We might not be the fastest, but we're certainly robust when it comes to analyzing, deciphering, and processing data brought to and found in space.

At the two-minute mark, Jericho says on the main display, "*Sagan Explorer*, this is *Kogarashi*. All support systems on *Telemine* Station are nominal and standing by."

"*Kogarashi*, all systems on *Parallax One* nominal and standing by," I respond. "Venture Probes One and Two are in position and ready for launch."

"Roger that, *Sagan*. Mission Control Helsinki, we are green on all systems. Please cross check and confirm."

Jericho's transmission, traveling at light speed, takes five seconds to cross the 1.5-million-kilometer distance; we wait for another five seconds to get the return message. "*Kogarashi*, this Mission Control," NUESSA Director Eric Johnson says. I spot Lemuel off his left shoulder. "We are seeing all systems nominal from here. Venture One and Two look good. You are clear to proceed."

"Copy that, Helsinki." Jericho busies himself with some display on his chair arm and then looks up at his bridge camera. "Evelyn?"

"Go."

"You wanna do the honors?"

"Me? But you—"

"Think it's only right."

I stifle a sudden laugh that forces itself past my lips. "Absolutely. I'd be honored." I glance over at Bhavna for a time check.

"Coming up on t-minus sixty seconds, Captain."

"Roger that. Stand by for *Parallax One* Infinita Gate activation in t-minus one minute."

After that, I mute the public audio transmission and sit back. I need a second, and the world and all its outlying habs, stations, and settlements will get the live audio again soon enough. In the meantime, everything goes quiet. I don't know what to do with my hands, so I flex my fingers and make fists a few times as the seconds count down. I wish I could box something right now. Palms are sweaty.

The main display shows all of *Telemine* Station's augmented hull with the three emissions nodes on the open end. All personnel have been cleared, and all ships have fallen back to minimum safe distances, including the Space Navy vessels, to stay clear of any negative energy pressure and potential gravity wave anomalies.

The clock passes t-minus forty seconds when Ramirez exclaims, "*Jesucristo*, he's releasing a blacklist!"

It's gotta be about Sallsworth. I want to tell Ramirez to shut up and focus, but I'd be lying if I said I wasn't curious.

I don't even have to ask Ramirez to expound; he does it anyway. "It's a list of all Tantum's incogs! He's... he's outing *all of them*."

"Right now?" Sam asks.

"Yeah! Just uploaded it live. It's *loco*, eh?"

"Alright, let's just stay calm, people," I say.

"You seeing this?" Jericho asks me over our private ship-to-ship comms.

"*Ramirez* is, but yeah." A memory of Adrian Wallace's betrayal flashes in my mind. "You think it has merit? Or just another desperate attempt to rattle us?"

"Timing feels too convenient to be legit," Jericho interjects. "And he's trying to shut us down for sure. But we can't take any chances. Can you have Natalie run that list against our rosters?"

"She's a little busy."

"I can do it," Sam offers instead.

"Thanks," Nat replies.

"I'll update both captains with anything notable," Sam adds.

I notice the time. "Twenty seconds. Public audio going live again. Bhavna?"

She nods and then announces herself to the whole human race. I smile at the act's beauty, seeing as how her name has been dragged through the mud just a few short months ago. "This is SESI Communications Specialist Bhavna Mishra for the *Sagan Explorer*. We are at t-minus fifteen seconds to gate activation."

"*Sagan*, this is *Kogarashi*," Jericho says. "Activation authority transferred. It's all yours, Dr. Park."

"Accepted. Thanks, Knight," I reply. "Let's make history, people. *Parallax One* coming online in five… four… three… two… one… Activate."

THE FIRST THING that happens is… well, nothing spectacular. Just a bunch of meters showing a massive amount of power flowing from the 7-X drive, through the station's newly expanded trunk lines, and into the three emissions nodes' pre-entry conditioners. Jericho designed the system to deliver a smooth and constant energy supply, one that would stay well within the safety margins that the simulations liked best. Too little power, or too many dips, and the oscillation pattern lost coherence. Likewise, too much, and the field grew distorted—yup, like overdriving the tubes in an antique guitar amp. Works great for orbital rock, but not for science experiments.

"Twenty petawatts and holding," Eddie announces

over the inter-crew V-cog channel. "All systems nominal. Time for the fucking magic show."

A moment later, Kit adds, "Holy biscuits! It's working."

Sure enough, the emissions nodes start presenting the extreme light infrastructure lasers. They're faint at first but growing by the second.

"Wavelength, 820 nanometers," Ramirez calls out. "Pulse length holding at 25 femtoseconds."

"Diameter?" I say. Sam doesn't reply. "Sam! Diameter?"

"I'm sorry. Sensors… confirm 100-centimeter diameter. Hydrogen banks are fully saturated."

I check the pion-to-kaon ratio and watch the reaction climb. Back on the visual feeds, a faint blue glow appears in the triangle's center.

"Landau singularity detected," Natalie announces with excitement rising in her voice.

"Just like the sims," I reply, trying my very best to stay calm. Eh, who am I kidding? I'm freaking out. *Just keep it professional, Evelyn.*

"PK ratio passing forty-seven to one," Nat says. "All systems nominal."

"Power?" I ask in the *Koga*'s direction.

"Twenty petawatts and holding," Nairobi replies. "Looking good."

The blue aura inside the triangle is expanding. And getting denser, to the point that it's obscuring the inside of the *Telemine* behind it.

"Is this really happening?" Nat asks.

"Yes. Stay focused."

"Roger."

"PK ratio?" I ask.

"Passing, uh… sixty-one."

"Copy that. Sensors, what are you picking from the gate window?" When Sam doesn't respond, I turn in my seat to look at her. She's pale. "Sam?"

"Right. I'm sorry, I just... I don't know what these readings are."

"I got it," Ramirez replies. "Photon emissions, negative gravity waves, frame-dragging. It's... all there..." He shakes his head. "There's gotta be an active galactic nucleus in there somewhere, just... in micro-miniature."

"Any cause for concern?" Jericho asks me.

"No. Nothing that models haven't predicted."

"PK passing seventy-five," Natalie says.

"Our ship hull temperature is increasing," Eddie says from the *Koga*. "But *Telemine* looks cool. Nothing visual on the anomaly's ass end either."

"We're reading the same here," Seb adds from our bridge. "Sensors aren't seeing anything out of the ordinary."

"Copy that," Jericho says. "Keep an eye on those temp sensors."

As the pion-to-kaon ratio passes eighty to one, the light mass in the triangle's center starts taking on a spheroidal shape.

"I'm seeing an oval mouth out there," Ramirez says. "Anyone else?"

"Tits, yes," Igor exclaims. "Is very much shape of mouth!"

"I'm seeing it too." I bring up a closer image of the Landau window and expand the spectral analysis sweep. "I've got Aharonov-Bohm QG effect. Ramirez, confirm?"

"Copy that. Blueshift, traces of Hawking radiation, and a Maxwell field too."

Something else catches my eye. "I'm also detecting

three-dimensional architecture on LIDAR. *Koga*, confirmation requested."

"Oi. Stand by."

I keep watching the anomaly grow as the PK ratio passes ninety percent; the lasers' effects are almost at their peak.

After a few more seconds, Eddie says, "Non-conforming secondary surfaces detected apart from *Telemine*'s inner hull."

Ramirez leans in closer. "There's some sort of… negative mass holding the throat open. Dios mío!"

"Evelyn?" Jericho asks, sounding concerned.

"We're still good," I reply. "It's all been predicted, just… never seen."

"The throat of what?"

"A wormhole."

The only thing keeping me in my seat right now is that I don't wanna screw this up and miss first contact. "How's power, Nairobi?"

"Nominal. Everything's good."

As the PK ratio reaches one hundred to one, an electromagnetic wave of both visible and invisible radiation pops from the Landau window. The corona passes the *Sagan*, causing a momentary brown out, but doesn't kick anything offline.

"*Holy bajoly*," Kit exclaims. "It's a tunnel!"

Sure enough, all sensors, including our own eyes, are showing a fully formed perfectly clear tube of swirling blue light starting at the gate's hazy laser-edge and peeling away toward infinity, right past *Telemine* Station's endcap.

"Evelyn," Ramirez says in a hushed tone. "We have an EPRB." He looks back at me. "I don't know how. But it's there. Just need—"

"Confirmation. I know."

"Layman's terms?" Jericho asks me.

"EPRB." I can't take my eyes off the anomaly. "It's an Einstein-Podolsky-Rosen bridge. We… did it. *They* did it. Helsinki, requesting EPRB reading confirmation."

No one moves on our bridge for the interminably long ten-second round trip. Finally, a voice comes back; fitting that it's Lemuel's. "*Sagan Explorer*, this is Mission Control Helsinki. We confirm EPRB detection inside *Parallax One.*"

Comms flood with distorted shouts and cheers. I look around at Seb, Ramirez, Bhavna, Natalie, Igor, and Cheng, each pumping their fists and shouting… all but Sam. She's even paler than before. I cast her a questioning look, but she doesn't even see me. There's no time to ask questions though; we have a job to do.

Back on the team channel, I say, "Alright, people. The clock is ticking: fourteen minutes thirty-five seconds remaining until the automated sequence shutdown, unless there's a new factor in play we don't know about. So we stick with the plan. All sensors trained on the gate window. I want to know of any anomalies the moment they're detected. And for the love of Jupiter, would someone please make sure the Navy has their fingers off their triggers?"

"Roger that," Jericho says. Just then, something flashes in his eyes. A look of recognition. A look of being startled.

Stars, no. "Jericho? What is it?"

He looks at me, but before he can say anything, Johnson comes over our team V-cog channel, voice somber and face flat. "Uh, to the joint teams of the Infinita Gate Project, this is **NUESSA** Director Eric Johnson at Mission Control Helsinki…"

The formality combined with Johnson's hesitancy makes my stomach turn. His eyes track something… a virtual cue card. He's reading a statement. I scramble to bring up the verb headlines, guessing that's what Jericho saw. But Johnson delivers the news just as my eyes run down the list of media notifications.

"By executive order of NUE General Secretary Sir Nigel Sallsworth, you are… hereby ordered to cease and desist all activity in and around *Parallax One* and shut down the enemy portal. Failure to do so risks immediate reprisals from NUE First Fleet currently stationed at your position. Upon review of the gate's successful opening, the project and any further actions to support it have been deemed…" Johnson twists his head to the side and closes his eyes. "…have been deemed a system-wide security threat level one. I repeat, failure to abide by this measure will be considered an act of war against humanity and will invite swift repercussions." Johnson is visibly shaken, a sight reinforced by the presence of military leaders stepping in behind him.

"Oi! What kind of flippity flying fuckery is this?" Eddie shouts over V-cog, then bangs his hands on his workstation.

I couldn't say it better. "Sallsworth," comes the word from my barely parted lips. *He knew.* He planned this all along. If he couldn't stop us with sanctions, couldn't intimidate us with the military, then his only choice was an executive order to protect system security. I should have seen this coming! *Dammit*, I'm pissed. We're making history, and Sallsworth wants to take it away.

"Evelyn?" Jericho asks. He's switched to a private channel. "What's going on in that head of yours?"

I look from the gate, to his face, to my team. Natalie nods at me as if reading my thoughts. Seb too. Ramirez and Bhavna both give me a thumbs-up. Sam just looks terrified but still offers a weak smile. Igor and Cheng both nod in consent. There are more people on this ship—fifteen other scientists in all. They need to have a say, but there's no time. I have to trust that they knew what they were getting involved with the moment their shuttles pointed toward L2.

"Evelyn? Talk to me. Let's just launch the probes as planned and then we—"

"I'm stealing it, Jericho. I'm taking what belongs to us."

"Evelyn! Wait. You—"

I block him on V-cog. "Ramirez? Max thrust, eye of the storm."

"Maximum thrust. Aye-aye, Captain."

JERICHO

THE *SAGAN*'s engines burst to life. In the void of space, there's no sound to accompany them, but the heartbeat in my chest makes up for that, filling my ears with the loud rush of pulsing blood. "Shit."

"Oi. Orders?" Eddie asks.

"Stand by."

The *Sagan* can only max out at three g's, if memory serves. It's a Horizon-class, and an old one at that. Which means it'll reach the gate in three minutes.

Three minutes. That's what we have to work with here. And my options are… what?

Evelyn's shut me out, so if I want to speak to her, I'll need to ping someone else in her crew. But what good will that do? She's committed. I could sooner alter a tornado's path by standing in front of it than change Evelyn's mind on something this big. So that's pointless.

I could kill the 7-X on *Telemine.* That would close the gate… at least, I think it would. Unless the Makriá are keeping it powered from their end now that we've made a connection. But it's worth a shot if it stops Evelyn from doing the insane.

And then what? It shuts down and she's arrested?

Maybe the courts get tied up with arguments about the legitimacy of the executive order, and things stretch on for months. Maybe years. All the while, Evelyn dies slowly on the inside. Even if she gets exonerated, Dr. Evelyn Park comes out the other side as a shell of a person, and I have only myself to blame—someone she'll never speak to again.

Which leaves me with only one other course of action: to try to stop the possible and probably impending violence about to be dispensed by the Space Navy. The *Sagan* doesn't stand a chance. Forget a snowball in hell. This is a single ice crystal against the whole of Danté's blistering *Inferno*. The point defense guns on one corvette alone would chew through the hull in seconds.

I ping Rook and cut straight to the chase. "They're gonna fire on her?"

"Roger."

"Can you stop them?"

He clenches his jaw twice. "Working on it, Knight."

"What about your CO?"

"Call lasted ten seconds."

"And the Navy?"

He just shakes his head.

"Dammit." I take a breath. "We have to do something."

He nods grimly.

Images of drastic measures form in my head. My emotions rise in the words, "I am *not* gonna stand by and watch my own government take out her whole goddamn ship. I just can't let that happen. Can you?"

"No."

"Then figure something out, Master Sergeant. Because we're running out of time." I terminate the call and look around the bridge. Everyone's staring at me. Waiting for orders.

I lied. There is one more course of action I can take. But I need consensus. "Listen up, people. I'm about to propose something nuts."

"Oh, I'm so totally in, Cap," Kits says.

"You don't know what I'm—"

"You're gonna suggest we go after 'em, right?"

"Well, what I was gonna say was—"

"Then I'm in."

"Same," Nairobi offers from her chair.

"I'm also good with it," Magellan states.

Alice shrugs. "As your PA, I'm contractually bound to go wherever you do."

"I owe you my life," Afumba adds.

"And I," Fergus One says, "am duty bound by sacred oaths to adhere to your royal decrees regardless of whatever mortal danger they may place me in, your majesty."

"What he said, only less fucking poetic. Might as well die doing something I love: pissing off the crows and flying fucking fast. Plus, we can't let that wanker Sallsworth shut this all down. You know we might not get another shot at this, right, Foxy?"

Well, I guess that settles it. Still, I feel a moral obligation to make sure they understand what we're about to do. "Just to be clear, we're gonna track with the *Sagan* in order to make the Navy's and the NUE's job of pulling the trigger that much harder." When no one seems to object, I add, "They're probably still going to pull the trigger."

"We got it, Captain Obvious." Eddie reaches inside a Velcro pouch on his chest, pulls out something, and tosses it to me. "Give the fucking order."

A meter before the small black object floats into my hand, I make it out: a knight from a chess board. I study the piece and then look back at him. "Mr. Carr? Take us in. Match speed and course."

"Matching speed and course. Aye-aye, Knight."

Rook

THE MASTER SERGEANT knew he had to act on Evelyn's behalf. He'd given her his sacred word. The obstacle was figuring out the most effective way in the shortest amount of time.

The good news was that the NUE *Bellerophon* was short-staffed. As a frigate, its 6,300-tonne displacement supported a maximum crew of twenty-five sailors, which wasn't a lot to begin with, plus capacity for up to fifty ride-alongs or cargo equivalency. Automated systems, excipion maintenance, and V-cog integration meant many of the ship's tasks didn't require the human touch like older vessels did. Furthermore, due to the last-minute nature of its recent assignment to pull overwatch for Dr. Park on *Telemine* Station and the subsequent need for both Navy and Marine personnel elsewhere during the Tantum Wars, as they were being called, the *Belle* only had nineteen souls onboard, twelve of which were Rook's, plus himself. The other six were the frigate's skeleton crew needed for basic ship operations. And of those, only the *Belle*'s captain and XO outranked him. As for Space Marine Corps personnel, Rook was the highest-ranking member of the crew and certainly had more clout than the lieutenant in command.

Rook was already on the bridge, accompanied by Sergeant Geller to monitor the Infinita Gate's activation. But the situation had quickly escalated into something he hadn't expected, though he supposed he shouldn't have been surprised. Uncanny events seemed to follow both Evelyn and Knight around like bees on honey and bears on salmon. And, yet again, here he was right in the middle of it all: a salmon stuck to a goddamn honeycomb.

Geller had observed the conversation with Knight. "What's the play?" he asked the master sergeant when it was over. Any second now, the fleet would bring RAGE systems online and open fire. The *Sagan* wouldn't stand a chance against rail assault gatling equipment.

Rook ground his teeth. As he'd said to Jericho, he'd already tried to bypass Sergeant Major Greenwood, who was still on Earth, and ping Captain Madriff, currently commanding Second Company onboard the NUE Destroyer *Bucephalus*. But that call had lasted for precisely ten seconds: three of which he spent trying to make his case, and seven of which was the expected asschewing he got in reply. Appeals to the Navy side of things would be even more pointless. With Knight powering up the *Koga* to pursue the *Sagan*, and with less than ninety seconds before the two vessels either entered the portal or got shredded by RAGE fire and guided torpedoes, Rook knew there was only one option left if he wanted to save his friends. It meant throwing away his career and probably dying, which was the more positive of the two options. Better to face the Devil in a boxing ring than the Colonel in a court martial.

"Son of a bitch," Rook said to Geller.

"Roger that." The sergeant, decked out in full combat kit, turned effortlessly toward the bridge's main door and sealed it shut using V-cog in conjunction with the touch panel. The combination made the lock that much harder to override.

At the same time, Rook floated up beside the ship's captain. "Lieutenant Jaffa? What do you say we go after those two ships?"

"Negative. We have orders to sit tight."

"I know that, and you know that. But we also know, based on the Sec Gen's exec order, that our fleet is gonna open up on those civilian vessels if somebody doesn't do something. Now, I don't know your politicast or if you like to piss in the shower instead of the head, but I believe that you trust that crow in Oslo about as far as you can throw him in Jupiter's gravity. Oorah?"

"What are you suggesting, Marine?" Jaffa's generic use of military branch didn't bode well. Neither did the stern look in the LT's eye. "I advise you to return to your position and get secured."

"So that's a no-go from you?"

"There're some crayons stashed under the seat if you're bored."

Rook glanced at Geller, who stood behind the executive officer at the helm and a petty officer behind comms. Back to Jaffa, Rook sighed. "I really didn't wanna have to do this." In one smooth motion, he unholstered his HG-11, selected the stun setting using the weapon's V-cog integration, and fired fifty-thousand volts into the side of his neck.

The XO reacted first, going for the console alarm. But Geller stunned the man before he'd even gotten his arm fully extended. At the same time, the petty officer on comms had the good sense to raise his hands, seeing the fates of his fellow squids. Sadly, Rook couldn't risk the petty officer sending out a silent distress signal, so he motioned for Geller to put him to sleep.

"Think you can fly it?" Rook said Geller.

"Think you should've asked me that before we took out the helmsman?" But then Geller smiled and pulled himself into the nav chair. "Give me ACE."

"Stand by." Rook, already connected to the *Belle*'s V-cog interface with executive privileges, entered a rank override used to grant unit leaders secondary helm control in situations where the pilot was incapacitated. Without the captain, XO, or petty officer conscious, the ship's AI naturally recognized Rook as a viable successor. Part of the deal included a nice bit of onboard automation called ACE, or an artificial control engineer. Basically, a smart pilot for dummies in situations where the new pilot lacked a full working knowledge of the flight systems. Again, AI wasn't permitted to run wild on any system, military or civilian, but ACE would more than supplement Geller's limited understanding of flying the frigate. The software also gave Rook an option to firewall ACE against any outside incursions, which meant that none of the other ships could retake control without his consent. And when the LT finally came to? The system would prompt Rook to hand back control… when the commander was cleared by a fleet surgeon. Rook smiled.

Not many of those where we're headed, he guessed. *Wherever there* is.

"I'm in," Geller said.

With the bridge secure, and Geller at the helm, Rook sent an update to his squad. He finished with, "If you wanna jettison, I'll keep the airlock open. No questions asked, and I fully expect you to tell Command the truth after they collect you. All those staying, we're most likely getting our asses shot to hell, but for the right damn reasons. If you're in, sound off."

The team channel came alive:

"Geller," he said from beside Rook. "All in."

"Grabowski, hell yeah."

"Rodgers, let's do it."

"Ibrahim."

"Korvich, all in."

"Hatch, all in."

"Engleman."

"Wijaya."

"Popov, fuck yeah."

"Dregs, oorah."

"Krutz."

"Horowitz, let's get some."

"Guess opening the airlock was a waste of time. Secure the remaining three feather heads. Everyone else, get ready for burn. Engines hot."

"Engines hot," Geller called back.

And away the *Bellerophon* went, speeding after the *Kogarashi* and the *Sagan Explorer*.

"God, help us," Rook said as the ship accelerated. "And crows be damned."

29

JERICHO

"Uн, Cap? I… think they're targeting us," Kit says from his workstation crash couch. He's fighting the pressure of three g's like everyone else. But the discomfort is about to end since we've almost matched the *Sagan*'s speed. "I'm getting more grid alerts than the day Aunt Sandy lost her cat and pinged the heck out of Old Cheyenne."

Nairobi adds, "I'm also detecting laser guidance hot spots from the PDGs. Turrets are moving with us."

"We need to buy them some time," I say.

"Uh, don't ya mean us too, Cap?" Kit asks.

I nod, but my head is too busy trying to think of a solution to say anything more. At their current acceleration, the *Sagan* will reach the gate in sixty-four seconds, according to the telemetry holo I'm watching. The *Koga* can obviously sprint the remaining distance even faster, but neither ship can outrun the Navy's guns and guided torpedoes. So we need a diversion.

"Magellan, take us past the *Sagan*. I've got an idea."

"Aye-aye."

"You wanna beat it to the gate, Cap?" Kit says, eyes wide.

"Only for show, Kit." Back to Magellan, I add, "As soon as we're past, flip us for decel, but don't slow us too much."

"Roger."

I shoot Evelyn a private V-cog message that I hope she plays sooner rather than later: "Whatever you do, don't reply publicly to what's about to happen. Stay on course."

Ten seconds later, we overtake the *Sagan* on our port side. Magellan kills our acceleration, throwing us forward in our seats, and then flips us with thrusters. The mains kick back in, wrapping my stomach around my spine.

"Picking up EM waves from several torpedo bays," Nairobi says, fighting the decel g's. "It's now or never, Knight."

I open a wide-beam emergency channel to the *Sagan* and make sure it's broadcasting to the verb and every government line I have access to. "*Sagan Explorer*, this is the *Kogarashi*. It appears that your engines have misfired. We are attempting to couple and slow you. Please maintain course to the best of your ability." I close out the channel, trusting Evelyn got my message, and hoping to God the magnetic rail cannons don't decide to tear us apart.

Evelyn

"WHAT THE HELL IS HE DOING?" Ramirez says as the *Kogarashi* flips past our bow and starts a decel burn.

I'm about to respond publicly to his wild-ass orders when I spot a message alert in V-cog. I play it and then tell my crew, "He's making the Navy think twice. If they open fire, it's on a civilian rescue attempt."

"So we're not stopping?" Sam asks.

"No way. The *Koga* is coming with us." Then I add in a whisper, "Thanks, Jericho."

"Think it'll work?" Nat asks.

"We're about to find out."

"Twenty seconds to threshold," Ramirez announces. "It's pucker up time."

"Now? I've been there for the last hour," Sebastián replies.

Sam sounds like she's about to jump out of her seat. "I'm tracking a third ship matching our trajectory. Navy vessel!"

"Put it up," I say.

The 3D telemetry shows *Parallax One* in relationship with all vessels in the area. The *Sagan* and *Kogarashi* are nearly to the gate, with First Fleet further back, and the rest of the science and private vessels further still. Sure enough, a small ship has left the fleet and is burning hard toward us. I'm about to ask for more detail when the drive signature and V-rec appear in an ID tag.

"The NUE frigate *Bellerophon*," Natalie says.

I smile. "It's Rook."

"You… think he's… gonna shoot us?" Sam asks.

"I think he just threw away his career so *no* one shoots us."

"Five seconds," Ramirez says. "Shit's about to get real!"

The gate's blue tunnel fills the entire display, prompting me to lean back in my seat as if that will help me take it all in. Then, out of my lips comes an involuntary mantra, "Forging paths through the darkness," and we cross the threshold.

Rook

THE ORDERS TO stand down or be fired upon paused only long enough for an all-channel emergency transmission from the *Kogarashi*. As soon as Jericho made his announcement, the hails to the *Belle* picked back up. The *Koga*'s captain may have come up with a genius way of saving their own hide, but that didn't do a thing for Rook. They were committed, and there was no going back.

"Say we're going to help too," Geller shouted. "The more the merrier."

"That's insane." Rook glared at him through his

helmet's HUD data. "But it might work. Open the channel."

Geller nodded.

"Command, this is… Lieutenant Jaffa," Rook said, hoping they would believe he was the currently incapacitated commander. "We are in pursuit of the *Sagan Explorer*, attempting to aid the *Kogarashi* in their rescue efforts. Stand by."

Geller closed the channel, and both men stared at each other like teenage boys hoping they fooled their mom about doing something they shouldn't have. Ironically, it wasn't death that scared them. That monster had been slain a hundred times over. Instead, it was the odd thing of being found in a lie, shitting in a firefight, or caught drinking a beer on deployments that topped their list of worries. Years of combat did strange things to a Marine's head.

"Negative, Lieutenant," came the voice on the other end. "Your orders are to burn back to the fleet and hold position."

"So the Navy doesn't want to lend any hand toward a rescue operation? Seems kinda negligent, if you ask me."

At that same moment, Captain Madriff pinged Rook over a secured SMCC—Space Marine Combat Channel. Rook stepped into a white V-cog base construct and answered the call, rendered in full armor.

"Farooq," Madriff said in his gray orbital SMC fatigues. "SITREP."

"Ship's commander is attempting to aid the *Kogarashi* in their—"

"He's gone AWOL. You are to proceed to the bridge and relieve Lieutenant Jaffa of command using any means necessary."

Rook glanced at Geller in the real and then replied, "Yes, sir." As soon as the channel was closed, Rook pointed at Jaffa's body strapped into a chair, and said, "Hey, you. You're relieved of duty."

"Hey, Sarge?" Geller said. "I just got something interesting here, running Sallsworth's blacklist against our rosters."

"Jaffa's an incog?"

"Negative. But it seems someone on the *Sagan* sure as hell is." Geller swiped the file to Rook.

The Master Sergeant's gut twisted as he registered the face of the woman he knew as Dr. Samantha Collins. But according to the blacklist, she was actually a TT operative named Olivia Tomlinson.

Son of a bitch.

"Hold on," Rook said and pushed the *Belle* past ten g's at the same moment he recorded and shot Evelyn a message marked urgent. He prayed she'd get it before crossing the gate's threshold.

Evelyn

EVERY EXTERNAL CAMERA on the ship displays the same blue light rushing past us from bow to stern. We're in… we're actually *inside* an Einstein-Podolsky-Rosen bridge, coasting at zero g's through a tensor network to… well, somewhere. Stars only know. Literally.

"Are we much disintegrated?" Igor asks from the back of the bridge while patting himself down.

"Not yet," I reply.

We're still getting ship position data from RADAR and LIDAR tracking the *Kogarashi* and *Bellerophon*, but V-cog signal strength is dropping to unusable levels fast. Likewise, our RADAR's rear-facing X/Y axis is shrinking by the second as the tunnel constricts the range. Then the ident tags on all vessels in our telemetry map blink out.

"We've lost grid connection," Bhavna says.

A second later, I get a Signal Lost notification in my suite. The only thing V-cog can do now is connect us with other users by personal area networks or by a more robust ship-hosted local area network. We're also limited to whatever data we've preloaded in our personal drives and whatever's backed up on the *Sagan*.

"Switching to V-cog LAN now," Bhavna announces.

The lost signal notification symbol in my suite changes to a LAN icon, and I get a list of connected crew through the *Sagan*'s internal comm relay. At the same time, I spot a message notification. Since it's probably an old "don't stop" warning from Jericho, I ignore it.

"Negative energy density is increasing," Ramirez says. "But that correlates with tunnel integrity theory."

"Keep an eye on it," I reply. "And watch for red-shifting. I imagine we'll be approaching the AGN soon."

"AGN?" Igor asks.

"Active galactic nucleus. But it's not that same as it would be with a black hole. In this case, light from our destination is coming toward us. But eventually, that will reverse, and the light will redshift as it moves away from us."

"Ah. I will be taking your word for this, yes?"

"Sounds good."

Something catches my eye in augmented overlay. More names are appearing in my LAN roster. "We've picked up the *Kogarashi*."

"I see it," Sam says.

"What about the *Belle*?" I ask her.

"Probably still out of range."

The *Sagan* continues to coast through the tunnel when Ramirez calls out the changes in the sidewall density and light spectrum. "We must be approaching the midpoint."

"Time?" I ask.

"Four minutes, sixteen seconds."

"Mark."

"Roger."

Igor points toward the main display. "Is redshit, yes?"

"Red*shift*. And yeah, that's what we want to see."

"Is meaning end of tunnel?"

"In another four minutes. Didn't you pay attention at all to our briefs?"

"Hey. I do biology of persons. You do biology of spaces, yes? We ask each other many question. Is normal. I'm sure you ask me about foot, knee, spleen, and do *I* see *me* complaining? *Nyet*."

"Got it. Just hold the rest of your questions for later, okay?"

Igor pantomimes zipping his lips shut and throwing away the key.

"Evelyn?" comes Jericho's voice. A second later, an augmented reality window appears in my vision about fifty centimeters away. His face captures all the excitement and horror that I'm sure each of us is displaying too. I also wonder how much anger he might be harboring toward me over the way I left things minutes ago.

I hit accept on the incoming LAN request. "Jericho."

"Evelyn. Jesus. Are you… okay?"

"Oh, you know, just bending the reality of space-time on a boring old Saturday afternoon in April. How about you?"

"We're all… stable. Physically. Emotionally? Maybe slightly anxious. What you did back there—"

"Impulsive. I know."

"But still probably the right call if we didn't want Sallsworth to shut this down forever." Jericho pauses, and a worried look crosses his face. "If he closes the tunnel behind us?"

"We still shoot out the far side. I think. This is all very theoretical for us. But good luck getting back."

"Right."

After another few seconds of watching him digest my words, I add, "Thanks for what you did back there."

"No problem. I couldn't let you have all the fun. Plus, I didn't think the Navy really wanted to fire on civilians—I just made sure they had a good excuse."

"And you wanted to piss off Sallsworth."

He holds up his thumb and index finger. "Maybe a little." After another moment, he says, "Looks like Rook wanted to join the party too."

"I'm surprised the Navy didn't blast him out of the void."

"Or maybe they sent him to do that."

"Nah. We'd be dead already if that was the case."

"Can you raise him?"

I shake my head. "He's still too far back for our LAN, and radio isn't working."

"Same."

"Anyway, we're almost through. Keep the line open?"

"Definitely. Oh, and"—he lowers his voice as if we were being overheard—"did Sam make any progress with the blacklist?"

I look back at Sam. "Hey. Any matches on the incog list?"

"Fortunately not. We're in the clear."

I tell Jericho, and he looks relieved. "Cross that possibility off our crisis list."

"And prepare to meet a brand new species," I add. "Talk to you in a minute."

"Same." The window minimizes, but our connection signal stays solid.

The crew grows quiet as the countdown timer passes the sixty-second mark. Just one minute to go. Forward-facing exterior cameras show the redshifted light converging on a center point that extends to infinity even though I anticipate the tunnel spitting us out wherever it ends. The suspense is killing me. I... I've waited my whole life for this moment. For every moment of discovery up 'til now. *And...* every moment yet to come. Okay, so it's like my own personal tensor network of constant freakishly exciting discoveries from now until the moment my self-awareness is annihilated and joins the infinite. Which could be any second depending on what we fly into. Better sit back and enjoy the ride while it lasts, Eves.

Just then, a fleeting thought hits me. Jericho didn't ask me if I got his second message. Not that he needed to. I'm assuming he either covered whatever it was that he wanted to tell me or else it had become irrelevant. Still, with half a minute left to go and nothing but red-shifted light to look at, I decide to check the message.

"Evelyn." It's *Rook*. "Dr. Samantha Collins is on the incog blacklist. Stay away from her." The message ends with a file depicting Sam wearing very different clothes and makeup and bearing a completely different name than the one I've known for the last four years.

Olivia Tomlinson.

30

EVELYN

"Projected tunnel ejection in ten seconds," Ramirez announces, but his countdown fades away as I try to grapple with the implications of Rook's message.

He could have misread the list. This is a high-pressure situation, after all.

Or it's bad intel. Nothing is below Sallsworth at this point.

Then there's the fact that Rook is biased. He all but said he wanted Sam to be guilty.

Or... Rook is right, and Sam... Sam has betrayed me for our entire relationship.

I can't even look back at her. Fog is building on my helmet's visor faster than the fans can suck it away.

"We're through," Ramirez exclaims. "The *Kogarashi* is too."

My throat is too tight to speak. I clear it and then ask, "Life-support?"

"All systems nominal," Natalie replies.

"What's our location?"

Seb is working fast. "Cross-referencing star charts against present view now. Stand by."

"That's a red dwarf out there," Ramirez says,

pointing to a star in the distance. "M-type. Really close."

"Um, Evelyn?" Sam says. I don't want to answer her. I can't. Fortunately, she goes without me. "There's a planet to our stern."

"Flip and bring us to rest," I order Ramirez.

"Roger."

A wave of vertigo plays with my equilibrium as Ramirez fires thrusters and brings us about. The *Sagan*'s mains kick back in and decelerate us at a rate of three g's. Then a hazy orange-hued planet fills the camera feeds. It seems Earth-sized. Maybe a little bigger. But guesses are relative until we know how far away we are. A chill goes down my spine. I'm having trouble sorting my emotions and hate that something is robbing me of the joy of this moment. Hate that Rook might be right. That Sam might be… a traitor. And that I fell for it.

"I've got a lock," Seb says after a few seconds, voice rising. "We're at Kepler! *That's Kepler-1649c!*"

"Hell, yeah," Cheng shouts.

Natalie claps her gloves together, laughing hard. "We made it! I can't believe we made it!"

Others cheer too, but I'm speechless. I can't see through the tears in my eyes… can't tell if they're from the wonder of having just crossed four light-years in nine minutes or from the pain of Sam… of *Olivia*.

Stars, why should that matter anyway? We just did the unimaginable. Experienced in reality what three-centuries of science said *might* be theoretically possible. *And* we're alive. In light of this moment, betrayal is… nothing.

And yet it's everything.

"Eves?" Sam asks over the sound of everyone celebrating. "You okay?"

I can't bring myself to say anything yet. Because I honestly don't know what to say. Last time things hurt this bad was in Seoul, lying in an alley with a broken wrist and bloody face. I glance at the decel burn clock; still two whole minutes before we're at a stop. But we're also at three g's. I need to deal with Sam. Dammit. *Olivia*—assuming the intel checks out and isn't a scam from Sallsworth to throw us off.

"Slow us to one g," I say. "Is anyone picking up any satellites, vessels, space stations—anything we need to be worried about?"

"Possibly," Sebastián says. "Scopes are detecting a…"

"A what, Seb?"

"I think it's an orbital debris field. Massive one. But no energy readings at all. And the planet… looks quiet. Something must be wrong with sensors."

"Ramirez," I say wanting the eyes of our chief dynamicist on the scopes. "Confirm."

"On it."

Something about the readings sends up a flag in the back of my mind. But gravity is easing, and I need to deal with Sam head-on before we get any further. As soon as I'm able to keep my arms up, I remove my helmet and gloves, undo my harness, and push out of my seat. Everyone else removes their helmets too now that the critical mancuvers are coming to an end. But I haven't taken the items off because of the diminishing safety concerns. I'm doing this because I don't want there to be anything between me and whoever the hell this person is when I stare her in the eyes.

All at once, the crew seems to notice that I'm not celebrating with them. The bridge gets quiet, and three steps later, I'm in front of the supposed traitor.

"Mind telling me what's going on, Olivia?"

"I'm just updating the star chart with—" Her eyes meet mine and register my use of the name. "Evelyn, I…"

"Is it true? Are you… working for the enemy?"

"Eves, listen. I can explain."

A surge of adrenaline floods my chest and makes my face hot. She… didn't deny it. Which means she's guilty. But after all this time? All these years? This can't be happening. "Get out of your seat."

"Evelyn, Please."

"*Get. Up.*"

Her hands shake a little as they work the buckles. Eventually, the harness straps slip off her shoulders, and she stands.

"I'm going to ask you these questions one time," I say with all my grief and anger directed into my words. "And I want answers, or so help me cosmos… *Who is Olivia Tomlinson?*"

"I am."

"And you work for?"

Her eyes dart around but settle back on me. "The Tantum Terrae."

My face reddens more, and I cross my arms to keep myself from attacking her. But the flutter in my breathing betrays the anger welling in my chest. The rage. The embarrassment and exposure of betrayal. "How long?"

"Evelyn, I didn't mean—"

"*How long?*"

"Since before we met."

I turn away and bite the inside of my cheek until I taste blood. I want tear into her like a punching bag. But I want answers before that happens because there might not be anything left of her when I'm done. "And your objective?"

Tears well up in Olivia's eyes. But they don't move me. *She* doesn't move me. "To stop your research," she says.

My research? We've been together for *four years*. I suddenly wonder how many setbacks she's responsible for. How many reports she's tampered with and in what ways, and… Shit, how much of *Astraea* she's responsible for! The security breaches, helping Stamos, framing Bhavna … even erasing the data archives in our final battle against Stamos. That was… *that was her. Stars*, this can't be happening right now. But it all makes sense. And she, *Olivia*, was at the center of it.

"This whole time? It was you?" My mind reels. Mouth goes dry. Waiting for her to respond.

But there's something more. This wasn't just about stopping our research. The attack on the SESI building in St. Johns. The press conference in Helsinki. Maybe even events surrounding the gate's activation that I'm unaware of. She's hiding something. I feel it.

"And?" I finally ask.

"And what?"

"You were sent to kill me, weren't you."

"Evelyn, I never—"

"*Weren't you?*"

"If you knew how many times—"

"TELL ME NOW, DAMMIT!"

"YES! I was ordered to kill you," she yells with tears streaming down her cheeks. "But I didn't! And I never would."

"Why not?"

"Because, I… God, I cared about you too much."

"But you didn't give a damn about all the people you killed on *Astraea*?"

She balks. Shock. But it's too late for remorse. For apologies. And if she so much as tries to—

"I never meant for anyone to—"

"Fuck you, Olivia." My right fist delivers all the pent up anger in my body to her face. Her nose cracks under the blow, head jerks back. She slams into her chair. Then the crew undo their buckles, start swearing, and yell at me to stop.

But I'm far from done.

I descend on Olivia like a raptor on a mouse, pummeling her as she tries to cover her head. Only, she's *not* trying. Her arms fall limp to her sides, giving me an open target. She even seems to lift her chin and keep her head straight as my blows come fast. Blood flings from her nose, lips, and the gash above her eye just as much as it does from the cuts on my knuckles. Fluids splatter on the deck as I keep punching her, but I don't feel the pain; the hole in the middle of my chest hurts too much.

Hands grab my arms, yanking me away. I still swing. Still yell something that I can't understand.

"Goddammit, Evelyn," someone shouts in my ear. It's Ramirez I think. But even as he pulls me away with Seb on my other arm, I manage to kick Olivia in the chest and head.

"You traitor," is all I can manage. My chest heaves. Hands throb. The guys pull me further back, come around front, and hold me against a wall. Meanwhile, Igor tends to Olivia while Bhavna stands over the traitor looking as though she's ready to tag team my assault.

"You framed me, didn't you," Bhavna says in a seething tone. But Olivia is too bloodied to speak.

Cheng moves in to keep Bhavna away. "Stand down, Mishra. Please."

"*But she framed me.*"

"I know. And you'll get your justice. But not now. And not like this."

I yank my arms free of Ramirez and Seb's holds and sneer at Olivia. "Do you have anything to say for yourself?"

"No."

"And any reason why we shouldn't flush you out of an airlock right now?"

"Evelyn," Nat says. "Maybe we—"

I silence her with a hand and point to Olivia. "*Answer.*"

A tear slides out of the corner of her eye before she says, "No."

The traitor's simple one-word admissions irritate me. I want to charge her a second time just to make her fight back. But she didn't then, and I doubt she will if I attack her again. Instead, she looks resigned. Sad even, beneath all the blood. I still have so many questions. So much anger at how exposed I feel. All the things I confessed to her. All the secrets we—

"We don't have time for this," I say as the adrenaline rush fades. "Cheng, Igor, remand her to her quarters and tend to her injuries as best you can. Put two people on watch until I can deal with her myself. Understood?"

They nod, lift Olivia off the floor, and turn her toward the ladder leading below decks.

Before she descends, Olivia says, "I'm sorry."

"Congratulations," is all I can think to say back. "Get her out of here."

Jericho

WE ALL WATCH through the *Sagan*'s bridge camera as Evelyn takes her seat and accepts some nanodermal spray and a bandage packet from Mishra.

"Oi. Remind me never to piss her off," Eddie says to our team. The mood is too somber for this to get any laughs. The fact that Sam is an incog, that she's been hiding in plain sight among us for so long, cuts deep. Evelyn isn't the only one who's feeling it, but God knows she's taking it the hardest.

I'm about to ask how she's doing when the *Bellerophon* appears between us and the planet.

"Whoa. Did you see that?" Nairobi says, looking at the main display. "Roll that back."

Kit, currently in charge of all the holo projectors, reverses the time to show the *Belle* emerging from nothing, stem to stern.

"It's like it just materialized out of nowhere," Nairobi adds.

"Not nowhere," Magellan says. "Look." He directs our attention to three points of light... three *nodes* affixed inside a massive ring.

"My God." Nairobi leans into the display's data analysis sections. "I think it's safe to say we're all looking at our first alien artifact. According to the sensor data, that thing is almost twenty kilometers across. Ring thickness at approximately 600 meters. Surface looks metallic, smooth, and the nodes appear to be molded into the radial interior." Sure enough, the nubby protrusions with glowing apexes looked a whole lot like the ones we'd constructed.

"Guessing the ring supports and powers them," I say.

"So *that's* how they're supposed to work," Kit replies. "Guess we got it a little wrong, huh?"

"Definitely more elegant than our design, that's for sure."

"And *that* Landau window doesn't look anything like ours did," Alice adds from behind me. "There's no blue light. It's just… see through."

Eddie, who'd been monitoring the sensors back on *Telemine*, answers before anyone else can. "Which is exactly what ours probably looked like from inside the station. No radiation. No light. Nothing."

Kit scratches his head. "So, so… Does that mean, when we go back, that we, ya know, need to go slowly? 'Cause we're gonna be inside the station when we arrive?"

"We'll save those questions for Evelyn and her team," I say. "Right now, we need to make sure that we're safe and that whoever this *Olivia Tomlinson* is hasn't sabotaged our expedition." The *Koga's* V-cog LAN auto connects with the *Belle's*, and I ping Rook as soon as his name appears. "Rook?"

"We gotta warn Evelyn," he says in a rush.

"It's done."

"What?"

"The incog is confined to quarters. How'd you know?"

"Geller got a hit on the list. I sent Evelyn a message before we went through, but I'm not sure if she got it."

"Oh, she got it."

"And? How'd she take it?"

One eyebrow climbs my forehead. "Once she confirmed it was legit, she beat the ever-loving shit out of Sam... *er*, Olivia."

"So she didn't deny it?"

"Nope."

Rook takes a breath. "I feel bad for Park."

"We all do. But pity has to wait. We've got a job to do."

In V-cog, I group all forty-nine names across the three-ship LAN roster, title it P1, and ping Evelyn. It takes her a few seconds to open the multi-ship team channel, and she appears remarkably composed. The only thing that betrays any sign that she just beat up someone is a smudge of blood on her cheek. Once everyone else has joined via hardware camera or V-cog monitoring, Evelyn is all business and starts the discussion.

"The Tantum operative known as Olivia Tomlinson has been remanded to her quarters. Dr. Natalie Mason is running a full diagnostic check of the *Sagan Explorer*, and Dr. Cheng Liu is conducting a physical search with a team as we speak. Rook, to you, I think the more immediate question is what's the likelihood that the military might follow us here?"

"You sure you're okay, Dr. Park?" I ask.

She gives me a cold stare. I know she doesn't like me asking in front of the whole team, but we all saw what happened, and I know it's on everyone's mind. Evelyn seems to get this too and finally says, "I'll be fine. My personal issues can wait. Rook? Chances of military intervention?"

"Minimal, if any." Rook seems cautious, as if searching Evelyn's face to make sure she's really alright, as she claims. "They're not about to pull a stunt like we just did. And they have little reason considering that the apparent threat is back there, not here."

I add, "So the more pressing question is what will Sallsworth do about the gate now that we're through."

"Probably turn it off, right?" Kit asks. "I mean, we're the big pain in his caboose, aren't we? So all he needs to do now is, *foowiph*, flip the switch and, *poof*, we're gone forever. Problem solved."

"God, I hope we're not *that* disposable," Natalie says.

"I would not put it past him," Afumba adds.

"Right," I reply. "He's all about political expediency. So then the question becomes, how will he do it?"

"Easiest way would be to destroy the nodes or the energy module hab," Rook offers.

"But then he loses leverage," Evelyn says. "And he wouldn't give up a chess piece that valuable so easily."

"But he was going to blow it up anyway," Nairobi says.

"Oi. That's before we got the fucking Rainbow Bright idea to fly through it, now ain't it."

She shrugs. "Fair enough. What's Rainbow Bright?"

"The point is," I say, "that every spacer alive is going to be rooting for us now that we've gone through, which includes the Viatoribus and Sentia Aux, who will be fighting on our behalf in the joint session. I have to imagine the Preservationists will also throw in now that the gateway exists and constitutes a discovery that they'll want to protect."

"All hail the champions of convenience," Magellan says.

Evelyn taps the end of her nose with a blood-stained finger. "So the easiest thing for Sallsworth to do now is wait for the fifteen-minute auto shutoff to kick in and then power down *Telemine*. That's what I would do if I were him."

"No you wouldn't," Kit says with a laugh. "You'd beat the snot out of each and every one of—"

"Kit?" I say.

"—of us with love and affection."

"Better."

Evelyn offers a weak smile that passes quickly. "Come to think of it, we're past that time allotment now." She turns to look at the *Sagan*'s main holo projection on their bridge. "Any way we can tell if the far side of that gate is emitting?"

Ramirez floats to the sensor's workstation and enters some commands. "I'm not reading anything like we did from *Parallax One*. Just background radiation from the planet and the star."

"Well, that's not conclusive," Evelyn says. "We'll need to circle back for a full scan. But my guess is that our ring shut down as predicted."

"Question," Kit says. "If activating ours turned this one on, couldn't it work in the opposite direction?"

"Anything's possible," Evelyn says. "And that's a fair hypothesis."

"Won't know until we try, right?" he adds. "Assuming we know how to read the instruction manual for the alien version of *Parallax One*, which, by the way, looks way cooler than ours. Anyone else?"

"I shall endeavor to read said instruction manual for you, my liege," Fergus One says. "Simply point me in the direction of my quest and—"

"Kit?"

"On it." He turns to face his pet excipion. "Hey. Hey! You gotta cool it, okay? No talking until I say you can."

"May I now?"

"No. *Jeez*, no."

Sebastián raises a finger. "Assuming the gate stays off for a while, might I suggest we tend to the most pressing issue?"

"Get accurate scans of the planet and this debris field?" Evelyn says.

Seb nods. "We are, after all, on a discovery expedition, aren't we?"

Evelyn looks back at the camera. "What say you, Captains?"

"We don't have your sensor capabilities," Rook replies. "But we'll be a third pair of eyes as best we can, and we'll pull overwatch in case anything decides it doesn't wanna play nice."

"Thanks. Jericho, while the *Kogarashi*'s sensors aren't much better than the *Belle*'s, you do have—"

"Speed," I say. "You want us to take a quick run around the backside of the planet?"

"It would help us get a more comprehensive picture to start, yes."

"Consider it done," I say.

"Just... be careful," she adds. "Everyone. Be careful."

Rook folds his arms. "Says the woman who flew into the first alien portal she laid eyes on."

⋮

"Looks pretty quiet down there," Kit says from his crash couch. "*Too quiet.*" We're burning hard around what everyone's taken to calling just *Kep-C,* and we've reached the quarter mark in under fifteen minutes.

"Are you recording yourself?" I ask him.

"Maybe. Figured people might like a documentary about my life as the youngest spacer to ever explore another star system. Might also make a good action movie too, depending on what happens. So I'm just, ya know, recording all possible lines for my part."

"Mmm. How about you keep your eyes on the scopes."

"Oi. And tell him to change out of that fucking ugly-ass smock already. It right pisses me off, it does."

"What, this?" Kit looks down at his self-styled #saymekit t-shirt. "It's not ugly."

"Back to work, Kit," I say.

"Aye-aye, Captain Fox." He gives me a crisp salute and then turns back to his workstation.

Kit is right about one thing though: the planet's surface looks quiet, as is all the wreckage we're picking up in orbit. No lights, no motion, and no reception of any kind. Granted, we're 400 kilometers up, so detail is scant. But there is some sort of civilization out there—at least there *was.*

That said, I still can't believe I'm here, orbiting through a star system that I would never reach using conventional propulsion, not for millions of years. I wish my father could see this. But some part of me says he can. Says he is now.

We're minutes away from losing line of sight comms

with the *Sagan* and *Belle*, so I decide to check in with both captains, but not at the same time.

"Rook. You there?"

"Roger." He steps into our locally hosted V-cog lobby dressed in black and grey combat armor with a helmet tucked under one arm. "Find something?"

"Just more junk, and more signs of massive infrastructure on the planet. But it looks old. Abandoned."

His face grows sullen. "I was afraid of that."

"What are you thinking?"

"Won't know until we get all the data."

"I'm not asking the data."

Rook lets out a sigh and then works his jaw. "This kind of destruction? I've seen it before. Smaller scale, of course. But…"

"Don't leave me hanging, Master Sergeant."

"This was war."

"I was afraid you'd say that."

"Me too. But we're already seeing signs of blast marks on some of the scraps in orbit. Too soon to know what made them, of course, or what these vessels were. But I'm guessing the destruction is planet-wide. Already spotting impact craters on the surface."

"Meteorites?"

He shakes his head. "Placement is too strategic. It's not good, Knight. The only positive is that, as you indicated, it looks like it happened a very long time ago."

I let the silence grow a little before saying, "We'll be in touch when we come around."

"Roger. Stay frosty."

I close the channel to Rook and then ping Evelyn. It takes her a second to appear in my V-cog lobby, but when she does, her distraught face tells the tale. Before I can even say hello, she falls into my chest and lowers her head. I'm a dumbass and just stand here, but then I wrap my arms around her and let her cry.

Half a minute goes before I ask how she's doing. I expect her to pull away and punch the wall. Or me. But she doesn't. She just lets me hold her. So I keep my mouth shut and wait for her to do or say whatever it is she wants. We've only got three minutes before we lose the ship-to-ship laser LAN connection, and I don't just want to vanish on her in V-cog. So I decide to try and say something, even if it's stupid.

"Do you wanna talk about it?"

"I'm mad," she says and rubs her nose on my shirt. Then she pulls back, giving me a good look at her tear-stained face. "But I'm also…"

"Sad?"

She nods and looks away. I can see more tears filling her eyes. "It hurts, you know?"

I don't dare say anything comparative. Just nod.

"I mean, how badly do you have to want to hurt someone to keep a secret for *four years*? And then to be complicit in the deaths of everyone who died on *Astraea*? And you live with that?" She rubs her face with a hand. "But then she… she's saved my life too. It's… it's just so confusing. Like my best friend just died in a car accident or something." She makes fists at the same time that more tears run down her cheeks, but she seems to have run out of words. Finally, her face and body relax, and she leans into me again.

"Well, in a certain way," I say, "your best friend did just die. At least the one in your head and heart. So I think the grief and confusion are all real."

Her head moves up and down against my chest.

"Evelyn, I wouldn't wish what you're going

through on anyone. And I can't imagine the pain and frustration you're feeling right now. It's sorrow, for sure. And more. All those things that a good counselor would probably say. But I'm not one, and I don't have any good advice. I just… want you to know I'm here for you. And that if I can make anything better, I will."

She nods again, sniffs, and then stands up straight. "Thanks."

"You're welcome."

But then anger flashes in her eyes again, and her fists rise to hip level. "And then there's this stupid planet!"

"Whu… uh…"

"It's hot."

"Okay?"

"No, like, too damn hot." She starts pacing.

I realize we've changed gears, which is probably for the best. "I take it that's not what you were expecting."

"Last we knew, Kep-C was 234 Kelvin. Uh, that's negative thirty-nine Celsius."

"So, how hot is very hot?"

"You familiar with Venus?"

"Can't say I've vacationed there."

"We're reading over 400 degrees Celsius. Hot enough to melt lead. Riverbeds, lake basins, ocean canyons, all dry as a bone. That's why we're not seeing any water down there."

"I was wondering about that. So am I wrong to assume that didn't bode well for the Makriá?"

"Not unless they could thrive without liquid water. Regardless of what caused all the orbital debris, it looks like this planet experienced a runaway greenhouse effect or something. If someone was here before, they're gone now." She lets out a long sigh. "I just… I don't get it. How could… send us a… from a dead …"

"Evelyn?"

Her avatar in V-cog flutters. "…advanced species that…"

"Evelyn, I'm losing you."

"…wormhole generator?"

"Evelyn?"

She blinks out of my lobby, and the audio goes quiet.

"We're out of range," Kit says. "Sorry, Cap."

As we dive behind the planet, Eddie adds, "Welcome to the fucking dark side,"

Evelyn

I'm grateful for Jericho. For his friendship. And for him not trying to ruin the moment with stupid advice. I'm also glad he let me cry without interrupting. While this situation is far from over with Olivia, at least I feel like I regained some headspace. And that I have someone who I can actually trust in my corner. I'll deal with her later. For now, I've got a new mystery to solve.

"I want a complete LIDAR scan of the surface, klick by klick," I say after reviewing the atmospheric results with Seb and Ramirez again. "We need a better picture of what happened here."

"On it," Ramirez replies.

"What about sending some drones down?" Natalie asks behind me. "We did a project in one of my astroarchaeology classes where we mapped the inside of a dormant volcano with RD-24s, just like we have onboard. All they needed was some shielding upgrades and modifications to the battery cooling matrix."

"I like it. How long do you need?"

"An hour?"

"Good. Grab anyone else you need."

She nods and pushes back to her workstation. At the same time, Igor floats through the bridge hatch, returning from his time below decks tending to... *Olivia.* Stars, I hate that name.

"Status?" I ask.

He rubs the back of his neck. "Many laceration, contusion. You do much damage in short time, Dr. Park. Is reminding Igor never to fight you."

"So she'll live."

"Oh, sure, sure. With bad memory of having shits beat from her. But is puzzle, no? Why not defend? Why take such bad beating laying downs? Is not Old Russian way. Is not even good way. Just bad. Very much bad. I think something wrong in head, no? Broken."

"Thanks, Igor. See if you can help Cheng."

"Oh, he is done doing searches. Coming up soon. He find nothing. All clears."

"Good to know."

"If ask me, I not so sure Dr. Collins—"

"She's not a doctor."

"Ah, sorry. Uh, this Olivia person is here to harm."

"Didn't ask. Take a seat, Igor."

"Of course."

Back to Ramirez, I ask, "What's the ETA on the *Kogarashi*?"

"Should be coming out of blackout any second."

I push away from his workstation, land back in my command chair, and pull up the 3D model of the *Koga*'s predicted flight path. The dotted line around the planet's dark side is nearly complete. I double check to make sure we're still scanning the radio frequency we left off on. The dotted line turns solid as the *Koga*'s trajectory puts it in our line of sight.

"*Kogarashi*, this is *Sagan*," I say.

Static.

"*Kogarashi*, this is the *Sagan Explorer*. Do you read?"

Still nothing but static.

"Scopes?" I ask Natalie.

"I'm not seeing anything. Maybe they're checking something out?"

"Ramirez, power up. Intercept course." I ping the *Belle*. "Rook, we're headed to Jericho. They're not where they're supposed to be."

"Roger. On your six."

"Copy that."

Ramirez is just about to push us forward when Jericho's voice breaks the static. "*Sagan*, this is the *Kogarashi*. Come in. Over."

"Stars, Jericho. What took you so long? You okay?"

"You sound worried about me."

My cheeks redden. "I was worried about Kit."

"Awwww, see? Thanks, Miss Evelyn. I was worried about you too," Kit replies in the background.

"You find anything new back there?" I know what

he's gonna say, and I ready myself for the disappointment.

"Nothing of interest…"

"That's what I thought."

"…unless you'd like to have a look at a second orbital gate."

"A what?"

BOOK 3

KOGARASHI'S RUN

What will the explorers find at the second gate?

Will Secretary General Sallsworth destroy *Parallax One*?

And how will Gemma fill the power vacuum left by her mother's death?

Find out in book 3 of the Infinita series: *Kogarashi's Run*

Available in trade and mass market paperback, hardcover, audiobook, and ebook at **christopherhopper.com**.

Or your favorite retailers:

Amazon | Apple | Kobo

INFINITA BOOK 3
KOGARASHI'S RUN
CHRISTOPHER HOPPER
SECURE YOUR COPY NOW!

CHRISTOPHER HOPPER
BROKEN BLADE
AN INFINITA SPIES
SHORT STORY

VIP

Become a VIP Club Member Today!

Membership is free, and you'll receive an official club poker chip, short story, and 10% off Christopher's store for life. Plus, you'll be signed up to get exclusive club perks in the mail and invited to join the private social media groups.

Visit christopherhopper.com to sign up now.

BECOME A VIP FREE

10 % OFF
ALL MERCH

VIP
MEMBER
POKER CHIP

SHORT STORY

PLUS
EXCLUSIVE ACCESS TO
PRIVATE SOCIAL MEDIA GROUP

SCAN NOW

GEAR UP IN THE SHOP

Show your spacer spirit by purchasing the officially licensed Infinita t-shirts, hats, challenge coins, and more. From NUESSA and SESI to the Tantum Terrae and Sentia Aux, find your faction and chose your side at christopherhopper.com.

INFINITA
COLLECTION

FIND YOUR GEAR NOW!

ACKNOWLEDGMENTS

Once again, this book would not be what it is without Matthew Titus, Jennifer Sell, Christie Strahler, Gary Guilmette, Tracey Beattie, and Neil Rubenking. Special thanks also goes to Dan Wong for his sharp attorney's eyes.

To my faithful alpha and beta readers for the thankless job of sweeping up the sawdust after the lights go out: Shane Marolf, David Seaman, Mauricio Longo, John Holley Jr., Kevin Zoll, Steve Janulin, John Walker, Jon Bliss, Mike McDonnell, Sean Ross, Eric Earley, Elijah Cole, George Hain, John Vermillion, Beverly Raymond, John Holley Jr, Brian Sinks, Joanne Sinks, Kathy Simonet, and Julia Camacho Monzon.

A heartfelt thanks goes to all the amazing spacers in my VIP club. Your encouragement and enthusiasm keep me positive and employed. I'm so grateful to have you as my most loyal fans.

Rebecca Woods and Daniel Wisniewski, thank you for bringing my characters to life for the audio version of this story. Once again, you have created a new piece of art from the rough medium of my words. Thank you for sharing your time and talents with us all.

I'm thankful for my fellow writing companions who know and share the highs and lows of publishing: Wayne Thomas Batson, Jeremy Davis, Jason Anspach, Jeff Chaney, Ken Lozito, Nicholas Smith, Gerry Riddle, Scott Moon, and Jonathan Yanez. Your friendship is a blessing.

Thanks to my daughter, Evangeline, for running my store and taking care of our customers, and to my son, Luik, for populating the Infinita Codex with all my world building content. You guys rock. Your dad couldn't do this without you.

And to my wife, Jenny. Thank you for charging through gates with me. I would be lost in the void without your hand to hold.

christopherhopper.com/infinitasecrets